W9-AMB-833

AiD

Dear Reader,

The Victorians made Christmas celebrations so much their own that it wasn't easy to find details of the Georgian/Regency Christmas. But I very much enjoyed tracking them down, and Jane Austen was a great help. Of course there had to be snow, and huge fire logs, and groaning tables.... I once visited a large country house when it was decorated for Christmas, and I've put into my story the enticing smells of apples and oranges, and herbs and spices and cooking that were all there! Lovely!

So much for the background! What about the twins and their heroes? Which will you prefer—gentle, vulnerable Rosabelle or fiery, feisty Annabelle? Philip, the perfect gentleman, with his desire to defend and protect, or Giles, the impatient man of action, who is so hard on his cousin's widow? It might even depend on your mood at the time. But I hope I'm not giving too much away when I tell you that on occasion Rosabelle can be feisty and Annabelle vulnerable, Philip a man of action and Giles tender.

Also, I hadn't really appreciated how slow communication was in 1818, how much our air travel and fast cars, our e-mails and faxes have spoiled us. In 1818, letters took a lot longer to arrive, and actual travel in a carriage, especially if you wished to keep your own horses with you, even longer than that! So there are some compensations for living in the twenty-first century.

I hope you enjoy the twins' adventures—and the development of their love affairs. Of course they all end happily—just as a pair of Christmas tales should.

*Sylvia Andrew*

**Sylvia Andrew** has taught modern languages and became vice principal of a sixth-form college. She lives in Somerset, England, with two cats, a dog and a husband who has a very necessary sense of humor, and a stern approach to punctuation. Sylvia has a daughter living in London, and they share a lively interest in the theater. She describes herself as an "unrepentant romantic."

# Sylvia Andrew

# The Christmas Belles

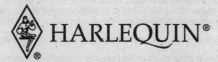

HARLEQUIN®

TORONTO • NEW YORK • LONDON
AMSTERDAM • PARIS • SYDNEY • HAMBURG
STOCKHOLM • ATHENS • TOKYO • MILAN • MADRID
PRAGUE • WARSAW • BUDAPEST • AUCKLAND

If you purchased this book without a cover you should be aware that this book is stolen property. It was reported as "unsold and destroyed" to the publisher, and neither the author nor the publisher has received any payment for this "stripped book."

ISBN 0-373-83368-7

THE CHRISTMAS BELLES

First North American Publication 2000.

Copyright © 2000 by Harlequin Books S.A.

The publisher acknowledges the copyright holder of the original works as follows:

ROSABELLE
Copyright © 1998 by Sylvia Andrew.
ANNABELLE
Copyright © 1998 by Sylvia Andrew.

All rights reserved. Except for use in any review, the reproduction or utilization of this work in whole or in part in any form by any electronic, mechanical or other means, now known or hereafter invented, including xerography, photocopying and recording, or in any information storage or retrieval system, is forbidden without the written permission of the publisher, Harlequin Enterprises Limited, 225 Duncan Mill Road, Don Mills, Ontario, Canada M3B 3K9.

All characters in this book have no existence outside the imagination of the author and have no relation whatsoever to anyone bearing the same name or names. They are not even distantly inspired by any individual known or unknown to the author, and all incidents are pure invention.

This edition published by arrangement with Harlequin Books S.A.

® and TM are trademarks of the publisher. Trademarks indicated with ® are registered in the United States Patent and Trademark Office, the Canadian Trade Marks Office and in other countries.

Visit us at www.eHarlequin.com

**Printed in U.S.A.**

# CONTENTS

# ROSABELLE

# Chapter One

*London—Christmas 1818*

'I don't care what you say, Giles! I have bowed to your opinion enough. This time I shall do what I know to be right—'

The young woman had been standing at the window contemplating the snow-covered scene outside, but now she turned and looked at the man in the centre of the room. Her expression was an uncertain mixture of defiance and a plea for understanding. But her companion remained unmoved.

'A rare event, Rosabelle! Or will you manage to convince yourself yet again that what you wish to do is conveniently what you ought to do?'

There was a short silence while Rosabelle Ordway struggled to remain calm. This was no time for one of those bouts of helpless weeping which had of late be-

come such a hazard to her composure. The gentleman
standing before her would have no patience with such
weakness. Giles Stanton was a hard, uncompromising
man. She drew a deep breath.

'Giles, my sister is alone at Temperley and my father
is not in good health. Surely it is not unreasonable for
me to want to be with them this Christmas?'

'To say nothing of the fact that it is really rather dull
here in London, since convention, if nothing else, demands that you are not seen in Society during your pe-
riod of mourning!'

'I have no wish to be seen in Society, Giles. I merely
wish to spend Christmas at Temperley.'

'Such devotion! Tell me, when did you last visit
Temperley?'

She bit her lip and turned away. 'Four years ago.'

'Four years? So not since you married my cousin, and
became the rich Mrs Ordway? I do not find your present
impatience to see them very convincing.'

'We…we went to see them once… But there were
reasons at the time—'

'Of course there were!' he said derisively. 'Why
should anyone wish to leave a doting husband, a fond
mother-in-law, and such a very comfortable home in order to visit a recluse of a father and a country mouse of
a sister? How could a shabby and probably draughty old
manor house compare with all this?'

His eyes travelled round the vast white and gold drawing room in which they stood. Rosabelle's eyes followed
his. Huge gilt-framed mirrors reflected walls covered in
silk, glittering chandeliers, and delicate French furniture.
The collections of snuffboxes and other valuable *objets
d'art* which had been one of Stephen's passions covered
most of the surfaces.

Rosabelle shivered. It was not a room she liked. She looked into the mirror opposite. Dressed in mourning, a wraithlike figure against all this magnificence, she was lost against the tall figure standing at her side. The room did not suit Giles either, she thought. But he dominated it all the same.

'Well?'

'Giles, why do you hate me so? You were away for those four years, so how can you possibly know anything about them?' She tried to speak reasonably, but her voice trembled and started to rise. She clasped her hands firmly together to stop their shaking. She had discovered that Giles despised any display of emotion. But she must get away, she must. Much as she loved Aunt Laura, she herself must have time to recover her strength and spirits. It looked as if she was going to need them.

'An unnecessarily theatrical word, Rosabelle. I do not "hate" you. But I certainly distrust you. Any fool could see why you want to escape from London at the moment. It is now two months since I first met you, and I have yet to observe any sign of genuine regret that my cousin is dead. I could hardly expect that you would stay merely because Aunt Laura depends on you. Life must be very dull for you now that the routs and balls and all the other frivolous pursuits you once delighted in are denied to you. But, for once in your idle life, you will earn your keep.'

'But I still don't understand why you think of me like this! What have I done?'

'Lady Ordway took you in and brought you up as her own daughter—'

'She was my godmother, Giles! When my own mother died—'

'She took you in,' he went on inexorably, 'and you

soon found you could wind her round your little finger. She was so captivated that she let you marry her only son—before Stephen reached his majority, even. I am not surprised at your haste—he was always easily led, and you might well have been uncertain that his affection for you would last. But what a blow it must have been when Stephen died before he actually inherited the Ordway fortune!'

Rosabelle was stung into reply. 'But this is madness! I was as young as Stephen. And I certainly had even less knowledge of what I was doing—' She stopped short. She had sworn not to talk of such matters to anyone.

He ignored her words, his voice full of bitterness as he went on, 'You couldn't keep your side of the bargain, could you?'

'Bargain?'

'Yes, Rosabelle. A life of ease and comfort for a girl who had nothing to offer of her own, in return for loyalty and a little affection for my cousin. But you couldn't do it!'

Consciousness of her own shortcomings caused Rosabelle's voice to falter. 'What…what do you mean?'

He nodded. 'You know very well what I mean. Stephen was still a boy—a sweet-natured, delicate, trusting boy. You betrayed and eventually destroyed him. Don't shake your head, Rosabelle. I have proof.'

'You can't have!'

'I may not have been in London, ma'am, but I have my cousin's letters. Your faithless behaviour broke his heart. He is quite explicit.'

'What faithless behaviour? With whom? I can't possibly have broken Stephen's heart!' Rosabelle cried wildly.

'Does the name of Selder mean anything to you? Ah! I see it does.'

'But it wasn't…it's not what you….' Rosabelle fell silent. A great weariness overcame her. What was the point of denying anything? Stephen had always been able to twist facts to suit himself. He had always been so plausible. No one would believe her, except Aunt Laura. And in her present state, the last thing Aunt Laura needed was to be confronted, reminded of the truth about her only son. So she shook her head, but made no effort to defend herself further. 'You are wrong, Giles, so very wrong, though I cannot hope to persuade you of that.' She looked away and said forlornly, 'I…I cannot understand why you wish me to remain here. Would it not be better for everyone if I went to Temperley and stayed there?'

'Oh, no! I am sure that escaping to Temperley would suit you very well for the moment, though what you would live on would be a problem. I can hardly imagine your father would want to support you again after all these years. But no, you will not go to Temperley. You are still needed here. My aunt no longer needs nursing, but she does need constant and sympathetic companionship. What little good there is in you seems to lie in your feeling for your mother-in-law…'

'I love Aunt Laura,' Rosabelle said passionately. 'She was my godmother before she ever became my mother-in-law, and I shall never forget her kindness to me when I was a child.'

'Brave words, Rosabelle! And now you can live up to them,' Giles said calmly. 'If you really mean what you say, you will stay here in London to look after my aunt, until she has fully recovered from the shock of Stephen's death. She will be your first priority, but you will also look after the running of the house. The task is not onerous—you have servants enough for your needs.'

'But you don't like me! You said you didn't trust me!'

'I don't have to like someone to make use of them. And I shall make sure that a careful eye is kept on you.'

'I can't do it, Giles! I cannot live in such an atmosphere of suspicion and dislike, I cannot!' She heard her voice rising once again and she took a deep breath. She must stay calm, she must!

'I think you will find you can. Otherwise…otherwise, my little schemer, I can still refuse to honour my cousin's debts. I need hardly remind you that they are now your debts. Yours and Aunt Laura's. Your husband ran through an astonishing amount of money in his short life. By the time his creditors are finally paid you will be a very poor widow indeed, my dear. So will Aunt Laura, who, I gather, supported you both in your extravagances.'

'You wouldn't! You couldn't! You're bluffing!'

'Are you about to call my bluff? I don't advise it.' The sight of the pathetically slender figure before him, hands clasping and unclasping, dark blue eyes huge in a pale face seemed only to enrage him further. 'Don't try your tricks on me, Rosabelle! Good God, you deserve anything that happens to you! Stephen had more money than anyone should need, and my uncle left Aunt Laura with a very generous jointure. I have spent the last two months trying to establish where it all went, but you have consistently refused to help me.'

'I…I don't know where it went,' she said faintly.

'What? No donations to the poor?' he jeered. 'No contributions to your poverty-stricken family? I had expected a better tale than ''I don't know where it went''.'

Rosabelle closed her eyes. This was all part of the

continuing nightmare of the past few years. The thing to do was to ignore the malice, and concentrate on saving what she could from the situation.

'And…and…if I do stay? Where will you be? Are you going abroad again?'

'Not for long, my dear.' Giles's smile was unpleasantly grim. 'Don't pin your hopes on my continued absence! I shall be leaving next week for France, but it won't be all that long before I am back. I don't intend to abandon Aunt Laura and the Ordway treasures to your rapacious little hands for longer than I can help.'

Rosabelle fought to control the shaking which was threatening to take over her whole body. She had always found it difficult to cope with disapproval, dislike, hard words. Her life had been governed by the desire to please, a search for love and security, and this man with his harsh voice, his bitter contempt, frightened her as she had not been frightened before—not even with Stephen.

Of course, she was not completely herself. Nursing Aunt Laura on top of what she had been through in the year before had wrecked her nervous system. And now, for two months, ever since Giles Stanton had first come to the house in Upper Brook Street, she had been battling with his prejudices and threats. He had arrived convinced of her guilt, and nothing she could say or do had caused him to change his mind about her.

It was all so unjust. She sat down suddenly and put her hands to her face. She was ill. But where could she go for help or even understanding? She must get away, just for a short time. Panic rose again, constricting the air in her throat. She must be calm! She must keep her head. If Giles would only give her a breathing space!

'Giles!' She took a deep breath. 'Giles, I will look after Aunt Laura—I would have done so without your

threats. But…I need a little time to myself first. You
need not fear I wish for dissipation or gaiety—I'm only
asking to go to Temperley to visit my family.'

Giles felt a sudden surge of impatience. Why didn't
the woman say she intended to go and have done? He
would have respected her more if she had, though at the
moment it would be damned inconvenient. The whole
business was most unsatisfactory. What his aunt and
Stephen had seen in this pale, nervous creature he would
never know. But, he reminded himself, she must be a
consummate actress. This air of helpless vulnerability
was very well done, and if he hadn't known better it
would have taken him in completely. She had certainly
led his poor cousin a pretty dance. And others, too, if
what Stephen had written was true. Well, young Mrs
Rosabelle Ordway would soon find that she had met her
match at last. Life at Upper Brook Street was going to
be a lot less to her taste! Still, though he had no intention
of changing his present plans to suit her whims, he ought
to let her visit her family some time.

'Giles?'

'You can go for a month later in the year,' he said
abruptly. 'At the moment Aunt Laura needs your help
more than the people at Temperley, and she is as much
your family as they. Besides, for the next three or four
months, until the Duke's move back to England is complete, I might be anywhere. Easter is the earliest I can
be reasonably sure of having time for my own concerns.
Even you will agree that Aunt Laura cannot be left alone
during that time. If she continues to improve you can
arrange to go to Berkshire for Easter.'

'But—'

'That is my final word, Rosabelle. And don't plan to
stay for longer than the month, either. Even though I

hope to be back permanently in England by then, you will have obligations to fulfil here. If you don't return to time, you might find your creditors on Temperley's doorstep.'

Rosabelle bowed her head. Where had her old energy and spirit gone? In the old days she would have found things to say to him, protested at his cruel treatment of her. But nowadays she was tongue-tied, nervous, the consciousness of what she had to hide inhibiting all her normal responses. Could she stay in Upper Brook Street till Easter? It appeared that she would have to. Giles was right in one thing—Aunt Laura could not be left alone. And if he was to be away in Paris for most of the time, she would at least have more peace.

'Thank you, Giles,' she said.

'Don't thank me—I'm not doing this to please you. I still intend to see that you pay what you owe to my family.'

Rosabelle escaped from his presence with a sense of profound relief. But outside the door to her godmother's room she stopped and took several deep, calming breaths. Four months! Four long months to Easter. How could she bear it? However, all thought of escape left her as she trod softly into the dimly lit room. How could she think of abandoning her godmother while she was looking so pale and old? Of course she must stay with her till she had recovered. Lady Ordway's eyes opened, and she said sleepily, 'Is that you, Stephen?'

Rosabelle picked up the glass on the table by the bed. 'No, Aunt Laura. Stephen can't come at the moment. It's Rosabelle. Shall I hold you up so that you can have a drink of this?'

'Rosabelle!' The sick woman's face lit up with a smile. 'What time is it?'

'Two o'clock. And it's snowing again.'

'Two o'clock? That's late.'

'You've been asleep all morning.'

'I thought you were Stephen.' Lady Ordway's face changed, and she turned her head into the pillows. 'How silly of me. Stephen's dead. How long is it now? Six months?'

'Seven, Aunt Laura,' said Rosabelle quietly.

'Is Giles still here?'

'I think he's just about to go. Do you wish to see him?'

'Not at the moment. He will soon have to go back to finish his work in Paris, I know. And he still has so much to do for the estate—dealing with the lawyers and...and all the rest. It's all his now, of course. He was to inherit if Stephen didn't have a child. And Stephen didn't.'

'No.' Rosabelle's voice was still quiet, but there was pain and revulsion in it. There had never been the remotest possibility that she and Stephen would have a child.

'I'm sorry, I shouldn't have said that. I'm sorry, I'm sorry—' Lady Ordway was getting very agitated. Her hands were plucking at the quilt and tears were rolling down her cheeks.

Rosabelle stretched to still those hands. 'Have some more of your drink.'

Lady Ordway sipped a little, then lay back. 'I...I forget, Rosabelle. I'm a stupid old woman.'

Rosabelle kissed her godmother's cheek. 'You're sick. Things will be better soon, you'll see.'

'Giles was always a kind boy. Very fond of my poor Stephen. I'm sure if he had been here Stephen would not...would not...'

Rosabelle put her finger to her godmother's lips. 'Don't talk of it, Aunt Laura. It upsets us both.'

'I should never have made you marry my son. I just hoped… You were always such a happy little soul—and so beautiful. I thought it might save him… And look at you now.' She took Rosabelle's hand. 'You've done your best to keep it from me, but I still have eyes. You're so pale and thin, and your nerves are in shreds, like mine. I did that to you, Rosabelle. Can you forgive me?'

'Of course I can! I love you, Godmama.'

They sat in silence for a while. Then Lady Ordway said, 'I've been thinking. Giles will soon have things under control—you should pay a visit to Temperley.'

'I…I can't at the moment. You said yourself—Giles has to be away quite a lot. He says I can go at Easter, if you are well enough.'

'Then I shall make sure I am! You know, lying here, thinking of what I can say to Giles, and realising how much I have to hide—all this has brought me to my senses. I was wilfully, wickedly blind—and though I loved you, I tried to use you. Now I want you to be young again. I want to hear you laugh as you used to. I think you should spend some time at Temperley—say, three months. Spend the summer there, perhaps, as you did in the old days. I shall miss you, but I'll manage.'

'I shan't stay away as long as that! Giles has given me a month.'

'It isn't enough!'

'It will have to be. Giles is quite…adamant.'

'He always was a little arrogant. It comes of being in command in the army. He's with the Duke, you know,' said Lady Ordway with a touch of pride. 'The Duke of Wellington. He always has been—fighting in Spain, then

France. Then, after the war, the Duke took him on his staff. He's very used to having things his own way.'

'So I've noticed,' said Rosabelle drily. Lady Ordway looked at her with a smile.

'Well, if you need longer, you must take it.'

'I can't! He would never allow it. And it just isn't in me to defy him, Godmama.''

'Really? We must think of something, then.' She gave Rosabelle a small grin. 'You could always send Annabelle back in your place. She's your identical twin, and heaven knows, you played enough tricks on me when you were children. Giles would never know the difference.'

'It would certainly serve him right—he is something of a bully. But I know you can't be serious.' Rosabelle sighed. 'No, I shall do as he says.'

'He has never married, though he must be well over thirty now—he was a good bit older than...than Stephen.' A shadow fell over her face again, and Rosabelle held the glass once more to her lips, until it was drained. Lady Ordway sank back against the pillows. 'Giles is basically a good man, Rosabelle dear. And he was always fond of me, too. We're safe in his hands, in spite of his domineering ways.'

'I'm sure we are, Aunt Laura,' said Rosabelle, putting as much conviction into her voice as she could manage.

A week later Giles Stanton had gone back to Paris. Rosabelle sat in solitary state in the dining room while the servants brought her course after course, very little of which she touched. They had decorated and dressed the table with greenery and fruit, but the room was cheerless. Christmas Day! She wondered what her sister Annabelle was doing today. Christmas was always an important day for countryfolk, and Temperley would be looking its best—tables piled high with food, rooms decorated with masses of holly and ivy and the rest, and… She sighed. There would be ordinary, uncomplicated, cheerful company, with laughter, and song, and…life.

She surveyed the dismal formality of the room she was in, and a wave of nostalgia swept over her. She wished passionately that she could go back to Temperley, to her childhood, to a time when the world had been bright with promise… Oh, if only she could have gone to Temperley for Christmas! Rosabelle sat up straighter and made an effort to pull herself together. There was no question of going to Temperley at the moment. She had written to tell Annabelle so. But Giles had promised she could go at Easter and she must just survive till then!

# *Chapter Two*

'Miss Belle, Miss Belle! Mr Winbolt is here.' Becky met Annabelle at the bottom of the stairs. 'I've put him in the little parlour.'

'Why didn't you tell him I wasn't here?'

'I couldn't do that! Now come upstairs again and change into your decent dress. I'll do your hair, too. He can wait a minute or two—I gave him a glass of wine and some biscuits.' She clucked and shushed a protesting Annabelle upstairs.

Becky Bostock had come to Temperley as a kitchen maid, long before Annabelle had been born. Now she was the housekeeper, rosy of face and ample in figure, and though she treated the young mistress of the house with suitable respect when others were present, neither of them ever forgot that Becky had been nurse, guide and companion to the lonely little girl throughout her childhood.

It had not been easy—Annabelle had always been a sturdily independent child, determined to go her own way. Her mother had died before she was six, and her father preferred his own company to that of his daughter. If Becky had not been there to guide her, scolding for her wilful ways, and comforting her when she suffered the consequences, the child might well have become unmanageable.

Now Annabelle had grown up and was managing the Temperley estate in place of her father, but Becky had remained Annabelle's chief support and confidante. The arrival of Philip Winbolt in the neighbourhood—young, rich and unmarried—had stirred Becky's romantic heart, but it had left Annabelle totally unmoved.

'You know what will happen, Becky!' she said resentfully, as Becky helped her with her dress. 'He'll ask to see Papa, and I'll tell him Papa is not in the best of health and cannot see him. I'll ask if I can be of any help, then he'll look concerned and hum and haw, and say something about females and business…'

'Hold yourself still, Miss Belle, till I get this hook done up. There! You know Mr Winbolt never says anything of the sort!'

'He may not say it, but it's perfectly plain that he thinks it! Three times he has called, and he still hasn't grasped the fact that Papa is indifferent to neighbours, estate business—indeed, anything but his books! If Mr Winbolt wants anything done, then I'm the one he has to talk to, single female or not! I expect he's come to tell me that the fence is down again in Four Acre field— as if I didn't know! If I were a man he'd lose his temper and tell me to get on with having it mended. But because

I'm a young lady he thinks he can't. I have no patience with him. He's an idiot.'

'You're not fair to Mr Winbolt, Miss Belle. You never have been from the moment he arrived.'

'Well, his uncle was so much more of a man,' said Annabelle impatiently. 'And less of a tailor's dummy! My hair is well enough, Becky—leave it! I can't hope to compete with Mr Winbolt's exquisite neatness.'

'There, that's better! There's no harm in looking tidy, Miss Belle.'

'Old Joseph never bothered, and he managed perfectly well! He never worried about propriety, either. If he felt like swearing at me he did—not that it made a difference. The fences on the estate are so old they're forever breaking. The whole lot need renewing. But Joseph Winbolt said what he thought, then simply had them mended, instead of paying morning calls and talking about it. Oh, I do miss him, Becky!'

'He was a good friend to you, that's sure.'

'He was. And this Winbolt is so different from his uncle! I suppose that's why I'm hard on him. But I find his excessively good manners very tiresome.'

'There's nothing wrong with good manners, Miss Belle! We could do with a few more round here, if you ask me. And I think you're wrong. I think Mr Winbolt makes the fencing and such an excuse to see you. He's quite taken with you—anyone can see he is. You'd better be nice to him—he'd be a feather in any girl's cap.'

'Becky, I know you're anxious to see me married off, but I swear to you this is the last man I would choose for a hu.band! He's far too gentlemanly for my taste— I've no desire for a doormat.'

'In my opinion, that's another mistake you're making, young lady. It's true that Mr Winbolt is a proper gentleman—I wouldn't disagree with you there. But he's no doormat. He may not shout and bluster the way Mr Joseph used to, but he gets things done just the same. He has a way of looking…'

'Oh, pooh, Becky! He's a doormat!'

Annabelle's voice was clear and carrying. By this time they were coming downstairs again, and it was slightly disconcerting to see that the parlour door was half open. It was very possible that the gentleman warming himself by the fire had heard this last remark. Annabelle's colour rose a trifle as she entered the room, but she remained calm as he took her outstretched hand and bowed over it.

She eyed him critically. Nothing could be faulted about his attire. He had removed his many-caped overcoat to reveal a beautifully cut tobacco-brown coat, immaculate buff breeches, and boots which had obviously been highly polished before he had ridden through the mud to Temperley. Above his intricately tied cravat his face wore a polite smile, with nothing to show that he had heard her comment. She concluded that he had probably been too busy admiring his reflection in the mirror.

'Mr Winbolt, what can I do for you now?' asked Annabelle somewhat less than graciously.

He considered her before replying. She had an uncomfortable feeling that somewhere at the back of his eyes lurked a slight smile. Then he spoke and she was sure she must have been wrong.

'I came to enquire after your father. Jardine says he is no better?'

'I'm afraid he isn't.'

'Is there anything I or my sister could do?'

'Thank you. You are very kind, but I really cannot think of anything at the moment. He never looks for company, not even mine, so that of a comparative stranger—' Annabelle stopped short. Had that sounded rude? 'I mean, sir—'

'Don't worry, Miss Kelland. I know what you mean. I am sure you will let us know if and when anything occurs to you. But I also came to tell you that Emily and I will be spending Christmas in town with my grandfather, so we shall be away for a few weeks.'

'Oh! Oh, how pleasant! For you, I mean. The…the neighbourhood will miss you, I am sure.'

'I doubt it, Miss Kelland. We have not yet found our feet, so to speak, among our neighbours. Six weeks is hardly long enough to establish a wide circle of acquaintances, and my uncle had the happy knack of offending most of them. We have only just started to have callers.'

Was he laughing at her? Surely not! His face was perfectly serious. But when would he get to the business of the broken fence? 'Well, sir, I must wish you and your sister a happy time in London. Well…' she paused. 'Is that all?'

'I think so. Er…may I finish my glass of wine? Perhaps you would drink a toast with me?'

Annabelle blushed scarlet with mortification. She had been guilty of gross discourtesy. 'Oh, forgive me!' she stammered. 'Pray be seated, Mr Winbolt. Another biscuit?'

He smiled, filled a second glass from the decanter Becky had placed on a small table, and handed it to her. 'Thank you, but I can't stay long—I have a great deal to do. If I can't be of help to you, I'll drink up and be gone.'

His smile was sweet, his manner gentle, but Annabelle rather thought she might just have been put in her place. The feeling was not welcome. She gave the traditional toast to Christmas in a stiff little voice, then, for the life of her, could not think of another thing to say. She waited in silence while he donned his overcoat, and then escorted him to the door.

She cut short his courteously expressed farewells and asked impatiently, 'Aren't you going to ask about the fence in Four Acre field?'

'It's mended, Miss Kelland. Goodbye.' She was still standing at the door staring when he rode off.

'Well? Do you think he heard you?' Becky's voice was anxious.

'Heard what?'

'Heard you call him a doormat, of course.'

'Of course he didn't. He's much too much of a gentleman to listen. You can stop being so excited, Becky. Mr Winbolt and his sister are going to London. They'll be away till after Christmas,' said Annabelle dismissively.

She would not have been so complacent if she had witnessed the scene between brother and sister at the Winbolt home.

'How did you get on, Philip?'

Mr Winbolt looked at his sister with a rueful smile. 'She thinks I'm a doormat,' he said.

'*You?* A doormat? She's mad.'

'No, just unused to polite ways. And for the life of me, I cannot behave differently, though I know it irritates her.'

'I should think not, indeed! You'd do better to abandon any ambition in that lady's direction—if she could be so described.'

'She's so lovely, Emily! I know she behaves like a termagant, but only think of the life she has led—brought up by servants, running wild, no training in the ways of polite society… But there's a sweetness about her na- ture—I know there is. And though she is so lovely she is not in the slightest vain.'

'I agree with you there. Miss Kelland is far too care- less with her appearance.'

He went over and took her hand. 'You're very cen- sorious, Emily. Do you not like Miss Kelland? She isn't easy to know, I agree.'

'I confess I would like her more if she was kinder to you! For myself I like her well enough. There's a di- rectness about her which is appealing. But I cannot feel that she is right for you, Philip.'

'In what way?'

She hesitated a moment, then said, 'You are far from being a doormat, but you do like a more peaceful life than Miss Kelland would be likely to give you.'

'I'd like you to explain that, if you don't mind!'

'She has an air of independence about her which would come into conflict with that highly developed sense of responsibility of yours for those you love. I am sure she would resent your desire to cherish and protect us.'

'Do I really stifle you? Am I over-protective?' he asked with a rueful smile.

'Of course not! You are the dearest of men and most women would feel themselves fortunate indeed to win your favour.' She went to him and hugged him. 'If Miss Kelland is your choice I shall welcome her into the fam- ily with all my heart, Philip. But I have great hopes of our visit to London. Five weeks might help you to change your mind about her.'

'I'm not sure I shall satisfy you, Emily. I doubt I will find a more beautiful girl in the whole of London!'

'But perhaps a more suitable one? Oh, Philip, don't look like that—I only want to see you happy—you deserve it so much. Let's talk of something else. Do you intend to set off early on Friday and make a push to arrive in Arlington Street before nightfall? Or shall we take a more leisurely pace and stay with the Verrinders on the way? What are the chances of snow, do you think?'

'Has John come back with the post yet, Becky?'

Annabelle stood by the window gazing at the whirling flakes of snow. The Winbolts had departed for their Christmas festivities, and in the household at Temperley life was going on as quietly as usual. Mr Kelland had decided to get up, and now spent some time each day in the large chair by the fire in his bedchamber. He was still weak, however, and no more sociable than usual.

Christmas was drawing very near. Annabelle had distributed small gifts to all the servants on December 6th, and now preparations for their modest Christmas were well on their way—parcels for the poor, food for the villagers for Christmas Day. Every day Annabelle stood like this, gazing out at the weather; every day she asked the same question and received the same reply.

'Just this minute, Miss Belle. But there weren't anything from London.'

'Oh, why doesn't Rosa write? I wrote over two weeks ago, and still no answer! It is too bad of her! And now it wants only three days to Christmas.'

'Perhaps the mail has been held up by the snow? John had a terrible time getting to the receiving office—and the stage was held up for an hour at Hounslow.'

'You may be right. But I doubt it. My sister doesn't seem to want to see us any more.' Annabelle cast a glance outside—the snow was falling more heavily than ever. 'And if she leaves it any later she won't be able to get here at all.'

'Aye, it looks as if we're going to have proper snow this year, and no mistake. A real Christmas.'

'A real Christmas? What is that?' asked Annabelle moodily. 'When have we ever had a real Christmas?'

'Shame on you! Why, we have the waits coming round every year, and we've always set a good table for anyone who wanted to feed themselves here. Your father has never denied the poor their Christmas feast.'

'I'm sure my father is happy for us to fulfil his duties as a landowner at any time of the year, and especially at Christmas. But it's always been a joyless occasion for all that.'

'It weren't always so, Miss Belle. When your mother was alive there was so much fun and laughter, such preparations, such feasts and games. And the house used to look lovely, it did, all polished and decorated.'

Becky's familiar, rosy face was so concerned that Annabelle abandoned her position by the window and drew Becky to the fire. 'Tell me about it,' she said.

They sat by the fire, as they had so many times before over the years, seeking comfort in each other's company. And Becky once again described the scenes of revelry and mirth which had filled the old house twenty or thirty years before.

'There'd be an expedition to go out and gather long strands of ivy, and great branches of holly and fir. Then we'd wind them up and down the oak staircase, and round the candlesticks and along the mantelpieces. And there'd be mistletoe as well...'

'And I'll swear you were kissed a good few times under it, Becky!'

'Well, I won't say as I wasn't in the old days,' said Becky with a reminiscent smile. 'But after my John came on the scene there wasn't anyone else who dared!'

'Does he kiss you under the mistletoe now, Becky?'

'Get away with you! Over thirty years married, and the children all grown! A fine to do that'd be! But I was saying there was mistletoe and apples and spiced oranges tucked in everywhere. My, we were kept busy! Baking and roasting—venison, mutton, beef—'

'And goose?'

'If there was one left over from Michaelmas, Miss Belle. The snow never kept folks away—they used to come from all over and stay till it thawed, or till Twelfth Night was over. Your mother used to make everyone dress up—Punch, and Punch's wife, King Cole, Red Riding Hood, Columbine. And she made names up for them, too—Johnny Piecrust, Mrs Croaker, Prince Toploft, Jimmy Rusty Trusty and the like. My goodness, they had some fun! Snapdragon and Bullet Pudding and Hunt the Slipper and I don't know what besides. The servants used to be invited in to watch the plays and charades the company put on, and many's the laugh I've had at their antics.'

'And now you and I eat in the kitchen, entertaining the people from the village…' said Annabelle gloomily with a return to her former mood.

'For some of them it's the only decent food they get all winter, miss. It's a good old custom. Don't you forget it.'

'Yes, but I'd like just once to have fun at Christmas, Becky! Or fun at any time, if it comes to it. The sort of fun Rosabelle has had in London, with parties and balls and concerts!'

'It hasn't been all that happy for her in the last seven

or eight months, though! You've no call to envy your
sister at the moment, Miss Belle.'

'No,' said Annabelle in a subdued voice.

Becky looked at her downcast face, and went on, 'You
were both not six years old when your mother died. Little
mites—both as pretty as a picture, and as like as two
peas. Both called after your mama, God rest her.
Rosanna Kelland. ''They're both so beautiful, Becky,''
she said. ''I'm going to put a 'belle' for beautiful on
their names—Rosabelle and Annabelle.'' You were always such an independent little thing, but even when she
was so young Miss Rosabelle looked…lost, as if she was
always looking to be loved, always wanting to be cud-
dled, bless her. I suppose Lady Ordway chose the one
she thought needed her most. And Miss Rosabelle was
her godchild.'

'She was the lucky one—my own godmother died
when I was ten, and all she left me was a hideous silver
epergne. Where is it now, Becky?'

'In the attic. There wasn't room for it in the dining
room.'

'The attic is the best place for it!' Annabelle returned
to her original theme. 'Then Rosabelle became Lady
Ordway's real daughter in the end—by marriage, at least.
I wonder what Stephen was really like.' They sat in silence looking at the fire for a while, then Annabelle
added, 'It's strange that Rosabelle has not been to see us
for such a long time—only once since she married, and
not at all since Stephen died. She always seemed to enjoy
herself when she was a girl and spent the summer with
us.'

'I expect she's led a busy life in London. And Mr
Ordway was such a rich young gentleman, brought up
in the city and all. The country didn't seem to be at all

to his taste.' The two women carefully avoided looking at each other. Stephen Ordway's visit had not been a success. 'Miss Rosabelle wouldn't have wanted to cross him.'

'But why doesn't she come now, when I asked her to? I told her Papa wasn't well. And it's Christmas! Lady Ordway could surely spare her for a little while. Rosabelle must have some feeling for us, she never seemed to blame Papa for giving her away.'

'No... but—'

'What?'

'Well, I've always thought that being taken away like that did something to Miss Rosabelle. There was no doubt that Lady Ordway loved the little girl, it weren't that, but...taking the child away from her home—and especially from you, her twin. You were so close, it must have given her a shock. She was always less sure of herself than you, Miss Belle, but I think she got worse after that.'

'I have this curious feeling, Becky—that Rosabelle isn't happy.'

'Of course she isn't! It's not a year since she lost her husband.'

'No, it's deeper than that. Rosabelle hasn't been happy for a long time. But she never says anything when she writes to us. Oh, I wish she would come!'

'She'll come if she can, my dear. She wouldn't stay away without good cause after she read your letter.'

'But what if the snow lies?'

'Now stop fretting and do something useful—have you been to see your father in the last hour?'

'No, I shall go now. But he doesn't need anyone, you know, Becky. Not for company.'

'I know, my dear. But you ought to stay with him for a little while.'

As Annabelle mounted the wide oak staircase to her father's bedroom, she tried to imagine what it would be like as Becky had described it, wound with holly and ivy, and scented with spiced fruits and dried herbs. The forlorn silence of the hall and landing would give way to the rustle of taffeta and silk and the sound of hurried footsteps and suppressed laughter. There would be a fragrance of lavender and perfumes from the bedrooms, honey and beeswax, apples and spices, mingling with the aroma of roast meat and baking from other parts of the house...she could almost smell it all.

She reached the top of the stairs, then turned and executed a deep curtsy to some imaginary tall, dark-haired beau, coming in through the door to be King of the Revels to her Queen for the twelve days of Christmas. He might even escort her to a neighbouring ball in a handsome carriage drawn by four perfectly matched horses.... But no one came up the stairs to meet her, no hand reached out to raise her, no admiring voice complimented her on her magnificent costume. The hall was empty and she was alone on the stairs.

Annabelle sighed, then laughed as she looked down at her simple house dress and practical shoes. No imagination could turn her into a fairy princess! The twelve days of Christmas would pass as quietly as any other twelve days of the year. A walk in the snow, visits to church, calls on the sick—those were her entertainments. She knocked on the door of her father's bedchamber. It was opened by his manservant.

'Is my father awake, Walters?'

'Yes, miss. But I'm not sure...'

'Nonsense. If he's awake, then I'll see him. You go downstairs for a while—I'm sure you need a break.' She walked past the gloomy, elderly man who had been with her father for as long as she could remember, and advanced to the fire. 'Papa! How are you?'

'No better than I was an hour ago, Annabelle. And no worse either. You can pour me a glass of water, since you've seen fit to dismiss Walters.'

Annabelle poured some water into the glass and passed it to him.

'Put the other candleholder nearer my chair. And fetch me the commentary on Donne I was reading yesterday.'

'But Dr Jardine said—'

'I know what he said. Fetch the commentary, there's a good girl.'

Annabelle sighed and brought the well-worn book from the bedside. Her father sat up with some difficulty, brusquely rejecting her offer of help. He opened his book and became absorbed.

'There is still no word from Rosabelle, Papa.'

'Hmm? Well, it doesn't matter. Close the door carefully when you go out, Annabelle. The draught is most unpleasant if you don't. And tell Walters not to be too long.'

Annabelle looked at him in some exasperation, then silently left the room, taking pains to close the door behind her. Becky and the others said her father had been a great charmer in his youth, but his daughters had never seen anything of it.

Mr Kelland had withdrawn from the world after his wife, Rosanna, had died, just five years after giving birth to a longed-for son. The child had been born before the twins, Rosabelle and Annabelle, were a year old, and the mother's constitution had not been equal to the strain.

She was never really well again and in the end, in spite of her indomitable spirit, she had simply faded away.

Henry Kelland had been distraught, he seemed not to know how to survive without his wife's gaiety and verve. The idea of bringing up three children, all under the age of six, seemed to overwhelm him, and Lady Ordway's offer to take one of the girls had seemed heaven-sent. So the twins had been separated—Rosabelle had gone to London, and Annabelle had been retained as a companion for the little boy. A useless exercise, as it turned out, for he, delicate from birth, had died before he was seven. Since then Mr Kelland had lived as a recluse, interested only in his books, attended silently by his manservant, and ignoring when he could the demands of the outside world.

Annabelle was left very much to herself, and when the various governesses and tutors finally departed no one suggested that she should see something of society. So she gradually taught herself, with Becky's help, to run the household and oversee the management of the estate, and sometimes it seemed to her that, except for a few short weeks each summer, she had never known what it was to be a child—carefree, without the burden of responsibilities.

Rosabelle, younger by twenty minutes and slightly less robust, would have gone under had she been subjected to such treatment. Her nature needed constant love and encouragement if it were to blossom. Her intelligence and sense of humour were as keen as Annabelle's, but quieter and more easily suppressed. Her imagination was as lively, but often dominated by fear of failure: failure to please, failure to conform to her godmother's standards, failure to make Lady Ordway proud of her.

The happiest times either twin knew were the sum-

mers spent together on the estate at Temperley. For three
months of each year Rosabelle had been delivered to her
family home and left in Becky's care to enjoy the companionship of her sister and the freedom and fresh air of
the country. And during this time the twins renewed the
bonds of their birth, trying, albeit unconsciously, to make
up for the separation which circumstances had forced on
them. Becky watched with pride in them both as the
sedate, grave little visitor from London turned into a
laughing, carefree girl, and her own reckless, impetuous
charge learned to match the grace and control of her
sister.

But the summer visits came to an end the year before
Rosabelle married, and since then Temperley had seen
her only once, in the company of her husband. It had not
been a happy occasion, and had never been repeated.

Three days later Annabelle stood gazing gloomily out
at dark skies heavy with the threat of yet more snow.
Christmas was nearly over. She had attended the midnight service in the church nearby on Christmas Eve, and
Mr Kelland had surprised everyone by coming with her
to morning service that day. He had returned to his room
immediately after, however. In spite of the weather, the
Christmas parcels had all been distributed to the poor of
the parish, and numbers of villagers and tenants had
trudged in to give them the season's greetings, and to
enjoy the traditional meal in the huge kitchen. Now they
had all gone, and the house had resumed its normal silence.

Rosabelle had not, after all, come. When the long-
awaited letter had finally arrived its message was disappointing. Rosabelle was deeply sorry—she only
wished she could come to Temperley for Christmas. But

there were too many difficulties in the way. Aunt Laura had still not recovered from Stephen's death and Giles Stanton, Stephen's heir, needed her presence in London for the moment. She had every hope that she would be coming to join them all at Easter.

'So that is that!' Annabelle had said to Becky. 'But this letter is too short and too uninformative. If there were not so much to do, and if I were able to leave Papa, I would post off to London to find out exactly what is going on. But I can't.'

'You can't anyway, Miss Belle. I think most of the roads are blocked now. It's just as well Miss Rosabelle isn't coming, if you ask me. She could easily have got stuck on the way. We must just look forward to Easter. The weather will be much better then.'

After Christmas the weather remained harsh. Winter lasted well into March, and the biting north-easterly winds continued even beyond that. Annabelle put aside her disappointment over Rosabelle's non-appearance, and taught herself to look forward instead to Easter. She went about her normal business in spite of the snow and wind, seeing to the estate, calling on her father's tenants and dependents. Mr Winbolt called several times after returning from his Christmas visit to London, but even his optimistic nature was wilting slightly in the chilly atmosphere of Annabelle's indifference—much to Becky's regret.

'I don't understand you, Miss Belle—you couldn't ask for a nicer, more gentlemanly gentleman. And it's not as if you were snowed under with offers.'

'I keep telling you, Becky! I couldn't bear to be tied to Mr Winbolt! I'm sure he would cosset me to death!'

'Well, what's wrong with that, I'd like to know?'

'It would stifle me. I like to fight my own battles.'

And an episode at the end of March illustrated just how much Annabelle's passion for independence was offended by Mr Winbolt's sense of chivalry.

At the time Annabelle was delivering a basket of eggs to one of her father's pensioners, a former servant who had married and now lived in a cottage at the edge of the village. Jenny's choice of husband had not been wise—he was a lazy good-for-nothing who spent a great deal of his time and wages in the Dog and Duck. His wife and children would have come off poorly except for the charity of friends and neighbours. Annabelle tried to avoid Sam Carter for he was almost always drunk and very often abusive. But on this occasion she was unlucky.

When she got to the Carters' cottage he was standing in the doorway, and refused to move. The thought of accepting her charity seemed to enrage him and he snatched the basket away and threatened to throw it to the ground. His manner was ugly, but Annabelle was perfectly prepared to do battle. As she well knew, Samuel Carter's blustering manner was mostly show, and a firmly worded request to return the basket was almost certain to succeed.

However, before she could utter it, Mr Winbolt, who was riding by at the time, leapt from his horse and strode over. Before either Annabelle or Carter knew what was happening, the basket was safely removed, and Carter was being held in the hardest grip he had ever experienced.

# Chapter Three

'Why aren't you at work, Carter?' asked Mr Winbolt curtly. Carter cowered and mumbled something about not feeling up to it.

'Go and dowse your head in the water butt, man! Go on!' Mr Winbolt gave Carter an almighty shove in the direction of the water butt, then turned to Annabelle. 'I hope he didn't hurt you, Miss Kelland.'

'Not at all. I am well used to Sam Carter's ways, sir.' The lady's tone was cold. 'I assure you, he would not have carried out his threat. He knows me too well for that.'

'He's drunk, however. And men in liquor are not always aware of what they are doing. You should be all right now—the cold water has sobered him up a little, and I shall see that he goes back to work.'

'You are very kind.' If anything the lady's voice was even colder. 'I am sure Carter's wife would be glad to see him go back to the farm. They need the money. But

I do assure you, Mr Winbolt, your help was unnecessary. I am perfectly able to deal with Sam Carter and his ilk, drunk or sober.'

Mr Winbolt seemed about to disagree. Then he glanced at the small crowd which had gathered, hesitated, then merely nodded his head. He regarded Annabelle with some amusement.

'I am relieved to hear it, Miss Kelland, but if you should need my help with Carter—or anyone else—at any time in the future I shall be ready to oblige. And I hope,' he continued, raising his voice a little, 'that Sam Carter knows as much!'

There were visible signs of approbation among the villagers round about. Respectful as they were of Miss Annabelle's authority, it was clear that they regarded the gentleman's intervention as natural and right. Annabelle was furious, but dared not show it. She gave the briefest of curtsies and turned into the cottage. Mr Winbolt stopped a passing wagon, arranged for Carter to be taken back to the fields, then continued on his way.

Annabelle received little sympathy when she gave an account of the incident at Temperley. Her father stirred uncomfortably, then said, 'John Bostock should have been with you.'

'Papa! I couldn't possibly have John nursemaiding me whenever I go to the village. What would they all think? I've been dealing with Sam Carter for years! You know he is harmless.'

'Not this time, apparently. Winbolt was right to intervene.'

'I would rather call it interfering! And I can manage perfectly well without it.'

'If you say so, my dear. Has the post arrived? I'm expecting a set of dictionaries.'

Becky's first words were, 'There, I knew it! I've always said John ought to be with you when you go into the village. Or that you have a groom of your own. It's not right.'

'Becky! Not you too! John can't be spared, and we cannot afford another groom just to dance attendance on me. The whole notion is ridiculous!' Annabelle stormed. 'I don't know what has come over you all. We were all perfectly satisfied till Mr Winbolt came along with his stupid London ways! I wish he would leave us alone!'

The Winbolts departed for London soon after, and Annabelle was left in peace as she wished. Mr Kelland had suffered a chill after his Christmas excursion to church, so he announced, with his doctor's full approval, that he would not leave his bedchamber until the weather became warmer, ordered a new supply of books from London, and spent his days in front of his fire, or resting on his bed. He was, if anything, even less sociable than usual. Annabelle visited him several times a day, but she was never made welcome.

Rosabelle had written regularly, but though her letters were usually straightforward enough, Annabelle suspected that some of them at least had been written and rewritten until all feeling had been removed from them. The planned visit at Easter was still in place, but, though Easter was now only a week away, they had heard nothing. Annabelle was growing anxious—Rosabelle must come, she must! She could not bear to wait any longer before seeing for herself what sort of state her twin was in.

Just a few days later Annabelle was on her way to her father's bedchamber, when she heard a strange sound from outside. She stopped and listened, but all she could hear was the wind whistling wildly through the chimney pots. She went on her way.

'Did you hear anything just now, Walters?' she asked as the manservant admitted her.

'I heard the wind, Miss Kelland. It comes through the windows. The draught is not at all what one would ask for an invalid, but though we have asked Bostock to mend them, he hasn't yet shown his face.'

Annabelle ignored this. Walters, jealous of the Bostocks' influence in the running of the house, seldom lost an opportunity to criticise them. 'That's not what I meant,' she said as she went over to her father. 'How are you, Papa?'

'Quite well,' he said absently. 'Have you any more candles? Walters asked the girl to bring some, but she hasn't appeared yet.'

'I'll look for her and tell her to bring them straight away. There's still some life left in these, isn't there?'

'A little. It's irritating if they run out. Thank you. You could pass me that dictionary, if you would.'

'I wonder if Rosa will come, Papa. Don't you?'

'I don't venture into useless speculation, Anna. You'd better find that girl. A dozen candles should do. And you might try to fasten those curtains more securely—Walters doesn't seem to know how.'

Annabelle sighed. Walters didn't want to learn, she thought, as she went over to fasten the heavy curtains. But what she saw from the window chased all thought of curtains and candles right out of her mind, and caused her to exclaim with joy. A handsome travelling coach was coming up the drive. 'Papa! Papa! It's Rosa! She's come, after all!'

Shouts from the coachman and grooms could be heard,

as the coach came to a halt. Annabelle flew down the stairs and pulled the huge oak door wide open.

'Becky, Martha, John, quickly, quickly! Mrs Ordway is here! Why didn't you write to let us know, you silly thing?'

She ran out to the elegant carriage, heedless of the icy wind, and stood impatiently waiting for her sister to emerge. It seemed to take an age, and when she did appear, she looked so fragile that a breath could have carried her away, let alone the present tempest. Annabelle heard Becky beside her murmur, 'Lord save us!' Then they moved forward and the sisters were laughing and crying and hugging each other as the servants bustled in and out with luggage and rugs, the wind catching Rosabelle's blue fur-trimmed travelling cloak and blowing it about like a banner.

They took Rosabelle into the kitchen, for she was shivering with cold, and it was the warmest room in the house. Becky hurried round muttering about beds and fires and warming pans, while Martha heated some milk for the traveller. John could be heard outside, telling the coachman and grooms where they could put the horses for the night.

'Shall I take your cloak, ma'am?' Martha asked as she brought the milk. 'The warmth of the fire will reach you better.'

'That's right,' said Becky, bustling up. 'Hang it up carefully, lass, then go and fetch the bottle of brandy from the cupboard in the dining room. A drop of cheer wouldn't come amiss for Mrs Ordway.' Annabelle sat on the floor beside her sister, rubbing the blue hands and gazing anxiously into the white face.

Rosabelle smiled at her sister. 'Oh, it's lovely to be here! Don't look so worried, Annabelle. We were held up at Maidenhead Thicket—there had been a landslip. I had to get out and wait while they got the carriage round on the road again. It was so cold! I had hot bricks and rugs when I set out, but they had lost some of their heat by then. I shall soon thaw out. How is Papa?'

'He's reasonably well—I was with him when I saw you arrive. Oh, Lord! That reminds me! Martha! Martha, get one of the girls to take a dozen candles up to the master's room. She's to tell him that Miss Rosa has arrived, and that I'll bring her to see him soon.' She turned to Rosa. 'I'm so happy you've come at last!'

As Annabelle brought her sister up to date on the state of affairs at Temperley, she examined her covertly. Rosabelle was bone thin, and her skin was transparent. The hands wrapped round the cup of milk must be warmer now, but they were still trembling. Something was very wrong—Rosabelle was sadly altered since she had last seen her.

Surely the loss of her husband alone could not have caused this transformation? Or was love a stronger force than she had imagined? Never having been in love herself she found it difficult to judge. The mystery surrounding Rosabelle was growing, and Annabelle resolved to fathom it before her twin returned to Upper Brook Street. But for the moment she needed love and attention and that she should have in abundance.

'There now, Mrs Ordway, your bed's made up in the room next to Miss Belle's—'

Becky stopped short as the twins smiled. 'Which Miss Belle, Becky?' they chorussed.

This was an old joke. Becky had over the years shortened Annabelle to 'Miss Belle', but whenever Rosabelle was visiting both twins quickly learned to answer to this, and Becky was forced to use their full names.

Before Becky could reply, Rosabelle said, 'Please, Becky, please call me Miss Rosa, as you did in the old days. I'd like it so much better. "Mrs Ordway" sounds so strange coming from you.'

'You and Miss *Anna* used to plague the life out of me in the old days, but I dare swear you've learned more sense since then. And, to be honest, it's not so difficult at the moment to tell which of you is which. Whatever have you been doing to yourself, Miss Rosa?'

Rosabelle's eyes dropped to her cup of milk. 'It's a long story, Becky.'

Becky's sharp eyes regarded her for a second, then she said briskly, 'Well, never mind it now! Suppose you paid a visit to your papa, and then went to bed? I'll bring you something to eat if you desire it, but what you need most is a good rest after that journey. Don't you agree, Miss B—Miss Anna?'

'I do indeed. I'll take you up to Papa now, Rosa, if you're ready.'

After a short and entirely typical interview with her father, the gist of which was that Mr Kelland was glad to see his second daughter, but not if she was going to disturb his peace too frequently, Rosabelle was happy to let Becky undress her and help her to bed.

'Another day tomorrow, my dear.' Rosabelle smiled sleepily at the familiar words. She hardly heard Annabelle's whispered goodnight before falling into the first undisturbed sleep she had had for many months.

'What are we to do?' asked Annabelle as she and Becky descended the stairs. 'Should I send for Dr Jardine tomorrow?'

Becky frowned. 'She's very pale and thin. And I don't like those shadows under her eyes, and that's a fact.'

'It may just be that she is overtired—she was telling me that Lady Ordway is still an invalid. I expect she has been spending a great deal of time with her. Shall we see what a few days' rest and good, wholesome food will do?'

'Maybe you're right—do you know when they want her back in London?'

'I don't care when they want her back! She's not going back before she is absolutely fit again, however long it takes. They must just do without her.'

Rosabelle stayed in bed for the next couple of days. A fire was kept going in the pretty little bedchamber, and the door to Annabelle's room was kept wide open all the time. Though she maintained each day that she was feeling considerably better, Annabelle was still undecided whether to call Dr Jardine or not.

Rosabelle slept heavily for the first day and a half, only waking to take a sip of water and a spoonful of Martha's broth. But then her sleep became more restless and Annabelle often woke in the night to hear desperate protests, followed by heartbreaking sobs coming from the next room. When she went to comfort her sister, Rosabelle would cling to her fearfully, even in her sleep, refusing to let her go.

On the third day after her arrival Rosabelle seemed to recover some of her spirits, and announced that she would get up. Becky and Annabelle had decided that they would make a particular effort this year to make Easter as joyful an occasion as they could, and the kitchen was redolent with spices for Easter cakes and Easter biscuits. Annabelle spent hours decorating the traditional Easter eggs, and raided the garden and copses

round about to fill the house with daffodils and fresh
catkins.

So Rosabelle came down to a warm fire in the small
parlour, the fresh scent of flowers in the hall and a delicious smell of baking from the kitchen. The dining
room was deemed to be too large and too cold, and a
small table had been set up in the parlour, which also
had its vase of flowers—late snowdrops, celandines and
wild daffodils.

Between them Annabelle and Becky had wrought
marvels, for time had been very short. Their efforts were
well rewarded. Rosabelle's smiles grew more frequent,
her cheeks acquired a little colour, her rest was less disturbed.

On Easter Sunday, as the bells rang out over the countryside, she startled Annabelle by announcing that she
would accompany them to church.

'But, dearest—'

'It's only a short walk, Anna. I shall be well wrapped
up. And look! The sun is shining. Please. I should like
to.'

The weather suddenly cooperated with Annabelle. The
wind dropped round to the west, the sun shone more
frequently, and the temperature rose. The buds on the
trees and flowers in the garden, which had been held
back by the inclement weather, began to swell. Rosabelle
was hesitant at first, but then she seemed to grow
stronger and happier with every day that passed and
Becky looked on with delight as the sisters laughed and
argued, came back with pink cheeks from walks which
grew longer each day, and played silly games with great
energy in the evening.

Though Dr Jardine came to see their father, no one

suggested that he should look at Rosabelle. Her sister waited patiently for any sign that Rosabelle was ready to confide in her, but none came. Rosabelle seemed to be determined to put London and all its associations behind her.

For a while all went well, then, towards the end of April, there was a sudden and dramatic reversal. Rosabelle grew quiet, started losing her appetite again, and was soon well on the way to her former nervous state. Annabelle sensed the turmoil in her sister's mind, but was at a loss to account for it. Eventually when she found Rosabelle sitting in her bedroom, gazing out at a landscape full of blossom with an expression of deep despair on her face, she decided not to wait any longer. She demanded to know what was wrong.

Rosabelle started to speak, then stopped. 'Nothing, Anna. Nothing you could do anything about. I must just face it again myself.' She gave a long, shuddering sigh. 'I just…I would like… It's hard, Anna.'

'What is? And what do you have to face? My dearest Rosa, whatever it is, you needn't face it alone! There are two of us, remember.'

'No. You can't help. No one can. I have to go back.' The low voice was lifeless, but when Annabelle looked at her sister's hands they were twisting the handkerchief that she held round and round her fingers.

'To London? But this is rubbish! I thought you could stay till the summer?'

'They're sending the carriage for me in one week. Exactly one calendar month from the day I left London. He's very exact. I expect it comes from being in the army… He said I had to return when he sent the carriage.'

'Who is "he"?'

'Giles Stanton—Stephen's cousin. He was Stephen's heir.'

'Why haven't I heard of him before?'

'He's been away in Europe for most of the past ten years. He came home only a few months ago.'

'But what has he to say to what you might or might not do? Rosa, it's clear that you are not yourself. Why do you take any note of what Giles Stanton says?'

'You don't understand, Anna. I have to take note. Stephen…left a lot of debts. Somehow or other he got hold of some of Aunt Laura's money, too, and spent that. I expect he would have paid everything off, if he had lived to inherit all the rest. But he didn't, and now Giles is…in charge.'

'Stephen was over twenty-one when he died, surely?'

'Yes, but under the terms of his father's will Stephen had either to have a son, or wait till he was twenty-five, before he could inherit.'

'I see! I didn't realise… Wasn't that…rather strange?'

'Yes,' said Rosabelle briefly. 'But there were reasons… Anyway, the result of it is that Aunt Laura and I will be practically penniless unless Giles clears Stephen's debts.'

'Mr Ordway is, however, honour bound to see that you and Lady Ordway are secure!'

'Not…not legally.'

'Perhaps not, but any man of feeling—'

'That's just it! He has no feeling.' Rosabelle's voice rose slightly and her fingers were now tearing the delicate handkerchief to shreds. 'He dislikes me, he thinks I'm a parasite.' She looked down. 'And perhaps I have been, all these years. Aunt Laura was always so kind, so loving. Perhaps I did let her spoil me. Then when she was so insistent that I should marry Stephen I felt it was the least I could do… It was never for the money…'

'Is that what Giles Stanton thinks? What a pleasant man he is, to be sure! But, Rosa…are you saying that you didn't love Stephen?'

'I…I loved him because he was Aunt Laura's son. It…it seemed the right thing to do. He was kind enough to me….when I was little. But—' Rosabelle came to a sudden stop, her lips firmly closed. Then she added, 'I must go back when Giles sends for me. He is going away to France again soon, and he needs me in London. So I have to go next week. I…I just don't feel… It hasn't been long enough to…'

Annabelle gently removed the remnants of the handkerchief and held her sister's hands. 'You mustn't go back till you are fit, Rosa. This Giles Stanton will surely understand that. You must write and tell him.'

Rosabelle shook her head. 'Giles Stanton wouldn't believe a word I said.'

'But *why?*'

'Stephen told him dreadful things about me.'

'Rosa—?'

'And that's all I can tell you. I've given my word not to talk about Stephen, and I've already said more than I should. No, I have to go back and there's an end!'

There was a silence. Annabelle didn't know what to say. The picture of Rosabelle's life in London was so different from what she had imagined.

'Then I shall get Papa to write to Mr Stanton. He would if I refused to leave him alone till he did. Mr Stanton must listen to reason.'

'I tell you, he won't! He made me promise that I would return to Upper Brook Street when the carriage comes to fetch me, and look after Aunt Laura, and run the house for him, while he's away. Otherwise he'll refuse to pay Aunt Laura's debts—'

'He's a monster!' said Annabelle, really shocked. 'He can't mean it!'

'I don't really think he would hurt Aunt Laura. He's fond of her. But I can't risk it! And when he jeers at me in his horridly sarcastic voice, and accuses me of being unfaithful to Stephen...I don't know how to answer him. To tell you the truth...I'm frightened of him.'

'The man is clearly out of his wits.'

'Out of his wits or not, he now has complete control of the Ordway fortune. Aunt Laura and I will live in penury, unless he agrees to pay Stephen's debts.'

Annabelle frowned as she considered her sister. 'You know, Rosa, you've allowed all this business to get you down. It can't have been easy—losing Stephen, Aunt Laura ill, and now these debts. But you are not usually so...so spineless.'

'Is that what you think me? I suppose I am. But, Anna, I've never had your...your enjoyment of a fight. I like to be friends, to be at peace with those around me. And...and...' Rosabelle's voice trembled. 'In recent years there seems to have been nothing but unhappiness.'

'Why didn't you tell us this sooner? Or come earlier?'

'I couldn't leave Aunt Laura. And then after Christmas Giles went away to France and things were better for a while. Aunt Laura and I were on our own, and the house was peaceful. Waiting till Easter to get away didn't seem so impossible. But then Giles came back again and started working on Stephen's papers. He found some diaries. It was much worse again after that. Stephen was ill. He hardly knew what he was writing, he ranted and rambled, and sometimes you can hardly make out what he has written. But Giles is sure he understands it all.

He only sees what he wants to see, of course. Anna, I swear I gave Stephen no cause to hate me—you believe that, don't you?'

'Of course I do!'

'Giles doesn't. It ought to be easy to convince him, but I just can't do it. I keep thinking of what he could do to Aunt Laura, and then I get in a panic and can't think straight. If only I felt better about going back!'

'You shan't go back!' said Annabelle decisively. 'Not until you are ready, at least. It is clear to me that you need time to build up your strength and spirits. I know—' She held up her hand as Rosabelle tried to speak. 'You feel you can't leave Aunt Laura. But tell me, Rosa, what will happen if you collapse—as I think you will unless you are given time to recuperate? No, you must stay at Temperley until you are fit. I shall get Papa to write to Giles Stanton tonight.'

'No! You mustn't! Giles is so determined to believe the worst of me, Anna. Indeed, I wouldn't put it past him to stop the payment of Stephen's debts out of sheer malice, and the bills are already overdue. He was so angry with me the day before I came away that he almost stopped me coming. I tell you, I had to give him my word that I would return when the carriage came for me.' Rosabelle grew even paler. 'He said he would tell my creditors where I am if I didn't. Or that he might even come himself to fetch me.'

'I wish he may! I would enjoy telling him what I thought.'

Rosabelle shook her head. 'Aunt Laura needs me, and Giles has the power to make her life a misery. I must go. That's the end of the matter, Anna.'

Her face was gentle but obstinate. Annabelle could see that her twin was determined to submit to Giles Stanton's

ruling, and nothing anyone said would persuade her otherwise. It was because of Lady Ordway, of course. Even
in her present state of health Rosabelle would have challenged Giles Stanton's threats if they had been directed
solely at her. But her sister had always been devoted to
Lady Ordway—apparently to the extent of tying herself
for life to someone she clearly had not loved, merely to
please her godmother. Giles Stanton's callous use of
Stephen's debts to threaten Lady Ordway was the lever
which was forcing Rosabelle back to London. The man
deserved to be punished!

If only they could find a way of letting Rosa stay at
Temperley without harming Lady Ordway... Quite out
of the blue an idea came to her—an idea so audacious
that she rejected it immediately. It would be *impossible!*...wouldn't it?

Over the next few days, as Rosabelle grew more and
more miserable, the idea kept coming back to Annabelle,
like an importunate gnat. What was the use of being an
identical twin if you couldn't use it to good effect? In
the past they had often played tricks on Becky and the
others for their own amusement. Now some active good
could come out of it. Eventually the idea no longer
seemed so out of the question, and she decided to try it
out on Rosabelle. Her twin stared at her as if she had
gone mad.

'*You* go to London in my place? Don't be absurd!
Aunt Laura suggested something the same, but she was
only joking. It's impossible, Anna! We couldn't carry it
off.'

'We've done it before.'

'But never for so long. Giles would be bound to suspect.'

'Giles Stanton has never seen me. No one ever believes how alike we are until they see us together—you know that! In any case, if he dislikes you as much as you say, he probably wouldn't even see that much of me. From what Lady Ordway writes, he is to be away for a month—perhaps we could change over again before he comes back! And, Rosa, didn't you say that Lady Ordway even had the same idea?'

'Yes, but I can't believe she meant it.'

'I think she did. Why should she mention it otherwise? I am sure it would be perfectly possible! Think, Rosa! You could have another month or so—the summer, even—down here with Becky, and no one else to cause you the slightest worry. We should have to tell Papa, but he wouldn't object, I am sure.'

'It would be wonderful!' Rosabelle's face was full of longing. 'But no! I can't let you do it.'

'Why ever not? The more I think of it, the more I like the notion.'

'But you don't know the servants, the house, your way about London…'

'You could coach me. We have a little time before the tumbril comes.'

Rosabelle chuckled. 'Anna! Things may be bad, but Giles wouldn't submit you to the guillotine!'

'Well, then, what have we to lose?'

'What about your neighbours? Mr Winbolt's nephew? And his sister?'

'It couldn't have worked out better—they are away again, spending Easter with their grandfather. You'll meet them very little before we change back. And you can always make some excuse. Since I hardly ever pay calls, I haven't seen much of Emily Winbolt at all. Philip Winbolt has visited us several times, but Papa has always

pleaded illness as an excuse for not receiving him, and
I haven't wasted time on entertaining him. Rosa, this is
the best idea I've had for a long time. You must let me
put it into practice.'

'Let me think it over. I cannot deny that it's very
tempting…'

One week later the twins stood in the little parlour and
gazed at one another. Rosabelle was no longer the pathetic creature who had so shocked Becky and her sister
on her arrival. The twins were once more almost indis-
tinguishable one from the other. Identical dark blue eyes
were surrounded by the same absurdly long lashes.
Identical dark golden curls surrounded the same delicately modelled faces, though one head was half hidden
by the hood of a travelling cloak. There was not a tenth
of an inch difference in the height of the two slender
figures. Each face even had the same half-excited, half-
apprehensive expression. They were saying their farewells, for the Ordway carriage had come as arranged and
was now waiting at the door.

'There's still time to change your mind, Anna.'

'What, and waste all those hours spent learning the
geography and customs of the Ordway mansion—not to
mention the streets of London? What a foolish suggestion! Besides, I am determined to enjoy myself—I
wouldn't miss it for all the money in the Bank of
England.'

Rosabelle was still anxious. 'You have my note for
Aunt Laura?'

'Safely tucked inside my reticule. She shall have it as
soon as I see her.'

'No, no! You must make sure she is strong enough
first. I know she suggested we should change places, but

she may not quite have thought we should actually do it. Take care of her, Anna! Make sure she understands why we have done this—I wouldn't hurt her for the world. And remember to call her Aunt Laura!'

'Rosa, I shall do everything necessary. Stop worrying, my dearest girl. You will best prove your devotion to Lady Ordway by getting fit enough to look after her yourself, and acquiring the strength of mind to stand up to Giles Stanton. Though by the time I have done with him he may well be more human.'

'Don't upset him, Anna! Please!'

'Of course, I shan't upset him,' said Annabelle reassuringly. 'I shall be the soul of discretion, I swear. You may trust me—I have learned a great deal from dealing with Papa, you know. I must go—we mustn't keep the horses standing. Don't come out with me—we don't want the Ordway servants to see us together, but tell me the names of the men out there.' They went to the window.

'I'm not sure of their names—they're all newly engaged. The one on the left is Roberts, I think, but they won't think it strange if you don't remember them.'

'Who is the man waiting by the door?'

'He's important. That's Goss.'

'Giles Stanton's man? The one who was a sergeant in the army?'

'Well remembered! Giles must have sent him to make certain that I do go back, as promised.'

'How charming of him!'

Rosabelle hesitated, then suddenly took Annabelle's arm and said in a rapid undertone, 'Anna, I gave my word to Aunt Laura that I wouldn't tell anyone about Stephen, but I can't let you go without warning you! He…he had some strange friends. Don't take any risks—

especially if you come across a man called…called Selder.'

'I shan't take any risks at all. Don't worry so, Rosa! I can't imagine Stephen's friends will bother anyone after all this time.'

'But you will take care?'

Annabelle took her sister's worried face between her hands and kissed her. Then she said slowly and clearly, 'I shall take every precaution not to receive any of Stephen's friends, I will remember to call Lady Ordway "Aunt Laura", and I shall treat Giles Stanton with great respect—for as long as I can manage it! Now will you stop worrying? I shall soon lose all patience with you, Rosa! Come, you can see me to the door, but no further. And you can take care to call me *Rosabelle* in public!'

'There you are!' Becky bustled up as they emerged from the parlour and made their way to the front door. 'Have you everything you need, Miss Belle?'

It was what was needed for this fraught moment. The twins looked at one another and smiled as they chorussed. 'Which Miss Belle, Becky?'

Becky frowned severely as she looked at the Ordway grooms, waiting just outside the door. She said, gazing hard at Annabelle as she spoke, 'Why, Miss *Rosabelle*, of course!'

The figure in blue embraced first her sister, then Becky and allowed herself to be assisted into the coach. The grooms leapt up, the driver cracked his whip and the carriage trundled down the drive. Annabelle Kelland was on her way to London.

# Chapter Four

Rosabelle sighed and turned back towards the parlour. She suddenly felt exhausted. The last week had been exhilarating but hard. Equipping Annabelle with what she needed to carry out her impersonation had taken every bit of their joint ingenuity. They had chanted and memorised, tested and re-tested, joked and laughed, had even come close to quarrelling once or twice, but in the end they had agreed that Annabelle had as much information as Rosabelle could impart, and Annabelle could absorb in the time given to them. She hoped it would be enough.

There were dark areas in her life regarding Stephen which she had not discussed with her sister, but they had remained undisturbed for some time now. And she had put Annabelle on her guard. In fact, the situation seemed to be under control…as long as Annabelle kept her head and didn't provoke Giles. She shook herself. She now had a month—perhaps more—to forget the tensions of

the house in Upper Brook Street and learn to relax. That
was the whole purpose of this daring escapade.

The small household soon learned to accept 'Miss
Belle', and indeed it was hard for most of them to remember which Miss Belle it was, so alike were the girls.
The present Miss Belle had a gentler air, perhaps, a more
ladylike manner, but not so that a casual observer would
notice, and Temperley's secret was well guarded by
Annabelle's loyal band of servants. There had not been
time for Rosa to learn about life at Temperley, so she
spent a great deal of her time working with Becky and
John in order to acquire the routines of the house.

Her father remained in his room. Mr Kelland's condition was pronounced not life-threatening, but his weakness, allied with his indifference to the world, made it
most unlikely he would leave his bedchamber in the foreseeable future. He had been told of the switch between
the twins, but it had not seemed to mean much to him.

Life at Temperley carried on in its quiet, uneventful
way—the best possible treatment for Rosa's shattered
nervous system. John brought news from the village that
the Winbolts had accepted an invitation from some
friends in Surrey, and were not expected back for another
few weeks. Rosa breathed a sigh of relief. Anna had been
dismissive about Philip Winbolt, but nonetheless it
would have been a strain meeting him. Becky seemed to
think he was more wideawake than he appeared.

May ran the rest of its course and the countryside
started to show signs of summer. Rosa went out most
days, walking or riding. She took to performing
Annabelle's duties with the people on the estate, gaining
more confidence with every day that passed. Fresh air,

peace and Becky's loving care had wrought wonders. Rosa's step had a spring to it, the shadows under her eyes had vanished and her cheeks had lost their hollows. She was now slender, rather than thin, and the fragile, transparent look which had so shocked Annabelle, had quite gone.

She began to believe that in a little while—quite soon, in fact—she would be able to cope once again with life in London. The thought was not a happy one. She had discovered that life in the country suited her far better than city life, and Upper Brook Street was a poor exchange for Temperley. However, it was her clear duty to look after Aunt Laura, and she prepared herself gamely for the changeover.

One day, leaving her horse tethered to a tree, she walked along the banks of the river which marked the boundary of the Kelland estate. After a while she came to a spot where the view was so beautiful, that she left the path and stepped down on to the river bank to admire it. Willows, bending their slender branches to trail and sway in the water closed the vista on either side. In the foreground, a family of swans made their stately way upstream in slow, rhythmic strokes. And beyond, on the other side of the valley, the green slopes of the Downs rose serenely to an azure blue sky. She stood lost to the world, breathing in the scented air, feasting her eyes on the idyllic scene.

'Miss Kelland! How very pleasant to find you here. I was on my way to call on you when I saw your horse. But—take care! You'll be in the river.'

Rosabelle had swirled round to find a perfect stranger standing on the bank behind her. With a cry of alarm she had taken a step back, stumbling over the skirt of her riding habit. If he had not caught her she would have fallen.

'I'm sorry to have startled you. I didn't think... Please forgive me!'

He assisted her up to the path, but released her immediately when she took a step away from him. Now she could see that he was quite the handsomest man she had ever met, with regular features, grey eyes and blond hair cut in a Brutus crop.

'Miss Kelland? Are you quite well?' He was regarding her with such an expression of concern that she forced herself to respond.

'Perfectly well, thank you. The...the sun was in my eyes. Thank you for rescuing me.' Who could he be? He obviously knew Annabelle. Was...was this Philip Winbolt? The doormat? She rejected the idea immediately, it was impossible! But who on earth could he be? Annabelle had not mentioned any other newcomers. He was looking at her as if waiting for her to say something. She must speak.

'I...wasn't expecting to see you here.' That was safe enough. But he still appeared to be waiting! 'Temperley has not seen you for such a long time.' That was safe, too. She had been home for nearly two months, and this man had not called in all that time.

'I dare not hope you've missed me! Emily and I have been visiting friends and relations, but I confess I am more glad than I can say to be back at Shearings.'

It *must* be the doormat! The Winbolts had owned Shearings Hall for as long as anyone could remember, and Annabelle had called Mr Winbolt's sister 'Emily'. Oh, how could Annabelle have been so blind? She decided to risk his name.

'Mr Winbolt...' That seemed to go down well. He had

smiled. She said more confidently, 'Mr Winbolt, did you say you were on the way to Temperley?'

'Yes, I did.'

'Shall we ride together?' A flicker of pleased surprise crossed his handsome face.

'Of course, Miss Kelland—I should like nothing better.'

Stupid, stupid Rosabelle! Of course! Annabelle would have been far less gracious. But she could hardly withdraw the invitation now. Think, Rosabelle, think! Annabelle had said something about fences... She set off along the path.

'I thought we could look at...at some of the fences on the way,' she said in a cooler tone, throwing the words over her shoulder. 'I believe you wanted them seen to?'

'Ah, yes. The fences. Shall we not leave John Bostock to deal with it?' He drew ahead to hand her over the stile. 'I confess I am still in holiday mood, Miss Kelland.'

There was a quirk to the corner of his mouth, and the grey eyes were dancing as he stood on the other side of the stile and looked up at her. She found the humour in them irresistible, and laughed. Mr Winbolt stopped short, gazing at her in wonder. Then he took a deep breath and helped her down to the ground. He appeared to forget that he still had hold of her hand as they set off along the road to the horses, and Rosabelle gently removed it.

Her mind was working furiously, but she was also conscious of a feeling of exhilaration such as she had never before experienced. It was clear that Mr Winbolt was more interested in 'Miss Kelland' than her sister had revealed. Annabelle had been somewhat scornful of the gentleman. Had her attitude been a screen to hide her real feelings? Rosabelle was inclined to think not—her sister had been too casual. But how had she come to underestimate Mr Winbolt so? This was no weakling— the hand which had grasped hers was firm, the voice, though perfectly polite, had an assured ring to it.

'Is your groom near at hand?' he said, looking around.

'I haven't one with me.' When he showed surprise she added, 'I've known Temperley and its surroundings all my life. I can manage perfectly well without one. He is better occupied working for John Bostock on the farm.'

'You could still have a fall,' he said gently. Then he held up a hand and said, 'But I know your independent spirit too well to say any more. Will you permit me to help you mount?'

Rosabelle nodded and in a few minutes they set off back to Temperley. She wondered nervously how she would fare in this unexpected test, and tried to remember what Annabelle had said about the Winbolts. After a minute or two Mr Winbolt broke in on her thoughts.

'You seem somewhat abstracted. I hope your father is not worse? I saw Dr Jardine in the village yesterday. He seemed to be of the opinion that Mr Kelland's condition was stable.'

Rosabelle seized on this unexceptional topic of conversation. 'You are kind to be so concerned, sir. Papa is as well as he is likely ever to be again. He has always been happiest when left to himself, and though his illness is undoubtedly genuine, it provides him with the best possible excuse to be unsociable.'

'So you have said—more than once,' he murmured. 'And I have to confess that I thought it a ruse to keep me at arm's length.'

'Oh, no! I am sure it wasn't!'

'You sound as if you no longer remember, Miss Kelland?'

Once again Rosabelle castigated herself for her stupidity. Her deception wouldn't last long at this rate. What had Annabelle said? She blushed and stammered, 'I meant that…that I intended no such thing—' She stopped short. Heavens, she was now sounding as if she didn't wish to keep him at arm's length! What a tangle she was getting in! She took a deep breath and said stiffly, 'I think you are aware that Papa is fairly indifferent to us all—family and acquaintance alike. Whatever my own feelings in the matter, there was no ruse attached to what I told you. You misunderstood, Mr Winbolt.'

He looked at her flustered face and shook his head ruefully. 'I apologise. I won't tease you any more. It's a bad habit I have, and a frequent source of annoyance to my sister.' There was a short pause. The horses ambled gently along, neither rider making any attempt to hurry them. The day was delightful—bright without being unduly hot, and the countryside was still freshly green and alive with the movement of small animals going about their business.

'But…' He stopped.

'But what?'

'I seem to have made it impossible for myself to find out whether you still object to my calling at Temperley. Now that I can no longer claim that I have come to call on your father.'

'Oh. I…I…' Rosabelle was filled with conflicting feelings. On the one hand she knew she should not encourage Mr Winbolt—Annabelle would not thank her for it. On the other… It was a long time since she had met anyone whom she found more agreeable. She compromised. 'In the country, Mr Winbolt,' she said primly, 'neighbours call on one another out of simple courtesy, with no particular significance attached to it.'

'Of course,' he said gravely. His face was serious, but she had the impression that he was amused. However, he seemed content to leave the question, for he went on, 'When I last saw you you were still uncertain whether your sister would be able to join you for Easter. Did she come?'

'What? Oh, yes! We had a very pleasant time. Quiet, you know. She…she is a widow.'

'Is she much older than you?'

So he didn't know that the Kellands were twins! So much the better. 'No, not very much,' she said, crossing her fingers and telling her conscience, which was distinctly uneasy, that twenty minutes was indeed not very much.

'Does she resemble you? I should like to have met her.'

Poor Rosabelle was becoming somewhat desperate. 'We are a…a little alike, yes, Mr Winbolt,' she stammered, thanking her lucky stars that Mr Winbolt had never met Rosabelle Ordway before. Had he seen the twins side by side, her present impersonation would soon have been discovered, for nothing much would escape this gentleman's sharp eyes, she was sure. How could Annabelle have been so wrong about him? She must get off the subject of the Kellands as soon as possible. It was too nerve-racking. 'Er…how is your own sister? Did she enjoy her stay in London?'

'We spent the Easter holiday with my grandfather in Arlington Street. I can't say we had a lively time there— he is an old man, Miss Kelland, and tires easily, but we are both very fond of him. We always spend Christmas and Easter with him. Afterwards we spent time with friends in Reigate, and that was more to Emily's taste. She is a sociable creature—we both are. I'm sure she enjoyed herself, but, like me, she is glad to be back at Shearings. Emily loves the countryside round here as much as I do. We hope to have some friends to visit us in the near future, and I should very much like you to make their acquaintance. Dare I hope you would come to Shearings again? My sister would be delighted to welcome you there.' When Rosabelle hesitated he added, 'Just as a matter of neighbourly courtesy, Miss Kelland. With no particular significance attached to it.'

She glanced at him sharply. How dare he quote her own words back to her! But he was regarding her with such a quizzical look in his eyes, inviting her to share in the joke, that she was hard put to it not to laugh again. She would not laugh, she would not! It was too dangerous. He was watching the telltale quiver at the corner of her mouth with great interest, to see what she would do. But when she suppressed it he smiled, as if he guessed what an effort it had been. What was there about this man? She had known him for less than half an hour, but he was already a danger to her peace of mind—and not just because he might see through her charade, either! With immense relief Rosabelle saw that they were at the gate to Temperley.

'Thank you for your company, Mr Winbolt. Pray give my regards to your sister. I hope to meet her quite soon. Goodbye.' She held out her hand in unmistakeable dismissal. He bent his head over it.

'I have enjoyed our ride together, Miss Kelland. But we still have much to discuss. May I call on you tomorrow?'

'What have we to discuss?'

'Why, the fences, Miss Kelland. Had you forgotten?'

'I thought you had decided to leave the fences to John Bostock, sir,' Rosabelle said, unable to decide whether she was pleased or sorry that he was being so persistent.

'That was today when I was in holiday mood. Tomorrow is another matter altogether. Seriously, Miss Kelland, I do need to clear up the matter of our boundaries. I'm sure John Bostock and my man can sort out the larger part, but there are one or two places where we need to come to some sort of agreement. I would have preferred to talk to your father, but you have always given me to understand that he leaves such decisions to you. May I come about eleven o'clock?'

'Of course. I shall expect you then. Goodbye, Mr Winbolt.'

Rosabelle rode up the drive at a good pace. If she was to learn about Temperley's boundaries before eleven o'clock the next morning she would have to begin at once. She rode straight round to the stables, where she hoped to find John Bostock. He was nowhere to be seen. She waited impatiently while the stable lad looked for him, then dismounted and ran into the kitchen.

'Becky! Becky, tell me quickly. Where's John?'

'My John, Miss Belle? He's gone to Reading Market.'

'Oh, confound it!'

'Miss Rosabelle!' said Becky, scandalised.

'I'm sorry, Becky, but it's so urgent! And you mustn't call me Rosabelle.'

'I'm not surprised I did,' said Becky austerely. 'Such language. But what's amiss?'

'Philip Winbolt is coming here tomorrow to catechise me on the boundary fences! That's what is amiss. And I haven't the faintest notion about any of it.'

'Dearie me! What time is he coming?'

'Eleven o'clock. I shall have to pretend I am unwell, that's all. Five minutes talking about fences—no, not even five!—would expose me for the fraud I am.'

'Now don't get in a fret, Miss Belle. The maps and all the other details are in the library. We'll go and get them out first of all. John should be back before long and he can spend some time with you then. And tomorrow you've got till eleven.'

'All the time in the world,' said Rosabelle hollowly. 'I still think it would be better if you told him I was prostrate. Indeed, it will probably be perfectly true.'

'Come, Miss Belle. If Mr Winbolt wants to talk to you about these fences you've got to face him sooner or later—I don't suppose he'll wait till Miss Annabelle gets back. Think of her! She could well be ashamed of you, the way you're going on. You're not ill now, young lady.'

Becky sailed off towards the library, Rosabelle meekly following. Annabelle proved to have been a methodical and efficient worker. The plans were kept in clearly marked folders, and the areas of dispute in the past were outlined in red. Rosabelle carried them carefully into the little parlour and laid them on the table by the window. Becky helped her to change out of her riding things and she was soon absorbed in the plans of the Temperley estate.

The names of the fields and woods were already familiar to her from her childhood summers. She and Annabelle had roamed freely through every corner of the estate and picture after picture unrolled in her mind's eye as she studied the documents. Dead Man's Spinney, Potter's Pit, Four Acre field, South field, Boundary field, Thomson's Wood and the rest—all known, all loved.

* * *

It came as a surprise to her when Becky interrupted her with the news that John was back.

'So you can have a bite to eat, and then the two of you can study the things together. Though he's not much of a scholar, my John, he knows the grounds like the back of his hand, and he's helped Miss Belle a lot in the past.'

After supper they worked till the light faded, and then fetched some candles and worked some more. It soon appeared that there were only two areas which might still be in question. John scratched his grey head.

'Though I don't understand what he wants to talk about, Miss Belle, I really don't. The other Miss Belle—' He looked sideways at Rosabelle and she nodded. 'The other Miss Belle sorted it all out with old Mr Winbolt and the lawyers...it must have been early in the autumn last year—a month or two before the old gentleman died.'

'All the same, we'd better make sure that I know what I'm talking about, John.'

So Rosabelle toiled till her eyes couldn't stay open, and she got up early the next day and went back to the plans, and worked some more. When the time came for Mr Winbolt's call, her eyes were sore and her head was aching but she was fairly certain that she had mastered the history and layout of the Temperley estate.

'Mr Winbolt, ma'am.' Becky ushered Rosabelle's new acquaintance into the parlour with dignity.

'Thank you, Becky. Perhaps you'd fetch some refreshment. What will you take, Mr Winbolt?'

There was a very slight pause, then her guest said politely, 'The Canary wine you...offered me before

Christmas was excellent, Miss Kelland. But a glass of wine of whatever sort would be very welcome.'

'The Canary wine, Becky—and some of those delicious macaroons Martha was making yesterday. I hope your sister is well, Mr Winbolt…'

Becky left the room and came back a couple of minutes later with the refreshments. Her face was impassive, but Rosabelle could tell she was perturbed, and wondered what she had done wrong. She tried to catch Becky's eye as the housekeeper placed the tray on the side table, but failed. Becky went out, and Rosabelle, mentally shrugging her shoulders, turned to Mr Winbolt.

'You see, I have all the necessary papers ready for you. Let me show you.' She took him to the table and opened up the large map of the estate. 'I understand the difficulty lies here—' she stretched out her arm and pointed '—and here.'

She became aware that Mr Winbolt was standing very close, and felt slightly breathless.

'Where did you say it was exactly, Miss Kelland? Here?'

His arm brushed hers as his finger touched the spot on the map. He seemed to have come even closer. She moved round the corner of the table, and looked hard at the places on the map, waiting for her pulse rate to slow down a little.

Then she said firmly, 'I am surprised that you do not seem to know where it is, Mr Winbolt! I believe the matter has already been discussed by the lawyers. Before your uncle died.'

'Ah!' He smiled at her apologetically. 'You have found me out.'

'Am I to infer, sir, that you knew this yesterday?' asked Rosabelle, with commendable restraint.

'No, no! I was told about it by my agent this very morning. I went to see him before coming here—something I should have done before even mentioning the matter to you. It was careless of me and I am truly sorry, Miss Kelland. I could have saved you the work of getting these documents out.'

Rosabelle resisted a strong impulse to throw the map at him. If he only knew what his 'carelessness' had cost her! Getting the documents out indeed! That was nothing, nothing at all, compared with the real work she had done since speaking to him the previous day! The whole of the evening before and half the morning spent slaving to master details which he was now dismissing so light-heartedly as unnecessary! It was too much!

She was about to say so when she suddenly saw the pitfall before her. She could not possibly vent her wrath on him, or on anyone else! It would have to be suppressed. The real Annabelle would not have had all that work—she would have had all the details at her fingertips without reference to any maps or documents!

Something of her struggle to contain her feelings must have reached him for he went on, 'I am truly sorry. But why didn't you tell me yesterday that it had all been dealt with? I thought when you mentioned fences…'

'I was thinking of the broken fences, Mr Winbolt,' Rosabelle said with an undeniable snap in her voice.

'They are all mended. You know they are.'

This took her by surprise. 'I do?' Then she pulled herself together and said firmly, 'I mean, I do! Of…of course I do! But…but it is all very vexing!' As soon as these words left her lips Rosabelle regretted them. She knew exactly what she meant by them, but she hoped Mr Winbolt did not.

She was lucky—Mr Winbolt merely looked anxious

as he said, 'I have made you angry again, and we were dealing with one other so well, too. How can I make up for it? You…you wouldn't consider coming out for a ride? It's too lovely a day to spend indoors, and I enjoyed our short meeting yesterday so much.' She hesitated and he went on, 'Be generous, Miss Kelland. Forgive my thoughtlessness and come. Will you? Or do you think it too hot?'

Rosabelle was fully conscious that she should refuse this invitation. Her sister would never have accepted it, she knew. Annabelle would not welcome a closer acquaintance with the Winbolts. And every moment spent in this man's company threatened the safety of their charade. Most important of all, she was more strongly attracted to him than anyone else she had ever met. It was all too disturbing!

Even if he felt the same attraction, nothing but disappointment could come of it, for her time at Temperley was already drawing to a close. No, not only for Annabelle's sake, but also for her own happiness and perhaps even his, she should not go with him. She opened her mouth to refuse him, and, when their eyes met, she said weakly, 'Thank you. I should like to. I shall only take a moment to change.' Then calling Becky she went upstairs.

'You shouldn't do it, Miss Rosabelle,' said Becky when they were safely in her bedchamber. 'There's bound to be trouble. I shouldn't be surprised if Mr Winbolt is a touch suspicious already. You certainly had him puzzled.'

'Yes! Why? What did I do just now in the parlour? You were frowning.'

'You made him welcome, that's all. The best Canary,

Martha's macaroons, enquiries about his sister, one of your best smiles…'

'I didn't smile! Or if I did it was a conventional smile of welcome. Not in the least a…a best smile, Becky!'

'If you say so…but it looked very like one to me. Miss Annabelle wouldn't hardly have given him the time of day. No wonder he was a bit taken aback.'

'I cannot understand why Anna was so determined to dislike him. To my mind he is charming.'

'And no fool, either, Miss Belle,' said Becky, her voice heavy with warning. 'What's going to happen when Miss Annabelle comes back, that's what I'd like to know. What will he think then? Going for rides day after day, entertaining him in the parlour—you'd best be more careful in future! There! It's a bit loose, but I've pulled the string as tight as I can. You're still a touch thinner than Miss Annabelle.'

In spite of her strictures Becky looked with pride at her charge when she had finished dressing her. On the whole Annabelle paid little attention to her appearance, but her old riding habit, which Rosabelle normally wore when she went out by herself, had recently been replaced with a new one, and today Rosabelle had donned it for the first time. Its lines were simple, all the fullness of the skirt being gathered to the back, and the severity of the cut, the slate-blue colour of its fine wool cloth, its tiny white ruff at the collar were immeasurably flattering—a perfect foil for Rosabelle's slender lines and her delicate colouring.

As Rosabelle stood there, in the middle of Annabelle's bedroom, dressed in Annabelle's clothes, Becky knew that it would be impossible for anyone who didn't know the twins as she knew them to tell the difference. But the signs were there for those who knew what to look for. Life had treated the Kelland twins very differently, and it showed. Annabelle had an air of decision, impatience almost, trained as she had been to run Temperley efficiently and well. She had a kind heart and a very ready sympathy for those in need of it, but she was as yet unaware of the more complex human emotions.

Rosabelle, as intelligent, as quick of understanding as her sister, had always seemed more lost, more in need of affection, and the years had only served to increase her air of vulnerability. If Mr Philip Winbolt spent very long with Rosabelle he would surely begin to suspect something, though whether he would dream that the Kelland sisters were capable of such a mad escapade was doubtful. But what about Rosabelle herself? She was showing a reckless liking for Mr Winbolt's company. Becky shook her head. There was only one consolation in this dangerous situation—Annabelle was now due to return as soon as a suitable opportunity for the changeover arose. Becky prayed that this would take place before any serious damage was done.

It was another day of brilliant sunshine, with just enough wind to keep it agreeably cool. Rosabelle was resolved not to let Becky's anxieties spoil her pleasure. Let the future take care of itself! The long term prospects for this delightful acquaintance did not look promising, for the time was rapidly approaching when she would have to resume her former life in London. She was chilled at the thought. She had had little enough enjoyment in recent years, and the prospect of life in London was not pleasant. All the more reason, she told herself firmly, to put all thought of the future aside and make the most of the present!

However, if she was to relax enough to enjoy the day

then she must direct the conversation into safer channels
than those of yesterday.

'Mr Winbolt, I am like you yesterday—in a holiday
mood. Shall we…shall we forget any difficulties of our
past acquaintance, and begin again? Shall we play a
game? That we have never met before?'

'If it means that you will look more kindly on me than
you have in the past, I should be delighted.'

'It's only for today, mind!' Rosabelle said hastily.

'Then I shall make the most of it. Miss Kelland, I am
enchanted to make your acquaintance. Are you familiar
with the countryside round about? Or may I show you
the beauties of this corner of Berkshire?'

'It is always pleasant to see familiar places through
someone else's eyes, Mr Winbolt. Pray do.' Their eyes
met, and they both burst into laughter. 'Please don't stop!
I know it is a ridiculous pretence, but I am enjoying it
so much,' Rosabelle said as soon as she could speak.

'Then may I take you to the little piece of woodland
by Harden Lane? If you haven't been there recently
there's something you might like to see.'

# Chapter Five

They rode along sometimes speaking, sometime in silence, but always with a feeling of companionship. They passed fields scattered with grazing sheep, tall trees echoing with the harsh sounds of rooks busying themselves in their untidy nests, hedges filled with the flutterings of small birds. Rosabelle looked at it all with a smile of contentment on her face, and Philip Winbolt looked at Rosabelle and wondered why he sensed sadness behind the smile. He made an effort to amuse her, and met with success, for soon the sound of her laughter filled the narrow lane. They reached the copse, tethered the horses and walked to the stile a few yards away.

Rosabelle had fallen silent, for she was still conscious of the strange sensation she had experienced when he had put his hands at her waist in helping her to dismount. She was trembling as she climbed over the stile, and would have stumbled had he not grasped her hand firmly and held her till she had regained her balance. He ap-

peared to be a little short of breath, but he said nothing.
Nor did he this time hold her hand longer than necessary.
Colour rose to her cheeks. What an idiot she was!

'I...I...' Mr Winbolt cleared his throat. 'I wanted to
show you these.'

'Oh, how lovely! Oh, thank you!' Rosabelle gazed in
rapture at a rare carpet of flowers and ferns, a symphony
of green, silver-grey, pale pink, white, mauve and purple.
She bent down to touch with gentle fingers, caressing the
pale lilac florets, the delicately veined petals, the spotted
leaves of an orchid. 'I haven't seen anything like this for
years...!' She stopped short. Of course she hadn't—but
Annabelle would have! 'Anything quite so beautiful, I
mean,' she added hastily. 'I wonder how I came to miss
them?'

'It's easily enough done. I only came across them by
accident.' His tone was easy, but slightly puzzled, and
Rosabelle berated herself inwardly. Yet again she had
been careless. If she made many more such mistakes, Mr
Winbolt was bound to start suspecting something.
Delightful as his company was, the risk of being discovered was always there, however harmless the conversation appeared to be.

'You look unhappy. Does the thought of the flowers
depress you, Miss Kelland?'

'Oh no! They are exquisite. The orchids above all—
they are such a rare sight.'

He gave her another look. 'I suppose you mean rare
in the sense of beautiful? As you must know, such flowers are quite common round here.'

Once again Rosabelle laboured to retrieve the situation. 'Yes, yes! Beautiful. Such fine specimens—such a
beautiful setting. The ferns look as if they have been
arranged by an artist!' It was no use, the sun was still

shining, the countryside looked as beautiful as ever, but her happy confidence had evaporated, and the charm of the day quite vanished.

'What is it, Miss Kelland?'

'N…nothing,' she said nervously. 'Shall we go back?'

'Why, of course, if that is your wish. But…will you not tell me what is wrong?'

'I…I suddenly feel rather tired.'

'Then we must go at once. Do you need my arm?'

'No! That is to say, thank you, but the path is too narrow for that. I can manage, thank you.' She gave him an apologetic smile and started back for the stile.

The ride back to Temperley was not as comfortable as their outward journey. Rosabelle was dejected, making one banal remark after another, confining herself to comments on the farms, the state of the track, the weather, refusing to respond to Mr Winbolt's attempts to amuse her. After a while he gave up, and gave her a selection of politely conventional replies. The silences between them were constrained.

As they drew near to Temperley he said, 'I was about to ask you if my sister could call on you tomorrow. But perhaps you would prefer a rest?'

'Yes,' said Rosabelle, eager to seize on this excuse. 'Yes, I think I need a rest.'

'Could she come later in the week, perhaps?'

'I…I'm not sure…'

He regarded her closely, then said, 'Tell me, Miss Kelland, have you been ill while we were away?'

'Wha…what makes you think so?' Then, fearing that he might find the question strange she added, 'Yes, I was. It wasn't serious, however. I am now fully recovered. Except that I…I tire easily.'

'You should have told me—I should not have taken you so far.'

'No, I enjoyed our ride, Mr Winbolt. Those orchids were a cure for any ills!'

'But not for melancholy, it appears,' he murmured.

'I beg your pardon?'

'Nothing, nothing. I spoke without thinking. Miss Kelland, my sister is not a demanding visitor. I think she might well amuse you. And you would be doing her a very good turn, for she has yet to make any real friends in the neighbourhood. Could she not call—later in the week?'

'I should be delighted to see her,' said Rosabelle weakly.

'On Friday then? In the afternoon?'

'On Friday, Mr Winbolt.'


Becky was full of disapproval when she heard that Miss Winbolt was to call. 'I told you, Miss Belle—no good will come of it, you mark my words.'

'But what was I to do, Becky? In the nicest possible way he made it impossible for me to refuse him without appearing to be very churlish. I'm not quite sure how he managed it, but he did! I simply couldn't say no!'

'I always said that young man knew what he was doing. Miss Annabelle wouldn't have it—she thought he was weak, but I always knew! He wasn't here more than a couple of weeks before the people at Shearings were doing as he said. And it can't have been easy—they were that set on old Mr Winbolt's ways. No, he's a determined young man for all he's so soft-spoken. You...you're not getting too fond of him, are you, Miss Belle?'

'I am as aware of the situation as you are, Becky!' Rosabelle spoke with a touch of hauteur. Becky was a privileged servant, but there were some matters which were not for discussion. 'I will not do anything to compromise Annabelle's position. I know that she will take over in a very short time now. But receiving Miss Winbolt on a simple afternoon call can surely not commit Annabelle to anything but perfectly normal neighbourliness! In fact, I am surprised at my sister for not showing such a commonplace piece of politeness long before now!'

Becky gazed at Rosabelle in amazement. The twins had always been undivided in their loyalty to each other—they might quarrel among themselves, but they would never criticise one other to an outsider. Miss Rosabelle was right, of course. Miss Annabelle had been remiss. But it was extraordinary that her twin should say so. She tried to defend her mistress.

'Your father was ill, Miss Belle. And visitors were never welcomed here—you know that.'

'Well, it's time Annabelle did something about it! My father's illness was severe at first, but he no longer gives us cause for concern. He will remain what he has always been—a natural recluse. But Temperley should begin to live again, take part in the life of the neighbourhood. As far as I can learn, Annabelle has called on the Winbolts only once, though they arrived in the district some time ago. She is in danger of becoming as much a recluse as my father, Becky!'

Rosabelle's face was flushed and her manner was more spirited than it had been for a long time. She looked more like Annabelle than she had ever done before.

Becky would have spoken, but Rosabelle swept on, 'And I intend to do something about it. I shall receive Miss Winbolt on Friday, and what is more, I shall return

the call, too—and pay other calls. When Annabelle returns she will find that a normal social life has been
created for her, and she will thank me for it. When I
have gone back to London, she will be able to enjoy the
company of the Winbolts at parties and go for drives and
rides with them in the country, and laugh, and look at
flowers, and other…other delightful…delightful pursuits…'

Rosabelle's voice suddenly quavered and she fell silent. There was a pause. Then she repeated quietly, 'Annabelle will thank me for it, I am sure. So look out the
best china, Becky and get someone to polish the silver
teapot. There must be somewhere in Reading where we
can obtain macaroons and cakes…'

'You may safely leave the arrangements to me, Miss
Belle,' said Becky, very much on her dignity. 'Temperley will not let you down—and Martha's hand is as light
as any pastrycook's in Reading.' But she softened at the
despair in Rosabelle's next words.

'Oh, Becky, how soon will Annabelle come, do you
think?'

'I don't know, Miss Belle. I should have thought she'd
have written to warn us before this. But I don't suppose
she knows herself exactly when it will be. It's awkward—I mean she has to wait till she can get away without rousing suspicion.'

'And Colonel Stanton is a naturally suspicious man.
But it can't go on much longer.'

'There might be something tomorrow,' said Becky.

There had still been no communication from
Annabelle by the time Miss Winbolt's carriage drew up
at Temperley's door the following Friday. Becky had set
a whole series of preparations in train—the little parlour,

which had always been a favourite with the ladies of the house, warm in winter and cool in summer, had been swept and garnished. The ancient woodwork in the hall was shining with beeswax polish and elbow grease, and Rosabelle had filled the alcoves and side tables with roses from the garden and masses of greenery. A delicious smell of baking wafted through from the kitchens.

Miss Winbolt proved to be a sensible looking young woman in her middle twenties. It was clear that the good looks in the family had gone to the brother, though she had the same colouring, but the sister's face wore a similarly pleasant, open expression, and her widely spaced grey eyes were friendly. She looked round as she came in,

'So this is the famous linenfold panelling—how lucky you are to have such a fine feature in your house!' She gave her pelisse, and a small basket to Becky. 'Philip says you have been overdoing it, Miss Kelland. He was quite anxious about you. Are you more yourself after your rest?'

'I feel very well, Miss Winbolt. Your brother is kind, but you must tell him that he need feel no further concern on my part.'

Miss Winbolt's quizzical look reminded Rosabelle strongly of her brother. 'Telling Philip not to be concerned is as fruitless as King Canute's efforts to tell the tide not to come in. Whatever we say or do, his instinct is always to regard himself solely responsible for the welfare of his friends and relations. And to blame himself when things go wrong.'

Rosabelle smiled as she ushered Miss Winbolt into the parlour and said, 'Solely?'

Her visitor laughed. 'I may exaggerate a trifle, but I assure you it is very nearly true.'

'But surely such concern cannot be a fault!'

Miss Winbolt had been arranging herself in the chair
Rosabelle had offered her. But she stopped at this and
stared. 'Now that is strange! I would have sworn you
would be just the sort of person to resent it. Oh, forgive
me, Miss Kelland. That was impertinent. I rattle on too
much. But you surprised me, you see. And I must admit
that I myself have occasionally been forced to demonstrate to Philip that I am more capable than he allows.
But he's a good brother, for all that. He sent you some
strawberries from our own beds, by the way.'

Rosabelle flushed with pleasure, but when she saw
Miss Winbolt's eyes on her she merely said primly,
'How very kind. Would you like some tea, Miss
Winbolt?'

After that slightly awkward beginning the afternoon
went surprisingly well. Philip's sister was direct in her
speech, but her manner was friendly, and she had a
highly developed sense of humour. In spite of her earlier
words she was clearly very fond of her brother, and the
phrase 'Philip says' was frequently heard in her conversation.

Except for Lord Winbolt, their grandfather, the
Winbolt brother and sister were the last of an old, highly
respected family. They had inherited Shearings Hall
from an uncle who had never married, and their own
parents were dead. But it was clear that both brother and
sister loved the country, especially that part of Berkshire
in which they now lived.

'Have you ever lived in town, Miss Kelland?'

'Er…no. My sister has made her home in London for
some time. But I have never been there.' Once again
Rosabelle's conscience was uneasy at the lie. This masquerade had been embarked on for the best of reasons,

but it involved a web of deceit which was not at all welcome. But what else could she do? She prepared herself for further prevarication, but fortunately Miss Winbolt did not pursue the question of Miss Kelland's sister.

Instead, she went on, 'Up to now, I have never been able to make up my mind whether I preferred city life to that of the country, but now I am quite sure. I shall always be happy to spend time—and lots of money—in London's theatres and shops, but though life there is exciting, it cannot compare with life at Shearings.'

Rosabelle smiled with a touch of wryness. Her recent life in London had fluctuated between extremes of dullness and terror. She had no wish at all to return there. The thought pulled her up short. Had she really no desire to return? Not even to Aunt Laura?

'Miss Kelland?'

Rosabelle came to with a start. 'Oh, forgive me! My wits were wandering. What did you say?'

'I can see I've done just what Philip forbade! I've over-tired you again.'

'No, no, no! I've enjoyed our talk immensely.'

'Then may I ask you to come to Shearings? Quite soon? To tempt you further, I can promise to have all the latest versions of the *Ladies Magazine*, *La Belle Assemblée*, and other fashion journals. Philip is going to London next week and he always finds them for me.'

Following the decision she had expressed so forcibly to Becky a few days before, Rosabelle smiled warmly and said that she would come with pleasure.

Miss Winbolt left shortly afterwards.

'So what is your opinion of Miss Kelland now, Emily?'

The day after Emily's visit to Temperley the Winbolts were walking in the grounds of Shearings, enjoying the air and sunshine. They had taken to doing this quite regularly as the weather grew warmer. On these walks they usually discussed Philip's plans for the grounds and estate, but today the talk was of Temperley and its mistress. Philip was eager to hear Emily's impressions of Miss Kelland, and because they had had company the night before, this was his earliest opportunity.

'I have to say I may have been wrong about her, Pip. Of course, she has only been to Shearings once since we arrived, and her call then was very brief. The Courtneys were here, too, if you remember. I didn't talk to her for any length of time.'

'I thought you saw enough then to disapprove of her?'

'I didn't disapprove of her! I simply thought she would not be a good choice for you. But now…'

'Yes?'

'You said she had been ill. I think it must have been more serious than she has acknowledged. She is…less forceful than I remember.'

'But she doesn't lack spirit!'

'No. She was just as amusing, just as quick to appreciate my—our—somewhat quirky sense of humour. But her personality has…I don't know how to describe it. Softened? I found her very charming, which is not a word I would have used of her before. Perhaps her sister's visit had something to do with it? Her company manners have certainly improved.'

'Her manners have always been delightful,' said Mr Winbolt, somewhat stiffly.

'Philip! How can you say so? I know you have a partiality for Miss Kelland, which not all my efforts in London and Reigate could weaken, but you are usually prepared to be more honest than this. You've quite often given me a description of her behaviour to you which has shocked me, you know it has. Whatever her opinion of you, good manners alone would forbid some of the things she has said and done in the past. Calling you a doormat indeed!'

'You might be right, though she didn't intend me to hear that.' Philip laughed, but grew serious again when his sister asked, 'And what about the incident with Sam Carter? From what I hear she was almost rude about it.'

'That was different, I agree. She was remarkably determined to fight her own battle with Carter. And though I am very much more willing than you will admit for a woman to have her independence, I thought she was foolhardy—and surprisingly touchy. But I have to say one thing, Emily.' He stopped.

'We would be doing Miss Kelland a grave injustice if we forgot that the poor girl has had little opportunity to learn to depend on others. As far as I can tell she has been fighting her own battles since she was a child. And when has she had a chance to learn how to behave in company, confined to that house with a hermit for a father?'

'You are right, as usual, dear brother! But your Miss Kelland has recently acquired quite a few graces. So what is it which has brought about this present change? Can it possibly be that your persuasive charm is having an effect at last?'

'Much as I would like to think it, I can hardly believe it to be so. There hasn't been time for it to work! No, I believe the change is due to Mrs Ordway's visit.'

'The sister? She was here at Easter…I suppose you might be right. Someone who resides in London, and has a greater knowledge of the world than your Annabelle, was bound to make every effort to cure her sister's country manners. She appears to have had some success. Although…'

'Although?'

'I am reluctant to say this…but I must. If Mrs Ordway is even more worldly than we think, she might just have pointed out to her sister the advantages of marriage to a very rich man.'

'No! How can you suggest such a thing? Miss Kelland may be everything you say, Emily, but she is no fortune hunter. I'd swear to that.'

'I'm inclined to agree with you. But she would not be the first by any means to seek to improve her position in life by marrying a fortune.'

Emily's tone was bitter and her brother took her hand and held it comfortingly. Six years before, Emily's considerable fortune had attracted a man who was as charming as he was unscrupulous. Fortunately she had found him out before actually marrying him, but it had been a hard lesson, and she had taken a long time to recover.

But Philip said now, 'Dearest Emily, Annabelle Kelland is not such a one as Harry Colesworth. I know it.'

They walked in silence for a minute or two, then Emily asked, 'What about you? What is your opinion of the lady, now that you have seen her again?'

'I…I…' He laughed at his own lack of words. 'Emily, she is the loveliest, most desirable creature I have seen in my life. And I intend to marry her.'

'Such arrogance. How do you know she will have you?'

'It might take time, but she will have me in the end.'

'I know you too well to have any real doubt about the outcome. And on yesterday's evidence I think Miss

Kelland might turn out to be just the wife you need, darling Philip. There's a lost look about her which I missed completely when we first met. I rather think she might turn out to be a perfect subject for cherishing!'

Meanwhile, unaware of the Winbolts' discussions, Rosabelle continued to perform Annabelle's duties to the best of her ability. And, eventually, she inevitably came across Samuel Carter. Carter's son had been off colour for some days, and though Rosabelle was no expert, she was not satisfied with the treatment little Sammy had been receiving. She expressed her doubts to the boy's mother.

'Jenny, I really think you should consult Dr Jardine about little Sammy. I am not sure that Granny Carter's cordial is doing him much good.'

The boy had a fever, though it was not a high one, and Mrs Carter had been dosing him with an evil-smelling, black, viscous liquid, which previous generations of Carters had sworn by for all ills. On this, Rosabelle's second visit, the boy seemed to be, if anything, worse.

'But Miss Belle, the boy's father won't hear of the doctor! He swears by Granny's mixture—they all do! Besides, Miss Belle, we ain't got the money.'

'If Sammy has caught some sort of epidemic fever, then Dr Jardine will be only too pleased to come and check on him—without payment. He's a great believer in stopping these things before they take a hold.'

'Epidemic fever? My Sammy? Oh no, Miss Belle!' Mrs Carter looked as if she might burst into tears.

'Please, Jenny, don't get upset! Sammy doesn't look to me to be seriously ill, but I just think it would be a wise precaution to consult Dr Jardine. Why don't I call on him on my way home? And, I promise you, that if there is anything to pay I shall deal with it.'

After spending some time persuading Jenny Carter to agree, Rosabelle picked her way out of the dark cottage and out into the light. Here she was confronted by Jenny's husband, who stood on the threshold, blocking her way. He was swaying slightly, and there was a strong smell of beer about his person.

Rosabelle was nervous, but said pleasantly, 'Good morning, Carter.'

Samuel was surly. 'Marnin!'

'I'm sorry Sammy is ill—I've arranged with your wife that Dr Jardine should call.'

'There baint no need fer that! Granny's mixture 'll do the trick—the boy'll be foine. 'E don't need doctors and such.'

'I'd like to make sure of that, Carter,' said Rosabelle.

'You'd like to make sure! What call have you to come interferin'? I tell you, we don't need no doctors!'

'You do if there's a question of fever, Mr Carter,' said Rosabelle with determination. 'I'll call on him now on my way home. Please let me pass!'

'Fever!' Carter's face darkened. He stayed where he was. 'There's no fever in my house! Don't you go frightening honest folk with your talk of fever and the loike! We ain't got money fer quacks.'

'There'll be no charge. Now let me pass, if you please!'

'I'm not sure I want to, your ladyship! I told you last toime, we doan't need your charity—'

'Get out of Miss Kelland's path, Carter.' The quiet voice behind him caused Carter to turn round. 'If there's a risk of fever in the village, Dr Jardine must be notified—immediately! Miss Kelland, I'll escort you…if you wish.'

'Thank you!' With a sigh of relief Rosabelle stepped round Carter and took Mr Winbolt's arm with a smile. Then she stopped and turned. 'Don't be hard on Jenny, Carter. She's worried enough. Why don't you go back to the farm and leave her to deal with the child?'

'Why don't you, Carter?' asked Mr Winbolt with a steely look in his eye.

Carter shuffled off with a malevolent glance at Mr Winbolt. Rosabelle's eyes followed him down the street, and she sighed. 'What an unpleasant man he is! Will he go to work, do you think?'

'Unless I'm mistaken he's on his way to the Dog and Duck. But at least he'll be out of his poor wife's way for a while. I…I am relieved to see that you do not seem to be offended at my intervention. When I saw you both, I'm afraid I acted quite instinctively again.'

'Why on earth should you think I would be offended? I was extremely grateful!'

'Good! I'm glad to see you've acquired a little sense.'

'Sense?'

He regarded her with the half-rueful, half-quizzical smile that she was getting to know. 'You seemed to think on a previous occasion that you were invincible, that my help was completely unnecessary. And though I said nothing at the time I'm afraid I disagreed.'

'Oh. Er…this occasion. With…with Sam Carter, was it?'

'Yes. Don't you remember?'

'Yes, I do now,' said Rosabelle quickly. 'Of course I do! But…but Carter was worse today.'

'He was quite drunk last time, too, Miss Kelland. He was capable of anything.'

'I…I had forgotten. Well, perhaps I am feeling less invincible today? Or more favourably inclined to you?' She smiled at him charmingly, willing him to forget the subject. 'Shall we call on Dr Jardine?' There was a slight frown on his handsome face, but it cleared at her smile, and he agreed willingly enough.

A few days later Rosabelle was once again getting ready to meet the Winbolts, this time at their home. As Becky looked out one of Annabelle's dresses and tried it on her, Rosabelle was delving into what she could remember of Shearings. She had been there as a child but her memories were vague—far vaguer than Annabelle's ought to be, for her twin had frequently visited old Mr Joseph Winbolt before he died. Becky made little effort to help her—she was more interested in making the direst prophecies about what would come of it all.

'I wish you wouldn't do this, Miss Belle! Sooner or later it will all come out, and then we'll be in a mess, without a doubt! Oh, I do wish we'd hear from Miss Annabelle! It must be over a month since she last wrote.'

'And she didn't say anything much to the point then! I wonder if she's afraid someone in Upper Brook Street is reading her letters? I wouldn't put it past Giles Stanton—though he should have been off to France weeks ago.'

'You shouldn't say such things, Miss Belle. Colonel Stanton wouldn't read anyone else's letters, I am sure!'

'Colonel Stanton is capable of anything—anything at all, Becky. And I have noticed that Annabelle is always very careful to write as if she really is me. There is nothing in them to reveal her true identity. She must have a reason for being so cautious. But…are you so anxious to be rid of me?'

Becky shook her head vigorously. 'There's no doubt that your stay here has done wonders for you, and if I could have you both here—openly and without any of this play-acting—I'd be more happy than I could say. But since that cannot be, it's time you went back! High time! No good will come of all this visiting and the like.'

'I've told you, Becky. I'm doing Annabelle a good turn.'

'And yourself no good at all, if I'm any judge.'

Rosabelle's lips set firmly. She was not going to pay any attention to Becky. Let the future take care of itself—that was her motto now. 'Have you nearly finished the dress, Becky?'

Becky was working on one of Annabelle's walking dresses, taking it in where she could. 'It's not so bad now, Miss Belle. You're filling out. Soon I won't have to take anything in at all.'

Rosabelle gave a laugh. 'If Annabelle has been crossing swords with Giles Stanton she might well have lost a few inches herself!' Then she was serious. 'I hope she hasn't provoked him. She may not realise just how ruthless he can be. Oh, I wish we could have a proper letter from her, to learn what is really happening in London! But she has at least let us know that Aunt Laura is improving, and that is very good news indeed. Do make haste, Becky! I don't want to be late.'

'You don't want to seem too eager, neither, Miss Belle. There's no need to fuss. John will get you there in time. There!'

The dress was slipped over Rosabelle's head and Becky fastened the inside tapes and started to hook it up. It was a round dress in white jaconet muslin, plainly

cut except for a flounce of scalloped work round the
hem. Over it Rosabelle wore a close-fitting spencer in
cerulean blue silk, with long, narrow sleeves, puffed at
the top and trimmed with rouleaux of satin in the same
colour. There was even a very pretty bonnet to go with
it—pale straw, trimmed with bands of light blue silk and
a bunch of marguerites, and a fetching parasol.
Annabelle had looked ravishing in it, and so did her twin.

'There!' said Becky. 'You'll do.'

Rosabelle, impatient to be off, gave Becky a reassuring smile and whisked down the stairs. Becky followed
at a more sedate pace, shaking her head as she did so.

As soon as Rosabelle's carriage drew up at Shearing's
imposing portico, the master of the house appeared and
took her himself into the entrance hall. Here he gave her
parasol to the footman and gave him some instructions.
Then he walked with her to the drawing room. 'I'm so
glad you came,' he said simply, and smiled at her, his
eyes telling her how well she looked in her blue and
white outfit. 'And I have an agreeable surprise for you.
We have other neighbours—or almost neighbours—here.
They called quite out of the blue.'

Rosabelle's heart missed a beat. The afternoon suddenly seemed full of pitfalls—other neighbours? Another
session of walking a tightrope, keeping guard on one's
tongue, fencing with words? At best, these neighbours,
whoever they were, might be astonished at how little she
remembered of them. At worst they might ask about
'Rosabelle', mention the word 'twin'—even comment on
the likeness between them! It was truly said that the liar's
path is fraught with danger!

Desperately rallying her forces—she must just keep
the conversation in channels of her own choosing!—she

entered the sitting room. An elegantly dressed gentleman was standing by the mantelpiece, one well-shod foot resting on the fender. The lady sat on a chair nearby, her green silk gros de Naples dress, her curled feather bonnet, her fine kid gloves and slippers proclaiming the lady of high fashion. As far as she knew she had never seen them before in her life. They were complete strangers.

# Chapter Six

Feeling rather like Mary Queen of Scots mounting the scaffold, Rosabelle advanced into the room. Miss Winbolt came forward and greeted her kindly.

'Miss Kelland! I'm so glad you came! May I introduce you? Miss Kelland, Mr and Mrs Harpenden.'

Heavens—she had never even heard of them! But…her hostess had said 'introduce'. There was a chance, after all! Hardly knowing what she was doing she gave a vague smile in the Harpendens' general direction and curtsied.

'Mr and Mrs Harpenden are the proud new owners of Adwell Park, near Reading, Miss Kelland. So apart from yourself we are all newcomers to the area,' said Mr Winbolt.

'Oh!' Rosabelle's smile grew warmer, and she joined in the ensuing conversation with a pleasure unmarred by any fear of discovery. The afternoon passed quickly. The only difficulty Rosabelle encountered was in suppressing her own knowledge of London when the company talked of the amusements, the theatres, the parks, the customs of the capital. But since their manners were very good they only touched lightly on experiences that they did not expect her to share.

Questions about Temperley, Shearings, the countryside generally, she was able to deal with comparatively easily, and for the rest she found they had a style of conversation and behaviour which was totally to her taste. The company was in such good accord when the time came for the visit to end that the Harpendens pressed her to join Emily and Philip Winbolt when they next visited Adwell Park.

'Thank you. I...I...' Rosabelle hardly knew what to say. She did not expect to be in Berkshire for very much longer, but she could hardly say as much. In the end she fell back on the state of her father's health. 'I hope to be able to come. It is very kind of you.'

'Of course she will come, I shall see to it myself.' Mr Winbolt gave Rosabelle a smile, but spoke quite firmly. Rosabelle flushed as she saw Mrs Harpenden look surprised, then cast one discreetly raised eyebrow at Miss Winbolt. Philip's sister smiled blandly back, but a message had been received and understood, and, though the Harpendens were too well-mannered to say anything there and then, it was clear from their attitude as they took their leave that they were intrigued by the situation. Rosabelle was left to wonder what they said to Philip as he escorted them to the door. After they had left the room Emily Winbolt insisted that Rosabelle should stay a little longer.

'They have a journey to make, and you live practically next door. You can surely stay half an hour more—I

have some fashion plates to show you. I cannot say that
I like many of the new styles, but one has to keep up!'

'In London, perhaps, but surely not here in the country!'

'My dear Miss Kelland, when one is as lovely as you,
one can wear anything at all and still look entirely delightful—though, if I may say so, that is a very pretty
dress. But since the good Lord saw fit to give Philip all
the looks in our family, I have to take more pains—
wherever I am!'

'Are you talking nonsense as usual, Emily?' Philip
Winbolt came into the drawing room, shaking his head
and looking amused. 'It must be in the air. Mary
Harpenden talked a lot of nonsense, too. Oh, surely you
are not yet going, Miss Kelland? Can you not wait until
it is a little cooler?'

'I really ought to be ready to go when John comes,
and he should be here any minute.'

'I...I...er...I'm afraid I have a confession to make.
When you arrived I took the liberty of telling John not
to return for you. I shall take you back to Temperley
myself.'

Miss Winbolt looked with interest to see how her
guest would take this, but her brother paid her no attention. With a glance at the colour rising in Rosabelle's
cheeks he went on, 'I have a great deal of respect for
your independent spirit, Miss Kelland, but this is a very
trivial matter. It was really not sensible to take up your
servant's time when I have all the leisure in the world,
and would take pleasure in performing this small service.'

Confusion, not anger, had been the cause of
Rosabelle's colour. But since it seemed to be expected
of her, she simulated annoyance. 'He is, however, my

servant, Mr Winbolt,' she said coldly. "I should have preferred to have been consulted.'

'I've done it again,' Mr Winbolt said ruefully. 'I've offended you. Will I never learn?' He looked so cast down that Rosabelle's tender heart was touched. She exerted herself to reassure him.

'It was a very kind thought, both for John Bostock and for me. I am sure you meant well, Mr Winbolt.'

Mr Winbolt's sister seemed to be having difficulty in suppressing a laugh, but when her brother gave her a look she turned it hastily into a cough. Philip turned back to Rosabelle and went on, 'No, you are annoyed with me—and with reason.'

'I…I assure you that I am not at all annoyed…any longer, that is. Allow me to thank you for your thoughtfulness, Mr Winbolt.' He still looked uncertain, so she added persuasively, 'Please, let us forget the matter.'

Miss Winbolt shook her head in amused disbelief, as Philip gave Rosabelle a sweet smile with no hint of satisfaction in it. 'You are very generous. Er…may I show you something? It's in the winter garden.'

'But, Philip,' exclaimed Miss Winbolt, 'Miss Kelland and I were talking fashions before you came in! I wanted to show her the journals you brought back from London.'

'Can that wait till the next time, Emily? I want to show Miss Kelland something which won't last even as long as the fashions in the fashion plates.'

He was regarded with exasperated affection. 'Very well. But I hope you realise what a good sister I am. You don't deserve me.'

He came back to her and kissed her. 'You are the dearest, most deserving, kindest sister that ever was, Emily. Now, Miss Kelland, prepare to be amazed.'

He led Rosabelle through the house to the south side.

Here the somewhat neglected glasshouse of Joseph
Winbolt's day had been transformed into an oasis of
greenery. Tropical shrubs and plants of all sorts flour-
ished in the warm and slightly humid air.

'It's…it's…I've never seen anything like it before,'
said Rosabelle, gazing round in wonder.

'I am pleased you like it. I would have shown it to
you when you last came, but we had so little time—and
besides, it wasn't really ready for visitors. There was
practically nothing here then.'

'Nothing here?' said Rosabelle, gazing round at the
profusion of plants. Mr Winbolt smiled.

'Things grow very quickly in this atmosphere, and I
have numbers of friends who know of my interest and
send me plants, as well.'

He led her to a bench on which was a mass of delicate,
starlike, white flowers. They were small, but filled the
air with a sweet scent. Rosabelle was entranced. 'Oh,
how beautiful! What are they?'

'Orchids. Epidendrums. A friend at Kew sent them to
me. They're a distant cousin of the orchids at Harden.
And over here there are some special ferns…' He took
her over to another bench, then another, and another,
pointing out the rarities, and waiting while she examined
them, one by one. They came back to the beginning, and
Rosabelle looked around her.

'If I had not already forgiven you for sending John
back, I would surely do so now, Mr Winbolt. I would
not have missed this for the world.'

She looked up at him, her delight still reflected in her
eyes. What she saw in his made her tremble. Panic-
stricken she stammered, 'Mr Winbolt, I… We must go
back! Please….'

Her voice died away as he took her hand and raised

it to his lips. A mixture of enchantment and desire almost overcame her, and when he released it she could not stop herself from letting the hand rest against his cheek.

'Please,' she whispered. 'Please. You mustn't…'

He took her hand again and drew her closer, slowly, almost reluctantly, as if he knew he ought not, but could not help himself. Then, still holding her hand, he put his other arm round her. They stared into each other's eyes, like two people in a trance. Mr Winbolt tightened his arm and bent his head… Their lips met. After an initial hesitation Rosabelle found herself returning his kiss with fervour.

'My darling!' he murmured. There was an unusual unevenness in his voice, as if a struggle was taking place behind the calm exterior. 'Darling Annabelle!'

Annabelle? But she was not Annabelle! Rosabelle came to her senses with a shock, and wrenched herself free. 'No, no! You mustn't!' she cried. 'Oh, you've spoiled everything! How dare you, Mr Winbolt!' She could not continue. It was too much! She had betrayed not only herself but her sister, too! Taking refuge in anger, she said bitterly, 'I did not think you were the sort of man to take advantage of a guest in such a disgraceful manner! Pray let me pass—I wish to return to the drawing room! Immediately!'

Mr Winbolt looked surprised, then a dull red rose in his cheeks. 'Forgive me,' he said stiffly. 'I…I don't know what came over me. I thought you…' He stopped and pressed his lips firmly together. Then he said, 'I apologise for my behaviour, Miss Kelland. I assure you I had nothing of this sort in my mind when I invited you to see the winter garden. I thought only of giving you pleasure.' They both found his choice of words unfortunate. Rosabelle gasped and tried to look angrier than ever, Philip hastened to explain. 'I mean—'

'I know what you mean, sir. But I still wish to go back to your sister. Indeed, I should never have left her. It is not at all suitable for me to be here alone with you. I suppose I have only myself to blame for what happened.'

'You must not blame yourself, Miss Kelland! The fault was all mine…the sweetness of your response went to my head.'

The unpalatable truth contained in this remark resulted in a complete and perfectly genuine loss of temper. 'That is too much!' Rosabelle cried. 'I have heard enough! I did not respond, sir! You misunderstood me. *I did not respond!*' She stormed out of the winter garden, and ran back along the corridor to the drawing room. Outside the room she stopped short. What could she say to Mr Winbolt's sister?

Fortunately that lady was immersed in a journal and did not hear her. When Rosabelle finally entered the room, she merely looked up with a smile and said, 'I hope the winter garden had more to offer than these journals, Miss Kelland. I have seldom seen so many hideous dresses.'

By the time Rosabelle had made some reply and examined the page Emily had open in front of her, Mr Winbolt had arrived. He looked composed but unusually stern. Rosabelle refused to meet his eyes.

'I think I must go,' she said, trying to sound natural. 'My father will wonder where I am.'

'I shall see you home, Miss Kelland,' Mr Winbolt said, and added when Rosabelle looked doubtful, 'You will be safe with me, I assure you.'

'Of course,' she said nervously. 'In any case, it isn't far.'

Mr Winbolt looked grimmer than ever. 'Shall we go?' he asked.

Rosabelle took her leave of Miss Winbolt, and was escorted out to the carriage. It was a curricle—Mr Winbolt intended to drive her himself. Reluctantly she allowed him to help her in, withdrawing her hand as soon as she could balance. Emily waved them goodbye and they set off.

They drove in silence for a mile or so, then Rosabelle decided that she must make an effort to speak. Something had to be done about the difficult situation in which they found themselves. Accordingly, she began rather shakily.

'Mr Winbolt, you must be wondering what...'

He interrupted her. 'Forgive me, but I do not really feel any need for further discussion of the events in the winter garden. Except to say that I am sorry. You were right—I did misunderstand you, but, in any case, the fault was mine. I assure you my actions will not be repeated.'

He sounded so decisive, so final, that Rosabelle was not sure how to continue. In any case, what could she say? Her false identity made it impossible for her to say what she really wanted to say. Left to herself, she would have found some way of telling him that she would welcome a closer friendship between them, a friendship which might in time grow into something warmer. But she could not plunge into a confession without thinking very carefully of the possible consequences. No, it was better to remain silent, to let him think she was still angry. She stole a glance at him. He looked calm enough, but she sensed he was not happy.

'You took me by surprise in the winter garden,' she said softly.

'Really? I have said I am sorry,' he said stiffly.

'I…I may have given you some reason to think I was encouraging you…'

'I now know you were not. Can we not put this tedious subject aside, Miss Kelland?'

In spite of his continued coolness she persisted. 'I…I would like to think we were still friends.'

'Friends!' This time his tone was so bitter that her tender heart smote her. She made an impulsive movement towards him, but hastily put her hand back in her lap. This was no time for weakness. But the gesture had caught his eye, and a small frown of mystification appeared on his face. There was a silence after which he seemed to come to a decision.

'I have to confess that you puzzle me, Miss Kelland,' he said thoughtfully, looking at the offending hand. 'You made your indifference to me clear enough at the start of our acquaintance, but I had come to believe…that there might be some hope for me in the future.'

'No, no!' Rosabelle cried, her own regret causing her to speak with great emphasis. 'You must not hope—I can offer you nothing but friendship. Anything else is quite out of the question.'

'Do I repel you, perhaps?' She shook her head, and he went on, 'In that case, need you be so…so very final?'

'I must! I cannot permit you to indulge in hopes which can only be disappointed. Believe me, I cannot regard you in…in any light other than that of a friend.'

'I see.'

Conscious of his intent gaze she managed to keep her face under careful control. Finally he said, 'I am disappointed, naturally. However, let that be forgotten. My sister would be sorry to lose your company.'

'And I hers,' said Rosabelle a touch sadly. It was hard—oh, how hard it was!—to insist on friendship, largely with his sister, when the thought of this man's love was so tempting.

There was silence in the carriage again for the rest of the journey. Then he said, 'We have reached Temperley. I hope you will not let your mind dwell too much on what happened today, Miss Kelland. I assure you that I regret it. You will have my friendship, if that is what you wish.'

His voice lacked its normal sympathetic flexibility, that undercurrent of humour and understanding, which she had learned to depend on. Their farewells were briefly conventional. Rosabelle was anxious to escape to her bedroom, where she could give way to her misery, and Mr Winbolt seemed abstracted. She left him at the door and went in, full of doubt, self-reproach, and a fierce, bitter regret.

One of the girls had let her in, but when she was halfway up the stairs Becky came hurrying up towards her.

'Becky, I'm very tired. I think I shall just go to bed—perhaps I'm coming down with a cold?'

But Becky paid no attention. 'There's a letter, Miss Belle. From Miss Annabelle. It came this afternoon, by special delivery.'

'What? Where is it?'

Rosabelle opened the missive with trembling fingers. She scanned the pages eagerly, half relieved, half dreading what she would find.

My dear Sister
What a surprise we have for you! Aunt Laura's

doctors have suggested that she should seek a cure at a watering place, and Giles has given his consent. I believe he intends to take us to Bath, and this means that I shall be able to leave Aunt Laura in his care while I pay you all a quick overnight visit. Temperley is only a few miles out of our way. What a pity it is that you are unable to accommodate us all! But Aunt Laura insists that Temperley is no fit place for a second invalid. She and Giles will stay with friends of hers in Reading while I am at Temperley, and I will rejoin them there. It will be delightful to see you and Papa again.

Aunt Laura sends her love—and so do I. I shall write again to give you the exact day as soon as the details have been settled to Giles' satisfaction. It will certainly be within the next week or not long after. What a great deal we shall have to talk about!

                                                   Your loving Twin


'She's coming. Annabelle is coming back,' Rosabelle said. She was stunned. Coming on top of the recent scene with Mr Winbolt, this seemed to be both a deliverance and a thunderbolt. She didn't know what she felt.

'When?'

'Very shortly. Colonel Stanton is taking my godmother and Annabelle to Bath, and they will stay at Reading on their way. Annabelle has arranged to come here alone on a short visit. We shall be able to change over again then.'

'Thank goodness for that! Oh, don't look like that, Miss Belle. I shall be sorrier to see you go than I can well say, but it's time you went back where you belong. Before any real damage is done.'

Rosabelle had recovered from the initial shock and feeling was returning to her numbed senses. 'I rather think,' said Rosabelle wearily as she turned away, the letter fluttering to the ground, 'I rather think, Becky, that the damage has already been done.' Slow tears started trickling down her cheeks as she went on up the stairs, and shut the door of her room behind her.

Philip Winbolt was hardly in a better frame of mind as he drove back to Shearings. He was angry with himself for his disastrous loss of control in the winter garden. It had not been his intention to reveal his feelings so early in their friendship. On several previous occasions he had noticed that Annabelle withdrew from him when he showed his admiration, and he had decided that his courtship of her must be patient and slow. So why had he acted so impulsively? It was quite out of character—he normally prided himself on his self-discipline.

The truth was that Annabelle's pleasure in those plants, the intimate atmosphere of the winter garden, her obvious delight in his company, had totally unnerved him. He had quite simply lost his head. Perhaps the heady perfume of those damned flowers had played a part? And he had ended up apparently having destroyed any chance of winning her. But...

But that was the puzzle! His instinct, which was usually sound, told him that Annabelle was not indifferent to him! His instinct had led him to believe that Annabelle Kelland's early feelings towards him had changed materially—so much so that she would at least listen to him with patience, if not yet with pleasure. The last thing he had expected was that she would dismiss his aspirations altogether!

His mind returned to the scene in the winter garden.

Surely her anger had been somewhat overplayed? Whatever she said afterwards, she *had* encouraged him—her response to his kiss had been surprisingly ardent. And what was the significance of that gesture in the carriage? Though she had withdrawn it immediately, he would swear that her hand had stretched out of its own accord towards him. But, in that case, why had she then refused so adamantly to regard him as a possible suitor? It was all a mystery…

Had she some secret attachment unknown to the neighbourhood? An unwise early marriage, or something of that nature? But from what he had heard Annabelle Kelland had never left Temperley in her life. There were no hidden corners, nothing on which to base such a suspicion. So why, why, why? As he drove on he grew impatient with the lack of answers. His faith in the girl he had grown to love battled with doubts about her sincerity, her honesty. Was Annabelle Kelland the girl he thought he knew? Or was she a tease, a woman driven by caprice, or worse, a woman with some sort of shameful past, which made marriage impossible? He resolved to find out.

But Mr Winbolt was forced to leave his plans in abeyance, when his sister told him the next day that Annabelle was ill.

'What happened in the winter garden yesterday, Philip? Or is it tactless of me to ask?'

'I showed Miss Kelland the plants. Including the orchid Charles Dantry sent me.'

'And?'

'And what?'

'Did she like it?'

'Very much.'

'Did you talk of…anything else?'

'A little, but not much.'

Miss Winbolt looked at her brother with some sympathy. 'I can see that this is forbidden ground. Very well. But I think you ought to know that I've just had this note from Miss Kelland putting off our rendezvous on Thursday because she is ill.'

'Ill! Let me see!'

The note was polite but brief. Miss Kelland thanked Miss Winbolt for the very pleasant afternoon she had spent with them. She had much enjoyed meeting their friends, and the winter garden had given her a great deal of pleasure. Unfortunately she was now confined to her room with a particularly virulent cold. She sincerely hoped that she had not been infectious the day before. It would clearly not be advisable for Miss Winbolt to call as they had arranged on Thursday. The note concluded with suitable greetings, but there was no mention of a future meeting.

'I wonder…'

'What?'

'She might really be ill, I suppose…'

'What reason would she have for pretence? But ill or not, this note makes it perfectly clear that, for the moment, the lady does not wish to see either of us.'

He walked to the window and without turning said, 'I…I made a mistake yesterday, Emily.'

'In the winter garden?'

He turned and nodded. 'I told her of my feelings for her. It was far too early.'

'Is that all?'

'I kissed her.'

'You brute! Is…is that all?'

'Yes! Except that she became quite distressed. And very angry.'

'You kissed her and she became distressed? So distressed that she is ill today? Either you were very clumsy, Philip, which I refuse to believe, or there is something wrong with the woman! I swear I would be extremely flattered if a personable young man—who, by the way, would have every reason to think that I was attracted to him—kissed me and told me he loved me, whatever I actually felt about him. I certainly shouldn't take to my bed the next day, and refuse to meet even his sister!'

'So you too think there is something odd about it?'

'Very. I don't know what to make of Miss Kelland. She seems to change with the wind! I could not have imagined the girl I met in October being such a coward. Yet I was not half so attracted to her then, either. It's very strange… You…you don't think she's a tease, do you, Philip? There are such women—they enjoy being chased, but dislike the consequences.'

'I don't know. I wouldn't have thought Miss Kelland like that at all. And there were not even any significant ''consequences'', as you so charmingly call them. I am not an animal.'

'Of course not. I was being foolish. But I have to confess I am at a standstill. I simply don't understand our Miss Kelland. Would you like me to try calling at Temperley? I could take some fruit for her.'

'Would you? I would value your opinion on the situation. For all we know she might be really ill.'

'I shall call this afternoon.'

There was never a chance that either of the Winbolts would see Rosabelle, for she was determined not to be seen. The letter from Annabelle had brought home to her how vital it was that she should avoid all contact with them until she left Temperley. If the change back to the real Annabelle was to remain unremarked, the immediate impact of Rosabelle's personality must have a chance to fade. The present situation had come about by accident, but if it had been planned it could not be bettered—a cooling off between herself and Philip Winbolt, an excuse to see less of them in the future. Annabelle could quite naturally let the acquaintance gradually fade if she so wished, and in time Philip would forget his love for Annabelle Kelland. In the seclusion of her bedchamber Rosabelle wept bitter tears over the loss of love and future happiness, but she rose the next day fully resolved— the Winbolts would not meet Rosabelle Ordway again.

Miss Winbolt duly arrived at Temperley with her gift of fruit, but was told that Miss Kelland was unable to receive visitors. Becky took her into the parlour, and offered to deliver a message or a note, if Miss Winbolt wished.

'I shall not disturb the invalid. Pray give her my best wishes for a speedy recovery, if you will, Mrs Bostock. Is there anything we can do? You must be very busy with two invalids on your hands.'

Becky looked slightly uncomfortable. 'Thank you, ma'am. You're very kind. But Miss Kelland's sister is due to arrive any day now. She will take charge, I'm sure.'

'Her sister from London? That's good news.'

'Yes. Being so close, they understand one another wonderfully well.'

'So close?'

'Miss Annabelle and Mrs Ordway are twins, ma'am.'

'Twins! How interesting! I don't believe I knew that.

And how fortunate for Miss Kelland at this time. Will the neighbourhood see anything of Mrs Ordway while she is here?'

'I couldn't say, ma'am,' said Becky stolidly. 'But I do know that she can't stay long.'

'That's a pity. I should have liked to meet her. Well, Mrs Bostock, I'm sure Miss Kelland is in good hands. Have you already sent for Dr Jardine, or would you like me to call in on my way home?'

'Thank you, ma'am, but I'm not sure he's needed yet.'

'Then I'll take my leave. Perhaps you'd be good enough to let me know when Miss Kelland is well enough for visitors?'

'Certainly, ma'am,' said Becky.

'However, I am not sure she will,' said Emily when she got home. 'There was something distinctly off-putting in the good Mrs Bostock's manner. Whatever we have done, we seem to have offended Miss Kelland beyond present forgiveness. You may set your mind at rest on one score, at least, Pip. I do not believe her to be seriously ill at all.'

'I don't understand it,' said Philip. 'Almost her last words to me were that she valued her friendship with us. What has happened in the meantime?'

'I agree it's odd… They've heard from her sister—but that can hardly be it.'

'Mrs Ordway? There were some nasty rumours circulating about Stephen Ordway, the husband, at one time. But that's a year or two back, and the man's been dead for some time. I doubt that has anything to do with it.'

Emily was growing tired of the subject. She was fond of her brother and would help him all she could, but she was beginning to think that he ought to forget Annabelle Kelland. The girl was proving to be disappointingly capricious.

'Well, she is coming next week on a short visit. If Miss Kelland needs further care, I think we can leave it to Mrs Ordway to provide it. Do look at these bonnets, Philip! I think the milliners have gone mad!'

# Chapter Seven

Though she had known happiness in her childhood, from the time of her marriage to Stephen Ordway, Rosabelle Ordway's life had been one of self-doubt, shame and misery. During the marriage her unhappiness had bordered on despair, and her anxieties had once or twice turned into pure terror. Stephen's death had brought a measure of relief, though worry over his debts had overshadowed her life. Then Giles Stanton had taken over with his threats and jeers, his implacable determination to see nothing good in her.

Her lack of self-esteem reinforced by his presence, her nervous system shattered by the events surrounding Stephen's death, her health affected by time spent nursing her godmother, she had been near to collapse. She had escaped at Easter just in time—or so it had seemed. Escape, freedom for a while from the atmosphere at Upper Brook Street, had been all she had wanted.

Then she had met Philip Winbolt, and the brief moments of delight she had recently experienced in his company had been an unexpected, a miraculous bonus.

But now she was filled with a pain she had not experienced before. For the first time in her life she had fallen in love, deeply in love, with a man who was everything a woman could desire—honorable, kind, amusing, energetic, and with sufficient standing in the world to offer his wife security along with all the rest... She had good reason to believe that he would have married her, if only... But it was impossible. She had embarked on a deception which ruled out any happy end—indeed, she would not see him ever again. And she had no one but herself to blame.

How could she possibly tell him that she was a liar and deceiver? A married woman, not the girl he thought her. And if he forgave her for that, what sort of wife would Stephen Ordway's widow make for a distinguished man such as Philip Winbolt? No, better by far not to let herself be tempted. At first she wept bitter tears, and, when her tears dried up, she lay awake into the small hours, staring hopelessly into the dark...

But she was no longer the poor, nervous creature she had been before Easter. She faced her pain with courage and determination, bolstering her rediscovered self-respect with the thought that a man like Philip Winbolt had nearly loved her... She refused to allow her mind to dwell on what might have been. Instead she began to make plans for the future, wondered what Annabelle had done about Giles Stanton's blind prejudice, and made a decision that, whatever had happened in London, she would cast off once and for all the black heritage of Stephen's malice and deceit. She would go to Bath, look after Aunt Laura, and, when they returned to London, she would run Giles Stanton's house for him so well that he would be forced to respect her.

As the week wore on Rosabelle grew increasingly impatient to be gone from Temperley, anxious to be free of the risk of meeting—or seeking—the Winbolts. She was prepared to face whatever might be waiting for her in London and her sole aim was to get away as quickly and as quietly as possible. So it was with relief that she saw John coming up the drive with a letter. It must be from Annabelle and would contain news of her release. She met him at the door, took the letter from him and opened it eagerly. It was indeed from Annabelle. She hurried through to the parlour and sat down, impatiently scanning the sheet of paper.

> Dearest Sister
> This will be as great a shock to you as it is to me. Colonel Stanton—for I cannot bring myself to call him anything else, unless it is The Monster—has decided in his wisdom that we should be better off going to Buxton! He is quite adamant. Apparently, he intends to visit his father in the vicinity, though he has not informed me of the fact. I had to learn even that much from Aunt Laura! I suspect that this is not his only reason, however, though I cannot imagine what any other could be. He can surely hardly be serious when he hints that my character may have something to do with his decision! I wonder whether Aunt Laura and I made the mistake of appearing too pleased with the notion of going to Bath? For such a killjoy as Colonel Stanton, the temptation to change his plans must have been quite irresistible. But let us forget the less

pleasant aspects of life in Upper Brook Street!

The sad truth is that by the time you receive this letter we shall be on our way north to Buxton, and it will be impossible for me to see you for seven or eight weeks! Words cannot express how sorry I am. I assure you, my darling sister, I would have hired a chaise and come alone if it had been possible, but the change of plan was sprung on us with hardly a day's notice, and I have been kept exceedingly busy. Colonel Stanton is all consideration! I expect he wanted to spare us the pain of learning too soon that we were not to enjoy the excessive dissipations of life in Bath! I understand that Buxton will provide me with 'fewer opportunities to parade' myself. I quote.

Since I shall not be seeing you in person for some time, I send you my love, and best assurances that I am happier than I may seem! Life with the Monster in the house is at least never dull. And you may have an easy mind about Aunt Laura. She continues to improve, and, however little I deserve it, she seems to be very happy with

Your loving Twin.

'What is it, Miss Belle? You're as white as a sheet! Has something happened to Miss Annabelle?' Becky came in to the parlour to find Rosabelle staring at the wall.

'She isn't coming, Becky.' Rosabelle's voice was devoid of life. 'She's on her way to Buxton. Giles Stanton has changed his mind about taking them to Bath,'

'Not coming? Why ever not? Where's Buxton?'

'It's a watering place in the North. There isn't the slightest possibility that Annabelle can come to

Temperley before the end of August. Even then it is quite
possible that Colonel Stanton will change his mind again,
and take her to…to the Antipodes or the even to the
moon! I shall never get away! Here, read the letter!'
Rosabelle got up and walked agitatedly about the room,
while Becky put her glasses on and read Annabelle's
letter.

'It's too much, Becky! Much too much! I can't bear
it! I've worked so hard to discipline myself to look forward, to forget… And now it will be two months or more
before I can escape. What am I to do? Oh, what am I to
do?' Rosabelle threw herself down on the sofa and burst
into tears.

'There, there, my dear.' Becky took Rosabelle in her
arms and stroked her hair as if she was a child. 'You'll
manage. You've managed all this time without a foot
wrong, and you'll do it again. Hush, Miss Belle! There's
no need for this, my honey.'

After a while Rosabelle grew calmer, and Becky got
up to go. But Rosabelle clutched the housekeeper's hand.
'No! Don't go. I need you, Becky. There's no one else
I can talk to. I don't know what to do. Help me!'

'It's Mr Winbolt, isn't it, Miss Belle?'

Rosabelle looked at the kindly, rosy face, regarding
her with such concern. Becky had been right, after all,
in her gloomy prophecies. 'Yes. It's Mr Winbolt. You
were right to warn me… I should have heeded you
more.'

'As to that, I hardly expected you to, Miss Belle. Mr
Winbolt is as fine a gentleman as I've seen.' Becky sat
for a while in thought, then she said, 'Have you tried
speaking to your papa about this, Miss Belle?'

'Papa? No, of course not!'

'I think you should. He's ever so much better than he was. And he is your own father.'

'But he would only be annoyed at being disturbed—you know what he's like, Becky.'

'I should try all the same. He's a clever man, your papa. And you need someone to talk to—you said so yourself. You never know. Why don't you try?'

At first Rosabelle rejected the suggestion out of hand—it seemed absurd. Her father had not taken the slightest interest in any of them for years, so why should he start now? But as the day wore on the idea of consulting her father grew more tempting. Becky was right—Papa was clever. Moreover he would certainly take a dispassionate view of her case—if he gave any opinion at all, it would be realistic. Besides, who else was there to consult?

Becky was a darling—she gave comfort to her former nurslings whenever they needed it, and had been the recipient of many a childish confidence. But this was no childish matter. It concerned the personal affairs of a neighbour, a local landowner of some importance, and it would be unfair to involve Becky in such a business.

By the evening, when her daily visit to her father was due, Rosabelle had almost made up her mind. She would see what sort of mood her father was in, and if he seemed at all receptive she would consult him.

When she first entered her father's bedchamber she thought he was asleep and her heart sank. But as she went quietly over to his chair, she saw that his eyes were open and he was staring into the fire. The candles had not been lit, and his book was lying neglected on the table nearby.

'Are you feeling well, Papa?'

'Yes, yes.' Mr Kelland roused himself and looked at his daughter. 'It's Rosa, isn't it?'

'Yes, Papa. I'm afraid Anna can't be here for some time. Lady Ordway has taken her to Buxton.'

'Buxton, eh? Well I suppose it's time Anna saw a bit of the world. I've been a bit selfish in keeping her here. It's an odd place to go, though, Buxton.'

'Papa,' said Rosabelle, taking a deep breath. 'Papa, I wish to talk to you—may I?'

'Why not? I've finished my book. I was just sitting here...thinking...'

'You looked sad when I came in—what were you thinking about?'

'The past. But it's a useless occupation. What did you want to say?'

'It's rather private, Papa. May I tell Walters not to interrupt?'

'He's in his room. You can tell him that I shan't need him for an hour or two.'

This accomplished, Rosa sat down by her father and said, 'Papa, I'm in something of a quandary. I don't know what to do.'

'Being in a quandary means you don't know what to do, Rosa. Don't waste words.'

'Forgive me.' Rosabelle took another breath and began again. 'I need your advice.'

Mr Kelland frowned, but said, 'Go on.'

'The fact that Anna's return has been delayed has caused me some difficulty...' She hesitated, trying to choose her words. But when she saw her father shift impatiently in his chair she hurried to tell him of her friendship with the Winbolts, and its latest development.

'It never does any good, mixing too much with neighbours. You should have followed Anna's example, and kept clear of them. Still, it's done now. So what do you want me to say? Did you tell Winbolt that you and Anna changed places? Is that the trouble? I notice he hasn't been round here this past week.'

'Papa! I didn't think you paid much attention to what went on!'

'It's difficult not to, when horses and carriages are forever crunching up the drive and the damned doorbell is ringing all the time! I should be in a room overlooking the back—that would be more peaceful.'

'Not with the stables close by, Papa,' said Rosa patiently. 'But I haven't told Mr Winbolt anything. I wanted to go back to London without him ever knowing.'

'His,' said Mr Kelland.

'His?'

'His ever knowing. Go on.'

'So I've been keeping out of the Winbolt's way to make it easier for Anna to take over...' Her lips trembled. 'And now she's not coming for weeks and weeks...'

'If you're going to cry, go somewhere else, Rosa! Crying won't help, and I can't stand it.'

Rosabelle got up, wiping her eyes. 'I'll go, Papa. I'm only disturbing you.' She started to walk to the door.

'You can stay if you promise to keep calm. You need to make some decisions. Is that why you want my help?'

'Yes, Papa.'

'Then sit down here and talk sensibly.'

'Yes, Papa.'

'Your problem is that you've got yourself into some sort of tangle with Winbolt, from which you thought you could extricate yourself by going back to London. Is that it?'

'Yes, Papa.'

'And how was Anna going to manage when she took your place again?'

'Oh, I didn't compromise her, Papa! I was always careful to…to keep my distance. Mostly.'

'What does that mean?'

'It wouldn't be difficult for Anna to resume her former relationship with the Winbolts when she returns. Though I did think originally that it would do her good to mix a little. She's getting to be as much of a recluse as…oh! I beg pardon, Papa.'

'As much of a recluse as I, eh?'

'Well, yes! And she's still too young to shut herself away! Before we changed places and she went to London she hadn't seen anything of life in Society.'

'It doesn't seem to have done you much good.'

Rosabelle bit her lip and looked down. 'That was different. I was…unlucky.'

'It was obvious that you didn't love Stephen Ordway. But Laura Ordway wanted the match, and you would have flown over the moon for her. I should never have consented to it.' Rosabelle was silent, and after a moment he asked abruptly, 'What about Winbolt? Do you love him?'

'Yes,' said Rosabelle. 'Yes, I do.'

'Enough to want to marry him?'

Painful colour rose in Rosabelle's cheeks. 'Yes. But that is impossible.'

'Because of your deception? He'll get over that.'

'I wish I had your confidence. But there's something else. Stephen was…was…'

'I can guess what Stephen was, Rosa. And you think that Winbolt would repudiate you because you were married to such a man?'

'Yes,' she whispered. 'Or feel he had to…to withdraw from Society himself if he married me.'

'I can reassure you on the first question: a young man in love—really in love—will forgive almost anything, including the small deception you and Anna have practised. Love makes idiots of us all. And on the second… Only you can know how closely you were associated with Stephen Ordway's activities. I would think not at all. I doubt you could be held to blame for them in anyone's eyes—whether Winbolt's or those of Society. You're being over-scrupulous, Rosa.'

'What am I to do?'

'It's my opinion that you ought to take the chance fate has given you, and use your extra months to fix Winbolt's interest. It shouldn't be difficult. You're a beautiful young woman, and he's a warm-blooded male.'

'Should I confess the truth?'

Mr Kelland had taken up another book. 'Whatever you think best. I should give yourself a little while before doing anything rash. Make sure he's besotted enough first.'

'But how can I face them?'

'You can't play at being sick for months, and you can't avoid the Winbolts if you're not—unless you wish to become a recluse, like me. You're going to have to meet them again, aren't you?' He opened his book, and started leafing through it.

'I…I suppose so. Thank you, Papa.'

'Think it over by yourself. Make up your own mind. Er…take Walters down with you and give him some more candles, Rosa. I expect he's sulking. He hates to be shut out of anything. The exercise will do him good. And Rosa! Make sure you close the door carefully on your way out—'

'I know, Papa! The draught is most unpleasant when I don't.'

Rosabelle collected Walters and went thoughtfully downstairs, and on into the kitchen to see that he was given the candles. Here she found Becky who waited till Walters had shuffled away again, then asked, 'Well? How did you get on?'

'You were right. It did help to talk to Papa. But I'm still not sure what I should do.' She told Becky what her father had recommended.

'Why don't you try? It's better than moping in the house for two months. And you couldn't be much unhappier than you are, Miss Belle. What have you got to lose?'

'Not much, it's true.'

'There's no need to rush it. Take your time, and it will come right, you'll see. I'm a great believer in Providence—you haven't been given this time without good reason.'

'I hope you're right. But whether I succeed or fail...'

'You won't fail, Miss Belle! But you must have it all in the open before Miss Annabelle comes back, mind.'

'Of course, I will! I wouldn't leave Anna with a problem like that!'

'From the bits I've seen of that letter, Miss Annabelle is solving a few problems of her own, and enjoying it!'

'What do you mean?'

'It seems to me that there's rather a lot of Colonel Stanton in it.'

'But that's because he's so awful!' Rosabelle was horrified. 'No, Becky, you're wrong! You must be! Anna and Giles Stanton? Impossible!'

* * *

The weather turned somewhat cooler that week, and Rosabelle was able to work in the garden, following Becky's advice and taking her time. And as she gradually put the flower beds in order, she tried to do the same with her thoughts. In the evenings she visited her father, and though he never referred to their conversation and was as taciturn as ever, she now felt his support was there if she should need it.

Slowly, in the calm after the storm of her outburst earlier in the week, influenced by her father's talk of fate and Becky's of Providence, her spirits lifted by an idyllic spell of clear skies and temperate breezes, she adopted a more philosophical approach to her problems. She would carry on as before, trying where she could to show Philip Winbolt that she was not the adventuress he might otherwise believe her to be when he learned the truth. The rest was up to fate. Let the future take care of itself!

Miss Winbolt was invited to tea and shown round the garden. Though there was a degree of stiffness in her manner at first, she gradually unbent, and before the visit was halfway through the two young ladies were enjoying each other's company almost as much as ever.

'And…your brother? Is he well?' asked Rosabelle, somewhat self-consciously.

'Very well, thank you. He was pleased to hear you had recovered from your…indisposition.'

'I'm sorry I couldn't see you. I had no desire to offend you, believe me,' said Rosabelle. 'But I received some bad news, and felt much worse as a result.'

'Bad news? Not too serious, I hope.'

'Not really. My sister has been forced to postpone her visit. She has had to go to Buxton.'

There was a pause, then Miss Winbolt said, 'Buxton?

I haven't ever been there. Philip and I intended to call there when we visited the Lake District some years ago, but it somehow didn't happen.'

Happy to turn the subject away from her sister, Rosabelle said, 'The Lake District? Oh, I should love to see the Lakes! Do tell me about it!'

The visit passed off as well as could have been hoped, and a return invitation for the following Thursday was given and accepted.

'My brother will be in London for the day, so I shall be glad of your company, Miss Kelland,' said Emily blandly.

'He won't be there?' Rosabelle was not sure whether to be sorry or glad that her first encounter with Philip Winbolt was postponed.

'I confess I chose the day deliberately.' Miss Winbolt studied her hostess. 'It was my impression,' she said carefully, 'that when you were last in his company you were…not at ease. I thought you might prefer to see less of him in future. Or am I wrong?'

The sensitive colour flooded into Rosabelle's cheeks, but she spoke with dignity.

'Your brother was everything that was kind, Miss Winbolt. I will not hide from you—nor from him—that there are…circumstances which caused me some difficulty, and continue to do so. But I hope to overcome them in time. I believe I would enjoy his company as much as I do yours. On the other hand I would perfectly understand if he wishes to regard me as more your friend than his.'

'We shall see! I'm glad to have settled that slight awkwardness. Shall we keep to Thursday for this time, however?'

'Miss Winbolt—'

'Could you see your way to calling me Emily? I am not one for great ceremony.'

'I should be very pleased to, Emily! My name is—'

'Annabelle. Yes, I know. May I call you Anna?'

'Er…yes. Of course.'

If Miss Winbolt was surprised at the reluctance in Rosabelle's tone, she did not allow it to put her off. Instead she merely said, 'Till Thursday, then. I shall ask your advice on our ornamental pool. Philip wants to fill it with carp. Goodbye—Anna.'

However, Rosabelle was to see Philip Winbolt sooner rather than later. Only a couple of days later she was working in the garden as usual, when she became aware of a tall figure standing behind her.

'Mr Winbolt! Oh, you startled me.'

'It seems to be a habit of mine. I'm sorry.' Rosabelle had scrambled to her feet, and he held out his hand. 'Emily tells me you are better.'

'No, don't shake hands with me. Mine are covered in earth. Look.' She held out a grubby hand. He took it, and released it quite normally.

'A little dirt never hurt anyone. Do you think me such an exquisite?'

'No! But…'

'Emily also told me that you might enjoy my company, after all. As a friend, of course.' He seemed to be waiting. There was still a coolness in his manner which was very different from his former warmth.

'I…I should like that,' said Rosabelle somewhat nervously.

'It's all I am asking of you, Miss Kelland! Friendship. Nothing more. You needn't look so frightened,' he said, somewhat impatiently. 'I've taken note of your wishes.'

'It…it wasn't that at all,' she stammered. 'But I didn't expect to see you today.'

'I had some business down the road, which I wanted to complete before going to London. Emily said you were working in the garden, and she asked me to bring you some plants—John Bostock has them.'

'Thank you!' They fell into step up the path to the house. 'Do you often have business in London?'

'I like to keep in regular touch with my grandfather. And he insists that I take a full part in any discussions with our agents and trustees. The Winbolt estate owns some property in London near St Giles, and I'm trying to persuade my grandfather to get rid of it. It's in a terrible state, and I will take no rents from the poor devils who have to live there.'

'So you will sell it to someone else who will?'

'Wrong! It's being pulled down. But it all takes discussion and time.' He looked around him. 'And it seems such a waste of this glorious weather to spend it in a city!' He hesitated, then said abruptly, 'Are you fit enough for a walk, Miss Kelland? I feel like stretching my legs a little. But perhaps you would rather not?'

Rosabelle looked down so that he should not see the delight in her eyes. 'I shall wash this dirt off my hands and fetch my hat,' she said demurely. 'May I suggest you could use a little water yourself?'

He looked down at his hands and smiled. 'It might be as well.'

They took the lane down to the river. The river population was out in force. Ducks, moorhens, coots were parading their families, a kingfisher was busy in the reeds, and as they walked along the bank sudden plops and splashes ahead of them gave evidence of escaping water rats. They even caught sight of an otter, twisting and turning in the river.

'It's so beautiful here,' sighed Rosabelle. 'I never want to leave it.'

'You love the country so much?' Rosabelle nodded, and he continued, 'My sister and I both prefer life in the country, but she occasionally feels the need to see what is happening in the city. I'm not sure what she will do if she ever marries.'

'*If* she marries? How unbrotherly you are! Miss Winbolt is bound to marry one day.'

'My sister said that you were going to call her by her given name.'

'Emily, then.'

'Emily was engaged once, but she broke it off. There were good reasons. It was several years ago, but though I think she is very nearly over it, it has made her wary. She hasn't shown much interest in anyone else since. The path of true love doesn't seem to run very smoothly in our family, Miss Kelland—' He stopped. 'I'm sorry,' he said. 'Have you seen the swans?'

He said no more about Emily's personal affairs, or his own, for the rest of the afternoon. Instead their conversation ranged widely, from reforms on the Shearings estate—about which Rosabelle knew nothing, but believed she managed to conceal her ignorance rather well—to a lively argument on the rival merits of *Waverley* and *Emma*, about which she knew a great deal.

In the heat of the discussion he regained some of his natural warmth, and she found herself once again drawn to him—his humour, his sympathy, his love of life. He never once gave the slightest indication that he regarded her as anything but a friend, however, and afterwards, when she turned the walk over in her mind, she could not remember that he had ever touched her unnecessarily. When they reached the house again she held out her hand.

'I enjoyed our walk, Mr Winbolt,' she said.

'So did I. Though I still think that Miss Austen's technique and restraint in *Emma* far outweigh the big guns in *Waverley*.'

'Oh, pray do not open that subject again! I am exhausted!' Rosabelle laughingly protested.

'You defended your position manfully. And what is conversation for, if not to debate our likes and dislikes?'

'Say our preferences, rather. I, too, rate Miss Austen's works very highly. Good night, Mr Winbolt. And have a safe journey to London.'

'I shall be back quite soon—and then we can debate more preferences, perhaps. Good night, Miss Kelland.'

After that Rosabelle saw one or both of the Winbolts nearly every day. Walks, rides, drives, and visits to each other's houses occupied many happy hours. Perhaps Rosabelle would have been less carefree if she had known that Philip Winbolt kept a more careful eye on her than she realised. In spite of his open manner and gentle ways, Mr Winbolt was far from being a fool. He may have appeared to seek nothing but friendship from Miss Kelland. He certainly treated her much as he treated his own sister.

But he soon found that, in spite of his suspicions and doubts, he was still as much in love with her as ever, and, since that was the case, he was determined to unravel the mystery which surrounded her. He gathered tiny facts and inconsistencies, and hoarded them as a squirrel hoards nuts. For instance, why did Annabelle, who had successfully run Temperley for so long, know nothing of the new systems in farming—even though one or two were in place on her own land?

Why was her behaviour in the second episode with Carter so inconsistent with her behaviour in the first? Why, since then, had she appeared to be ill at ease whenever she met any of the villagers in his company? She visited them regularly alone, and was popular with them, he knew that from hearsay. So why be uneasy when she met them in his or Emily's company?

Why was she so reluctant to be involved with their other neighbours? She usually found an excuse not to be present at larger gatherings. Was she company-shy? He hadn't forgotten how tense she had become when he told her that the Harpendens were at Shearings. But she had relaxed afterwards, and the Harpendens had been charmed by her.

He did not share his thoughts with his sister, though he made a careful note of what she said about Annabelle.

'Why do you suppose Annabelle Kelland objects to being called "Anna", Philip?'

'Does she?'

'She seemed rather hesitant. I wondered whether she thought me too forward. Yet…she was very friendly otherwise…I tell you, Pip, I feel like a weathercock when I think about her. At the moment I like her as much as anyone I have ever known. But there have been times… She puzzles me. She appears to have humour and courage and spirit. But why was she so cast down when Rosabelle Ordway couldn't come after all? She said it had made her ill, and I have to say she looked it when I first saw her afterwards! I can't believe the mere absence of a sister would do that to any normal person. I'm prepared to wager that you wouldn't take to your bed if I didn't visit you when I ought! And fond as I am of you, I certainly wouldn't refuse to see other callers if you went away.'

Philip laughed, 'I should hope not, indeed!'

'Perhaps it's different if one is a twin.'

'A twin?'

'They're twins—didn't you know?'

'No, I didn't,' said Mr Winbolt thoughtfully. 'Who said so?'

'Mrs Bostock. She was their nurse at one time.'

Philip was silent for some time, then he said slowly, 'That might just be it!' He thought again. 'No—surely not! I can't believe it! But...but it would account for a lot...if there was a twin sister.' He saw his sister looking at him, and smiled at her cheerfully. 'I mean, it would account for her being ill, perhaps.'

# *Chapter Eight*

The thought was fantastic, but Mr Winbolt could not dismiss it. The apparent inconsistencies in Annabelle Kelland's behaviour could be explained by the existence of a twin who had changed places with her. If such an exchange had taken place, it was an outrageous piece of trickery—though it would not have been for mere amusement, he was sure. He tried to tell himself that it was all the product of an over-fertile imagination, a result of his anxiety to get to the bottom of the mystery surrounding the girl, but it was no use. He knew the notion would continue to plague him until he gave it closer examination. He would treat it as a pastime, an exercise in logic, such as he had enjoyed at Cambridge. 'First assemble your data, Winbolt,' his tutor had exhorted him, 'examine it carefully, and then produce a hypothesis.'

What were the facts? Annabelle Kelland, an intelligent girl who had spent years running the Temperley estate, had tried and failed to hide her complete ignorance of even the basic notions of modern farming. Annabelle Kelland, who had met him at least ten times before, had seemed not to recognise him after Easter, when they had met for the eleventh time. Annabelle Kelland, who had previously been indifferent to him to the point of rudeness, had changed her attitude to him between one meeting and the next—a change which had taken place so arbitrarily that he could not possibly attribute it to his powers of charm and persuasion, much as he would have liked to.

Annabelle Kelland, who had never before wasted a moment in his company, had agreed—no! *suggested* that they should ride back to Temperley together, and when they arrived she had offered him wine and biscuits and the like, welcoming him with a grace and charm which he had never before observed in her. There were the two episodes with Carter. Before Easter, Annabelle Kelland had resented his assistance with the man, but after Easter, she had accepted it more than gratefully!

Emily's suggestion, that the sister from London had exercised a civilising influence during her visit, might explain some of it, but not all. He went over in his mind other small incidents which had disconcerted him at the time, and came to the conclusion that they could all be explained if the girl at present at Temperley was not Annabelle Kelland at all.

Over and above all these details there was evidence of a different kind—not suitable for a court of law, but convincing, nonetheless. He had admired Annabelle Kelland before Easter, had thought that with time she could turn into the bride he was seeking. But he had fallen in love with her, quite suddenly, quite arbitrarily, but with no doubt or reservation, when he had helped her over the stile by the river in early June. She had seemed a different woman altogether—and perhaps she was!

So what else? It was a fact that Annabelle Kelland had a sister, and it was beyond reasonable doubt that they were twins. Though the girl at present at Temperley had implied that this was not the case, she had not actually said so. Her 'not very much older' could have meant a matter of minutes. But *why* had she prevaricated, if not to lead him off the track?

Were the Kelland twins identical? If the girl at present at Temperley was *not* Annabelle, then they must be for the imposture to succeed as it had. That was something which shouldn't be difficult to find out.

Furthermore, if the girl he had first met was the real Annabelle, and the one now at Temperley was not, then they must have changed places some time after Easter. He knew both girls had been at Temperley then, and the wrong girl could have gone back to London. The difference in 'Annabelle', which Emily and he ascribed to illness, would thus be easily explained!

Though Mr Winbolt had begun this exercise with scepticism, the more he thought about it, the more convinced he became that it was the case. If he could confirm that the twins were, in fact, identical, that would clinch it. He pondered over this for some time, for the last thing he wanted was to let the girl at Temperley, or Emily, or anyone else, become aware of his interest.

An unexpected opportunity came during a visit to one of his tenants. It had been his uncle's practice to make regular calls on the farms on the estate, and Mr Winbolt had followed his example. On this occasion the lady of the house had invited him in for a glass of ale. The day was hot, so he sat down gratefully at the kitchen table, and chatted comfortably with the family. The conversation turned to his Uncle Joseph.

'He was a fine man, Mr Winbolt. Not soft, but you knew where you were with him.'

'I'm sorry to say that I hardly knew him, Mrs Pegg. Just towards the end he invited me down to see the place. But he didn't seem to want me to stay more than a night.'

'Ay, that's Mr Winbolt for you,' said the farmer's wife. 'The kindest man you could ask for if you were in trouble, but he never wanted company. He and Mr Kelland up at Temperley made a right good pair, though your uncle at least cared for the land, and you can't really say that about Mr Kelland. It's young Miss Kelland who runs the estate at Temperley. And that's what I meant about your uncle, Mr Winbolt. He was kind to Miss Kelland and spent a lot of time with her, teaching her what she needed to know. They had some rare arguments—about fencing and draining mostly—but they understood each other, they did. She was really upset when he died.'

'It's a novel idea to me—a young lady looking after the estate. It can't happen often.'

'Well, she had to, more or less, Mr Kelland not being interested, like. And from the time she was a child Miss Annabelle was always eager to learn about the land. Mr Winbolt taught her a good bit, and John Bostock the rest. She was a bit of a tomboy, mind, but…well, she had to be, didn't she? Not like her sister.'

'Was she not like her sister? I thought they were twins.'

'They're like two peas out of the same pod! But Miss Rosabelle was taken away when she was nobbut a little child to live in a grand house in London with her godmother. A Lady Ordway. She only spent the summers here. She was…gentler. Quieter. Both lovely girls—but then the late Mrs Kelland was a lovely lady.'

'I expect they played tricks, did they? There were some fellows at school—twins—and they used to have the masters at sixes and sevens.'

'I won't say as they didn't, Mr Winbolt. Monkeys they were, sometimes—Miss Annabelle pretending to be Miss Rosabelle, and the other way round. Even Becky Bostock who reared them couldn't always tell which was which! Not always. But they were good-hearted children, all the same. I often wonder how Miss Rosabelle is getting on. She married Lady Ordway's son, but he died and she was left a widow, poor thing. She was here for a while at Easter, and folk said as how she looked very frail. But still the image of her sister. Did you never meet her?'

'We were away at the time, Mrs Pegg.'

'Ah, yes. She went back just about the middle of May.'

So the Kelland twins were identical—his case was just about complete! Now what? For the first time Philip Winbolt started to think of the consequences of his investigation. Having proved the theory to his own satisfaction, what was he going to do about it?

Somewhat to his surprise he found that he had no desire to expose Rosabelle Ordway for the fraud she undoubtedly was. He had admired Annabelle Kelland during his short acquaintance with her, and, because the inheritance of his uncle's estate had brought thoughts of marriage and of founding a family, he had even thought of her as a possible wife. But the girl he loved, more deeply with every day that passed, was the girl at Temperley now—gentle, vulnerable, and in need of help.

His discovery had not changed his feelings for her, not by a hair. Indeed, he felt a greater need to protect her, to shield her from disgrace and exposure.

But though he had proved his theory correct, his work was not yet finished. The reason behind this reckless attempt to deceive him and the rest of the neighbourhood was still a mystery. Not for one instant did he believe that it had been undertaken lightly. It was no trick for the sisters' amusement, nor, he thought, for any frivolous cause, such as giving Annabelle an opportunity to see London and town life. No, he suspected that it had been born of desperation, and his instinct told him that the desperation had been Rosabelle's. Nothing could have appealed more to Philip Winbolt's chivalrous nature. Rosabelle Ordway, not Annabelle Kelland, needed a champion. And one was to hand.

Having sorted out his feelings in the matter, Mr Winbolt considered what he would do next. Should he confide in anyone else? Rosabelle herself? Emily? The household at Temperley certainly knew of the substitution—now that he knew the truth he could see that there had been several indications of that. But, on balance, he thought it best to keep his discovery strictly to himself until he knew more about this masquerade. If, as he suspected, it had something to do with Stephen Ordway's misdeeds, it was possible that Rosabelle might take fright if he confronted her—he might well lose her completely. And it was tempting to think that, given time, she might learn to trust him, even confide in him of her own accord.

So Philip Winbolt embarked on a deception of his own. And, though he was as anxious as ever to help Rosabelle, there was no denying that the situation intrigued him, even appealed to his sense of humour.

* * *

'Tell me, Rosa, has Philip Winbolt succumbed to your charms yet?'

'Not yet, Papa,' said Rosabelle. As usual she and her father were sitting one evening in his room, though now that it was hotter they were by the window, catching a faint breath of air. There had been a change in Mr Kelland in recent weeks. Instead of remaining in his chair all day he had started to walk about the room, and the pile of books on his table had diminished.

'Why not?'

'I…I don't know. He seems to have taken what I said to heart. That I wanted a friend, not a lover.'

'Rubbish! Either he's cooling off, or he's biding his time, and I'm inclined to believe the latter. You're still interested in him, are you?'

'Oh, yes, Papa! That will not change. I love Mr Winbolt.'

'Then you'd better do something about it!'

'I…I don't know what that could be.'

'Good God, girl! Didn't your godmother teach you anything?'

'Not really, Papa. She said it wasn't necessary. She arranged for Stephen to marry me before I was brought out. So you might say that I never learned the arts of attraction.'

He looked at the face in front of him, dark blue eyes with a hint of sadness in their depths, sensitive mouth which could curve into a totally enchanting smile, dark gold hair framing the delicate lines of cheek and throat. He frowned.

'She was right. You don't need any arts. But what was the woman thinking of, marrying you off to that misbegotten son of hers, before you were out of the schoolroom? I should have realised…'

'Oh, no, Papa! You mustn't blame yourself. I was very ready to oblige Aunt Laura.'

'And afterwards?'

She turned her head away. 'We realised we had made a dreadful mistake, Aunt Laura and I. A dreadful mistake.' Then she looked back at her father. 'You know, Papa, whatever happens between Mr Winbolt and me, this stay at Temperley has done me a lot of good.'

'I'm glad to hear it—the imposture has had its merits, after all. In what way has it done you good, precisely?'

'Being here, and talking to you and Becky, and the people round about—especially the Winbolts and their friends—has taught me so much. I had never realised before how extraordinary my life in London was. I was always so close to Aunt Laura, that I didn't meet many other people. Then marriage to Stephen followed as soon as I was old enough. And though I can see now that the marriage was doomed from the start, I was convinced at the time that the fault was all mine.

'He was always telling me I was a failure… The atmosphere in that house just before he died was…the stuff of nightmares. And after his death Giles Stanton came, and made me feel even worse. Here at Temperley I've had time to reflect, and I can now see that I was far too young, and far too inexperienced, to help Stephen. I think it was an impossible task anyway—certainly towards the end no one could have saved him…' She fell silent.

'And that thought makes you feel better?'

'Of course not! But I've learned to stop blaming myself!'

'I hadn't realised how bad it was for you, Rosa. But then, I've haven't taken much notice of anything in recent years. Perhaps I, too, have learned something from

your stay here.' Mr Kelland moved restlessly in his chair.
'Well, what about the Winbolts? What are we to do
about them? I think you should ask the young man to
come and see me. It's high time.'

'Papa! You won't...'

'I'm not about to ask his intentions, if that is what
you're afraid of!' he said testily. 'I'm not a complete
fool. But I do want to see the fellow for myself. I don't
intend to fail you a second time, Rosabelle. Ask him if
he plays chess.'

The upshot of this conversation was that Mr Kelland
had an evening's chess with Mr Winbolt which he enjoyed so much that it was repeated. It became a regular
engagement, and each player soon learned to respect his
opponent—and not only in a game of chess. Philip
Winbolt discovered to his surprise that Rosabelle's father
had the same quirky sense of humour as the Winbolt
family, though he was somewhat out of practice in using
it. Mr Kelland found Philip Winbolt to be what he called
sensible, a man who seldom spoke or moved without
thinking, but when he did, it was to the purpose. Just the
man he would have chosen for either of his daughters—
but especially Rosabelle.

Time was moving on, and news of Annabelle's return
from Buxton was already overdue. Communication between the sisters had continued despite the distance between them, and in her letters Rosabelle had been
open—more open than she perhaps realised—about her
feelings for Philip Winbolt. Not that she was indiscreet.
When writing to one another, the sisters still kept up the
fiction that Annabelle was in Berkshire and Rosabelle
with the Ordways, and anyone reading them would only

learn that Annabelle Kelland of Temperley was finding
companionship, and perhaps more, with her neighbour,
Philip Winbolt. The difficulties this attraction brought in
its train were not mentioned, but they would be obvious
to both sisters.

In fact, Rosabelle felt that her friendship with the
Winbolts, and Philip Winbolt in particular, was becoming more securely founded with every day that passed.
But when she asked herself if it was secure enough to
stand the test of a confession, she hesitated. Philip
Winbolt, to use her father's word, did not yet appear
'besotted' enough. Indeed he had every appearance of
having forgotten his passion, replacing it instead with a
rather placid friendship. And try as she might, she could
not bring herself to employ any arts to change it—not
while the secret of her true identity lay between them.
She was caught in a circular trap of her own making.
She could not confess without feeling absolutely secure
of his regard; she could not work to secure his regard
without having told him the truth! And time was running
out. Any day now she expected to hear news of
Annabelle's departure from Buxton.

But when the expected letter arrived it told her that
her sister had been delayed yet again. Much later, when
she learned the true reason for Annabelle's continued
absence, Rosabelle realised that she ought to have been
worried beyond measure, but at the time she only felt
she had had a reprieve.

My dearest sister,
I am writing this note in great haste before we
are whisked away yet again. You will begin to think
that I have little desire to see you and Temperley
again! But I assure you that I have no intention of

letting another four years elapse before my next visit, though I have found myself unable to keep my word to come in August! Giles is taking us both away from Buxton, though not back to London. He remains as high-handed as ever, and has not yet deigned to inform us where we are going. I daresay he would not even let me send this letter if he knew I had written one!

But however mysterious our destination, you may be certain that we shall all be comfortably lodged. One of Giles's redeeming features—perhaps the only one!—is his care and attention for Aunt Laura. Sadly, this courtesy does not always extend to me. I sometimes think he would be quite happy to see me lodged in a cow byre. However, you may be easy in your mind—Aunt Laura would not permit it.

Aunt Laura and I have found Buxton society more interesting than we had expected, and we have on occasion enjoyed ourselves immensely. Once or twice I have even found myself basking in Giles's approval. He can be surprisingly agreeable when it pleases him!

I am afraid I can give you no firm date for our reunion—I cannot even slip away for a day or two to see you and Papa, as I would wish. But take comfort in the thought that entertaining me would limit the time you could spend in Mr Winbolt's company! I regret I cannot talk to you face to face about such an important matter, but I do not need to tell you that your happiness is very important to me. Aunt Laura and I both feel it may well lie with a man like Philip Winbolt, and we shall look forward to meeting him when the time is ripe.

Meanwhile I shall do my best to earn Giles's approval more often. The trouble is we fall out so very frequently!

Aunt Laura sends her love, and I mine. We are both in perfect accord on your situation, so do your best to acquire me a brother-in-law as soon as possible, my darling twin.

Your loving Belle

PS Does Papa know? Please give him my love—I am pleased he is so much better.

Rosabelle was still examining this letter when Becky came to tell her that Miss Winbolt had called.

'Emily, what a pleasant surprise! I thought you were going to be in Reading all day.'

'Philip had to come back earlier than expected—he has to see someone at Shearings. So I asked him to drop me here while he went on. He'll call for me in an hour. I hope it's all right?'

'Of course it is! Can Becky get you anything?'

'Thank you, no. We ate so well at the Harpendens that I may well not feel hungry till the day after tomorrow! Anna, are you free on the last Saturday in September? It's my birthday, and I've decided I'd like to have a party. The Harpendens are coming, and one or two other friends of ours. Do say you'll come!'

Rosabelle hesitated. She had always avoided going to parties and large assemblies where she might meet numbers of local people—especially if the Winbolts were to be present, too. But this sounded as if it would be harmless enough—an affair with their own friends... She could hardly refuse an invitation to Emily's birthday party.

'I'd love to,' she said, trying to sound as if she meant it.

'Good! I'll send a proper invitation as soon as I have them. We've ordered them from a place we know in London. And I'm ordering a new dress, too.'

'Another one?'

'Of course! Anna, you have no idea how lucky you are. You look enchanting whatever you wear, whereas I...'

'What nonsense you talk, Emily! I shall look forward to seeing the new dress—what colour is it?'

'I haven't quite decided—we're going to London to-morrow for about three weeks, so I shall have time to consult with the dressmakers and have one made up.'

'Three weeks?'

'Yes. Grandpapa has sent for Philip—that's why we left Reading early. He wants him to see to some business. I don't know what it is. The lawyers are involved again—a tiresome affair. So Philip has decided to take some time and finish whatever it is off properly. As it is, some time in London suits me very well, though we've had such short notice. Anna! I've had a splendid idea! Why don't you come with us? We could have such fun, and you could get your dress for my party at the same time!'

'Oh, no!' There was panic in Rosabelle's voice, and Emily stared. Rosabelle forced a smile and softened her reply.

'I should love to come to London with you, but it will have to be on another occasion. You know very well that I'm not as free as you are, you....butterfly!'

'A very mundane one—a cabbage white, perhaps?'

'No, no! In your new dress you will be a peacock and dazzle everyone! Now tell me your ideas.'

They became involved in a discussion of sleeves and flounces, trimmings and waists, and when Philip Winbolt arrived they were deeply immersed in sarsnet and zephyrine, satin and Urling lace.

'I'll go away again, and come back in a couple of hours, shall I?'

'No, no! I've finished, Pip. Anna and I were just discussing our dresses for my party. She thinks I should go to Fanchon.' A thought struck her and she turned to Rosabelle. 'How on earth did you know about Fanchon, Anna? I thought you had never left Temperley and she is purely a London phenomenon—I doubt she has ever heard of Berkshire!'

There was a fractional silence, then Rosabelle said hastily, 'I…I must have heard the name somewhere…'

'I expect Mrs Ordway has patronised her,' Mr Winbolt said, easily. 'And mentioned it in conversation. Are you coming to London with Emily? To order a dress?'

This time Rosabelle was prepared. She smiled and shook her head. 'I shall make do with our local dressmaker and what I can find in Reading.'

'But you shall have my pattern book from which to choose your style!' said Emily. 'I shall get one of the servants to bring it over tonight! We must go, Pip. I have a thousand things to do, and we set off early tomorrow morning, remember.'

'I promise to remember if you do, sister dear,' said Philip, smiling.

Emily shook her head at him, and took an affectionate farewell of Rosabelle. 'I shall see you as soon as I get back,' she said, 'and you shall be the first to see The Dress.'

Rosabelle shook hands with Philip and wished him a

pleasant journey. He hardly replied. He seemed to be more concerned with helping Emily into the carriage.

Rosabelle went upstairs for her usual half-hour with her father, but she was feeling a little low. The Winbolts were going to be away three whole weeks! If it were not for her wretched situation she could have accepted Emily's invitation, gone with her to shop, be fitted for new dresses, visit the theatre—and spend time with Philip. Though she would not lack occupation at Temperley, the prospect of three weeks without the Winbolts was dreary.

'Wasn't there to be a birthday party when they come back?' asked her father. 'I thought girls liked parties.'

'I do!'

'Well, think of a present for your friend and stop moping. Or is there some other reason?'

There was, though Rosabelle didn't feel like mentioning it. Judging by this evening's performance, Philip Winbolt was still far from losing his head over her. His farewell had been noticeably cool.

Mr Kelland suddenly sat up in his chair and stared out of the window. 'Good Lord! I haven't forgotten the day, have I? Did Winbolt say he was coming for a game of chess today?'

'No, Papa. Why?'

'He's coming back again up the drive. You'll have to tell him I haven't the time. No, I'll see him myself.'

But, as Mr Winbolt explained, he had merely brought the promised pattern book for Miss Kelland.

'Good!' said Rosabelle's father. 'I don't feel like chess this evening. It's too hot.'

'It is indeed, sir. I confess I'm not looking forward to spending time in London.'

'Madness! See Mr Winbolt out, my dear. You might take a turn with him to the gate—you haven't been out today.'

Rosabelle felt the colour rising in her cheeks. 'Mr Winbolt rode here, Papa. He doesn't want to have to lead his horse the length of the drive.'

'If you would keep me company, Miss Kelland, I will do so with pleasure. If you haven't been out today as your father says, then you need the air. Shall we go before it is dark?'

When they reached the door Mr Winbolt said, 'I have a better idea. I'll leave Thunderer where he is—he's happy in your stables. We can take a turn round the gardens, even go into the park, then I shall see you to your door and collect my horse. How does that strike you?'

'I'd…I think it an excellent idea,' Rosabelle said, trying to sound calm. 'I'll fetch my shawl.'

They went out into the garden. Though it had been hot during the day, summer was now looking slowly towards autumn, and the days were beginning to draw in. Swifts were wheeling and twisting through the air, a gaggle of rooks were noisily seeking out their favoured roosting spots, and the song of a blackbird or thrush could be heard from the other side of the garden. It was that time of day when the sun has disappeared but the sky is still light, and the merest whisper of a breeze freshens the air.

'You are not cold?'

'No, I have my shawl. Thank you for coming with the pattern book. It was kind, when I know you must be busy. You should have let one of the servants bring it.'

'And miss an opportunity for a few minutes' chat with

you? We don't seem to have been alone together for weeks. I love Emily dearly, and I enjoy your father's company immensely—but I sometimes wish them a hundred miles away.'

'Mr Winbolt!'

'It's true! You probably don't realise it, but when more than one person is present you seem to disappear into the background, and I lose you.'

'I…I didn't think you noticed such things—not now.'

'Oh, I notice.' Rosabelle glanced at him. He was smiling at her, quite in his old, half-teasing, half-serious manner.

She felt the colour rising in her cheeks, and said, 'I'm not used to company, you see. But I…I am always glad to talk to you, Mr Winbolt.'

They had reached the edge of the garden. 'Are you tired? Or shall we go a little further?'

'I'm not tired,' was all she said, but Philip Winbolt smiled, raised an eyebrow and took her hand in his. She left it there.

They went out of the wicket gate and turned down the lane. The light was now fading and, with the exception of the solitary blackbird, the birds had fallen silent.

'Listen!' They stood while the exquisite trills and flourishes were borne to them on the breeze. When the song came to an end they waited for a moment still held by its magic.

'London has nothing to compare with all this!' said Rosabelle softly.

'Nor with you.'

She looked round, not sure she had heard him correctly, but his face was in shadow. 'Mr Winbolt—' she began nervously.

'No, don't say it!' He put a finger on her lips. 'You

remember the second time we went out for a ride together? You wanted us to pretend we had never met
before.' She nodded and he went on softly, 'Now it's
my turn. Can we not pretend tonight that there are no
secrets between us, no barriers? Can you pretend—just
for a few moments—that we are two young lovers out
for a walk in the twilight, listening to the sounds of the
night... If I were to take you into my arms, like
this...would you be shocked and angry?' He waited, but
when she said nothing, he drew her closer and gazed
into her eyes.

'My love,' he said. 'My very dearest love.' He kissed
her carefully at first, almost as if he was afraid she would
fly away, but then his arms tightened and he kissed her
again.

'Philip, no—' Rosabelle's protest, which had come too
late for any conviction, was silenced by his third kiss.
'Philip...' she breathed, and suddenly found herself responding to him, lost in such a tumult of feeling that she
hardly knew what she was doing. When he lifted his
head she gave a little cry and pulled it down again so
that his mouth covered hers once more...

When the kiss finally ended, Rosabelle still held on to
Philip's arms, not trusting her legs to support her. They
were both breathing rapidly.

He said, 'I swear you have the strangest effect on me,
you...you enchantress! I start with every intention of
treating you as the rare and wonderful being you are, I
tell myself I mustn't hurt you, mustn't frighten you. But
when I have you in my arms, when you respond as you
do, I forget everything except your witchery!'

Rosabelle shook her head. Reaction was setting in.
She had behaved disgracefully. Nothing in her upbring-

ing had ever sanctioned behaviour like this. She tried to pull away, but he wouldn't let her.

'Don't! Don't tell me that you didn't want me to kiss you. Don't spoil that moment! You can't tell me that you don't love me this time. I really wouldn't believe you. Not this time.'

'I couldn't do that! I do love you. But I'm...I'm ashamed of myself. I don't know what happened to me. What must you think of me?'

'Everything that is good, believe me.'

She hardly heard him. 'I...I have never behaved like that before—never even felt like that before,' she said miserably.

He hesitated, then said in a curious voice, 'Never?'

'No.' The memory of her farce of a marriage to Stephen Ordway flashed into her mind, destroying her calm. 'Useless, devoid of natural feeling, shameless, wanton...' Her voice rose in panic. 'What sort of woman am I?'

'Stop this, Ro—role playing! You can't seriously believe what you're saying! Listen to me!' He took her by the shoulders. 'You are like no woman I have ever known. Lovely, gentle, amusing, kind...and totally desirable—do you want me to go on?'

She looked at him dully. 'But you don't know...'

'Then tell me! Trust me!'

# *Chapter Nine*

Rosabelle looked at Philip Winbolt in confusion and distress. Was this the long-awaited moment? Had the time come to tell him the truth? She was still off-balance, unable to think clearly, governed by strong emotions never before experienced—or even suspected. In spite of his reassuring words she still had a sense of shame at her passionate response to his kisses, her loss of all control; the memory of her husband's cruel taunts and lewd suggestions had been vividly resurrected in her mind.

How could anyone love her so much that he could forgive her deception? If he asked to know more about her marriage, what could she tell him? Would he turn away in disgust if she revealed the sordid details, the degradation that marriage to Stephen Ordway had brought? Was she brave enough to risk it? She stole a glance at Philip Winbolt. It was now nearly dark, and the newly risen moon slanted across his face, giving it an unfamiliar sternness.

'I…I *can't*!' she said and hid her face in her hands. A shuddering sob escaped her.

The air was heavy with Philip's disappointment. He seemed about to protest, even to force the truth out of her. But then his face softened and he took her into his arms again, this time cradling her gently in them. 'Don't! Please! I didn't mean to upset you. It's just that I want so badly to help you, to have you trust me. And I'm sorry that you don't seem able to.'

'I will, Philip, I will! But not yet!'

'I suppose I understand—after all, you have not known me for all that long, though it seems like a lifetime to me. But, *whatever* your secret is, my love and friendship for you will not change. Believe me.'

Rosabelle turned away and shook her head. Philip refused to let her hide from him. He took her face in his hands and said firmly, 'Listen to me! I could persuade you to tell me if I really tried. You love me, I know, and I've told you what I feel for you. But I'm foolish enough to want you to confide in me of your own free will, without any persuasion or pressure. Am I being mad?'

'No! But I can't tell you tonight! It's…it's late—and I need time!'

He looked at her for a moment, then nodded. 'I can understand that. I didn't mean to bring matters to a head tonight, I wanted to take things slowly, carefully, but now I've rushed you, after all! It's all because of my call to London, of course, and the fact that I found I couldn't go away for three weeks without seeing you once more. If I could ignore my grandfather's summons, I would, I assure you, but I can't! Something which has been brewing for a long time has reached a crisis, and he needs my help in sorting it out. And this time we must put an end to it once and for all. But three weeks seems a very long time before I can see you again!'

Rosabelle nodded. 'It is a long time,' she said softly.

He smiled and bent his head to kiss her again, very gently. After a moment he cleared his throat, and said firmly, 'Perhaps it's as well that we have to postpone our discussion, otherwise I really might not be able to concentrate on Winbolt business as I should! But, listen to me—while I'm away, I want you to remember that I have sworn to you that I love you. Hold on to that and let it give you courage to tell me everything. It will make no difference to my feelings for you, I promise you. Will you do that?'

He continued to hold her, waiting until she looked into his eyes.

'It's hard...I wish you weren't going, Philip...'

He kissed her gently on the lips and silenced her. 'So do I.'

She took a deep breath. 'I will tell you—when you come back,' she said gravely. 'I promise.'

He saw her safely back inside the house, raised her hand to his lips and kissed it, and it was as if the fervour of the kiss passed through the hand, into the rest of her body, bringing new hope and new life.

'Miss me a little,' he whispered. 'And smile for me now.'

Putting aside her doubts and fears, Rosabelle smiled at Philip Winbolt. If the smile was a little uncertain at first, it grew in answer to the old familiar quizzical gleam in his eye, until her face sparkled with love and laughter.

That smile haunted Philip throughout his weeks in London. He was fond of his grandfather and normally enjoyed time spent with him on business connected with

the Winbolt estates. But on this occasion the sessions
with lawyers and agents seemed unusually long and tedious. Lord Winbolt was in his eighties but, though phys-
ically frail, he was still in full possession of his considerable faculties, and he was at first surprised and then
annoyed at his grandson's lack of concentration.

'What the devil is wrong with you, Philip? You're
usually bang up to the mark, but Harrison has twice
made an error which passed you by, and it is quite obvious that you can hardly wait to be finished! What's
going on?' He grew sarcastic. 'Or does all the business
involved in your inheritance of half a million pounds or
more bore you? Not to mention the title.'

'I hope the title won't be vacant for some time yet,
sir. But no, I'm not bored.'

'You must be in love, then.' He gave Philip a hard
look. 'Is that it? Who is she?'

'I…I'm not absolutely sure.'

'What? What on earth does that mean? You'd better
explain yourself, sir! I'm not having my heir marrying a
nobody!'

'Grandfather, I promise you I have no intention of
disgracing the family name! But I would rather not discuss the lady with you until…certain matters have been
cleared up.'

He remained adamant in this refusal though Lord
Winbolt tried to move him with promises, pleas and,
finally, threats.

'Trust me, Grandfather. When the time comes I will
tell you everything—I'll bring her to see you. You will
approve, I am sure.'

'Oh, very well, very well. You were always a head-
strong, obstinate young puppy. But I never found you

lacking in sense. What about your sister? Any beaux in that direction?'

'No, but there's time yet.'

'She's five-and-twenty, sir! High time she was married. She'd make a good wife, though it's a pity she didn't take after her mother—she was a real little beauty! Emily isn't still pining for young Colesworth, is she?'

'I think she's over him now, though it took some time. His defection was a shock.'

'A sad business. Very sad. But it must be five or six years ago now. Has it made her difficult to please?'

'No, but it *has* made her cautious. She's a very rich young woman since my mother's fortune became hers, and past experience has made her a touch suspicious of young men who pretend to admire her.'

'I said no good would come of that money, and look what happened! What did your mother mean by leaving it to Emily, not you?'

'She knew very well that I already had more than enough, sir! But rest your mind about Emily. She'll find someone when the time comes.'

'I hope she may not leave it too late! Where is she now, by the way?'

'At her dressmaker's. She's having a new dress.'

'Another one? She ordered three the last time she was here.'

'This one is for a party we're giving at Shearings—to celebrate Emily's birthday.'

'No cause for celebration there! Twenty-five and not married yet. Better to keep quiet about it. Remind me to see about a small gift for her.'

Philip's time was not totally taken up with business matters. When Emily was otherwise occupied, he enjoyed several convivial sessions at various London clubs. Here, during the course of conversation with his friends and acquaintances he managed, quite casually, to introduce the name of Ordway. But though he heard numerous rumours, and a certain amount of speculation, there was nothing definite. Whatever Ordway and his circle had been up to, they had kept it very quiet. However, the picture he began to form was bad enough to explain why Rosabelle Ordway would be reluctant to talk about her husband.

'You seem to be interested in Ordway and his cronies—I can't imagine why. They were never your sort, Winbolt,' said one acquaintance. 'But I'll tell you one thing. Ordway wasn't the ringleader. That was a man called Selder, but no one outside ever saw him—we only ever heard the name. He came out of nowhere and stayed well in the background. I don't know what became of him—the group seemed to split up after Ordway died and I haven't heard a whisper of Selder since then. But if you ever do come across him, I'd advise you to treat him with caution. From what I've been told, he's the nastiest customer you're ever likely to meet.'

One thing Philip made time for early in his stay was to visit the Ordway house in Upper Brook Street. But the knocker was off the door, and the house was closed. The family were clearly away, along with many other London families at this time of year. He turned away, and came face to face with a well-dressed gentleman, who was standing at the foot of the steps.

'Excuse me, sir. Were you hoping to see Lady Ordway? I'm afraid they're out of town.'

This agreed with what Rosabelle had told him—that her sister was going to Buxton. The stranger seemed to

be well-informed, and Philip decided that he might learn
more from him. He joined the gentleman and they started
to walk towards Grosvenor Square.

'That is a pity. I had hoped to deliver a message from
Mrs Ordway's sister,' Philip said, 'You know the
Ordways, perhaps? Can you give me their direction, sir?
My name is Winbolt.'

'I am delighted to make your acquaintance, Mr
Winbolt. Julian Falkirk at your service.'

Mr Falkirk appeared to be about the same age as
Philip, a dark-haired man of average height, but powerful
build. He had an air of distinction about him, and his
voice was curiously agreeable—husky and deep. Philip
would have described him as an ugly man, but when he
smiled, as he did now, his face was transformed into
something magnetically attractive. He went on, 'But I
regret I am unable to oblige you with the Ordways' address. I believe they intended to go to Bath, but they
appear to have changed their minds. Is Mrs Ordway's
sister with you in London?'

'No. Only my own sister.'

The two walked across the square and down towards
Piccadilly. Mr Falkirk proved to be an intelligent, inter-
esting companion, and very knowledgeable about
London life. When they reached the corner of St James's
Street Philip paused and held out his hand. 'Goodbye,
Falkirk. I turn off here. I might well follow your rec-
ommendation and take my sister to *The Taming of the
Shrew*' tonight. I don't believe she has seen it staged
before. Thank you.'

Mr Falkirk smiled. 'I've half a mind to see it again
myself. You might well find me there. Goodbye,
Winbolt. I hope you manage to trace the Ordways.

Would you care to tell me where you're staying—in case I hear anything?'

'In Arlington Street with my grandfather. But the matter is not urgent. It can wait.'

Mr Falkirk strolled away down Piccadilly. But once out of sight he abandoned his casual air, and walked quickly and purposefully towards the maze of small streets beyond Leicester Square. Here he searched through several disreputable-looking taverns until he found the man he wanted.

'Burrows, find out all you can about a certain Philip Winbolt. He's asking a lot of questions about Ordway, and today I found him at the house in Upper Brook Street.'

'Where does he live?' Burrows asked laconically.

'Not in London. That's something I'd like you to find out. But he and his sister are staying in Arlington Street at the moment. With a grandfather.'

'Winbolt…let me think… That'd be Lord Winbolt. He lives in Arlington Street. When d'you want it?'

'Before tonight.'

'Have a heart, Selder—' There was a sudden silence during which the air fairly crackled with menace. Burrows grew pale.

'I'm sorry. It slipped out.'

'Did it? How dangerous. For you, I mean.'

'It won't happen again…Falkirk.'

'Good. I wouldn't like to lose you—you're quite useful. I want to know about the Winbolts before tonight, Burrows.'

The result of Burrows's researches was so interesting that Mr Falkirk dressed with particular care that evening, and set off to see *The Taming of the Shrew* for the second time.

* * *

Somehow Philip was not surprised to see Mr Falkirk at the theatre. He had appeared to be a man who liked company, and, as he had explained, most of his friends were out of London at the moment. The play proved to be everything he had claimed, and at supper afterwards, he and Emily speculated with much imagination, and a great deal of amusement, on the possibility of future happiness for the hero and heroine. Emily was more animated than Philip had seen her for a long time.

'But, sir, Katharine was merely pretending to be submissive! I'm sure she is still a clever, strong-minded woman. She had not changed essentially at all, and I fear Petruchio is due for an unpleasant surprise.'

'Not at all, not at all! Petruchio knows very well what sort of wife he has acquired. It's a game they are both playing.'

'You mean he *wants* a termagant for a wife?'

'No, no. But he wants a wife who knows her own mind. I think most intelligent men do.'

Philip had been content to watch the sparring match, but now he intervened. 'I think some men do. But if someone has to have the last word, then it should surely be the husband.'

In the argument that followed Philip watched Julian Falkirk closely. The Winbolt brother and sister had been orphaned at an early age, and Philip was accustomed to guarding his sister's interests. When Colesworth had nearly broken her heart, Philip had supported his sister in her distress, had taken her away on a long tour of the Lake District to help her recover, and had, since then, discreetly vetted any would-be successors. As it turned out, his efforts had till now proved unnecessary—Emily had never taken an interest in any one of them.

Julian Falkirk seemed on the surface to be eminently

suitable—presentable, amusing, and, from what he said, of the same sort of background as their own. Since the Winbolts were not great mixers in fashionable circles, and since Falkirk had met Philip only by chance that morning, he was unlikely to be a professional fortune-hunter. There hadn't been time for him to hear gossip about Emily's inheritance. Still, it wouldn't do any harm to set some enquiries in motion.

The time came for them to part company. 'Goodnight, Miss Winbolt,' said Falkirk. 'Today, when I found that the Ordways had still not returned to London I was somewhat cast down. But see! It has resulted in a very pleasant evening.'

'You know the Ordways, sir?'

'Slightly. But more by way of business. Mrs Ordway might be able to help me with some papers I need.'

'Her sister has told me that they are in Buxton at the moment. But they should be back before long, I think. Goodnight, Mr Falkirk.' Emily smiled and offered him her hand. He took it and touched it fleetingly with his lips.

'Goodnight, Miss Winbolt. And thank you for a most…interesting evening.'


Philip met with only moderate success in his enquiries. Julian Falkirk was very popular at the clubs, being someone who had a fund of excellent stories, held his wine well, and, though willing to play deep, never played beyond his ability to pay. He had been a captain in the Army, and had fought with distinction at Waterloo. After the war he had remained abroad and had been a frequent, though elusive, visitor to London. Until recently.

But then a radical change had taken place in Julian Falkirk's fortunes. He was a distant cousin of the present

Lord Banagher, a very distant cousin, but a series of misfortunes in the Banagher family had resulted in a disastrous lack of heirs. As a result, when the present Lord Banagher died, which report said could be at any moment, Julian Falkirk would inherit the title.

The matrons of society now regarded him with benevolence, and were looking forward to cultivating his acquaintance when Society returned to the capital. Heir to a barony, moderately wealthy, charming in company, not even the worst of the tabbies could claim that there had ever been any scandal associated with him. His only fault seemed to be that he was still somewhat elusive, and though he danced and conversed amiably enough during the last season, he had never seemed particularly interested in any of the young ladies who were paraded before him.

It had to be said that Mr Falkirk did not parade his interest in Miss Winbolt, either. He was apparently in no hurry to pursue the acquaintance, for neither Philip nor Emily saw anything of him for over a week after the theatre visit. He might almost have been out of town. But on his return he was so charming that Emily grew more interested in him with every day that passed. Though their conversations may not have been exceptionally long, she found them more stimulating than any others. He teased her about her love of shopping, he shared her intense interest in drama and the theatre, and he listened sympathetically to her enthusiastic descriptions of the beauties of Berkshire.

A more handsome man would have made her cautious, but Mr Falkirk's lack of looks disarmed her. The fact that he obviously prized intelligence and initiative in a woman was most reassuring to someone who thought of herself as plain. Philip watched and did his best to hide his anxiety. With all his heart he wanted Emily to find someone with whom she could be happy. He was not yet certain that Julian Falkirk was that man.

Then, to Philip's dismay, on the eve of their return to Berkshire, he heard his sister issue an invitation to Falkirk for her birthday party. This development was as unexpected as it was unwelcome, but he found it impossible to think of anything to say against it. It was highly out of character, for Emily was usually a cautious creature. She was clearly more interested in Julian Falkirk than he had realised. To do Falkirk justice, the fellow demurred, hesitated, said everything that was proper…but the end result was that Julian Falkirk's name had been added to the list of those invited to the party at Shearings on the following weekend. He had friends nearby, he said, with whom he could stay.

'You don't approve, Pip?'

The Winbolts were in the carriage on their way back to Berkshire. It had become clear to Philip that Emily was having second thoughts about her invitation to Mr Falkirk, and was looking for reassurance.

'I don't exactly disapprove, Emmie,' said Philip, deliberately using an affectionate name from childhood. 'I was a little surprised. We don't know much about him.'

'That's because he has lived abroad a great deal of the time,' said Emily eagerly. 'He was at Waterloo, and before that he fought alongside the Prussians.'

'Ah. That might account for it. Er…where has he been since 1815? Did he say?'

'I gathered that he's been with the Army of Occupation.'

'Has he said anything about his family? The Banaghers haven't the best of reputations.'

'Philip! I don't like you in this mood! There isn't the slightest need to be so suspicious. Mr Falkirk is only a distant connection of the present Lord Banagher. You mustn't tar him with the same brush. His family own a castle on a lake in the south, which he is due to inherit any day. It's very beautiful there. He has always been something of a rover, but now he is beginning to feel that he ought to settle down.'

'He appears to have plenty to live on,' said Philip, trying to find something positive to say. 'Just…just don't rush into anything, Emmie. It isn't like you.'

'I know, Pip dear. You're afraid I'll make another mistake. Don't worry—I'm not going to lose my head over Mr Falkirk. But I have to confess that he's the most interesting man I have met in a long time! And he is not coming to stay for a month—only a few hours on my birthday.'

The warm weather held throughout the weeks the Winbolts were in London. Rosabelle ordered her dress, made her usual visits to the sick round the Temperley estate, sat in the garden in the shade of the trees, went for walks along the river, and quite failed in all of this activity to put Philip Winbolt out of her mind. Sometimes she could picture herself living forever more in idyllic happiness at Shearings, but at other times she was despondent, unable to see a future with him anywhere. Then she would remind herself of his words and take heart again. Her father was getting more active. He even came down one afternoon to sit with her in the garden, and said several times how pleasant it was.

'I had quite forgotten how agreeable it can be in the

open air. My room is very hot in the afternoons. I should
do this more often. When is young Winbolt coming
back?'

'On Friday, I believe, Papa. Emily's party is the day
after.'

'Hmm. Leaving it a bit late, aren't they?'

'They have a very competent housekeeper, she will
see that the servants do everything necessary. Emily says
in her note that Mr Winbolt has too much to do to leave
London earlier.'

'I take it that you haven't yet spoken to him?'

'He did ask me a little about it—the night before he
left. But…I wasn't ready. Don't say anything, Papa! I
know it was foolish, but when it came to the point I just
couldn't do it! It was he who suggested waiting till he
came back, not I! He…he is very kind.'

'Kind? Bah! I told you. He's in love with you! Don't
waste any more of his time, Rosabelle. Tell him! I'll
warrant he'll take you in his arms and swear it makes
not an atom of difference. Tell him soon.'

Rosabelle's smile, her enchantingly sweet, sparkling,
vulnerable smile, lit her face. 'I will, Papa. I will.'

Her father's face softened. He stretched out his hand
to hers. 'I want to see you made happy, my dear. And
Philip Winbolt is the man to do it.'


Philip and Emily arrived home in a carriage laden
down with packages and parcels of every size. Rosabelle
had been warned of their arrival and was at Shearings to
greet them.

'Emily! How many dresses did you intend to buy?
There's more than one here, I'll swear!'

'Well, it would have seemed such a wasted opportunity, Anna dear. Three weeks with nothing to do but look at the shops and choose materials!'

'During the day,' said Philip. 'She had better things to do in the evenings. How are you?' He came over and took Rosabelle's hand. 'Have you missed me?' he said softly, taking her hand to his lips.

The look in his eyes caused delicate colour to rise in Rosabelle's cheeks. 'I…yes, I have,' she said.

Emily had been busy with her boxes and parcels, but now she looked sharply at her brother. She seemed about to say something, but he gave a faint shake of his head, and she changed her mind. Then she turned to Rosabelle.

'Anna, I have to show you my dress—it is a dream! You were quite right about Fanchon. Come! We'll go to my bedchamber right away.'

Laughing, Philip said, 'I can see that my sister has her own priorities. Who am I to interfere? I'll go and see what's been going on at Shearings while we've been away. I'll be back in less than an hour, however, so don't linger over your rhapsodies!' With that he left the room and the two young ladies ascended the stairs to a handsome room on the first floor.

The new dress was produced and greeted with awe. In truth, its rich, wine-red silk top and thin cream gossamer skirt were extremely flattering to Emily's colouring, and her figure was shown to full advantage by the slightly longer, closely-fitting bodice.

'You don't think the waist is too low?' Emily asked anxiously. 'Madame Fanchon said it was going to be all the fashion, but I'm really not sure.'

'I shouldn't argue with her. That bodice is absolutely right for you. I hadn't realised what a tiny waist you have, Emily. I like the little point in front—that's very elegant.'

'I was very taken with the sleeves—see?' Emily lifted up the short oversleeves of wine red, to display the short, delicate, gossamer silk undersleeves ending in a pointed fall of lace and silk. Every detail was pored over and admired by Rosabelle, delighted that her friend had been so successful in her search for a dress worthy of the occasion.

'And what have you found, my friend?' asked Emily when the dress had been given, along with all the rest, to be put away.

Rosabelle smiled and said. 'Guess the colour!'

'Blue,' said Emily promptly.

'Wrong—it's azure! Blue is far too commonplace a name for the colour of my dress—according to the silk merchant in Reading. And I've taken some lace from one of my mother's old dresses to trim it. You'll like it. But you're the important one on Saturday, and that dress makes you into a star. It is truly beautiful!'

'Anna, I've invited someone I met in town. He's Lord Banagher's heir. His name is Falkirk. Mr Julian Falkirk.'

'Oh?'

'Don't say "Oh?" in that significant way! You mustn't read more into a simple invitation than there is! I simply like him, and I think you will, too. He isn't particularly handsome, but he's a sensible man and very easy to talk to. I shall look forward to hearing your opinion of him.'

'What about your brother? Does he like him?'

'Philip's protective instincts are always aroused when I show interest in anyone. He's reserving judgement. But I'm sure he'll like Mr Falkirk more when he sees him here at Shearings. I might call on you to support me. Philip will listen to you.'

Rosabelle grew pink and said, 'What makes you think that?'

'Oh, Anna! I have eyes! And I've known Philip a long time. He's besotted with you! And there is no one I would rather have as a sister—you must know that. But I won't say any more until one of you tells me that it is all settled. I have a feeling that I won't have long to wait.'

The maid came back at that moment to say that Mr Winbolt was asking for them. Emily gave Rosabelle an unladylike wink, and hugged her. They both collapsed into laughter, then calmed down and descended the stairs in a dignified manner.

'It's a great nuisance,' said Philip as they entered the drawing room. 'I have to ride over to Johnson's farm tonight—apparently Johnson injured himself pretty badly yesterday, and I need to see him and settle what we'll do while he's out of action.'

'But Johnson's farm is miles away!' exclaimed Emily. 'And it's already late!'

'I know,' said Philip, looking at Rosabelle. 'It's… inconvenient. There are other, more important, things I wished to do.' He turned to Emily. 'But I can't put it off till after the weekend—and tomorrow is your birthday. I'll go tonight and stay at the Falcon in Theal. That way I can see Johnson early tomorrow, assess what to do and be back in time for the party.'

'I'll tell Mrs Hopkins to pack a bag for you,' said Emily and hurried out.

Philip went over to Rosabelle and took her into his arms. 'I've missed you. Oh, how I've missed you!' was all he said, but Rosabelle felt his love enveloping her once again. She gave him her enchanting smile.

'I've missed you, too, Philip. And I'm ready now to

tell you everything. But it will take some time—it's a long story.'

'We'll have all the time we need tomorrow, my love—no, confound it! It's Emily's party! I'm sorry, but all this time I have looked forward to seeing you; I arrive home to find that you are ready to trust me as I had hoped—and I cannot stay to hear you!'

'Johnson is bad?'

'Very. He's likely to lose a leg. I have to see him and do what I can to reassure him.'

'Of course. We can wait. After all, we have the rest of our lives.'

'But now that I know you love me, I want the rest of our lives to begin as soon as possible!'

'So do I, Philip—oh, so do I! But it seems we must wait till after the party—and, after all, it is Emily's day tomorrow.'

'So I must wait till Sunday then?'

'On Sunday I shall tell you the whole sad story. And then—'

'And then…' He drew her to him.

There was a sound of loud coughing from outside the door and Emily entered the room. 'It's all ready. When do you expect to be back, Philip?'

'I shan't know till I see Johnson. However, I shall certainly be here in time for your party, Emily. I wouldn't dare miss that! But perhaps you should get that cough of yours seen to?'

Rosabelle had many dresses equal to Emily's in style and modishness in the house in Upper Brook Street, but she had seldom dressed there with as much pleasurable anticipation as she did at Temperley on the evening of Emily's party. The dress she wore was not ambitious in

style, for she had thought it better not to test the skills
of the local dressmaker too far. The bodice was plain,
and the skirt full and simply cut. But she had been very
fortunate to find the length of 'azure' silk at the silk
merchant's in Reading. The beautiful material shim-
mered in candlelight, and the intense blue kept its colour
where paler shades would have faded. Her mother's lace
was valuable and the dressmaker had draped it over the
bodice and round the hem with considerable success.

The whole of Temperley's small household shared
Rosabelle's pleasure—they had all watched her increasing confidence and happiness in the past weeks, and
thought they knew how to account for it. Even Mr
Kelland insisted on seeing his daughter before she set
out for Shearings.

'My dear girl!' he said. He was not accustomed to
emotion, and found difficulty in expressing it. But the
sight of his gentle, anxious daughter's transformation
into a laughing, radiant beauty overcame his inhibitions.
'My dear girl—you look...wonderful! Irresistible!
Enchanting! I am so proud of you.'

'Papa! Thank you! And thank you for looking out
Mama's jewellery for me.'

'You look just like her, Rosabelle. Just like my
Rosanna. That diamond collar was my wedding present
to her.' Mr Kelland coughed and cleared his throat. 'I
should have come with you. But I daresay John will see
you safely there and back. And I have no doubt whatever
that young Winbolt will keep an eye on you at the party.
Enjoy yourself.'

Rosabelle went over and hugged him, without thought
for her finery. 'Thank you, Papa. Not just for the jewellery, but for everything else.'

'Well, well. That's enough. Off you go. Don't keep
the horses standing about.'

# *Chapter Ten*

Shearings was *en fête*. All the huge double doors which linked the rooms on the ground floor were open. Hundreds of candles burned in the chandeliers and wall lights, and the house was full of great bowls of autumn leaves and flowers. The Winbolts had brought Mrs Hopkins, the housekeeper, with them from London when they had first come to Shearings, and she had proved more than worthy of their trust in leaving her to it. Extra help had been engaged locally, and Maynard, Lord Winbolt's butler, had condescended to join the household for the week leading up to the party. He and Mrs Hopkins were old friends and together they had worked to produce superb food and wines in fitting surroundings. Emily might well be pleased with the preparations for her birthday celebration.

Rosabelle had not realised, when she had accepted the invitation, that it was to be such a huge affair. She would have been far more reluctant to come, had she known that practically the whole neighbourhood had been invited. But she comforted herself with the knowledge that Philip, who was the most important person in her life after all, would soon know the truth anyway. So she came into the hall, after leaving her cloak with the footman, prepared to enjoy the evening.

'Annabelle! Where've you been all these months? We've hardly seen you! Y're looking deucedly well, girl!'

Rosabelle turned round to find a large lady beaming at her. She had a weatherbeaten face, was dressed in purple satin, and had two lavishly curling feathers waving in her hair. The face was dimly familiar, but the name eluded her. Lady Harbury?…Harbottle? Har… Heavens! What was the woman's name?

'Ah, Lady Harwarden! There you are!' Philip Winbolt appeared at Lady Harwarden's side. 'And I see that our neighbour from Temperley has arrived, too. You are both very welcome.'

'How are ye, Winbolt? This is a splendid affair, indeed it is! I never saw anything like it when y'r Uncle Joseph was alive! Not that he was mean, mind—he just couldn't stand a lot of noise and fuss. Where's your sister?'

'She's in the drawing room, ma'am.'

'I'll seek her out straight away. Oh, by the by, Annabelle—what about the horse?'

'Horse?' said Rosabelle blankly.

'Y'can't have forgotten! How much d'ye think she's worth?'

'I…I haven't—'

'Come on, girl! You've had long enough to think about it!'

'Now, ma'am,' said Philip smoothly, taking Lady Harwarden's arm. 'I won't let you bully my guests in this shameless manner. It's not the right occasion for business matters. And if you don't find Emily soon, you won't see her at all—she'll be dancing. Talk to Miss Kelland some other time. Come, I'll find you a glass of wine and then take you to my sister.'

'Y're quite right, of course, Winbolt. I'll see you later, Annabelle!'

Philip bore Lady Harwarden off and Rosabelle breathed again. She mingled with the other guests, finding with relief that she remembered most of them quite well—especially when she could take her time about it. In due course, when she thought that Lady Harwarden would be safely out of the way, she went in search of Emily.

Emily was surrounded by a group of young people, most of whom Rosabelle could remember from the summers spent at Temperley during her childhood. She joined them with fair confidence. The young woman holding the stage at present was Georgiana Smythe— Georgie, they had called her.

'Anna! You're late! And you live practically next door—shame on you!' said Emily, smiling and kissing her cheek. 'I sent Philip to find you, but he came back with Lady Harwarden.' She saw Rosabelle's eyes go over the group, and said softly, 'No, my guest from London has not yet arrived. He said he would be late.'

One of the young men asked Emily if she would dance and with a smile at Rosabelle she went off in the direction of the music.

'Will you dance, too, Anna? Or will you accuse me again of treading on your toes? I've been taking lessons—this is an easy one.' Rosabelle looked into the anxious eyes of a gangling youth and smiled her enchanting smile.

'And I've been learning manners. I'd be delighted to dance with you, Freddy!'

After the set was finished Rosabelle and her partner rejoined the group. Rosabelle was panting slightly, for Freddy Norland's energetic style had rather taken it out of her. She met Philip's quizzical smile with fortitude, however, and thanked her partner prettily. She turned to Philip.

'Stop looking at me like that!' she whispered. 'I shall burst out laughing, and that would never do. Poor lad!'

'If I looked at you the way I really want,' said Philip, equally softly, 'the poor lad and all the rest of them would be shocked.'

Rosabelle took refuge behind her fan and turned away. But after a moment or two she turned back. 'How is Johnson?'

'In a bad way. But I think he'll pull through. I've brought a man in to keep the farm running.'

A burst of laughter drew their attention back to the group.

'Anna,' said Emily. 'Georgie has been telling me such tales. Did you and your sister really get up to such tricks?'

'I'm not sure,' Rosabelle said carefully. 'Which ones do you mean, Georgie?'

'Well, Rosa wasn't there at all for the best one,' said Georgie. 'You remember, Anna? When we fell into the mill pond? That was a lark!'

'Oh, yes,' said Rosabelle. 'Yes, that was very amusing.'

Then Georgie said, catastrophically, 'I'm hopeless at telling stories—you tell it, Anna!'

'Er…'

'I'm sure Anna would tell it brilliantly,' said Philip.

'But if you get your story, I shall miss the dance I've been promised! The set is just being made up. I propose to take your Scheherezade away! Or—' he turned to Rosabelle with well simulated anxiety '—am I being presumptuous? Would you prefer me to forgo dancing with you?'

'No, no!' said Rosabelle. 'I'm sure Georgie can tell the story just as well as I could—or even better.'

'I would put money on that,' murmured Philip.

'I beg your pardon?'

'Nothing, nothing. Come, we shall miss it unless you hurry.'

'I didn't promise any dance to you,' hissed Rosabelle as he led her away.

'No, but you were glad I intervened, weren't you?'

'Wha-what do you mean?'

'My dearest girl—tell me honestly. Would you rather tell a stale old story to a bunch of people, most of whom know it better than you do—or would you rather dance with me? You look enchanting, by the way.'

'There's no competition, if you put it like that,' said Rosabelle and gave herself up to the enjoyment of dancing with Philip.

The party continued without any further crises. Though Philip was careful not to make too much of it, Rosabelle was conscious of his care and attention all the time. For the first time in years—perhaps the first time in her life—she felt she could look forward to the future with a light heart.

This happy situation changed dramatically halfway through the evening.

'My dear Miss Winbolt, what a splendid occasion! How fortunate for me that we met in London!'

Rosabelle heard the words from the flower-bedecked alcove in which she was sitting, somewhat hidden from view. There was a sound of breaking glass, and looking down she saw that she had dropped her wine glass. The wine had spilled out on the floor, and splashes of it were staining the hem of her dress. Red. The colour of blood.

'What is it? What's wrong?' Philip's voice broke through the waves of faintness which were threatening to overwhelm her.

'I...I don't feel well...'

'Come, I'll help you upstairs. One of the maids will take care of you. Put your arm through mine.'

'No! Not that way!' she whispered. He had begun to lead her past the owner of that hateful voice. 'I'd...I'd like some air. Take me into the garden, Philip.'

'But you'll be cold—'

'Take me outside!' Her voice was still low, but the intense feeling in it impressed him. He led her to the side door which opened into the garden room. Here he snatched up a wrap which was lying on one of the benches and helped her put it on. They went outside.

He took her to a small gazebo, set with ornamental stone seats. 'Sit here. Now tell me what caused all this.'

Rosabelle wasn't ready. Confused and frightened, she had to have time to think! 'I'd like a glass of water, Philip,' she whispered. 'Do you think you could fetch one? I'll be all right here.'

'Of course.' He strode away.

What was she to do? Oh, what could she do? She was well nigh certain that the voice belonged to Selder. He was here in the house. He had said he would be back, but he had disappeared after Stephen had died—more than a year ago, now—and she had come to think he had given up. She had apparently been mistaken. By what catastrophic coincidence had he come here to Shearings? Or was it a coincidence? Had Selder tracked her down as he said he would?

The thought terrified her, and she half rose, ready for flight. But second thoughts prevailed. She could not avoid him—even if she fled, questions would be asked and Selder would easily find out where to look next. She tried to subdue her rising panic—she must stay calm and think sensibly, if not for her own sake, then for Philip's. He must be protected at all costs from Selder's anger… She must think…

Selder had obviously met Emily in London. It was a Mr Falkirk who had made such an impression on Emily, but there had been no mention of a second stranger… Oh God, what was she to do? Falkirk *must* be the man she had known as Selder… She shut her eyes as the dreadful memories returned, the appalling state of Stephen's poor, battered body, his groans… Whatever happened, Philip must not be put in a position where he would do anything to arouse the man's enmity. She had seen what Selder did to those he regarded as a threat.

And yet if Philip learned what sort of man Emily had invited to Shearings there would surely be some sort of confrontation. But how could she prevent it…? Pretend not to know him! Continue to be Annabelle! That was it! She must…she *must* persuade Selder that he had found the wrong sister. It was the only way she could think of to protect herself and her friends.

'I'm sorry it took so long. I had to make a latecomer welcome—someone I would have sooner not welcomed at all to tell the truth.' Philip sat down at her side and put his arm around her. 'Here—I brought a little brandy, as well. Drink it.'

Rosabelle sipped the brandy. Its warmth spread

through her veins, but it could not dismiss her feeling of
dread. 'Who was it?' she asked.

'A man called Falkirk. We met him in London, and
Emily was rather taken with him. She invited him for
tonight, and he has just arrived. What's this? You're
shivering again. What is it, my darling?'

'Philip, hold me! Hold me tight.'

'Hush, Rosa, hush! You're safe with me. Nothing can
harm you.'

Rosabelle clung to him for a minute, drinking in his
warmth and the feeling of security in his arms. Then she
drew back and stared at him. 'You called me Rosa,' she
whispered.

'A…a slip of the tongue.'

'I don't believe you,' she said. 'Why would you make
such a mistake? That's not it at all! You know! You
know I'm not Anna.' He nodded, never taking his eyes
from her face. 'How long have you known?' she demanded.

'I haven't been absolutely certain till this moment. But
I've suspected as much for several weeks.'

'Who told you?'

'No one. You did.'

'Me?'

'Let's say I worked it out. I fell in love with you after
Easter, Rosa. It was you, not Annabelle, that I found
myself in love with.'

'Does Emily know, too?'

'I haven't told anyone else. Why did you do it?'

'I…I was ill. I needed a rest. There were reasons why
I couldn't simply abandon my godmother in London.
So—Anna took my place.' She paused, then asked, not
looking at him, 'Do you know about Stephen, too?'

'Know what?' he said carefully. 'I know you're his

widow, if that is what you mean. Do you…do you still mourn him, Rosa?'

'No,' she said sadly. 'I never did.' She looked at him sombrely. 'I was glad when he died—and so was he. He…he wasn't the sort of person someone…someone like you would want to…to associate with.'

'Yes, I know,' he said gravely.

Rosabelle let out her breath in a long shuddering sigh. 'I was so frightened of telling you. Are you sure that it doesn't make a difference to the way you feel?'

'Not the slightest in the world—didn't I tell you so?'

'Yes, but I didn't know then what you meant.' The relief was too much for Rosabelle's overstretched nerves. She burst into tears. 'Philip,' she sobbed, 'Philip, I love you so much!'

There followed an interval during which Mr Winbolt did his best to demonstrate that he returned these sentiments in full. After a while she grew calm again, and he said quietly, 'Tell me why you were so upset.'

'Before I do, will you promise me something first?'

'What is it?'

'I want to—I *must* carry on pretending to be Anna. For the moment. Will you help me?'

'Of course. But why?'

'I can't change back without telling Anna first.'

'That's understandable. But it doesn't begin to explain why you were in such distress. Tell me the real reason, Rosa. Don't put me off.'

'No. I…' Rosabelle took a deep breath and forced herself to speak calmly. 'I think I might know Mr Falkirk, though I didn't…didn't remember his name. And if he is the man I know, then he will recognise me. It would be better for everyone if I can persuade him that I am not Rosabelle Ordway.'

'Are you saying that it was Falkirk who caused that shock?'

'I heard his voice—and thought I recognised it. I can't be sure until I've seen him.'

'Tell me why you don't want him to know you.'

'I…I can't.'

Philip regarded her in silence. 'Did he make advances to you when you were married to Stephen Ordway? Is that it? Are you afraid he'll repeat them?'

Rosabelle stared at him. This might be as good a reason as she was likely to find, though it fell a long way short of the truth. It might keep Philip safe. She hung her head. 'Yes,' she said. 'Please, Philip. Help me to convince him I am Anna.'

Philip was silent, then he sighed. 'I'm sure there's more to it than this. Can't you tell me?'

'Not…not yet. I'll tell you later.'

'I have a double reason for it, you know—Emily, and now you.' He looked at the set face before him. 'But I think that's all I'm going to get out of you for the moment.'

'Promise you'll leave it,' said Rosabelle clutching his arm. 'If we can make him believe I'm Anna, he'll go away to London and we shan't see him again. We can convince Emily that he isn't for her, I'm sure. Promise, please promise! When he's safely away I'll tell you the whole story.'

He frowned at the note of desperation in her voice, then his face softened. 'Very well. For the moment. Now tidy yourself up, and we'll go in. Otherwise it'll be all over the county that I've seduced Annabelle Kelland— and then how should we manage?'

When Philip and Rosabelle returned to the house they

found Emily in the supper room, being plied with food by Julian Falkirk.

'Anna!' she cried. 'And Philip, too! Come here at once. I've been waiting all evening to introduce my acquaintance from London to my friend. Mr Falkirk, Miss Kelland.'

Julian Falkirk had been standing with his back to the room. Now he turned round. He stared for a long moment, then smiled. 'Rosabelle Ordway!' he exclaimed. 'What a very pleasant surprise! I quite thought I had lost track of you!' He turned to Emily. 'Mrs Ordway is an old friend,' he said. 'Her husband and I were very close.' He turned back to Rosabelle. 'Isn't that so?' he asked impudently, challenging her, threatening her, reminding her of the past and what he could do.

The man before her was indeed Selder. Drawing on all her strength, Rosabelle kept her eyes clear of any previous knowledge of the man and smiled apologetically. Philip came to the rescue. He shook his head ruefully. 'Falkirk, you have just lost me an argument. When I was told that this lady here and her sister were identical twins—"as like as two peas in a pod" was the phrase used, I believe—I refused to entertain the notion that two people could possibly be so alike. But you say you know Mrs Ordway?'

'I do,' said Falkirk.

'And you think to see her here?'

'I'm certain of it.'

'What if I were to tell you that this lady is her sister, Annabelle Kelland?'

'Of course she's Annabelle!' said Emily. 'She lives with her father at Temperley, quite near here. Mrs Ordway lives in London. Did you say you knew her, Mr Falkirk?'

'Er…yes.' Falkirk frowned. 'I thought so,' he said. He turned to Rosabelle, and eyed her speculatively. His eyes were hard, obsidian, like a snake's. She gave him a cool look in return and raised her chin. He suddenly smiled and said, 'Forgive me, Miss Kelland. I'm sorry I mistook you. The likeness is amazing, truly amazing.'

'You are excused, sir. I am well used to being taken for my twin, though it can sometimes be embarrassing.'

'Well, now that's settled, may we have some food? It's always the same—one never gets anything to eat at one's own parties,' said Philip. 'Come, my little case of mistaken identity! If I know Maynard, he has a few delicacies put away for the deserving. We'll see you later, Falkirk.' Philip offered Rosabelle his arm and led her away.

'You were very good,' he said as they made their escape. 'All the same, my love, we'll have to spend some time talking to him later. I don't want to give the impression that we're avoiding him.'

But all of Rosabelle's courage was required when later that night Falkirk asked her to dance with him. Philip was already dancing with someone else, and so was Emily. To refuse would be somewhat pointed, and he had a suspiciously watchful air about him. Mr Falkirk was far from convinced.

'Tell me, Miss Kelland,' he began as they started towards the room set aside for dancing, 'do you know your sister's present address? Or when she intends to return to London? She has something of mine in her care, and I should like to collect it.'

'I'm afraid I can't help you with either, Mr Falkirk. I haven't heard from my sister for several weeks. Indeed, I shall take her to task when I do see her. I believe her to be with her godmother still.'

'Ah, yes, Lady Ordway. Are the two ladies alone? It sounds a dangerous enterprise to me.'

'Dangerous? Surely not! I understand that Colonel Stanton, Lady Ordway's nephew, is with them.'

'I see…Giles Stanton, eh? Of course, the Stantons have an estate in Derbyshire, have they not?'

Rosabelle looked enquiringly at Mr Falkirk. 'I really don't know. You seem concerned?'

'Well, I shouldn't have said that Stanton was the best escort for two ladies in the wilds of the North.'

Rosabelle was just about to agree, when she remembered that Annabelle was not supposed to have met Giles Stanton. 'Really? You know Colonel Stanton?'

'No, but I've heard of him. He has the reputation of being a ruthless sort of chap.'

If Rosabelle had not been so afraid of arousing any sort of curiosity in this man she would have questioned him further. It was true that Annabelle's recent silence had worried her. But she would not give 'Julian Falkirk' an opening.

'He's Stephen Ordway's heir, after all,' she said airily. 'My sister seems to fall out with him quite regularly, but I can hardly believe he would do anything to give rise to scandal.'

'Of course not,' said Mr Falkirk. The irony in his voice was not lost on Rosabelle, though she gave no sign that she noticed. Instead she turned the conversation to talk of the rooms, the music, all the various topics in which comparative strangers can take refuge.

By the end of the evening Rosabelle was exhausted. The effort of keeping up a front in the face of Mr Falkirk's unremitting interest had taken its toll. Emily had noticed the manner in which her London guest's eyes had constantly followed Miss Kelland, and she was distinctly put out. Rosabelle saw it, but could do nothing to help her friend. Indeed, one small consolation in the affair was the hope that Julian Falkirk's behaviour would give Emily a distaste for him. When the Temperley carriage was announced Rosabelle was horrified to hear Mr Falkirk offer to escort it.

'I feel I owe it to Miss Kelland's sister,' he said smoothly. 'The roads are dangerous at night.'

'Not here, sir,' said Philip curtly. 'And, in any case, the lady has already accepted the offer of an escort from me. I promised her father.'

'Ah, then I shall wish you goodnight.' He turned to Emily, 'Thank you for a very pleasant evening, Miss Winbolt. If you would let me know the next time you are coming to London, I shall procure some theatre tickets for you. I can usually be sure of the best seats.'

Rosabelle was delighted to observe that there was nothing in Emily's manner to encourage him. 'Thank you, but I do not think I shall be in London for some time. Goodnight, Mr Falkirk.'

Mr Falkirk was unabashed. He smiled, that slow, magnetic, charismatic smile. Rosabelle could hardly restrain another shudder.

'Goodnight, Miss Winbolt.' A bow, another look at Rosabelle, and he was gone! Rosabelle could have cried with relief.

'Emily—'

'I see there's a stain on the hem of your dress, Anna. What a pity. I hope it will come out.'

Rosabelle looked down. She had forgotten about the wine. The marks had faded to a dull brown. 'Becky will know what to do. Emily, I hope you enjoyed your party. It was a wonderful occasion.'

'Of course I did! But I think my dress was a mistake. The colour doesn't really suit me. Goodnight. Philip will see you home.'

'Shall I see you tomorrow?'

'I expect so. I'm a little tired. Goodnight, Philip.' Emily turned away and went slowly up the stairs.

Philip looked at her retreating back with a frown in his eyes. Then he turned and took Rosabelle's arm. 'She's unhappy, but I don't think anything I could say at the moment would help her. I wish I'd never met Falkirk!'

'She's unhappy now, Philip, but she will be saved a lot of unhappiness in the future if she forgets him, believe me. He is not the sort of man she ought to know.'

'I believe you. Shall we go to Temperley?'

'There's no need for you to come! How will you get back?'

'My darling, dearest Rosa! I regard this evening as our unofficial engagement! If you think I would let you drive home alone, you are clearly deranged! I shall fly back on wings of love! Or, John Bostock will lend me a horse, if you prefer.'

Laughing, they ran out to the waiting carriage. From an upstairs window, Emily watched them, heartache in her eyes.

A whole week went by without any sign of Julian Falkirk, and Rosabelle started to breathe freely again. It had been a week of mixed fortunes. Emily was clearly depressed. The thought of being twenty-five had not seemed to trouble her before her party, but now she often referred to her age, and lack of prospects. However, she appeared to have forgotten her pique at Julian Falkirk's interest in Rosabelle, and was as friendly as ever. She brought up the subject of her future.

'One has to look facts in the eye, Anna. It is clear that you and Pip are made for each other. Indeed, I cannot imagine why you have not announced your engagement already. And when you marry, you will hardly want a third living with you.'

'Emily! Without wishing to discuss household arrangements which are still hypothetical, I swear that Shearings would be big enough for a host of sisters— and especially ones as nice as you! And I'm sure you will agree that we can make nothing official until I have managed to be in touch with my own sister! I have written to her three times at least, but I think the letters must have gone astray.'

Emily put her hand on Rosabelle's arm. 'Don't look so anxious. When Pip and I were in the Lakes no one heard from us for weeks! It is quite remote in some parts, you know. I expect your sister will write as soon as she returns to civilisation.'

'You make it sound like the moon! But it is October now. It's rather late in the season to be jaunting round in the wilds of the North! I am sure it cannot suit Lady Ordway.'

'You'll hear soon, I'll warrant you. Now, tell me. Are you coming with Pip and me to Lady Harwarden's?'

Rosabelle smiled. She had no intention of going near the good lady till she could find out more about that horse! 'I'm afraid I have a previous engagement,' she said, trying to sound regretful.

Rosabelle had much the same discussion with Philip.

'I want to tell the world that we belong,' he said. 'Is that so unreasonable?'

'My darling Philip, we do belong—isn't that what matters? And you must admit that you can hardly announce your betrothal to Annabelle Kelland, and then marry Rosabelle Ordway! It simply wouldn't do! What would the neighbourhood say?'

'Damn the neighbourhood!' Then he smiled. 'Yes, yes! You're right, I suppose. We can't have two Rosabelle Ordways roaming the country. Where is that sister of yours?'

Rosabelle's face clouded over. 'I don't know, Philip. I'm worried.'

'Darling Rosa, don't look like that. From what I saw of Anna when she was at Temperley I would say that she is very well able to take care of herself—and Lady Ordway, too.'

'But Giles Stanton went with them, and I am not at all sure she is safe with him!'

'Stanton? Giles Stanton? You say he is with them? Why?'

'He is Aunt Laura's nephew and Stephen's heir. His mother was Sir John Ordway's elder sister.'

'I thought Giles was in France, or Vienna. Somewhere in Europe, anyway.'

'He came back last year, when the Duke of Wellington returned to England, though he still spends time abroad.'

'Then Anna is in the best possible hands. I knew Giles Stanton in the Peninsula. A great fellow.'

'Really?' said Rosabelle doubtfully.

''I can imagine the ladies finding him somewhat harsh. He doesn't waste time on civilities.'

'No!' said Rosabelle with feeling.

'But he's absolutely straight. Anna couldn't ask for a better escort—and, after all, my love, they're not in the wilds of Estramadura, only Derbyshire!'

'So why doesn't she write?' demanded his love.

On the day that the Winbolts visited Lady Harwarden, Rosabelle, whose previous engagement was entirely fictitious, stayed at home. She felt restless. She was no happier than Philip about the delay in announcing their engagement, but until she could see Annabelle, or at least communicate with her, she was determined not to make their exchange of identity public. Her father agreed with her.

'Anna did this as a favour to you, Rosa. You can't end the deception without consulting her. You don't know how it might affect her.'

'No, Papa. But Philip and I—'

'Want to be engaged, get married all in five minutes! Heaven defend me from the impatience of lovers! You're not children—you can wait. Go out for a walk and leave me in peace.'

Now that the weather was less agreeable Mr Kelland had once more taken up his position by the fire, complete with his books. Though he was no longer quite so absorbed in them—Philip came several evenings a week to play chess and converse, and Rosabelle often stayed a while to talk with him—today he was impatient to finish a new criticism of the art of the Greeks and had little time for his daughter.

Rosa waited until she was certain that the Winbolts would be well on their way to Harwarden Place, then wandered out into the park. The day was overcast, with dark clouds scudding across the sky. The wind was tossing the branches of the trees, bringing down showers of leaves. It would soon be winter.

She had been at Temperley now for nearly six months. Half a year. What changes there had been in her life!

She wondered how Annabelle was getting on with Giles Stanton. Had he changed his opinion of 'Rosabelle Ordway'? Becky was convinced that Annabelle was attracted to Giles, but how could she be? And yet…Philip liked him.

It was strange that the two men should know each other. Not so strange, perhaps—they were of an age, and it was fashionable for young men of their generation to go into the army. Philip appeared to know him well, so perhaps she had been mistaken in his character…

'What would you say if I told you that I had found your sister, Rosabelle?'

She whirled round. Selder was leaning against one of the oak trees, looking at her mockingly. In spite of the shock Rosabelle kept her head—and remembered to call him by the right name.

'Mr Falkirk! What are you doing here?'

'I thought you might like to know where Annabelle is.'

Rosabelle kept her head. 'Annabelle? What do you mean? I'm Anna.'

'Are you? Well, that remains to be seen.'

'You are talking nonsense, sir. Did you say that you had Mrs Ordway's direction?'

'No, not exactly. The lovely widow Ordway is keeping well out of my way. She's not in Buxton. But if she's with Giles Stanton then I might know where to look next. Or am I wasting my time? Is Rosabelle Ordway in front of me here and now?'

'I can't stand here trading rubbish with you, Mr Falkirk. Either you know Rosa's address, or you don't. If you do, then I should be obliged if you would give it to me. If, in spite of what you say, you don't, then I will waste no more of your time—or my own.'

'I'm damned if I can decide… Let us say, for the sake of argument, that you are Miss Annabelle Kelland, Rosabelle. I'd like you to give her a message if you will.'

'I've already told you, sir. I have no idea where my sister is!'

'Tell her that she has something her husband gave her—something I want back. She'll know what it is. Tell her that I'll take it by force if I need to—she knows what that means, too. You're looking pale, Rosabelle. Have I brought back memories?'

'No, but I don't like the menace in your voice, sir. You are making me very anxious for my sister. And I wish you would stop calling me Rosabelle!'

'She's in no danger as long as she does what I say. You see she gets the message.' He turned to go.

'Mr Falkirk!'

'Yes?'

'I…I really haven't an idea where Rosa is. How can I tell her anything?'

'In that case, let's hope you find her before I do, eh? The message would come more…agreeably from you. I'll call again.'

'No!' But Rosabelle's cry was lost in the wind. Selder had gone.

# Chapter Eleven

Rosabelle sat down on a fallen tree trunk, her head in a whirl. What had Selder meant? What was it that he wanted? As far as she knew, she had nothing of his—Stephen had not given her anything. She and Aunt Laura had nursed Stephen constantly until he had died, his frail constitution unable to withstand the terrible beating he had suffered at Selder's hands. He had muttered in delirium, obviously desperate about money, but he hadn't been in a state to say or do anything coherent, and, even if he had, he couldn't have communicated with anyone outside.

No one else had been allowed near him—she and Aunt Laura had been desperate to protect the family name from the shame and scandal which would surely follow if his activities became public. Aunt Laura's doctor had treated him, but even he had never been alone with his patient. The story they gave the world was that Stephen had fallen down a flight of steps, and such was his reputation that no one had questioned it. Whatever the doctor thought privately, he had supported the tale—largely, Rosabelle was sure, for Aunt Laura's sake.

What was she to do now? It didn't take long for Rosabelle to decide that there was little enough she *could* do. She couldn't communicate with Annabelle, and it was too late to call Falkirk back. Her hands were tied. The temptation to confide in Philip, to lay her burden on his shoulders, was very strong... But the sight of Stephen's body rose in her mind's eye, and she buried her face in her hands. She could not! She could not expose her beloved Philip to the risk of suffering a similar fate. And to tell her father would be tantamount to telling Philip. She must work it out on her own.

Her thoughts ran this way and that, like a squirrel caught in a cage. What if Falkirk found Anna before she had been warned that he was searching for her, believing her to be Rosabelle Ordway, and in possession of something he wanted? The thought of what he might do to Anna, innocent of the background to all this, chilled her blood. But how could she prevent it? What could she tell him when he came? After a while she came to the conclusion that there was really no decision to be made. She had no choice.

She would write to Anna again that night, begging her to get in touch immediately. But if there was still no response before Falkirk returned, then she would have to tell him the truth—that she was indeed Rosabelle Ordway. If Anna was at risk, there was nothing else she could do. She realised she was chilled to the bone, and made her way slowly indoors.

Another week followed, a week of anxiety and tension for Rosabelle. It was difficult to meet Philip every day without letting him see how tormented she was—she had no idea what she would reply if he were to ask her what was wrong. But just as she was sure he was on the point of confronting her, news came from London that Lord Winbolt was ill. Philip set off for Arlington Street straight away and Rosabelle's immediate problem was solved. She grieved for Philip's grandfather for she knew how close the family was, but for herself, she didn't know whether to be relieved or sorry.

Though some of the tension disappeared with Philip's departure, she missed his quiet strength, the reassurance of his presence. A few days later Emily came to see her with the news that Lord Winbolt was no longer in danger, but that Philip was remaining in London for the moment to arrange his grandfather's affairs, and incidentally to make sure Lord Winbolt did not exert himself too soon.

'He had asked me to join him there in a day or two, when Grandpapa might need more distraction. He's a bad invalid and a worse convalescent! Meanwhile I am to look after you, Anna. Philip is worried about you— he says you are too pale. Is there something wrong? Something you can tell me?'

'Darling Emily—you mustn't let Philip's excess of concern infect you too! You have enough to worry about, without adding my problems to your list. I shall come about. Tell me, will Lord Winbolt make a full recovery?'

'We think so—though at his age nothing can be certain. I don't know how Philip will take it if Grandpapa dies. He is very fond of him.'

'When…when did you say you were to leave for London?'

'I'm not sure—as soon as Philip gives me the word. It won't be long.'

Towards the end of that week, however, Rosabelle had a most unwelcome return visitor. Falkirk appeared when she was out for a walk, almost as suddenly as he had the previous time.

'Well, well, if it isn't the beautiful Miss Kelland—or the lovely Mrs Ordway!'

Rosabelle braced herself. 'Mr Falkirk! You gave me a fright. You've found my sister?'

'Not yet, though I have people searching for her. Stanton has spirited her well out of the way. But perhaps you know where they are…Miss Kelland? Perhaps you managed to get a message to her. Did you?'

Rosabelle's heart was racing. The moment of decision had arrived. There had been no word from Anna, so she must tell Falkirk the truth. She wished fleetingly, passionately that Philip was beside her, but there was no point in delaying any further.

'There was no need to send any message, Selder. I will no longer prevaricate. You were right in the first place. I am Rosabelle Ordway.'

In one stride Falkirk covered the space between them and was holding her arm in cruel fingers. *'Don't call me Selder!'* he hissed. 'The name is Falkirk—get it?' He gave her a shake.

'Yes,' Rosabelle said. 'Let…let me go. You're hurting me.'

He released her, patting her arm in a travesty of concern. 'My apologies. I tend to lose my temper when someone reminds me of other, less fortunate, times. So you *are* Rosabelle Ordway, eh?'

Rosabelle nodded.

'Then tell me where the packet of papers is.'

'So it's papers you want?'

'Don't waste my time. You know very well what they are.'

'You're wrong. I know nothing of any papers. Stephen never mentioned them. He certainly didn't pass them to me. Nor to Lady Ordway.'

'No? I find that hard to believe!'

'You have to! I swear I have nothing, nothing at all, of yours! Ah!'

Falkirk had taken her wrist and had twisted it up behind her back. He said softly into her ear, 'I'll remember you're a lady and treat you more gently than others who lie to me. For the moment. But I shan't give up. I've a mind to become respectable, my dear, and those papers represent a threat to my plans. Tell me where the packet is.' He gave another vicious jerk.

Rosabelle cried out with the pain. 'You could break every bone in my body,' she cried, 'just as you did with Stephen. But I can't tell you what I don't know! Stephen didn't tell me anything of papers of yours. I swear that is the truth!' The desperation in her voice seemed to convince him. He released her again and took a step back.

'I think I'm beginning to believe you—you don't know,' he said slowly. 'You have no idea what I'm talking about. And shall I tell you why? Because you're lying to me now, not earlier. I don't believe you're Stephen Ordway's widow at all. You're out to save your sister, aren't you...*Annabelle Kelland*!'

Rosabelle stared at him in amazement. She had not expected this! 'You're wrong! I'm Rosabelle Ordway, I swear!'

'Swear away, darling!' He put his hand at the back of

her neck and pulled her towards him again. His other arm pinned her to him. 'You're beautiful enough, I give you that. But as you said yourself, the two of you are often confused. Identical twins, they all said that. Enticing little morsels, both of you. And if I had the time I'd find out if you had more go than your sister. At least you aren't saddled with a pathetic rat of a husband.'

Rosabelle stared into the black, snake's eyes so close to her own. 'Let me go!' she said, refusing to show any sign of fear. 'I have nothing to tell you, and nor has my sister.'

'I wonder...' He smiled, then bent his head and kissed her slowly. His arm held her to him so that she couldn't move, couldn't breathe, and the hand at the back of her neck was cruelly tight. Rosabelle felt as if she was suffocating...

'Mr Falkirk! Anna!'

Falkirk whirled round, holding Rosabelle like a shield in front of him. But when her tormentor saw who had interrupted them he let her go. She stumbled over to a tree and held on to it, drawing air, grateful, cool, fresh air, into her lungs in deep gulps. Falkirk bowed gracefully, smiling all the time.

'Why, it's Miss Winbolt. I thought you were in London with your brother.'

'Evidently.' Emily's voice was full of shocked distaste.

Rosabelle wanted to speak, to protest at the contempt she could see in Emily's face, but her throat was dry. She could only croak her friend's name.

'Emily—'

'Pray forgive me for interrupting this...this idyll. I had no idea you knew each other so well.' This time Emily's voice was icy.

Falkirk started to laugh. 'We don't! I was merely testing Miss Kelland. To see if she was as easy a conquest as her sister—any man's for the asking.'

'That's not true!' Rosabelle cried hoarsely, finding her voice in her outrage. 'I fought you off then as I tried to just now, Selder—' He turned back towards her, and the clearing was suddenly crackling with menace. She drew in her breath and went on, 'I mean…I mean Falkirk— I've…I've *seldom* met anyone who fills me with more repulsion and horror!'

'It's clear that your sister has confided a good deal in you, Annabelle, though not enough, it seems. Seldom such repulsion and horror, eh? Brave words. But does she mean them, Miss Winbolt?'

Emily looked from one to the other, at Rosabelle's pallor and the tension in Falkirk's stance. 'I am not sure, sir,' she said slowly. 'But I can see that Miss Kelland is not well.'

'Please, Emily, please help me back to Temperley.'

'Are you sure you wouldn't prefer Mr Falkirk to take you?' Emily's voice was still cool. It was clear that she was not altogether convinced.

Falkirk smiled and shook his head. 'Forgive me for my lack of gallantry, ma'am! But it's time I was away. There's work to be done elsewhere—in the North. If you should learn the whereabouts of your sister, or of any papers, Annabelle—then you can reach me in London through the landlord of the Swan with Two Necks. In Lad Lane.'

'No!' cried Rosabelle despairingly. 'Don't go! You must leave my sister alone! I tell you—I swear to you, I am Rosabelle Ordway!'

'Tell that to her poor fool of a brother,' laughed Falkirk, nodding at Emily. 'But take care! He might believe you—and how do think he would feel about having a shop-soiled widow for a wife, instead of the innocent, untouched bride of his dreams?' He untied his horse, mounted and rode away, still laughing.

Rosabelle collapsed against the tree and put her head in her hands. There was silence in the clearing. When she looked up again Emily was still standing there, looking at her expressionlessly.

'Did you believe him, Emily?'

'When I met Mr Falkirk in London he was…different. I thought that I might at long last have found someone I could trust—the way I trusted you. But he's not the man I thought at all.'

'Emily—'

'And apparently you are not the woman I thought, either.'

'Believe me, Emily. I am.'

'You swore to him that your name was Rosabelle.'

'It is. I was actually telling him the truth, but he didn't believe me,' Rosabelle said in despair.

'I find that strange. You have always called yourself Annabelle. Either you lied to him, or you've been acting a lie all this while to me, and to Philip. To everyone here, in fact.'

'I…I'm sorry. I had to. But Philip knows who I really am. And my father.'

'Does Philip know about Mr Falkirk?'

Rosabelle was weary, wearier than she had been for a long time. Once again the past was smearing her with its lies and guilt and deceit, and at the moment she was too heartsick to defend herself. 'Know what exactly?' she said. 'What do you think there is to know about Mr Falkirk?'

'That you had a liaison with him in the past.'

'That's not true, Emily. He was lying. But I'm not going to argue with you. You've known Falkirk for a month at the most. You've been my friend since Easter, and you must know how I feel about Philip. You will have to make up your own mind about Mr Falkirk and me.' She straightened herself up and took a step forward. She was shivering in the cool, autumn air. 'Now I'm afraid that I must get back to Temperley. Will you help me, or shall I go on my own?'

'I'll help you. I'm not a monster. I can see that you are exhausted. Besides, my horse is at the house. Mrs Bostock told me you were in the spinney, and I left him there and walked down. I came to tell you that Philip has arranged for me to go to London tomorrow.'

'I see.'

'Why did you do it, Anna...Rosabelle? Oh I don't know what to call you, what to think! It's impossible!'

They had been walking slowly back in direction of the house, but now Rosabelle stopped and faced Emily. 'You have had sadness in your life, Emily, it hasn't always been easy for you, I know. But believe me, your life has been a bed of roses compared with parts of mine. Try not to judge me harshly. At Easter when Anna offered me a respite from a situation which was very nearly intolerable I took it. We didn't think it would do anyone any harm—it was to be for a month or six weeks at the most.'

'So why haven't you changed back again?' Emily's voice had not softened.

'I don't know where Anna is! Somewhere in the North with my godmother and Giles Stanton, but I have no idea where. She hasn't been in touch for weeks.'

They resumed their path. 'So you changed over at

Easter. That would account for quite a lot. Has Philip known for all that time?'

'No, only since the night of your party, though I think he had guessed before that. I love him, Emily. I wouldn't do anything to hurt him.'

Emily said nothing until the house was in sight. Then she said, 'It has been a shock. I don't know what to say. It's a long time since I trusted anyone as much as I thought I could trust you. When I first met you I felt you were direct, open, frank. But was that you or was it your sister? You see, I don't know.'

It was Rosabelle's turn to be silent. There was something she wanted to say, though it was not easy in the face of Emily's hostility. She waited until Emily was about to take her leave and it could wait no longer.

'Emily, I'd like to ask you, for all our sakes, not to broadcast my real identity. I don't wish to deceive anyone for one moment longer than necessary, but Anna must be consulted first.' She paused but Emily did not respond. Rosabelle went on, 'Philip is in agreement with me on this.'

'Very well…Anna,' said Emily coldly. 'I'll try not to let anyone know.'

'And…and…'

Emily interrupted her, saying angrily, 'If you wish me to promise not to tell my brother about this morning, then I cannot.'

'But—'

'I'm no tale-bearer. I won't volunteer anything. But if he asks me then I shall tell him the truth. You are wasting your time if you're asking me to deceive him. Goodbye…Anna.'

Still with a face of stone Emily mounted and rode off,

without even pausing for her groom. He had to gallop to catch up with her.

When Emily arrived in London she found her grandfather very nearly back to normal. Philip was happy to leave him in her care while he attended to business in the town. But in the evening when they lingered over dinner she was not able to avoid all mention of matters in Berkshire, and she found it very hard to hide her hurt at the deception which had been practised on her, to pretend that all was well. She had never had secrets from her brother before. After several occasions on which she had evaded a direct answer Philip finally said, 'Emily, you are not usually so reluctant to tell me all the gossip. How is everyone at Temperley?'

'I...I didn't manage to see a great deal of them,' said his sister, taking a large sip of her wine.

'Why not? Why didn't you? I asked you particularly to keep an eye on...my lady love.'

This reproach from her adored brother was too much. Emily burst out, 'Oh, this is unbearable! Tell me, Pip, why do you never call your "lady love" by her given name?'

There was a pause. Then Philip said slowly, 'I...see... So that's it. Rosa has told you the truth. Or did you guess it for yourself?'

'Let's say I found it out,' said his sister bitterly.

'But how? No one else outside Temperley knows.'

Emily couldn't help herself. 'No one?' she asked with a curl of her lip.

'Who then? Who could you possibly have seen? Falkirk?' Emily took another sip of her wine, avoiding his eyes. 'Are you saying that Falkirk told you? That's impossible—we've convinced him that she's Anna. Why are you laughing?'

'It's all so terribly, ironically funny!' said Emily, laughing a little hysterically. 'I thought she was Anna, you know she's Rosa, she told Falkirk she was Rosa, and he said...' She could hardly get the words out for laughing. 'He said he didn't believe her. He thinks she's Anna! And afterwards she swore to me she was Rosa! Oh, Pip, how difficult it is to see the truth for the web of lies and deceit she has woven!'

Philip came round the table and took her glass of wine away from her. 'You're not making sense, Emily. When did this conversation take place? And where?'

She sat back and looked at him, half-wanting to tell, half-reluctant. 'The day before I came away. In the spinney.' When he seemed to be waiting for more, she said defiantly, 'Ask some more questions. I said I would answer questions, though I wouldn't volunteer anything. Ask me another question, Pip!'

'God damn it! This isn't a game! You tell me!' He saw her shocked face. She had never in her life heard such a tone from him. He took her hand and said more gently, 'It's not a game, Emily! It's deadly serious. I must know what happened. Try to tell me it all! Falkirk was in the spinney, you say.'

'He...he was kissing her. He said he wanted to compare her with her sister, to see if she...if she was as ready to receive his advances. He meant Rosabelle Ordway had...had kissed him, Philip. In the past.'

'Go on. What did Rosa reply?'

'She denied it, of course. She was angry. She said she had fought him off this time and before.' Emily thought a moment. 'It was strange. I didn't really understand what she said next. And just for a moment I thought he would…would kill her. But that's not likely, is it?'

*'What did she say?'*

'I thought for a minute that she had said something like ''selder''—but then she corrected herself and began again. She…she was really frightened. She said she had seldom met anyone who filled her with such…such repulsion and horror. I think those were her words. He repeated them afterwards.'

'Selder!'

'You know the word?'

'It's a name. My God! So that's it.' Philip had been crouching at her side, but now he got up and walked away. 'Selder!' He came back and crouched down beside her again, his face close to hers. 'What happened next?'

'Anna looked ill. She asked me to help her back to the house. I…I was angry and said something about Falkirk helping her, but Falkirk said he couldn't stop. That he had things to do in the North. He said something about her sister and papers…he asked her to get in touch with him.'

'Where?'

'At an inn in Lad Lane. The Swan with Two Necks.'

'I know it! It's a coaching inn. Anything else?'

'Falkirk started to go and Rosa screamed at him. She swore she was Rosabelle Ordway, that he should leave her sister alone.'

'My poor girl! What did Falkirk say?'

'He started to laugh. He…he didn't say much more.'

'I want everything, Emily. What did Falkirk say?'

'Pip, I don't want to tell you!'

'Come on, Emily. You've done wonders, my dear girl. Finish it!'

'He said that you would be disappointed. That you

wouldn't want to marry a...a shop-soiled widow instead
of the bride of your dreams.'

Philip got up, slamming one fist into the other. 'I'd
like to kill him! I may well, unless the hangman gets
him first.' He looked at Emily, who was gazing at him
with tears rolling down her cheeks. 'Don't worry,
Emmie. You were right to tell me. You've saved me a
great deal of heartache. As for you—you've had a luck-
ier escape than you could possibly imagine.'

Philip's first impulse was to go with all speed to the
inn, and throttle Falkirk until he got the truth out of him.
But second, wiser thoughts prevailed. 'Don't go at it like
a bull at a fence, Mr Winbolt!' his army instructor used
to say. 'A good officer uses strategy—that's what wins
the day. Don't let the fellow know what you're up to till
he's got it in the neck!'

So he sent one of the more cunning stable lads to The
Swan with Two Necks, and contented himself with mak-
ing enquiries of his grandfather's physician about
Stephen Ordway's death.

'A shocking business,' said Sir James. 'Cottrell is the
Ordway man. He said the injuries were quite dreadful.
Hardly an unbroken bone in the whole body. Those two
poor women—Lady Ordway and her daughter-in-law.
He was full of admiration for them. They nursed him
themselves to the end.'

'He is supposed to have fallen, isn't he? Down the
cellar steps.'

'Yes. That was the story.' Sir James thereupon closed
his mouth very firmly and refused to discuss the matter
any more, however cunningly Philip tried. It was obvious
that Stephen Ordway's death had not been all that it

seemed, but that the medical profession had closed ranks on it.

The stable lad came back with the news that Falkirk was still lodged in Lad Lane and had paid his shot for another week. So far so good. Then Philip started to visit the clubs and taverns he knew Falkirk frequented, never mentioning the man's name, but always looking to come across him as if by accident. But when he finally ran his quarry to ground it was truly by chance. He was on his way to leave a note at Giles's lodgings, asking him to get in touch as soon as possible. At the corner of Charles Street he met the very man he had been seeking. He should have thought of it! Falkirk had clearly been calling at the Ordway house again.

'Why, Falkirk!' he called genially. 'What a surprise! Have you been trying the Ordways again? Are they home?'

'No!' Falkirk was apparently in none too good a mood. 'It's time they were back.'

'I don't think Miss Kelland has heard from them, either, though it's some time since I spoke to her, of course.'

'You haven't seen her recently?'

'No—my grandfather has been ill. I came to London soon after Emily's party, and I haven't been able to go back since. I've hardly spoken to a soul.'

'What about Miss Winbolt?'

Philip allowed himself a puzzled smile. 'My sister? Well, yes, I suppose I've spoken to her—she came to London a day or two ago. But we've not had time for chatter. She's well, if that's what you're asking. A bit quiet, perhaps. But that's only to be expected.'

'Expected?' Mr Falkirk asked sharply. Philip allowed himself to look slightly surprised. He said earnestly, 'Of course! She's very fond of my grandfather. She spends all her time with him. Are you going my way, Falkirk? As far as Arlington Street?'

They fell into step. 'I've just been calling at Stanton's place to see if they know anything there. Miss Kelland asked me to, and I felt I couldn't return to Berkshire without having tried. I'm afraid the housekeeper there is as ignorant as we are. But tell me—why are you so eager to see them? You're not a friend of Stanton's, are you? It was Mrs Ordway you wished to see, if I remember rightly.'

Falkirk gave Philip another sharp look, but Mr Winbolt's face was innocent. 'Yes,' he said slowly. 'She has some papers…of mine.'

'Papers?'

Falkirk seemed to make up his mind. 'To be honest with you, Winbolt, it's a matter of some delicacy. Mrs Ordway and I…well, you know how it is. Stephen Ordway was a poor fish, and Rosabelle is a beautiful woman—and a passionate one. The affair is over now, of course, but at the time I wrote her some letters…'

'And you'd like them back?'

'That's it! I don't like to think of them falling into the wrong hands.'

'Has Mrs Ordway refused to let you have them?'

'No. She'd be very happy to return them, I think. But she's away.'

'But what is the urgency? Or are you contemplating matrimony?'

Falkirk gave his flashing, magnetic smile. 'There's nothing I would like more! Especially as I now have the Banagher name to think of! But I don't think Miss Winbolt would have me.'

Philip experienced some difficulty in keeping his feelings—and his hands—to himself. The insolence! The infernal nerve of the villain! But he said with a laugh, 'I can quite understand why you'd like to clear the record before attempting anything of that nature. Women can be peculiar about such things. Well, if I hear of any letters I'll let you know.'

They had now reached the corner of Arlington Street. 'By the way, Falkirk.' His voice dropped to a confidential level. 'If you should see Miss Kelland, you won't mention any letters to her, will you? I shouldn't like her to learn that her sister had had an affair—she's such a country girl *au fond*. And we don't want her to get any ideas, do we?' He winked.

It was clear that Falkirk thought he was a fool. 'No, of course not, Winbolt,' he said, quite failing to hide the mockery in his tone. 'Pray give her my regards when you see her. And remember me to your sister, of course. *Au revoir!*'

When Mr Winbolt told his sister that he was paying a fleeting visit to Berkshire, she clutched his sleeve and said, 'No, Pip! I shouldn't have told you about Rosabelle. I've thought a lot about it, and I now believe I was wrong. She's innocent.'

'What do you think I'm going to do, Emmie?'

'I thought you were going down to break off your engagement.'

'You're a fool, dear girl. I never thought for one instant that the girl in Berkshire, whatever her name, whatever her history, was anything but innocent! Pig-headed, perhaps. Ridiculously protective, certainly—'

'Protective!'

'Of me. Odd, isn't it?'

'Protective of you?'

'I think so. And that reminds me. I don't want you to
go out while I'm away. It will only be for a day or two.
Send Betty or one of the footmen for anything you want.
And if Falkirk calls, pretend you're not at home. I don't
want you to see him.'

Emily shuddered. 'I don't, either. I didn't like the
Falkirk I saw in that spinney.'

'You'll promise me, then?'

'Yes.'

'Good! Keep Grandfather amused while I'm gone. I'll
be back as soon as I can.'


Philip set off very early the next morning, taking the
Winbolt carriage with him, for he intended to persuade
Rosabelle to come back with him to London. It was high
time that all the mysteries which had bedevilled their
relationship were cleared up. The problem of Annabelle
would have to wait until they could trace her, but for the
rest, he was not going to be satisfied with anything less
than the whole truth.

He arrived at Shearings, changed and rode over to
Temperley straight away. Becky let him in.

'Why, Mr Winbolt! What a surprise! Miss Belle is
with her father—'

'Thank you!' said Philip grimly, and went upstairs to
Mr Kelland's room. Here he found father and daughter
engaged in a chess tutorial.

'Sir,' began Philip.

'It's good to see you, young man! But, from the look
of you, you have something serious to say. It's not bad
news about Lord Winbolt I hope?'

'No, sir.'

'Good! Pray get it over with, and then you can set

about cheering up this daughter of mine. I haven't seen a smile for days.'

'I'd like to speak to her in private, if you don't mind, sir.'

'Of course! Take her downstairs.'

Rosabelle had not been able to say a word. Philip's unexpected appearance so soon after Emily had arrived in London could only mean one thing—Emily had found it impossible, after all, to keep the events in the spinney to herself. Perhaps she hadn't even wanted to. Philip's manner was not encouraging. Was he about to repudiate her? Or worse, was he about to demand to know all about Falkirk's involvement with the Ordway family? That she would never tell him—it was too dangerous. It would be dangerous for him even to know Falkirk's real name.

'Now,' said Philip as he shut the parlour door behind him. 'Now, Rosabelle Ordway, I am not prepared to wait any longer. I want the truth! All of it!'

# *Chapter Twelve*

Emily must still have been angry when she told her brother about the scene in the spinney, thought Rosabelle. And now he was angry, too. He looked forbidding.

'You know that Mr Falkirk was here, Philip?' she asked tentatively.

'I certainly do—Emily gave me a graphic description of your meeting. What she saw of it, that is. I gather she came on the scene halfway through. What does Falkirk want of you, Rosa?'

She turned her head away. 'You know what he wants. He would like me to…to be kind to him.'

'You mean to kiss him? I thought you had.'

'*He* kissed *me*, Philip. Against my will. Whatever Emily said—'

'We'll leave Emily out of it, Rosa. She may have told me what she saw and heard, but she doesn't know what lies behind it, does she?'

'She knows I'm really Rosa. She was…angry with me. I expect that's why she told you.'

'She'll come round. In fact, she was pleading your case before I left. And you mustn't blame her for telling me—I made her tell. What are these papers Falkirk was talking about?'

Rosabelle's head came up with a start. 'Papers? I don't know, Philip! I don't know what he meant.'

'You haven't written him letters…or anything of that kind, have you?'

'No! Did Emily think they were letters?'

'I've told you. Leave Emily out of this.'

'I have never done anything or written anything to give…Falkirk the slightest encouragement. I find him repulsive,'

'Ah, yes! Repulsive. He fills you with repulsion and horror. Was that it?'

'I said that, yes. Emily has a good memory.'

'Is there nothing more you can tell me about Falkirk?'

'What could there be?' Rosabelle avoided Philip's eye. 'He was one of Stephen's friends. He's not…he's not a nice man. I am sorry if what your sister saw upset her, but if it means she has given up the thought of cultivating his acquaintance then it was worth it.'

'Emily is not at the moment my main concern, though I agree with you. Why are you fencing with me, Rosa? I thought you had promised to tell me the truth?'

Still avoiding his eye, Rosabelle said quietly, 'There are some things it is better for you not to know, Philip.'

'Falkirk's real name, for instance? Selder?'

'*What?*'

'Emily's hearing is better than you think. She heard you say ''Selder''. It didn't mean anything to her, but it does to me. And to you, I see.'

Rosabelle took him by the arms and gripped him hard, her knuckles white with the strain. 'Philip, please forget I said it! Please! And Emily must forget it, too. It's nothing, just a…a name. It has nothing to do with us.' She was deathly pale and shivering. Philip swore under his breath and broke her hold, wrapping his own arms round her. He held her close, trying to give her some of his own warmth. After a while the shivering stopped and she looked up.

'Rosa! Don't, don't be afraid. There's no need, there really isn't! Not while I'm here to protect you. Surely you know I love you?'

'Oh, Philip!' she said on a long shuddering sigh. 'I thought you had come to say that you wanted to have nothing more to do with me. What Emily saw and heard was so…so damning. I've been so unhappy.'

Philip sighed in exasperation. 'This has to stop!' He led her over to the sofa and made her sit down. Then he stood over her, tall, upright and challenging. 'Look at me, Rosabelle Ordway! What do you see? A fool? A rake? A braggart?'

She was surprised and indignant. 'Of course not! You're none of those! Why do you ask?'

'Then why do you keep thinking I shall behave like one?'

'I don't!'

'Oh, yes, you do!' He knelt down beside her. 'I have told you so many times that I have faith in you, that I honour you, that I want you to be my wife more than anything else in the world. I have said, more than once, I believe, that I love you and will continue to love you as long as I have breath in my body.'

'Oh, Philip—'

'No, I have to finish. I'm well past the age of being a

young hothead, swearing to what he doesn't understand.
I've lived long and fully in the world, Rosa. I've fallen
in love and out of it again, I've made mistakes and got
over them, I've fought hard in wars and worked hard
afterwards for the things I believe in. I know what I
want! Why won't you allow me to know my own mind?'

'I hadn't realised… Oh, Philip, forgive me!'

'No more doubts?' Her face was hidden in his shoulder, but she shook her head. 'Do you love me?'

'Oh, yes!'

'Then show me.'

She got up, pulled him to his feet and flung her arms
about his neck, casting caution and propriety to the
winds in her relief and happiness. She kissed him eagerly, passionate little kisses on his cheeks, his brow, his
eyes…his lips. Here she lingered, and then Philip took
over. The kiss lengthened, deepened until they were lost
in each other, sinking down on to the sofa, all the while
murmuring words of love and delight in each other.

Eventually Philip lifted his head. 'I…I think you've
shown me,' he said, somewhat unsteadily.

'Was it enough?'

'It would never be enough, my darling, my love, my
sweet life,' he said, lovingly putting her hair back from
her face. 'But it'll do for now.' He laughed at her exclamation of dismay when she put her hand to her hair
and found it falling down her back, at her confusion
when she looked down at her dress, which was in considerable disarray.

'Instead of laughing, my own, why don't you help me
find my hair pins?' said Rosabelle severely. 'Becky will
be waiting to serve some tea. When did you last eat?'

'I had something before I left.'

'That must be six hours at least! Come, help me with

this last hook, and I'll find Becky. No, Philip! Just hook it up!'

'Pity! In that case, while you see Becky I'll go to have a word with your father. I'll join you here in half an hour.' It was clear that his talk with her father was not to include her. Rosabelle was content. This was no more than normal procedure. Philip was about to ask her father for her hand in marriage. She went into the kitchen.

'Come in, Winbolt—don't keep the door open. Walters, disappear, man!'

Philip entered Mr Kelland's bedchamber, shut the door and advanced into the room. 'Are you busy, sir? I'd like to speak to you. It's about Rosa.'

'Oh?' said Mr Kelland with exaggerated surprise.

Philip laughed. 'As I'm sure you know, I want to marry her, sir. As soon as it can be arranged.'

'You have my blessing, if that's what you're asking. I like you, Winbolt, and I think you're the right man for her. But...'

'I know we have to wait till your daughters can take up their own identities again. And that can't happen till Anna's return.'

'Quite so. But after that I shall be delighted to welcome you as a son-in-law. You could hardly fail to be an improvement on the last.'

'Thank you, sir,' said Philip meekly.

Mr Kelland smiled thinly. 'I could have put that better, couldn't I? I ought to have said that you couldn't be improved on as a husband for Rosa.'

'Thank you. I shall be able to support her quite adequately. If you wish I can get my man of business to see you. Rosa will have settlements and all the rest.'

'Yes, yes. We'll go into that later, if you wish.'

'But…'

'But what?'

'There's the matter of her late husband.'

'I assure you that he's dead, if that's what you're worried about.'

'No, no! That's something I don't doubt. But how did he die? And why?'

Mr Kelland looked at him sharply. 'You feel there's a mystery, eh? Well, I can't help you. I don't know. I certainly don't believe the story the two women put about—that was an attempt to save the Ordway name. But Rosa has never confided in me.'

'I see…'

'But I agree with you. I've had my suspicions, too.'

'Do you feel you could share them with me?'

'Ordway was in with a very queer bunch of people. At one time I had enquiries made. He was a drug addict, of course—opium, laudanum, anything he could get hold of. And he was…' Mr Kelland grimaced. 'I read a lot, Winbolt. I am not easily shocked by what modern, rich, idle, young men get up to—it's mostly been done before. But when it concerns your own family… Ordway had…unnatural appetites.'

'You knew this? And you let your daughter marry him?' Philip didn't quite manage to conceal his disgust.

'Of course I didn't! Not until after they were married. And in any case, whatever suspicions I might have had beforehand, there was very little I could have done about it at the time. Lady Ordway practically forced Rosa to marry her son, and Rosa would have done anything to please her godmother.'

'All the same…'

'Yes, yes, you're right, of course. I failed in my duty towards my daughter. I should have refused to give my

consent. But I just wasn't sufficiently interested enough
to take a firmer stand. It would have caused a great deal
of fuss. Oh, you needn't look so shocked! Lady Ordway
had practically adopted Rosa. Except for the summer
months, I hadn't seen anything of the child from the time
she was six or seven. I've regretted it since, of course,
especially in the last few months.'

Philip exerted himself to speak calmly. 'So you can't
help me about Ordway?'

'Rosa is the one who knows the truth—or some of it.
Get her to tell you, if you really want to know. But if
you take my advice you'll leave well alone.'

'I'll…er…I'll think about it, sir,' said Philip briefly.
He got up.

'Shut the door on your way out. Winbolt. It's damnably draughty in this room,' Rosabelle's father said as
he picked up his book.

Philip went out, shutting the door very carefully behind him. Gentlemen did not slam doors.

After the substantial repast that Becky thought necessary, Rosabelle and Philip went outside. It was late in
the afternoon on a clear day in the middle of October
and the autumnal foliage was a blaze of red and gold in
the light of the dying sun. Philip turned in the direction
of the spinney.

'No, Philip. Let's go the other way.'

'Why? I want to see the spinney. I want to work out
what direction Selder could have come from.'

'Please, Philip, please don't say that name—not even
here! I tell you it's dangerous to know it. Why must you
talk about him, anyway?' she said desperately.

'Because, dearest, loveliest Rosa,' said Philip, stopping and turning to face her, 'I intend to scotch this snake.'

'No!' Rosa's voice rose in desperation. 'No, I won't hear of it. You must leave him alone!'

'I can't. What about Anna? The man is determined to get hold of those papers, whatever they are. He won't give up till he either finds them, or is stopped.'

'I know, I know! But you mustn't get involved. I'll manage somehow.'

Philip Winbolt seldom lost his temper, but at these words of Rosabelle's he exploded.

'What the hell do you think I am, Rosa?' he demanded fiercely. 'Your sister once called me a doormat, and, by Heaven, I think you regard me as one!'

'It's not that, Philip, it's not that at all!' she pleaded. 'But Selder is totally ruthless. I can't risk having you beaten unconscious, to die the way Stephen died. I couldn't bear it.'

'Good God, it's even worse than I thought! You don't think of me as a doormat. You think I'm like your rat of a husband. Ready to stand aside while you do battle with a villain like Falkirk! Abject enough to lie down, waiting to be kicked like a dog.'

Stunned by the strength of feeling in Philip's voice, Rosabelle couldn't say a word for a moment. But Philip didn't wait. He swept on, 'Well, I'm not about to crow like a cock on a dunghill about prowess in the art of defending myself. But I'm damned sure I'm not going to let you push me out of this fight. I've met worse men than Falkirk in my time, believe you me. And beaten them.'

Rosabelle found her voice. 'But you didn't see Stephen after Falkirk had finished with him,' she cried. 'I did! I tried to stem his bleeding, I bathed his head, I gave him more laudanum to ease the pain…' She couldn't go on. Tears were blinding her, her throat was constricted with feeling.

Philip took her into his arms. 'Hush. I know, I know. But Stephen wasn't a fighting man, my darling. He was no match for the likes of Falkirk. You say you trust me—'

'But not about this!'

'Yes, you must! This trust is just as important as any other—you can't separate them. Face the truth. Your troubles are now my troubles. I'm going to fight your battles whether you let me or not, and I know I can win. But I'll fight them a lot more easily if you are with me, if you help me to learn exactly who or what my enemy is. Have confidence in me. Tell me about Falkirk and the rest. Or I shall know that, for all your brave words, you don't really trust me at all.'

He held her eyes as she struggled to come to terms with this new Philip. This wasn't the charming, humorous, quizzical stranger who had captured her heart. Nor the passionate lover whose kisses could inflame her with strange and overwhelming sensations. Nor was this the sympathetic, undemanding friend on whom she had learned to depend. This was a man, ready to be her champion. It would be useless to deny him, for he would defend her whether she would or no.

She looked at him with new eyes, seeing the steel which was disguised by Philip's exquisite manners, the determination which lay beneath his air of charming diffidence, the authority which he had till now not found it necessary to parade. Philip was right. She had to let him make his own decisions about risk and danger. Security lay in working together. She took a step back and smiled.

'Where shall we start?' she asked.

* * *

They went to the spinney, where Philip took Rosabelle carefully through her second meeting with Falkirk.

'It's clear that he's desperate for those papers. Whatever they are, they must represent either a fortune, or a threat which can't be ignored. I wonder which it is…' said Philip, as they walked round the little clearing.

'It's a threat. He said so. They must incriminate him in some way.'

'He was here by this tree, you say, when you first saw him?'

'Yes. Both times he came, he seemed to appear out of the blue. He was…just there!'

'Horse?'

'He had one the second time. I didn't notice the first time he came.'

'Where did you meet him the first time?'

'In the park.'

'The park is on the other side of the house from here, further away from the bridle path… If you didn't see a horse then he must have walked across the fields. Right! Now think back again to his second visit. This horse— did it look as if it had been ridden far?'

'I wasn't looking…but I don't think so.'

'I'll get one of the men to start asking questions. The bridle path leads to Harden Lane and on to the Reading road. The road on the other side of the fields comes into the Reading road about ten miles further on. He can start along those ten miles.'

'Why are you doing this, Philip?'

'So far, my love, Mr Julian Falkirk has been a bit of a mystery. He seems to come and go as he pleases. I want to track him down—whether he stays at an inn, or whether he knows anyone in the neighbourhood apart from ourselves. But that's only the beginning.

Tomorrow, or the day after, I should like you to come to London with me. It's time you met my grandfather, and there's work we can do there.'

'London! But I can't!' said Rosabelle blankly. 'I'm not ready! I haven't any clothes...I can't leave Papa...'

Philip burst out laughing. 'You are a delight, Rosa! Mrs Bostock will help you to get ready, your father can do without your company, and as for clothes... You surely have some, and acquiring more can work to our advantage.'

'How?'

'You will have to gain admittance to the house in Upper Brook Street to look for the ones you left there! I assume there's a caretaker with keys?'

'The lawyers usually keep them. What...what do you want from Upper Brook Street?'

'Apart from your clothes? I want to look for some papers. Falkirk's precious papers.'

'They're not there!'

'How do you know? You didn't even know they existed when you were last in Upper Brook Street.'

'But what if Falkirk sees me?'

'Let me take care of that. Rosa! I'm serious when I say that I want you to meet Grandfather. Will you come?'

Rosabelle took a deep breath. It was a beginning, and she had promised to help him. 'Well, yes! I'd like to,' she said bravely.

However, she needed all her courage later that evening when Philip started to ask her about her life with Stephen Ordway. He was very patient, but the memories still had power to hurt. He led her gradually to the point where she had first started to suspect that her husband was engaged in unacceptable—or even illegal—activities.

'It was obvious to me very early that our marriage wasn't going to be a success,' she said.

Philip put a hand over hers. 'There's no need to go further into that, Rosa. Your father told me what Ordway was like.'

'Thank you,' she said. 'But it had an effect on what happened later. He…he did try, you know. He was devoted to his mother, and wanted above anything to please her. And he and I had practically grown up together. But…he didn't trust me. And…it didn't work.' She shut her eyes, and when she opened them they were full of misery.

'He blamed me. He used to get very angry with me. And for a long time I accepted what he said and blamed myself. I…I tried to make myself acceptable to him, however much it went against my…my nature. But then he…he found what he really wanted. He told me he was in love with someone called Selder. At the time, that was all he said.'

She got up and walked about the room, refusing to look at him. The words came out jerkily, tension and shame in every syllable. 'I was humiliated and hurt, of course, when I thought Stephen had taken a mistress, but at the same time I was relieved. It meant that I was left in peace! And at least he seemed to be happier.'

Philip hardly dared breathe. Rosa's painful story was filling him with pity and anger, but he dared not interrupt her—not because of anything she might tell him about Falkirk, it was far more important than that. Rosa was at last ridding herself of a canker which had blighted her life for years, which might well be the source of that

permanent look of sadness which he had seen at the back
of her eyes. She must be allowed to continue.

'Then one day,' she went on, 'Aunt Laura and Stephen
had a terrible quarrel. About me. And, as always, he
blamed me for it. He still loved his mother deeply and
he was badly upset at falling out with her. He...he
wanted to punish me. So that night after Aunt Laura had
gone to bed he brought Falkirk to the house. I didn't
understand at first. I had expected "Selder" to be a
woman. I was, in spite of everything, still so...innocent!'
This was said in bitter self-contempt.

'How old were you, Rosa?'

'I don't remember exactly. Nineteen? Twenty?'

'My God!'

'And when I did understand I was shocked beyond
measure. Stephen introduced us. He paraded his infatuation with the man in front of me. But Falkirk...he
wasn't like that at all. Falkirk treated Stephen at first
rather as you might treat an importunate puppy. He even
seemed kind. Can you imagine it—in spite of the shock,
I quite liked him!'

'When did you change your mind?'

'Stephen used to boast to me about his friends, and it
gradu-ally became clear to me that Falkirk would do anything for money. It was a matter of business for him. He
and one or two others were making themselves very rich,
providing...desperate people with what they needed—
drugs, and...the other. And worse things than those,
even.'

'Worse?'

Rosa's reply came out of the darkness. She was walking round the edges of the room, out of range of the light
of the candles, as if she could not bear to be seen. 'Ter-

rible…terrible things. Childre— I can't tell you. I won't!'

She stopped for a moment as her voice rose and her breathing became more uneven. Philip longed to go over to her, to fetch her forward into the light, to reassure her, but forced himself to sit still. Better to let the whole ugly story emerge as she wished to tell it. Then would be the time for the cure.

She went on, 'But that was when I changed my mind about Falkirk. I was desperate, but there was nothing I could find to do about it. I was on my own. Stephen was besotted, of course. I couldn't confide in Aunt Laura, and I had no one else.'

'What about Anna and your father?'

'How could I go near them? I felt…unclean. I didn't want to taint their lives with what I knew. So I thanked God that Temperley was so many miles away and kept clear of it.' She stopped suddenly and in spite of himself Philip went over to hold her. But she pushed him away. 'I'd like to finish,' she said.

'Are you sure? We could leave the rest to tomorrow.'

'I want to finish! Then matters came to a head when Falkirk became bored with Stephen's slavish admiration. He found my aversion to him more intriguing. So he decided to…to switch his attention to me.'

Rosabelle had been almost invisible, a disembodied voice, telling its nightmare out of the dark. But now she came back and sat down as if her legs would no longer support her. Philip took one look at her chalk-white face and shadowed eyes and decided that enough was enough. Rosa needed a rest, whatever she said.

'I think we'll stop there tonight, my dearest love. You've had enough.'

'Have I? Perhaps I have. I wanted to finish it, Philip,

but I don't think I can. I hadn't realised what this would do to me—living it all over again.'

'Would you like to leave it there altogether, Rosa darling? We can manage without the rest, I am sure.'

'No, no! I want to tell you everything now that we've started. A clean sheet.' She sighed. 'A clean sheet. Perhaps there'll be one after this. But perhaps it would wait till tomorrow.'

Rosabelle had expected to be haunted during the night with bad dreams and memories. But in fact she slept sweetly, undisturbed by nightmares of any kind, and woke the next morning feeling refreshed, and ready again to tell Philip anything he wanted to know.

He came over from Shearings at an hour which was only marginally acceptable in polite society. Becky was impressed.

'Well, bless me! I never expected to see Mr Winbolt at this hour. He used to be a very well-behaved young man before he knew you, Miss Belle!'

'Perhaps he doesn't feel he has to stand on ceremony with us any more, Becky. He…he's asked me to marry him. And I'm going to!'

'Oh, Miss Belle! I'm so pleased! Not that I didn't expect it, mind. But I did wonder, just occasionally, whether you'd manage to sort things out. Does he…does he know which of you he's marrying, Miss Rosa?'

'Yes, he does! And he loves me just the same. Becky, he wants to take me to London as soon as possible—to meet his grandfather. I'd like to go tomorrow. Can you and Martha start getting my things ready? I'll help you later, but I have business with Mr Winbolt first.'

'Business, is it?' Becky said to herself, as she watched Rosa run out to be greeted by Mr Winbolt. 'That's a very friendly form of business, if you ask me! Kissing in full view of anyone who cares to watch, indeed! Come along, Martha! There's work for us to do.'

Rosabelle put on a warm pelisse and she and Philip took to the park. It was still early and the sun was not yet warm, but they both wanted to be outside. There was less risk of being overheard in the fields, and the freshness of the country air helped to cleanse the effect of Rosabelle's story.

'You're sure you still want to do this, Rosa?' Philip asked.

'Quite sure. Besides, the most important part is still to come.'

'Very well. But you must stop the minute you've had enough.'

'It's doing me good, Philip. And I want now to rid myself of it all. I've kept quiet for so long.'

'Then tell me what happened when Falkirk turned his attention to you.'

'Stephen went wild. He wept, he raged, he swore vengeance—I think that's when he must have written those letters to his cousin.'

'Letters? What letters?'

'Oh, not what Falkirk wants. Just letters Stephen wrote to Giles Stanton, talking of broken hearts, accusing me of all sorts of misdemeanours. Giles believed what was in them, of course. And the fantasies Stephen had written in his diary.'

'Wait! That's not fair—Giles is a hard man, but he was never unjust.'

'I forgot. He's your friend. Though how a man like you could... Never mind! You've probably seen him under different circumstances. And I suppose he had no reason to suspect that it was all lies. He and Stephen had always been friends in the past. But I assure you, Philip, Giles could not have been more unsympathetic to me when we met.'

'I can see I'll have to have a word with him. But what happened between Stephen and Falkirk?'

'I kept well out of Falkirk's way, and he eventually forgot about me. But by this time Stephen had transferred his affections to another member of the group. At least, Kingsley used to frequent the house more often than Falkirk, so I assume that's what happened.'

'Kingsley.'

'John Kingsley. But you won't find him. He's dead. I don't know how, and I have no idea why, but I am practically certain that Falkirk either killed him or had him killed. That's what Stephen shouted that last evening. He was beside himself, shouting that he would ruin Falkirk, that he would see him hanged.'

'Is that why he had to die in turn?'

'I think so. Philip, that's why I'm so afraid. Those two, Falkirk and his henchman, Burrows, have nothing to lose!'

'Being afraid is useful, Rosa. It makes you careful. But it doesn't mean you have to give up and simply scuttle for cover.'

'I realise that. And Anna doesn't even know she has to!'

'Look, I'm not too worried about Anna. If Giles is with her she'll be safe. You may believe me on that. There's no one I'd rather have with Anna at this moment!'

'Very well, I'll try not to worry. When do we start for London?'

'Can you be ready tomorrow morning? All the dresses pressed and so on?'

'*All* the dresses! If I have a quarrel with Anna, it is on the subject of her wardrobe! She is obviously not interested in clothes.'

'My love, you have been entrancing me for six months in Anna's clothes! Don't criticise your sister too badly.'

They arrived in London the next afternoon. In spite of Rosabelle's strictures, the carriage was well laden with boxes and valises, much to Philip's amusement.

'It's as well we decided to engage a maid for you in London, rather than taking one of the girls from Temperley,' he said. 'She would have had to travel on the roof!'

'They're dear girls, all of them,' said Rosabelle. 'But I'm sufficiently well acquainted with London servants to know that an untrained girl from the country would be very unhappy among them. You're sure your sister will help me find one?'

'If I know Emily, she will be eager to make amends. Try to keep her feeling a little guilty about you—she'll do much more for you if she feels she owes you something.'

'You're an unnatural brother! I shall do no such thing!'

Rosabelle gazed eagerly about her as they came along the Bath Road towards London. She had travelled this road with her godmother, twice a year, once at the beginning of June and once back to London halfway through September. As a child she had eagerly counted the mile posts, the toll gates, the sights along the route which had indicated how much further they had to go—the bridge over the Kennet at Reading, Hounslow Heath

and the junction where the main road to Lands End
joined them, the Grand Junction Canal, the Star and
Garter Inn at Kew Bridge, and then as they drew nearer
to London, Holland House and the mansions along the
road opposite Hyde Park. Soon they were bowling along
Piccadilly and at last they turned into Arlington Street.

# Chapter Thirteen

For a few minutes all was bustle and noise as grooms, footmen and other servants went about their business, and Philip led Rosabelle into the imposing, rather gloomy house which stood before them.

Lord Winbolt's butler met them at the door, and was good enough to acknowledge Miss Kelland by a slight softening of his stately demeanour.

'How is my grandfather, Maynard?' asked Philip, as the butler relieved him of his outer garments.

'Very well, Mr Philip,' the butler said. 'Er…he is in the upper drawing room.'

Philip stopped and gave the butler a hard stare.

'Miss Emily did her best, sir,' Maynard said, almost apologetically. 'But his lordship did not wish to receive Miss Kelland in his bedchamber.' This was a fairly free paraphrase of his lordship's blistering statement to the effect that he would be damned if his grandson's future bride would see him in his bedgown and nightcap, sup-

ping cat lap and generally behaving like a confounded
dotard. 'Mrs Jackman is ready to take Miss Kelland to
her room, Mr Philip.'

'If you will come this way, ma'am.' The housekeeper
curtsied and then led Rosabelle towards the very handsome staircase.

'Anna! You've arrived!' Emily came hurrying down
the stairs, but at the bottom she paused and looked uncertain.

'Emily?' said Rosabelle. Then the two young ladies
laughed and embraced each other. Emily put her arm
round Rosabelle's waist and they followed Mrs Jackman
up two flights of stairs.

'I've put you in one of the rooms at the back, Anna.
It's quieter, and you have a view of the park. See?'
Emily ushered into a delightful room overlooking Green
Park.

'Thank you. But, er…Emily, I would like to straighten
things out between us—'

'There's no need. Philip explained a little—enough to
make me wish I had been more sympathetic that last
time. I'm sorry, Anna.'

'Don't say that! And let's forget that episode. It has
served its turn. But…my name really is Rosa, Emily.'
Rosabelle looked apprehensively at her friend.

Emily kissed her. 'I shall remember. Now tell me,
have you brought a maid? I've asked one of the girls
here to help you in case you haven't. Then, if you wish,
we can hire a proper ladies' maid tomorrow. I'll send
for her and then you can refresh yourself after your journey. Do you wish for anything? Something to eat or
drink, for example?'

'Thank you, but we stopped at Hammersmith.'

When the maid arrived Emily went downstairs and

Rosabelle set about making herself presentable. A short while later she descended to the first floor and was shown into a beautifully proportioned room with a bow window overlooking the park. Philip and Emily were both there, and in a large armchair by the fire sat a gentleman, who was eyeing her with a great deal of interest. Though he was extremely old, his eye was keen and his air distinguished.

'Rosa, I'd like you to meet my grandfather, Lord Winbolt.'

'Hmph, so you've decided who you are, have you, young lady? My grandson has been telling me he's not absolutely sure.'

'That was a long time ago, sir!' said Philip. 'I'm absolutely certain now. Of that and other things. I intend to marry Mrs Ordway.'

'Yes, well, that's not a name I'm particularly fond of, I'm not surprised you wanted to change it. I think I shall call you Rosa. If you don't mind?' He gave her a fierce look from under bushy silver eyebrows.

'I should be pleased, sir.'

'Yes, well, sit down here and tell me about Shearings and your place in Berkshire, what's it called... Temperley? You were a Kelland, so I hear?'

Rosabelle bore up pretty well as Lord Winbolt put her through a catechism, which told him more than she perhaps realised. At the end of it he said, 'You're pretty enough—a very good-looking girl, in fact. You say your sister is exactly like you?'

'Yes, sir.'

'You must be a striking sight when you're together. I gather there's no fortune?'

'No, Lord Winbolt.' Rosa bit her lip.

'There's no need to look so cast down. Philip has more

than enough for the two of you. And he'll have more when I'm gone.' Rosa blinked at this plain speaking, but Lord Winbolt smiled at her and called Philip over to him. 'She's pretty, she's modest—look at her blushes now!—and she's sweet-natured. And I think she's probably no fool.'

'She's also demonstrably patient, Grandfather! Do you have to subject my beloved to such a trial?'

His grandfather chuckled. 'It's the only pleasure left to me, my boy! You'd have had more to complain about thirty years ago—I'd have given you a run for your money then! I have to say that I don't like the Ordway connection, but that can't be helped, I can't believe she was to blame for that. In any case, there was nothing wrong with the rest of Stephen Ordway's family. And the Kellands are good stock. You have my blessing, my boy.'

Philip smiled and drew Rosabelle to him. 'Thank you, Grandfather. I was sure you would give it.'

'But you'd still have married her if I hadn't, is that it?'

'I'm afraid so, sir.'

'Very well, very well. When is the wedding? Not too long ahead, I hope? I haven't all that much time.'

'As I told you, Grandfather, we have to wait until we can find Rosa's sister. But it will be as soon as we can arrange it after that, I promise you. Er…meanwhile…Rosa will be known under her sister's name in public.'

'What? Oh, yes! Of course. Well, I don't go out much, Philip. In fact, not at all. So there's no difficulty there.'


Rosabelle found that London was now a different place. The busy streets, the new buildings, the old quarters—all took on an additional brightness when Philip was there to laugh with her, escort her, admire the sights with her. And shopping with Emily was an excitingly new experience, too. Never before had she had a person of her own age in London ready to advise her on a length of material or the shape and colour of a new hat.

Emily was quite shockingly extravagant, and it was sometimes hard to refuse her generosity when Rosabelle decided that she couldn't afford a particularly suitable pair of gloves, or a desirable scarf. And her efforts were frequently in vain, for the same gloves or the identical scarf would later appear in the form of presents from Philip.

'You are teaching me bad habits, sir!' she laughed. 'You're training me to be a very unthrifty wife!'

'We have many problems, Rosa, my sweet, but having to be thrifty is not one of them. And while we are on the subject…I should like to take you to the Ordway lawyers this afternoon. We still have a lot to do.'

'Yes,' said Rosabelle, her smile dying. 'Of course. I had almost forgotten.'

'Good! It was what I intended. You've enchanted my grandfather, helped Emily spend even more than usual, and, I hope, enjoyed your respite from Falkirk and his friends. But now we shall take up the chase with renewed strength. I haven't yet mentioned what my man found out on the Reading road.'

On the way to Lincoln's Inn, Philip told her that Falkirk had been an occasional visitor to a small tavern about nine miles west of Reading, near Woolhampton. The landlord knew him as Selder, and, being slightly on the shady side of the law himself, had never questioned his comings and goings. But Falkirk always met someone else at the tavern, a seafaring man, who had come along the Bath Road from the west.

'From Bristol?'

'It sounds like it, Rosa.'

'Do we know the second man's name?'

'Decoster. Or something like it.'

'What did the two men do? Did anything change hands, for example?'

'Clever girl! The innkeeper always thought it was gold. Selder was being paid.'

'Bristol, seafarer, gold… Did Selder give the man anything in return?'

'Not obviously. Information, perhaps? But what information would Selder have to sell?'

'Philip! John Kingsley worked for Lloyds!'

'Good God! Shipping information? And Bristol has a bad record for pirate activities.'

They stared at each other. 'Philip, if Falkirk was passing on information about ships—that's a hanging offence! What if Stephen got some kind of evidence from Kingsley?'

'Falkirk would indeed be desperate to get hold of that. But what did Stephen do with it?'

'I don't know!'

'I'll get the men on to it. But here we are. Now, remember, it's your clothes you want to collect. There's no need to mention anything else. What did you say the lawyer's name was?'

'His name is Keetham. And I'm not a fool, Philip!'

Once Mr Keetham had recovered from his surprise at seeing Mrs Ordway he was very helpful. 'Of course, of course. We are not at present in touch with Colonel Stanton, but I am quite sure that he would not object to your collecting a few of your belongings. I'll have my clerk find the keys right away.'

'Keys, Mr Keetham? Isn't there a caretaker in the building? Surely he could let us in.'

'Ah! There's a slight difficulty there, I'm afraid. It is most unfortunate, but the house has temporarily lost its caretaker. He had an accident a few days ago, and we are having difficulty in replacing him. We fully expect to engage someone tomorrow—or very soon after. Meanwhile, my men made sure that the house was well locked and the front door is bolted—you'll have to go in through the mews at the back. Most unfortunate—but a temporary state of affairs, I assure you. It would have been ready for you if I had known you were back in town, Mrs Ordway.'

He gave a few instructions to his clerk, then invited Mr Winbolt and Mrs Ordway to take a seat, and a glass of Madeira. His professional air of discretion could not quite hide his curiosity about their relationship, though the Winbolt name was enough to ensure his willingness to help, and Philip, as the future Lord Winbolt, was particularly desirable as a potential client.

'I hope Lord Winbolt is in better health than when I last heard, sir? We were all sorry to hear of his illness.' Philip reassured him. The lawyer then turned to Rosabelle. 'Mrs Ordway, since we last saw you, there have been a few changes in matters affecting the Ordway estate. Would you…would you like to hear about them now? Or…?' He cast a look at Philip.

'Mr Winbolt has my full confidence, sir. You may, if you wish, speak quite freely before him.'

'Mrs Ordway has agreed to marry me, Mr Keetham.' But when Mr Keetham started to express his pleasure at the news, Philip cut him short. 'Thank you. I am grateful for your good wishes, but I hope you will keep the news to yourself for the time being. And we are a little pressed for time at this particular moment.'

'Of course, of course!' He went to the door of his office and opened it. 'Bennett! Have you found those keys yet?'

'Coming, Mr Keetham, sir!'

Mr Keetham returned to his desk. 'I shall hope to see you again quite soon, Mrs Ordway. I think you will find that your affairs are in better order now that Colonel Stanton has taken charge. Though there will be new arrangements, of course, since you are contemplating marrying again.' He beamed on them both, then turned with a start as the clerk came in. 'Ah, the keys! Would you like my man to come with you?'

Refusing his offer of assistance and promising to return the keys as soon as they had finished with them, they extricated themselves, not without difficulty, from the lawyer's effusions and made their way back to Piccadilly and thence to Upper Brook Street. By this time it was past four o'clock and the light was beginning to fade.

'Damn that lawyer! It's too late to do very much tonight, Rosa. We'll have to come back tomorrow. And if the house is completely empty I should prefer to take a few precautions. I don't like the sound of that accident to the caretaker.'

'Can't we just fetch one dress, Philip? I should like to wear it at the ball tonight. I really haven't anything else that will do.'

'I suppose so. After all, it's what we told the lawyer we were going to do! But don't waste any time in there. It will be dark quite soon. Come!'

* * *

Since the front doors would be heavily bolted they were taken round to the mews at the back of the house and, after telling Philip's coachman to wait in Grosvenor Square for a quarter of an hour, they let themselves in. They went up the back stairs, emerging through a servant's door on to the landing at the top of the main staircase. Here they turned towards the bedrooms, but Philip suddenly stopped and grasped Rosabelle's arm. He put his hand over her mouth and pointed downstairs. Unlike the floor they were on, the lower floors were all shuttered, but they could see a flickering light on the landing below.

A voice came floating up out of the darkness. 'There's no one here,' it said.

Philip drew Rosabelle silently back against the wall.

'I tell you, Burrows, I heard something! Have you got your gun?' This voice was horribly, hatefully familiar and Rosabelle stiffened. But she nodded at Philip's warning look and made no sound.

'Look in the dining room,' the voice continued.

'Mebbe it was a rat?'

'Here?' The voice was full of contempt for the other's ignorance.

'Even the best houses get rats if there's no one to get rid of them. How long has this place been shut up?'

'Go and look in the dining room, Burrows. If you see a rat, leave it alone. We don't want to make a lot of noise for the sake of a rat, do we? But if it's anything else—one of the rest of the crowd, for example—then deal with him. I'll keep guard here in case the visitor is somewhere else.'

Footsteps were heard descending the stairs to the hall, then crossing the hall. Then silence for a moment. Suddenly a chair was knocked over and the footsteps came running out. 'I told you! It was a rat. It's gone now. I knew it wasn't anything else. We know the Ordway lot aren't back yet—we've kept a watch out for them. And no one else would dare come here. Besides, none of the others would be interested in a load of old papers.'

'They would if they knew what was in them. They wouldn't want to be transported any more than you or I do.'

'Transported!'

'Or hanged. I should have killed Stephen Ordway.'

'You did.'

'Before he got hold of Kingsley's confession, and my letter. That doxy must know where it is! I was soft with her sister, but by God I won't waste time on courtesies with the Ordway woman. She'll tell me, before she's much older.'

'You've got to find her first.'

'I will.' The deep, husky voice was full of menace. 'And when I do…'

'We'd better go.' Burrows was getting nervous. 'It's getting dark and the light from these lamps will be seen from outside through the shutters. I've had enough of this. We can't bribe a second caretaker to say he's had an accident, and they're bound to send another round soon. Anyway, we've been looking for nearly a week now and there's no sign anywhere of any papers.'

'Stephen Ordway hid them. And Rosabelle Ordway must know where.'

'Then let's wait till we find her. But for now let's go!'

The listeners heard footsteps descending the stairs and retreating to the back regions. The lamplight faded.

'The door!' whispered Rosabelle in fright.

'I locked it again behind us. They won't notice anything. And the carriage isn't marked. If they do see it, they'll think it's just arriving.'

'Philip! I'm so frightened.'

'Don't be. Fortune seems to be on our side. That rat was a wonderful piece of luck. I have to admit that the odds were worse than I normally enjoy if it had come to a fight tonight!'

'Don't talk of it!' Rosabelle shuddered.

'Come—they've gone. Fetch your dress and we'll go, too.'

Rosabelle fumbled in the semi-darkness for her dress, and then they cautiously descended the back stairs again and let themselves out. The carriage was waiting—there was no sign of anyone else.

When they arrived back at Arlington Street they found Emily in a great state of anxiety.

'Rosa! Where have you both been? You've left very little time to get ready. Is that the dress? Give it to your maid and let her smooth it out for you.'

'My dear Emily, four hours is too long for the most demanding toilette!' said Philip. 'I intend to make sure that Rosa has something sustaining to eat before embarking on anything so energetic.' He spoke lightly but, unseen by Rosabelle, he gave his sister a significant look and nodded slightly in Rosabelle's direction.

Emily took a closer look at Rosabelle's pallor and said, 'I was just about to have something myself, Philip. But on your own head be it if we are late. I will not hurry my preparations. I refuse to be seen at Chesterfield House in anything but a state of polished perfection, I warn you. Come, Rosa. We shall have a small, luxurious collation in my room, while your maid is getting your dress ready. Philip, you may send up some champagne.'

Philip smiled his approval at his quick-witted sister and promised to see to it.

There had been a certain amount of discussion over the evening's invitation to the ball at Chesterfield House. The problem of Rosabelle's identity made social appearances difficult for her, and so far she had avoided society, but Emily and Philip had between them persuaded her to risk it.

'You can go as my friend, Annabelle Kelland, and Philip will just have to exercise restraint!' Emily had said gaily. 'Please come, Rosa! It will make such a difference if I have someone else to talk to!'

So, half-dreading it and half-looking forward to an evening spent in the very highest society, Rosabelle had agreed to go.

Now, somewhat shaken by her experiences in the Upper Brook Street house, she would willingly have stayed at home that night, if she could have done so without disappointing her friends. But a peaceful half-hour with Emily, with a glass of champagne and a light supper, helped to restore her. And when Emily first of all approved wholeheartedly of her dress, then started laughing at its colour, she was able to join in. When Philip came to collect them he was puzzled to find them still giggling.

'But what is there to laugh about?' he asked. 'I have never seen you look better, Emily, and Rosabelle always looks enchanting in blue—azure, isn't it?'

'No, no…not azure, Philip,' gasped Emily. 'This time it's celestial!' And his two ladies went off into another gale of laughter. His perplexed look only made matters worse. By the time that the joke was explained and order restored, Rosabelle had quite forgotten her fears. And later, as they came into the entrance hall of Chesterfield

House and slowly ascended its magnificent staircase, she looked serenely lovely. Madame Fanchon had said herself that she had never made a more beautiful dress than the one Rosabelle was wearing that night—a clear blue *peau de soie*, worn over white silk, the bodice lavishly embroidered with small pearls and beads of crystal.

They danced and talked the night away and Rosabelle found that she was enjoying herself in a manner that, three hours before, she would have said was impossible. Philip was taking care to be discreet, aware that life could become very complicated indeed, if his name was linked with that of Rosabelle Ordway's sister. He danced no more than was conventionally polite with 'Emily's friend', but all the same he used his considerable powers of dissimulation to keep an eye on her throughout the evening. Julian Falkirk was accepted everywhere, even at social events as august as this one, and Philip was taking no risks. It was as well.

Halfway through the evening Rosabelle and Emily had repaired to the cloakroom to refresh themselves before supper, having arranged to meet Philip at the door to the supper room. When Emily was delayed by an elderly dowager who wanted to talk about Lord Winbolt, Emily signed to Rosabelle to carry on. But Rosabelle had hardly gone twenty paces before she was roughly seized. A hand was placed over her mouth and she was pulled into a narrow side passage.

'Don't try anything,' said Falkirk's voice. 'Or I'll break your neck.'

When Emily rejoined Philip, he was visibly restraining his impatience. 'Where's...er Anna?' he asked.

'She should be here,' said Emily. 'I was held up by Lady Grant, and told her to go on. Hasn't she arrived?'

'Oh, my God!' said Philip. 'No, she hasn't. Where did you say she left you?'

'Near the corridor to the library. But—'

Philip interrupted impatiently. 'Emily, stay here for a bit. I'll have to look for her.'

'But why—'

'Stay here, I tell you!' And with that he plunged into the crowd. He made his way back to the spot where Emily had last seen Rosabelle, then retraced her steps, looking for a likely place where she might have gone astray—or been abducted. He soon found the narrow side passage and hurried down it…

Rosabelle had no illusions about her plight. Falkirk's words that afternoon had painted a picture which had chilled her soul, and now it was harsh reality. But her faith in Philip kept her spirits up. She kicked and struggled as Falkirk dragged her along the passage, delaying their progress to the door at the far end which led into the garden. There, she knew, Falkirk would be able to do what he wished with her. His hand bruised her mouth, and his arm was so tight round her body that she felt her ribs would crack, every breath was agony, but still she fought, driven by a furious determination to survive.

'Be still, you little termagant! I don't intend to kill you, unless you make me. I need you!'

They had reached the door. Rosabelle was very nearly exhausted. When Falkirk slammed her up against the wall and held her by the throat with one hand, while he opened the door with the other, she had no strength to pull away.

'I'm…I'm—' she croaked.

'I don't give a damn who you are, you wildcat! Ordway or Kelland, it's all one to me. I'm going to keep you in my hands until I have the other one, too. Then we'll see who will talk!'

The door was open and Falkirk pushed her outside, and began to propel her along the path. Rosabelle asked herself frantically where all the servants, the waiters, the maids, the lamp attendants—where had they all gone? But Falkirk had chosen his spot cleverly. This was a dark part of the garden which was seldom used by anyone, a path leading to a disused mews block. There was no one in sight. She began to despair.

'Turn round, Falkirk!' The voice, icy, commanding, and crackling with menace, came from behind.

Falkirk jumped round, releasing Rosabelle as he did so.

'Run, Rosa! Run!' said Philip, keeping his eyes firmly on his opponent. It was as well. Falkirk leapt on him with a roar. Rosabelle screamed and put her hands over her eyes. It was happening! Her worst fears were about to be realised! Philip would be beaten, kicked, left to die, just as Stephen had been left. Oh God, she would not be able to bear it!

There were sounds of men breathing heavily, fighting, the crunch as blows met their target, a snarling sound from Falkirk. Suddenly Rosa took her hands away. She must not stand aside helplessly while Falkirk did his worst—Philip needed her help! She ran to the man standing over the recumbent body on the ground and rained blows on him, shouting and kicking...

'Rosa! Hey, Rosa! Wait! That hurts!' It was Philip's voice. Rosabelle froze.

'Can this be my gentle, ladylike Rosabelle? I don't believe it!' Philip's arms were restraining her, Philip's face was close to hers, Philip's eyes were gazing into hers with that well-loved, quizzical look. She glanced down. At her feet Falkirk was lying on the ground, groaning.

'Philip! It's you! Oh, I thought...I thought....' Rosabelle burst into tears.

'I know. You thought me too much of a gentleman to know how to fight a cur like Falkirk. I told you—I've lived a full life, Rosa. Not all of it has been among gentlemen. Calm down, my love, calm down! There's no need for this. Come, let me take you to Emily. I'll find someone to look after this *canaille* till I come back.'

Together they walked back along the corridor. Philip caught a passing footman and said calmly, 'There's someone lying outside in the garden back there. He...he has clearly met with some accident. Stay with him while I see that this lady is safe, will you? But...don't let him get away!'

The footman took note of Rosabelle's torn dress and disturbed state, Philip's ruffled hair and the rip in his coat and for a moment his impassive countenance showed a certain amount of emotion. Then he said calmly, 'Certainly, Mr Winbolt. Where did you say the gentleman was?'

Philip then sent another servant to fetch Emily, and when she arrived he delivered Rosabelle into her sympathetic hands. 'Take her back to the cloakroom, and do what you can with her dress. She has had a shock, but she'll be all right. I have some business to complete, then I'll take you both home.'

He went back along the passage, but when he went outside he found the footman somewhat painfully getting off his knees.

'You didn't tell me 'e was a bloody prize fighter!' he said resentfully. 'I 'adn't 'ardly got out 'ere when 'e clocked me one. Then 'e was over the wall and orf, before I could 'oller for 'elp! Beggin' your pardon, Mr Winbolt.'

Philip was furious, but not with the footman—the fault was his. 'I should have made sure he was properly out before I left him,' he said grimly. 'What's your name?'

'Jenkins, sir.' The footman had now recovered enough to be apprehensive about Philip's reaction to what had happened.

'Well, Jenkins, I'm sorry to have let you in for all that. I hope you'll forgive and, if possible, forget what happened tonight. Here, this might help.' He pressed a coin into Jenkins's hand.

'Cor! Thank you, sir!'

'Not a word about the lady, Jenkins. Remember!'

'Not a word about nothing, sir. Not h'ever. Thank you, sir.'

Philip went back into the house, followed by Jenkins. He was amused to see Jenkins about his work again later, looking as immaculate and as impassive as if the events in the garden had never taken place.

He soon found his two ladies again. Rosabelle was looking quite cheerful, and her dress showed no obvious signs of her struggle. Emily was the one who looked shattered. 'That man,' she said. 'Falkirk. What has happened to him?'

'Nothing,' said Philip. 'He got away.'

There was a shocked silence. Then Philip added, 'On reflection, I think that's just as well. It could have involved Rosa in a major scandal and, at the moment, that is the last thing we want.'

'But, Philip,' said Rosabelle, looking worried, 'Falkirk won't rest until he has taken revenge for the humiliation he suffered tonight at your hands. And you know now how vicious he can be.'

'Exactly, Rosa, darling. I am better prepared. And if I've beaten him once I can beat him again.'

'Not if he has company.'

'You're right. But you may rest easy, my love. I shall make sure you are safe—and I shan't risk my own neck, either. Emily, you look tired. Shall we go back to Arlington Street?'

'No,' said Emily slowly. 'I won't let that scoundrel spoil our evening. If Rosa agrees, we shall stay and have some supper. Then if there is any speculation later on about tonight, no one will be able to claim that the Winbolts—I include you in them, Rosa—looked as if they had been involved. What do you say?'

'I agree,' said Rosabelle firmly. 'As long as the pins in my dress hold together.'

Laughing, the three of them went in to supper. It would have seemed to the polite world at Lord Chesterfield's ball that Mr Winbolt and the two ladies with him hadn't a care in the world.

The polite world would have been surprised if it had followed Mr Winbolt on an errand he undertook the next morning before the ladies were up. His destination was certainly not one usually sought out by gentlemen of the *ton*. And when he left Bow Street to go back to his grandfather's house, he was accompanied by an undistinguished ferrety-looking individual, with a habit of looking round him with bright, keen eyes wherever he went. The ferret's name was Barnaby Stokes.

# Chapter Fourteen

Barnaby Stokes made a better bodyguard than he did a
spare groom or footman—the two roles he was ostensibly to play in the Winbolt household. When dressed in
Lord Winbolt's livery he looked the part well enough.
But he was woefully inept at handling carriage doors and
steps, and his bow-legged gait and aggressive demeanour
added nothing to the style of a lady's progress through
town. Nor did his habit of bundling her parcels inele-
gantly under his arm, or hanging them round his neck,
add to her consequence.

Any remonstrance brought forth the reply, 'Well,
ma'm, I arsk yer! 'Ow am I to save yer, if me 'ands is
full of bits and bobs? I trained with the Bow Street
Runners, not with a bloomin' domestic agency, beggin'
yer pardon, and no offence meant.'

After one or two minor disasters, Philip negotiated
with Lord Chesterfield for a temporary loan of one of
his footmen, and thereafter Barnaby Stokes acted as

Philip's groom, or merely followed the ladies at a discreet distance if they were out on foot. But whenever
they went out of the house Miss Winbolt and her friend,
Miss Kelland, were always accompanied by their new
footman, Jenkins by name.

Jenkins and Barnaby Stokes got on remarkably well,
and each learned a lot from the other. They were eager
to do the job they had really been engaged for—that is,
to protect their employers from harm—for they were
both in complete agreement that Mr Winbolt was a true
gent—a pleasant cove to work for, and generous with it.
And the two young ladies were as nice a couple of gen-
try-morts as they'd ever come across.

Protected by their two guardians, Philip and Rosabelle
had searched the Upper Brook Street house, in likely and
unlikely places, for anything that might be the papers
Falkirk wanted, but they found nothing. Whatever
Stephen had done with them, he had hidden them too
well for anyone else to find. So, when the new caretaker
came to take up his post in the house, they returned the
keys to Mr Keetham and resigned themselves to defeat.

'I had such hopes,' mourned Rosabelle. 'I thought we
might be rid of Falkirk and his threats, that our minds
could be set at rest. But now…'

'Don't despair. Stephen can't have been the only one
with a grudge against Falkirk. Tell me as many names
of Stephen's associates as you can remember.'

'Falkirk, Burrows, John Kingsley… There was a man
called…North?…Neath? No, Nairn! Samuel Nairn. And
there was another—a man called Fraser, I think, though
I never saw him.'

Philip had been writing busily. 'And I've got
Decoster's name down already. Rosa, I have some work

for Stokes and Jenkins for the rest of the day. You won't want to go out, will you?'

'No, Emily and I had planned to look at the latest *Ladies' Almanack*. She might be inspired to want to go out to Harding Howells to look at the new silks and muslins tomorrow, however…' They both smiled. Rosabelle went on, 'Why? What are you planning to do, Philip?'

'I shall send Jenkins and Stokes out on a fishing expedition. I want to know more about those men.'

However, when Philip showed Stokes his list, Stokes pronounced that he knew one name at least.

'Samuel Nairn to my own knowledge is in Newgate at this very moment. A friend o' mine put 'im there 'imself not a month since.'

'For what?'

'Pore devil was in debt up to 'is ears. All gone on drink and the poppy merchants.'

'Can you go to see him? Is he…is he still *compos mentis*?'

'I think 'e is. Course I don't know wot Newgate 'as done to'im. Terrible 'ard, Newgate, on a man. But I c'n go and see 'im. I'll soon tell!'

'Well, then, I want you to see Mr Nairn and, if you can, ask him some questions for me. I'll write them down for you. If Mr Nairn can help me, I might be able to do something for him in return, tell him.'

'Mr Winbolt, sir!'

'What is it, Jenkins?'

'Mr Kingsley's dead, sir, but I know his former manservant, sir. I'll have a chat with him, shall I, Mr Winbolt?'

'Right! Find out, if you can, what happened the night

Mr Kingsley died, and anything else that might be of use. Now, what about Burrows? Do either of you know anything about him? Or Decoster, or Fraser?'

They both shook their heads. But Barnaby Stokes offered to ask some friends in Bow Street about them, and Jenkins promised to make enquiries in The Footman's Friend and The Running Dog, and other places where valets and footmen congregated for gossip and relaxation.

The result of their labours was quite promising. Samuel Nairn was not only perfectly, one might say miraculously, still in his right mind. He was also ready to accept assistance from Mr Winbolt in return for information about Falkirk—to be specific, he was ready to swear that Falkirk had boasted to him of murdering John Kingsley. He would sign a document to that effect. Philip set that process in motion straight away.

John Kingsley's valet, after some persuasion, was now ready to swear that on the night Mr Kingsley had died, he had heard a quarrel between his master and another gentleman, though he had not seen the gentleman concerned. Mr Kingsley had called him 'Selly'. He had heard this 'Selly' threatening his master, and the following morning he had found Mr Kingsley dead. He had been too frightened to say anything at the time. But he had continued to mourn his dead master, and time had somewhat reduced his fear of 'Selly'. When pressed, he admitted that 'Selly's' voice was easy to recognise, and was remarkably similar to that of a certain Mr Julian Falkirk.

'I 'ave to say, Mr Winbolt, that the h'evidence of servants and convicted debtors is not going to go down well in a court of law. Not at all well. Especially if you're

trying to say that this ''Selly'' is really Mr Falkirk, wot
is about to become a lord.'

'That's 'oo it was! In the garden the other night!'
Jenkins was so excited that he interrupted them. 'I've
been wonderin' where I see'd 'im before. Well, I'm
blowed! Mr Falkirk!'

'I'm aware of the problem, Stokes,' said Philip. 'And
a court of law is not my immediate aim. But if I can get
enough to persuade Burrows that it would be better to
save his own neck by talking, then I'm sure we could
persuade a magistrate to act.'

'So Burrows is the one you want, is he?'

'He is Falkirk's right-hand man.'

'Right, governor. We'll find 'im for you.'

After some days, during which Rosabelle and Emily
had spent quite a bit of time exercising in the garden, or
reading indoors, Philip had gathered a fair amount of
information. He had Samuel Nairn's deposition, and
Nairn was now in the process of being released from
Newgate. He also had a signed statement from
Kingsley's valet. Bow Street knew nothing of any
Decoster, but one man remembered seeing something
about a Da Costa who had been involved with privateers
in Bristol.

Burrows had been traced to an ill-kept tavern the other
side of Leicester Square, and Philip himself had learned
about the last name on the list. Fraser came of a good
family and had been a well-known member of Society.
Then rumours had started circulating about his treatment
of his servants and others, and he had disappeared for a
while. He had recently reappeared, but not in any circles
recognised in good society. As for Falkirk, he seemed to
have vanished from sight, and Philip was still debating

what his next step should be when an unforeseen complication forced him to think again...

At the end of that week, London was in the grip of one of its periodical November fogs. It had been a miserable day—dark and cold—and the evening was no better. After one look out of his bedchamber window in the morning, Lord Winbolt had announced that he would spend the day in his room, and his grandchildren had not seen him. Philip had been out on business and the two young ladies had spent the day reading before the fire in the saloon. Now they were lingering over dinner, enjoying the convivial warmth of a good fire and the soft light of the branched candlesticks on the dining table. There were just three of them at the table—Lord Winbolt had remained in his room.

By common consent they had left aside their present problems and the talk was of books and the theatre, of travel and art. Suddenly, this agreeable moment of relaxation was interrupted by thunderous knocking at the front doors. It was not a time for casual visitors, and they waited with some curiosity to hear who or what it could be. Voices were heard in the hall and Maynard soon appeared at the door of the dining room.

'A Colonel Stanton, sir. He wishes to speak to you. I told him you were at dinner, but he was very insistent.'

'Giles!' Philip and Rosabelle spoke in unison as they both got up.

Maynard was brushed aside as Giles Stanton entered the room, saying, 'Excuse me for breaking in on you like this, Philip—' He stopped dead. 'Rosabelle!' he exclaimed. 'So you *are* here! What the devil do you think you've been doing? Oh, this goes beyond everything! To see you here without a care in the world while I…we've been sick with worry over you!'

He was clearly in a fury. He went over to Rosabelle and shook her. 'How dare you put Aunt Laura through all this distress! I thought you had given up your tormenting, ill-considered ways, but I see I was wrong…'

'Er…Giles, old fellow! Take your hands off my betrothed. Or I shall have to hit you, and that's the last thing I would wish for.' Philip spoke gently, but there was steel in his voice. He moved over and stood by Rosabelle.

Giles Stanton looked astounded. 'Philip! I… Am I mad? How can she possibly be going to marry you? It's her sister you're going to marry—Annabelle Kelland!'

'This is Rosabelle Ordway. But it's the girl I am going to marry.'

Rosabelle had gone very pale. 'Are you saying that you've brought my sister to London, Giles? Oh, how could you? After all my warnings and letters…'

'Giles, is she right?' asked Philip sharply. 'Is Miss Kelland in London?'

Giles Stanton looked from one to the other as if they had gone mad. 'I don't understand what the devil you're both talking about! You brought her sister to London! I haven't seen her sister! And this can't possibly be your betrothed, Philip, how can it be?' He turned to Rosabelle. 'Tell him, Rosa! Tell him about Annabelle's letters, how you and Aunt Laura hoped she would marry Winbolt here!'

Rosabelle tried to say something but found it impossible to speak. Confusion and anxiety for her sister were keeping her silent.

Giles exclaimed in exasperation and turned back to Philip. 'I'm beginning to believe you're all drunk,' he said, glancing at the wine on the table. 'Rosabelle Ordway—that is to say, this lady here—' he pointed at Rosabelle '—has been the bane of my life for the last six months. In all that time she has never once indicated that she had any kind of special interest in you, Winbolt. Indeed, she was delighted that you were going to marry her sister!' He turned again to Rosabelle, angry once again. 'Tell me why on earth you didn't wait for us at Temperley, Rosabelle!'

'Us?' asked Philip.

'Aunt Laura and me. We arrived at Temperley this morning. We stayed last night at Wallingford, and this morning Aunt Laura wasn't well enough to travel straight away. Rosabelle was very anxious to see her sister, so she went on ahead. But when we arrived at Temperley we heard she had already left again.' He turned to Rosabelle again. 'I'll have something to say to Goss about this. Where is he?'

Philip intervened. 'Giles, I…I don't know how to tell you this. I can see you have been as deceived as I was. You obviously don't know that the Kelland sisters are identical twins. This is Rosabelle Ordway, who changed places with her sister at Easter, and has been in Berkshire and London ever since. The lady with you in the North was Annabelle Kelland.'

Giles Stanton sank into a chair. He looked from one to the other. 'I've spent all day trying to get here—the fog is everywhere. And when I walked into this room I thought it had all been worth while. Rosa was here, safe and sound. Are you trying to tell me that this isn't Rosabelle, after all?' As he stared at Rosabelle, his face changed, and, for the first time he seemed to take in what Philip had said. He looked from one to the other. 'Does Aunt Laura know, too?'

'Yes. I'm sorry, Giles. We shouldn't have done it. But I was at the end of my tether…'

'I've been played like a fish,' said Giles bitterly. But after a moment he sat up and said, *'But in that case, where is Annabelle now?'*

Philip said gravely, 'If she's not at Temperley, and not here—'

Maynard came into the room, looking agitated. 'Forgive me, sir, but there's an individual at the back demanding to see Colonel Stanton. I thought it best to let you know straight away. He has ridden from Berkshire, sir.'

'It's Goss!' said Giles. 'Thank God! He'll know where she is.'

But it was John Bostock who came in. 'Colonel Stanton, sir, they found Goss, your man. He's been wounded. He says that he and Miss Belle were set upon shortly after they left Temperley by two men They shot Goss, and…and they carried Miss Belle off with them.'

'Falkirk's work!' They gazed at one another, stunned. Giles got up. 'I must go.'

'Wait, Giles! This needs planning.'

Giles would have argued, but he was brought to see the sense of this. Emily took John Bostock out to the kitchen to find food and a bed, and Stokes and Jenkins and Giles's groom were despatched to find reinforcements. While they waited Giles was also fed. But when the men returned the news was negative. Falkirk had not been seen in London for a while. Giles sat down and put his head in his hands.

'Giles, this isn't any good,' Philip said softly. 'Unless we alarm Falkirk unduly, I am sure Annabelle is safe for the moment.'

'But she's been in his hands since this morning! I'll go mad if I don't *do* something, Philip!'

'Remember what you told me at Badajoz? You have to know the terrain before you attack. It was good advice then and it's good advice now. Believe me, Giles, Annabelle is safe for tonight. Though Falkirk has searched the house in Upper Brook Street, he has failed to find his papers. He's desperate to have them in his hands, and his only hope is to get Annabelle to show him where they are. She's safe for tonight.'

'But Annabelle doesn't know anything about the papers, damn you!'

'We know that. But he doesn't.'

Giles turned to Rosabelle. 'Did Stephen say *nothing* before he died?'

'He was delirious,' she said miserably. 'He could only think of money. He said again and again that his bank account had failed him, after all. He said it over and over.'

'No, no!' Giles exclaimed. 'It's where he hid the papers. Why didn't I think of it before?'

'But—' said Rosabelle.

'Where?' said Philip.

'I'll show you. Tomorrow. But first we must find Falkirk. I'll swear he's somewhere in London.'

'I think I could flush him out,' said Rosabelle. 'They keep an eye on this house, I know they do. If I were to take a walk out in the open street, it's very likely Falkirk would have me followed. I feel certain that he keeps a watch on us all, and he wants both Anna and me—he said so.'

'No!' said Philip. 'It's too dangerous.'

'Why not? I put Anna into this mess. It's up to me to get her out of it.'

'No, Rosa. I can't let you take the risk.'

'The risk wouldn't be all that great, if you and Giles were at hand. And it would be by far the quickest means of getting Falkirk to show himself. Let me do it, Philip! I can't…I can't bear to think of Anna in Falkirk's hands for a moment longer than necessary.'

'I'm sorry. I understand your feelings, of course I do, Rosa darling. But so many things could go wrong. No!'

'He's right,' said Giles decisively. 'There must be another way.'

Rosabelle looked from one to the other. Two strong, determined men, knowing what was best. Anna would have argued further with them and even enjoyed it, she knew. But that was not her way, she was not clever with arguments and noise. Being Rosa, and knowing that she would not win, she said no more.

'Burrows! Burrows will know where Falkirk can be found, and I think I can put my hand on Burrows.'

'I'd like to put my hands on Burrows,' said Giles grimly. 'Both of them. Round his throat.'

'We'll go in search of him first thing tomorrow, Giles. But leave him alive long enough for him to lead us to Falkirk.'

A most unaccustomed spirit of rebellion stirred within Rosabelle. It might take a day or more to find Burrows and persuade him to betray Falkirk. Her idea would have been far more effective. Could she possibly carry it out alone? The thought was petrifying, but, in the circumstances, very tempting.

'What are Stokes and Jenkins doing at the moment?' she asked meekly.

'They can look after you,' said Philip. 'Giles and I together are more than a match for anything Falkirk can do—wouldn't you agree, Giles?'

'I'll say—remember that time at Almeida?'

'With the French on one side and the guerillas on the other? And that bandit Villanteo—'

'No, Villanteo was at Talavera...'

Rosabelle stood up. 'I'm sure you'll excuse me. I'll leave you two gentlemen to talk over old times, shall I?' The slight acid in her tone was lost on Philip and Giles. They were deep in reminiscence.

'Goodnight, my dear,' said Philip, looking up and rising to escort her to the foot of the stairs. 'Try not to worry. You'll be safer indoors. And we shall find Annabelle for you.' He kissed her hand, and presented her with her candle.

'Goodnight, my dear. Goodnight, Giles.' She started up the stairs. 'Safer indoors!' she muttered to herself. 'Safer indoors, not worrying about Anna in the hands of that villain while they take heaven knows how long looking for him! I think not, Philip, my dear. I may not be able to argue, but I am not a spineless idiot, either...! And Barnaby Stokes will help.'

The next morning the two gentlemen set out early on their quest for news of Burrows and Falkirk. Rosabelle watched them go, then found Emily.

'Emily, are you planning to go out today?'

'I don't think so. If it clears up I might want to pay a visit to Harding Howells again this afternoon, perhaps. Why?'

'I'd like to make use of Barnaby Stokes. I have to go out on an errand.'

'What are you up to, Rosa?'

'Nothing dangerous,' said Rosabelle, crossing her fingers. 'But I'd prefer to have Barnaby with me. Don't ask me any more, Emily. I can't tell you, and I'd rather not lie.'

Emily was not at all happy, but she eventually gave in. 'But I shall tell Philip the minute he gets in,' she warned.

'Pray do!' said Rosabelle blithely. She donned her heaviest pelisse, and the warmest of her new shawls. She paid particular care in selecting the right muff. It was not only warm—it had a slender pocket inside. Into this she slipped a wickedly sharp paper knife which usually rested on the desk in the library. Philip had only recently warned her about it. She hoped it was as dangerous as he had said it was—it could be useful.

She found Barnaby Stokes waiting for her. 'Now, Barnaby—I don't want you to carry any parcels, or help with crossing the road. Indeed, I very definitely want you to follow me a good few paces behind. I must appear to be on my own. Understand?'

'I understand what you say, miss. I'm not at all sure it's what Mr Winbolt would wish.'

'Mr Winbolt is not here, Barnaby. He has gone out looking for Mr Burrows.'

'Then why amn't I with 'im?'

'Because I need you, and Mr Winbolt doesn't—he has Colonel Stanton to keep him company. Now, are you going to do what I ask? Or shall I take Jenkins? I am going out in either case.'

'I'd better do it, then.'

'There's one more thing, and it is extremely important! If anything should happen to me, do not attempt to rescue me, but find Mr Winbolt, or Colonel Stanton, and tell him that I shall bring Mr Falkirk to Upper Brook Street within the hour. Within the hour—have you got that?'

'And what if I can't find either of the gents in that time?'

Rosabelle stopped to think. 'I think you will—you know where they are likely to be, you told them where Burrows was to be found yourself. But if you cannot trace them within the time, then you must send Jenkins after them and come to Upper Brook Street on your own. You…you mustn't fail me, Barnaby.'

'Wait a minute! I'm not sure I'm doin' right to let you go, at all!'

'You cannot stop me, Mr Stokes! Come!'

Rosabelle made her way on to Arlington Street and thence into Piccadilly. The fog had still not cleared— visibility was limited to fifty paces or less. She walked purposefully in the direction of Grosvenor Square. If Falkirk were as anxious as he had said to get hold of both Kelland twins, he would be keeping watch for her. She was very nervous, but the thought of Anna in Falkirk's hands kept her walking steadily on. A curricle loomed up out of the murk and she tensed. But no, it went on its way towards St James's. A couple of horsemen, another curricle…

Someone tapped her elbow. Rosabelle turned and looked down. A small boy, looking half-starved, dressed in rags and blue with cold, was holding out his hand. She fumbled for some coins. Suddenly her arms were gripped from behind, and the coins fell to the ground. A gag was thrust into her mouth, she was bundled swiftly into a closed carriage which had drawn up close by and it set off with a jerk. She fell on to the seat.

She was sore, she was frightened, but at the same time she rejoiced. Her plan had succeeded sooner than she could have hoped! Falkirk had surfaced and she would soon see Anna again. She tried to suppress any sign of

triumph as she turned her head to look at him—and saw
a complete stranger regarding her.

'Well, well!' he drawled removing the gag, 'I was told
what to expect, but I would never have believed it! Not
one, but two pieces of prime fare, and both exactly the
same. What a sight!'

Rosabelle took a deep breath. She did not have to act
a part. She was very frightened. 'Who are you, sir? And
wh…what do you want with me?'

'Don't worry, girl. Mr Falkirk would have my skin if
I harmed you before he has a chance to question you
himself.'

'Falkirk?' She pretended to make for the window of
the carriage. He pulled her back so roughly that her cry
of terror was perfectly genuine.

'If you try that again, I'll forget Falkirk's orders and
teach you to behave.' The voice was as smooth, but his
eyes were cold. He had enjoyed hurting her.

'Who are you?' asked Rosabelle, her teeth chattering.
It had been easy to be brave when drawing up her plan
the night before. The reality was so much worse than she
had imagined. 'And where are you taking me?'

'To join your sister, what else?' he said. 'Mr Falkirk
wants to ask you a few questions. I do hope you have
some answers. Mr Falkirk is getting rather desperate.
There's no knowing what he might do. He might even
hand you over to me.'

The carriage drew up. Rosabelle was bundled out, and
she saw that they were in a sort of yard at the back of
an inn. The gates were shut behind them and her captor
took cruel hold of her wrist and dragged her inside. They
went along a passage and into a dingy room.

'Thank you, Fraser. You've delivered Rosabelle
Ordway number two, I see!' Falkirk was standing at the

side of the room. In a far corner sat Annabelle, pale, dishevelled, but defiant. There was an ugly bruise on her temple, and her hands were tied behind her back.

'You've hurt her!' Rosabelle wrenched herself free, ran over to her sister and knelt down beside her. 'Anna! Are you all right?'

'I've felt better,' said Annabelle, trying to smile. 'But all things considered...'

'Oh, Anna! I'm so sorry...'

'Now, this is most enlightening,' said Falkirk. 'We seem at last to have solved the mystery. I gather that our latest arrival is the real Widow Ordway. So she's the one who can tell us where to look. Isn't that so?'

Rosabelle stood up. 'I told you, I was Rosabelle Ordway, but you wouldn't believe me. I'm not going to ask for any mercy, for I know you are without it—I saw what you did to Stephen. But there is no point in keeping my sister here, sir. Surely now you know which of us is which, you can release her?'

'Well, that depends a bit on what you're going to do for me, Ro-sa-belle,' said Falkirk. 'If I was going to do you a favour like that, I'd like one in return.' His manner changed, and he came over and hauled her to her feet. 'You've wasted my time for long enough!' he snarled, putting his face close to hers. 'You're going to tell me where your snake of a husband hid those papers, Rosabelle Ordway, or you'll say goodbye to your sister for good.'

'I...I...can't.'

Falkirk had himself in hand again. 'I hope that isn't true,' he said calmly. 'Oh, I do so hope it isn't true! The world will lose two of its loveliest stars if it is. Don't be cozened into believing I wouldn't do it, my dears. I've killed so many—two more deaths will make little difference. Men or women—they're all one to me.'

There was a tap on the door. Fraser talked to someone, then came over to Falkirk and whispered something in his ear. Falkirk nodded, then spoke briskly to the girls. His businesslike tone was somehow more frightening than anything else. It was clear that he now regarded them as objects, hindrances in his way, which he would remove without a moment's thought.

'You've got ten minutes for reflection. I don't propose to let either of you go until I know where to find those papers. If you really don't know, Rosabelle, then God help both of you!' He went out, taking Fraser with him.

# Chapter Fifteen

'Anna! What happened?' Rosabelle spoke in a whisper. 'How did you come to fall into Falkirk's hands?'

'He had men watching Temperley.'

'We heard. John Bostock came to tell us.'

'What about Goss? Oh, Rosa, is Goss dead?'

'No, he's alive. But we have to think about what we're going to do.' She dropped her voice even lower and put her lips close to Annabelle's ear. 'Anna, I have to tell you. I don't know where the papers are.'

'I thought as much,' Annabelle whispered back. 'But I don't think Falkirk believes that.'

'No, and he mustn't. He'd kill us here and now, if he did. We must persuade him that I know, but that it's too complicated for me to explain. I have to show him.'

Annabelle nodded.

Rosabelle went on whispering, 'Philip and Giles will be at Upper Brook Street in about half an hour. We have to get Falkirk there, but not too soon. We must stay together—tell him that we can't remember without each other. Pretend to be frightened.'

'I don't have to!' said Anna with feeling.

There were sounds of the men returning. Rosabelle put her arm round her sister and, as Falkirk entered, Annabelle gave a dry sob.

'Well? Have you decided? Tell me quickly—I haven't any time to waste.'

'I don't have to decide, sir. You misunderstood when I said I couldn't tell you.'

'I thought I must have,' Falkirk said with a sardonic smile. 'So where are they?'

'In the drawing room.' Rosabelle hesitated.

'Come on, come on! That's not enough!'

'I'm trying to remember!' cried Rosabelle, desperation in her voice.

'You have to, Rosa!' Annabelle said, convincingly desperate herself. 'Didn't you…didn't you say something about the mantelpiece?'

'Oh, yes! The mantelpiece. Did I say mantelpiece, Anna?'

'You said there was a knob, or a piece of wood which was carved in a strange way…'

'Whereabouts?' demanded Falkirk.

'In the drawing room,' Rosabelle said, looking a little puzzled.

'Good God! I know it's the drawing room, you featherhead! Where, on the mantelpiece, in the fireplace in the drawing room?'

'Yes,' said Rosabelle.

'Where, where, where?'

'I think Mr Falkirk means in what part of the carving on the mantelpiece, Rosa. Please, please try to remember, dear,' said Annabelle.

'Oh!' Rosabelle wrinkled her brow in a well-simulated effort to remember. 'It's been so long since I was there…' she said, and put her hand to her head. 'I think it was on the…right.'

'Good, good.'

'Or was it the left?' She extended her right hand, then her left. 'The left, I think.' She took one look at Falkirk's darkening countenance and faltered, 'I always get confused between my right and my left.'

'This is useless!' exclaimed Falkirk. He went to the door. 'Fraser!' he yelled. 'Get the coach ready!' He came back to the sisters. 'I'm taking you to Upper Brook Street. If we're stopped, you can tell them you've come to collect something. Meanwhile, your sister will stay here.'

'No!' cried Rosabelle in a panic. 'If Anna isn't with me I won't be able to remember anything at all! She has always helped me. I'm not leaving her here. I won't, I won't!'

It was clear that Falkirk was pressed for time. Whatever he had been told outside had created a crisis. 'She'll come. But she'll be tied up,' he said. 'Come on!'

'I won't go unless Anna is in the carriage with me. I'm too frightened—and I don't trust you, Falkirk.'

'You'd better produce those papers pretty quickly, you little shrew, or neither of you will live to go anywhere.'

'I've said I will, but I can't find where Stephen hid them if I'm not there to see the place,' stammered Rosabelle. 'I'm not very good at remembering if things aren't in front of me. And even then I won't be able to think straight unless Anna is with me.'

'That's right, sir,' said Anna, sounding eager to please. 'We have always been very dependent on each other— twins are, you know.'

Falkirk pushed both of them before him out of the room. Fraser produced a length of cord and Anna was bound up, feet as well as wrists, and put into the carriage. Rosabelle joined her, followed by Falkirk. Fraser sat outside. When Rosabelle sat down she felt something on the seat. It was her muff! She had left it in the carriage when they had arrived. While Falkirk was busy with seating himself close to Anna, she quietly slipped the paper knife out of its pocket and put it in her sleeve. She just managed it in time—Falkirk was turning to her.

'In case either of you decides to try anything, Mrs Ordway,' said Falkirk, 'we'll keep this on view.' 'This' was a short stiletto, and it was held to Anna's throat. A faint trace of blood, a graze, appeared on Anna's skin.

The next half hour was a nightmare. The road was rough, and each time the carriage lurched to a halt as something loomed out of the fog and crossed its path, the stiletto touched Anna's throat, and one more tiny drop of blood appeared. There was only one good thing about the journey. It was so slow that there should have been plenty of time for Philip and Giles to reach Upper Brook Street before them.

By the end of that journey Rosabelle had been tense for so long that when she got out of the carriage her legs would hardly support her. The fog swirled around them—there was no chance that they would be seen. Fraser slipped down off the box at the entrance to the mews and disappeared. A few minutes later the front door opened. So much for Mr Keetham's security measures!

They went straight upstairs into the drawing room, Rosabelle first, then Falkirk and the driver of the carriage half-carrying Anna between them. Here they paused a moment. The shutters were closed and there was very little light in the room. The place looked ghostly in the gloom, the mirrors reflecting the pale shapes of furniture shrouded in holland covers. Anna was dumped on to a chair, and then Falkirk sent the driver out again to stand guard.

'I...I can't see,' said Rosabelle loudly.

'Open the shutters, Fraser.'

'Is that wise?'

'She's an Ordway, isn't she? She has every right to be here. Open them.'

Then, when Fraser fumbled with the unfamiliar catches, Falkirk said impatiently, 'I'm beset by fools!' and went over to help him.

Rosabelle was standing next to her sister, and had the paper knife out before Falkirk had even reached the window. In seconds she had slit through the ropes which bound Anna's wrists, and put the knife down on a table next to her sister. Anna resumed her former uncomfortable position.

'Now!' said Falkirk. 'The mantelpiece.'

Rosabelle went slowly over to the fireplace. Where were Philip and Giles? Had Barnaby Stokes failed to find them? Had he got lost in the fog? Her blood ran cold at the thought of what might happen if they didn't arrive. Quite soon. But at least Anna had her hands free, and she would be able to cut the rope round her ankles as soon as Falkirk's attention was elsewhere. There might be a chance to run... No, she must have faith, she did have faith. Philip would come.

'Er...let me see...' she said. 'The right console...'

'You said it was the left one,' Falkirk said in a hard voice.

'So I did! But now I'm here, I'm sure it was the right

one.' Her gaze moved frantically over the carved wood. That cherub looked likely. Where, oh, *where* were Philip and Giles? She uttered a desperate prayer. Please God, let him come soon! Then she took a deep breath and said, 'I think this might be it.' Falkirk pushed her out of the way roughly and peered at the carving.

'Which?' he asked.

'That cherub there. His head turns,' said Rosabelle, trying to sound convincing.

Falkirk pressed frantically, pulling this way and that. Nothing happened. He regarded her murderously. 'If you are trying to hoax me...' he said.

Rosabelle's knees were trembling. 'You have to press it in a certain way,' she said. 'It's no good hammering it.'

'You do it!'

Rosabelle put her hand out and touched the cherub's face. It shifted. She gasped and jumped back.

Falkirk and Fraser pushed her away so hard this time that she stumbled, and Anna leapt up to save her. Falkirk paid no attention. He and Fraser were bending forward to examine the carving, their heads almost touching the bracket...

The door from the anteroom burst open and Philip and Giles came hurtling in. Their rush took them right up to the fireplace where they slammed Fraser and Falkirk against the ornate mantelpiece. There was a howl from Falkirk, but he turned like a tiger and threw Philip off. Fraser was struggling with Giles. All four men were powerful, and Falkirk and Fraser were fighting for their survival. They went back and forth, sending tables flying, ripping covers off the furniture to throw them over their attackers, hurling chairs wildly in an effort to trip them up. No trick was too low, no hold was barred. The fight was ferocious. The twins stayed in a corner watching the violence in horror, till they saw the driver of the carriage appear at the door.

'Quickly!' cried Annabelle, but her sister was already at the door. Together they threw themselves at it, and slammed it shut. A howl from outside suggested that the unfortunate man had not quite got his fingers out in time. 'Lock it!' panted Annabelle. After a struggle they got the key turned, and then they turned to survey the scene.

Fraser was lying unconscious on the floor. Philip was standing behind Falkirk, holding the latter's arm up behind his back. From the look on Falkirk's face, the grip was excruciating.

'Right!' said Giles, breathing rather fast. 'We'll get Burrows in.' As if it had been prearranged, Jenkins and Barnaby Stokes came in, with Burrows between them.

Falkirk's lips drew back in a snarl. 'You!' he said, staring malevolently at Burrows. 'I heard about you. So you told them all about me, did you…' And a string of curses issued from his mouth.

'That's enough!' said Philip. 'Move! You're going to the magistrates.'

Giles had taken a gun out, and was holding it on Falkirk. 'Search him for weapons.' Jenkins came over and examined Falkirk. The stiletto was produced and Falkirk released from Philip's grip.

'I should have used that thing on you, when I had the chance,' said Falkirk viciously, feeling his arm.

'Instead of on a woman who was bound hand and foot,' said Rosabelle scornfully.

'What do you mean?' Philip asked.

'He held it to Anna's throat in the carriage on the way here. He drew blood.'

'*What?*' For a moment Giles's attention was on Anna.

Now that the excitement had died down she was sitting sideways on a chair, holding on to its back. She was very pale, and the bruise on her head was very prominent. 'Anna!'

'Watch out!' Philip's cry came too late. Falkirk had taken the opportunity of Giles's lapse of attention to rush forward. He bent down to pick something off the floor and almost in the same gesture plunged it into Burrows's throat.

Burrows uttered a gurgling cry and fell forward. Rosabelle cried out. Barnaby Stokes and Philip threw themselves on Falkirk, and once again overpowered him. Falkirk offered little resistance. He stood between them, looking like a wild animal at bay, teeth bared. He nodded towards Burrows's body. 'He won't be able to tell tales about me now!' he said with satisfaction.

Giles had been bending over Annabelle, but now he went over to Burrows and examined him. He shook his head and straightened up. There was a cold, deadly calm about him. 'It's a pity there are so many witnesses here, Falkirk. I'd be glad to despatch you the same way Burrows went. You're two of a kind, you…'

Barnaby Stokes intervened. 'That's no way to talk, sir, if you'll pardon my saying so. It's best to let the law take its proper course.' He faced Falkirk. 'Julian Falkirk, also known as Selder, in the name of the Law I arrest you for the wilful murder of George Burrows. I require you to come with me…'

Rosabelle left Stokes to his work. She knelt down and gazed anxiously at her sister. 'Anna?'

'I'm all right. Truly. I'd like to go somewhere where it's more peaceful, though. My head aches.'

'We'll go back to Arlington Street. I'm sure that's what Philip would want.'

Philip had heard. He said, 'As soon as Jenkins comes back we'll send him for the carriage. He's fetching assistance for Stokes at the moment. Of course you must stay with us! I'll get Jenkins to warn Emily to have a bed for you.'

Giles was with Anna again, looking at her in silence. Rosabelle went back to join Philip. 'Is Fraser…is he dead, too?' she asked nervously.

Philip poked the recumbent Fraser with the toe of his boot. 'Unfortunately not. He'll have to be carried off when the men come for Falkirk. He might even be conscious by then. What I can't understand is how Jenkins came to miss Falkirk's other knife!'

'It…it wasn't his,' said Rosabelle nervously. 'I brought it. It's yours.'

'Mine!'

'Your paper knife. I took it in case I needed it. It must have fallen on the floor in the fight.'

'I'm glad to hear that you took some protection,' said Philip evenly. 'Though what you thought you might do with only my paper knife to protect you I cannot imagine.'

Annabelle roused herself. 'Don't! She cut my ropes with it so that we could join together to keep Falkirk's coachman out of the room. You'd have been outnumbered otherwise. Don't talk to Rosabelle like that!'

'Annabelle, you must save your voice!' said Giles, putting his hand over her lips. 'The sooner you can rest, the better.'

'I want to know something first,' she protested. 'What and where are these wretched papers?'

Giles went over to the merry little cherub on the right hand side of the mantelpiece. He pressed something and slid it to one side. When his hand reappeared it held a slender packet of papers.

'Here,' he said. 'Stephen's bank account. He used…he used to keep his pocket money here when he was a child.'

'But that was the very place I… Oh, heavens!' said Rosabelle.

'Exactly so,' said Philip curtly. 'You took an enormous risk, Rosa. How long do you think you would have lived after Falkirk got his papers?'

'I shall go mad,' said Annabelle suddenly. 'I've been chased, carried off, frightened half to death, rescued, beaten on the head and imprisoned, had my throat cut—'

'Anna!'

'Well, nearly—and all for the sake of that wretched bundle of papers. What are they?'

'You mustn't talk, Annabelle,' said Giles.

'Really? Well, silence me by telling me what I want to know.'

'It seems to be a confession signed by Kingsley.'

'Kingsley?'

'Ah! And here's a letter signed by Falkirk, thanking Kingsley for his information, and telling him it will be put to good use. He even calls himself Selder in it! Exactly what we wanted. It would have been enough to deliver Falkirk into the hands of the authorities.'

'Stephen's revenge,' said Rosa sadly. 'And his death warrant.'

'They would have been your death warrant, too,' said Philip. 'Thank God we turned up when we did!'

'But I *sent* for you, Philip!' said Rosabelle.

'Yes. So you did. Well, we'll leave that discussion for another time. I can hear a carriage drawing up.'

'I'll carry Anna,' said Giles.

'And I'll bring Fraser,' said Philip. Fraser was still lying on the floor. Philip took him by the heels and dragged him into the hall.

They made their way out down the stairs in a little procession, passing Barnaby Stokes and his prisoner on the way. Falkirk was standing in the hall next to his jailer, hands tied behind him, his face as if carved in stone. He ignored them as they passed. As they emerged through the front door, several men drew back and waited for them. Then the little band went inside to assist Barnaby Stokes with his prisoners.

The Arlington Street house was in a bustle when they arrived, but Anna's room was ready for her. Rosabelle noticed that Giles seemed remarkably reluctant to relinquish his burden. He brought her in, and brushed aside any offers of help in carrying her up the stairs. Annabelle's own protests he ignored, merely telling her to be quiet and rest her throat.

Philip smiled at the expression on Rosabelle's face. 'Leave them. They have some sorting out to do,' he said.

'I can't stand aside while my sister is carried off by a bully like Giles Stanton,' she said indignantly. 'Anna has more spirit than I have, but she's not well. He'll walk all over her! I've some experience of Colonel Stanton's ways. And from the way he talked to me last night when he thought I was Annabelle, time has not improved him.'

'You really think not? You're wrong. The boot is far more probably on the other foot! And, I assure you, you may safely leave Emily to see that they observe the proprieties. Forget them for the moment, Rosa. I want to talk to you.'

He led her into the library. 'I've lost my paper knife,'

he said idly. 'It's been taken as part of the evidence. Why did you do it?'

'Take the paper knife?' she asked, disingenuously.

'Don't play with me. The paper knife is the least of the matter. You knew you were taking a dreadful risk when you embarked on that escapade this morning. Falkirk is a ruthless killer—you knew that. Not many days ago, you could hardly bring yourself to talk about him, he had frightened you so much. But this morning you deliberately threw yourself into his path, although you knew that I would have stopped you if I could. Didn't you care what it would have done to me, if I had lost you? How much I would have blamed myself? How impossible I would have found it to *live* with myself? Why did you do it?'

Rosabelle saw that she had seriously hurt him. She remembered Emily's words to her—that Philip regarded the safety of all those connected with him as his personal reponsibility. She went over to him and put her arms round him. He stiffened.

'I'd like an answer to my question first, Rosa.' He gently put her arms down from him, and walked several paces away.

'Philip!'

'Oh, don't think I no longer love you as much as I did! The temptation to take you in my arms and kiss the life out of you, right now, is very strong! And it's very tempting, too, to gloss things over with kisses, and put what happened this morning behind us. But it wouldn't solve anything in the long term.'

'I don't understand...?'

'I thought I had your trust. It was a shock to find that I hadn't, after all.'

'That's not so! I do trust you! I put absolute trust in

you when I let myself be captured by Falkirk. No one could have had more faith in any other person, than I had in you this morning.'

'But not last night.'

'Ah!' Rosabelle paused, then she said slowly, 'Philip, you're talking now of judgement, not faith.'

'In what way?'

'You and Giles Stanton are both accustomed to making decisions which affect the lives of others—quick decisions, made in wartime conditions. About soldiers. Men.'

'Yes, but I fail to see—'

'Wait a little, I am still working it out. You decided last night that Anna, my sister, my twin sister, could wait until you had first of all found Burrows, had then persuaded him to cooperate with you, then have him take you to Falkirk, then work out a way of rescuing Anna. You didn't consult me, you didn't let me take part, you expected me to sit back and do nothing! Philip, I _could not_ sit back and do nothing while such a lengthy process was unwinding! Anna needed my help. She was only in Falkirk's hands because she had recognised my need for help this spring—long before I met you. I would have gone mad sitting here in Arlington Street, wondering what was happening. And...I'm sorry if this offends you...I thought you were wrong not to let me assist you.'

Rosabelle paused, but there was no reaction. She went on, 'I'm not a child, not a doll. I love my sister. This was the quickest way to rescue her, so I set about doing it. But to say that I didn't trust you is foolish. I put my whole life, and Anna's, too, in your hands... Can't you see that?'

She waited again, and this time when he didn't speak she went over to him. 'I love you, Philip. And six months ago I could not have done what I did this morning. I was too weak, too cowardly. You have given me the confidence I need, the trust in another human being, which is as necessary to me as breath. I'm not brave like Anna. I haven't her initiative. I need someone to love me…perhaps have faith in me… Then I can do anything, even…even use my own judgement. Don't deprive me of that—it's your greatest gift to me. Apart from your love.' Her voice broke on these words.

Philip gathered her into his arms. 'Rosa, Rosa, Rosa! Don't! You don't have to say any more! You're right! I'm an unfeeling monster. I should have realised what a bond there is between you and Anna. I was wrong. I promise, I don't regard you as a child—or as a doll. And I never will. To me you're a lovely, passionate woman— my treasure, my friend, my counsellor…and my adored wife. If you will still have me?'

'Oh, yes, Philip! Please!'

'When?'

At this point the door handle rattled and Emily came into the room. 'Colonel Stanton has left,' she said calmly, 'and your sister has been bathed and bandaged and is now asleep, I hope. I thought you must have had time to settle your quarrel by now, and I am come to play propriety. You've been alone long enough. Besides, I shall *die* of curiosity if someone doesn't tell me soon what happened today! But don't start yet! I've had some food put out in the dining room, and we can talk in there. Grandpapa is there already.'

When they had gathered in the dining room, Philip said, 'Before I begin, Grandfather, I want to tell you that Rosa and I are now at liberty to publish our engagement. I hope she will agree to marry me as soon as we can arrange a date.'

Lord Winbolt was delighted and supported this scheme with all his heart. Emily pulled the bell and Maynard came in with a bottle of champagne. 'I thought we might be needing it,' said Emily with a satisfied smile. 'But you must not think of marrying before next Easter!'

'Easter!' Philip was appalled.

'It would be just one year since you met. And if you think an important wedding such as yours can be arranged in a day or two—or even a month or two—you are very much mistaken! What about the bride clothes and all the other preparations?' Emily regarded the expression of outrage on her brother's face with some amusement. She turned to Rosabelle. 'Rosa will agree with me, I am sure.'

Having noticed the twinkle in Emily's eye, Rosabelle was emboldened to reply, 'I should think Easter would be almost too soon...'

'Oh, no!' said Philip with decision. 'I might, I just might, wait till Twelfth Night. But not a week longer. Don't tempt me too far, or I shall take you up before me on my stallion and whistle you off to Gretna tomorrow!'

'You're all talking a great deal of nonsense!' said Lord Winbolt irritably. 'Rosa must decide a time to suit the greatest number of people. I take it that the wedding will take place in Berkshire?'

'I would like that,' said Rosabelle.

'Very well. It looks as if I shall be seeing Shearings again before I die, after all. But I can't promise to wait too long. I may get a more pressing invitation.'

'The weather is always worse in January or February, Rosa,' said Philip persuasively. 'I think Grandfather should come down, at his leisure, but as soon as possible.'

'Christmas would be nice…' said Rosabelle pensively.

'Rosa!' shrieked Emily. 'Your clothes!'

'She only needs one dress in which to marry,' said Philip. 'It can't take long to make one dress.'

The issue was never seriously in doubt. It was soon settled that the wedding of Rosabelle Ordway to Lord Winbolt's heir would take place at Christmas, or very soon after.

'I shall tell Anna as soon as she wakes up,' said Rosabelle happily.

Annabelle swore that the news was the one thing to cause her to forget headache, bruise, sore throat and all the rest. For the rest of the day, she, Rosabelle and Emily spent a very happy time planning the celebrations.

'Rosa! What a wonderful Christmas Temperley will have once more! We must consult Becky. She can remember all the things our parents and grandparents did! Oh, it will be exciting beyond anything! A wedding at Christmas!'

Emily went off to arrange for more samples to be sent from Harding Howells, and to gather together all the copies of *The Ladies Magazine*, *La Belle Assemblée*, *The Cabinet of Fashion*, and others that she could find. The sisters were left alone.

They talked for a while of life at Temperley and Shearings, then Rosabelle asked, somewhat hesitantly, 'And what about you, Anna? Might there be another wedding at Christmas?'

The colour rose in Annabelle's cheeks, but she said composedly enough, 'I very much doubt it. I should need a husband, for a start.'

'And what about Giles Stanton?'

'Most unlikely! We seem to fall out with shocking regularity.'

'He seemed quite attentive yesterday.'

'Was he?' The colour in Annabelle's cheeks increased. 'But no! Let's just say that I shall be your bridesmaid, and hold your bouquet for you. Perhaps Philip will mistake me for you, and I shall have a rich husband after all!'

Annabelle refused to allow her sister to question her further on her relationship with Giles Stanton.

Indeed, the next day it appeared that there was more than one gentleman in London eager to pursue the lovely 'Mrs Ordway'.

When the first bouquet arrived, Rosa was excited and flattered—until she read the note attached to it.

'Who on earth is Peter Wainwright?' she asked. 'I seem to have made something of a hit with him, but I have no idea where!'

'He'd better take care!' said Philip. 'His admiration is natural, I understand it perfectly well. But he must learn to keep his flowers and his feelings to himself! Or find another object of his admiration.'

'Er…in fact, I think that the flowers are intended for me,' said Annabelle, in a little embarrassment. 'Colonel Wainwright was quite attentive before we went to Buxton. He must have learned I am in London again.'

Philip and Rosabelle exchanged a look. 'I see,' said Rosa slowly.

When a second floral tribute for Mrs Ordway arrrived, Rosabelle was better prepared. 'Colonel Wainwright appears to have a rival,' she said. 'Does ''Richard Pettifer'' mean anything to you, Anna?'

'Oh, yes! Captain Pettifer was very flattering. I think

he was the one who compared my eyes with bluebells—
or was that Major Dabney?'

'Annabelle! Were you a flirt?'

'Of course not! I was a "success", that's all. And you
have no idea how very pleasant it was to be in demand,
to wear beautiful clothes, to be complimented on my
appearance or the grace of my dancing! Most of it sheer-
est flattery, of course, but a welcome change from a life
in obscurity at Temperley, listening to compliments on
the yields of my tenants' fields, or the good condition of
the fences—or otherwise,' she added with a sly look at
Philip.

'Oh, those fences!' Rosabelle exclaimed in horror. 'If
you only knew how much trouble I had over those
fences!'

But a more serious contender for Annabelle's favours
appeared later in the day. Lord Monteith called, a most
eligible young man, the son of an Earl and heir to handsome estates in the West Country. But Annabelle refused
to see him, pleading that she was not strong enough for
visitors. Emily dealt with him, and he eventually left, but
he was not happy. It isn't often that such an important
young man is denied access to the lady of his choice.
But Annabelle appeared indifferent. She seemed to be
waiting for someone else.

# *Chapter Sixteen*

It was perhaps unfortunate that Colonel Stanton should appear just as Lord Monteith was taking his leave. However, Maynard took in the situation and showed the new caller into the library until his lordship departed. Giles was then taken to the small parlour where Annabelle was waiting…

When Rosabelle came into the parlour some time later she found the air bristling with hostility. 'Oh,' she said blankly, 'I thought I'd find Philip and Emily here. Forgive me.' And she made to go out again.

'Pray do not feel you have to go, Rosa,' said Annabelle in a high, brittle voice, quite unlike her usual tones. 'Colonel Stanton was just leaving.'

Giles Stanton's countenance grew even more forbidding. 'Annabelle—' he began.

'If you do not leave this room, sir, then I will!'

'In that case there is no more to be said,' he said furiously. 'Goodbye, Miss Kelland.' He turned and gave a brief bow in Rosabelle's direction, 'Rosabelle,' and strode out. There was complete silence in the room for a moment or two.

Then Rosabelle asked, 'May I…dare I ask what that was all about?'

Annabelle, twin flags of anger flying in her cheeks, exploded. 'Giles Stanton is an unfeeling, arrogant oaf! And I hope never to see him again!'

'Anna, he—'

'I refuse to discuss him, or anything connected with him, Rosa! If you wish to please me, you will not even mention his name. I do not wish to hear it.'

And Annabelle continued to be adamant. When Rosabelle, Philip, or anyone else brought the name of Giles Stanton into the conversation Annabelle simply fell silent until the discussion was over.

The rest of November was spent in London in a flurry of mantua-makers, drapers' shops, haberdashery stores, shoemakers, grocery supplies—three months' work crammed into three weeks. Rosabelle was in a happy daze for most of the time. She stood in a dream while Madame Fanchon or one of her assistants fitted and pinned and pulled. It was fortunate that she had Annabelle and Emily to keep her feet somewhere near the ground, for the wedding clothes would otherwise never have been finished.

Because of sundry delays, it was the second week in December before they got away, though there had been much to-ing and fro-ing between London and Berkshire in the meantime. They travelled in convoy down the Bath Road, with a large escort of grooms and postilions to see to their safety and comfort, and took the journey

at a leisurely pace, spending a night on the way, so that
Lord Winbolt should not get overtired. They were fortunate with the weather—the fog had completely disappeared, and though the days were cold, they were crisp
and bright. As a result the roads were dry and travel easy.
But though the sun sparkled on the traces of frost on the
trees and on the waters of the rivers they crossed, nothing
could rival the sparkle of eyes, laughter and wit as the
wedding party made its way to Temperley and Shearings.

At Temperley Becky was waiting with jugs of mulled
ale and spiced wine for everyone. Mr Kelland was downstairs with Aunt Laura, and the house fairly buzzed with
excitement and activity. As the little convoy wound its
way up the drive, children of the workers from both estates ran alongside, waving streamers and branches of
evergreen.

'Papa! Aunt Laura! Becky!' There were scenes of confused laughter, and many embraces, as both sisters were
welcomed back to Temperley. Philip waited with the second carriage, until some of the tumult had subsided, then
he gave a sign to one of the grooms to assist Emily and
Lord Winbolt out, and the three Winbolts walked forward. Some complicated introductions followed, then the
family party repaired to the large parlour, which was so
vast that it was hardly ever used. But Becky had seen to
it that the room was warm with huge fires burning at
each end, the flames bathing the panelled walls, plaster
ceiling and heavy furniture in a mellow glow.

'Now this is something!' said Lord Winbolt. 'None of
your fingle-fangling decoration here. Good honest wood
and plasterwork.' He sat down with a sigh of satisfaction
on a large armchair, made to accommodate the more
elaborate clothes of the previous century.

Philip smiled at Rosabelle. 'I can see he is going to

be hard on me for the alterations we've had done at Shearings!'

'I like them. Oh, Philip, we're home at last! I can't tell you how content I am!'

'Well, I'm not! Not yet. There's still the little matter of our wedding. And then I'll take you home. To our home.' He raised her hand to his lips and kissed it, his eyes never leaving hers.

'I can't help it,' said Lady Ordway, raising a hand-kerchief to her eyes. 'It's so lovely to see two young people so much in love.'

'Yes,' said Mr Kelland briskly. 'But do not, I pray, let us get sentimental. There is far too much to think of. Can anyone tell me exactly when the wedding is to be? Or is that asking too much?'

'I would marry your daughter tomorrow, sir. I have the licence.'

'I wish you would, Winbolt—it would save a lot of fuss. But I doubt we'll get away with that.'

'We shall be married during the twelve days of Christmas, Papa.'

'Well then, why not start the New Year together? Have the wedding on the thirty-first of December. That gives you all three weeks to settle in after your journey, send off invitations and announcements and there will still be time to enjoy Christmas. I'm assuming the licence is a special one, Winbolt, and that you can choose your own day.'

This idea met with general approval, and they began to discuss who else was to be invited.

Eventually the Winbolts set off to complete their journey to Shearings, and the Kelland family party were left alone.

'Is there…is there anyone else you would wish to invite, Anna?' asked Rosabelle.

'I don't think so,' her sister replied, listlessly. 'You've mentioned all the local people who should come. And there certainly isn't anyone else.'

Rosabelle looked at her in concern. For days Annabelle had joked and laughed with the rest, teasing Philip, conversing with Lady Ordway with whom she appeared to have a very good relationship, and adding to the general gaiety. But she had been unable to hide her unhappiness from her twin. Rosabelle wondered whether the rough treatment Annabelle had suffered at the hands of Falkirk and his gang was having a belated effect, and asked if her sister was well, but Anna replied, 'Of course I am! Pray don't worry about me, Rosa. I shall soon come about.'

Busy as Rosabelle was exchanging visits with neighbours, spending time at Shearings with Philip planning the household there, and, of course, working with Annabelle, Becky and the rest at Temperley, she still found time to keep a close watch on Annabelle. Annabelle did not seem to her to be 'coming about'. She talked to Philip about it.

'It's Giles Stanton, Philip, I'm sure of it.'

'So am I. What is more, I'm positive that Giles is as unhappy as your sister.'

'Then why don't they make it up?'

'How can they? They never meet. And unless something is done about it, pride and obstinacy will keep them apart permanently.'

'You're speaking very plainly about my sister, Philip.'

'I admire your sister a great deal, but I'm not sure she is the soul of forgiveness and patience. And Giles has always been pig-headed, though he usually comes round in the end.' Philip gave her a look. 'Shall I leave the matter in your hands?'

'For the moment, perhaps.'

A few days later the sisters were sitting alone in the little parlour. Aunt Laura was resting, and Mr Kelland was reading, as usual. Rosabelle took a deep breath and said carefully, 'Anna, I'm sure Philip would like Giles St—'

'No!'

'My dear, I can't carry on not mentioning Giles! He is Aunt Laura's nephew, and one of Philip's best friends. Why do you dislike him so?'

'Not even Samuel Carter at his worst ever spoke to me as that man has! You have no idea how unreasonable and…and cruel he can be,' Annabelle said bitterly.

'Believe me, I have. You forget that I knew him before you! But this is the season when we should forget and forgive past insults and injuries. I can't bear to see you so unhappy. Let me invite him to the wedding—you needn't speak to him, if you really don't wish to.'

'You're mistaken, Rosa. It is Colonel Stanton who would not speak to me! On the last occasion we met, he made his opinion of me perfectly clear! I am beneath his contempt. But I can do very well without him!'

'I'm sure you could, dear. But would you really object if I sent him an invitation?'

'I've told you a hundred times, Rosa! I do not wish ever to see that monster again!' Annabelle paused, then said, 'Besides, I don't expect he would come.'

Rosabelle said nothing more, but instead asked Annabelle to enlist Becky's aid in decorating the house. This she did, and soon all Becky's memories of how the

old house had been dressed for Christmas were revived
and followed.

On Christmas Eve the snow began to fall, large, gentle
flakes of white, floating on to the shoulders of the singers
as they wound their way through the village and up to
Temperley.

'Do you remember last Christmas, Miss Annabelle?'
said Becky. 'We had snow then, too.'

'But this year we're having a real Christmas, Becky,
darling. Everyone is here, and the house looks just as it
should.'

Annabelle looked at the ivy, the holly, the fir branches,
sniffed the air scented with spices and the fresh tang of
the greenery. Everything was now in place. The party
from Shearings had arrived that afternoon, and would
stay till after the wedding. The larders were piled high
with food for the feast, and fires were lit in every room.
The sound of church bells wafted in through the snow-
laden air.

She smiled as she observed Rosabelle and Philip,
about to come downstairs after an hour with her father.
They stood framed in an arch of greenery at the top of
the staircase, pausing for a moment, lost to the world.
She sighed and turned away. Such moments were private, not to be stared at, not to have their glory diminished by sadness or envy.

Christmas Eve passed in a flurry of activity, and
Christmas Day was already an hour old when the church
party returned to Temperley. Lady Ordway, Lord
Winbolt and Mr Kelland had elected to stay behind in
the house, but Philip had escorted the three girls through
the snow to the late night service. Though it had stopped

snowing several hours before, the paths and lanes were covered, and the four young people had slipped and slithered back to the house. There was much laughter and high spirits when they came into the hall, until they remembered that the older generation had probably retired.

'I'm quite tired, too,' said Rosabelle. 'There's a great deal to do tomorrow.'

'I'll see you to your room,' said Philip.

As they went up the stairs, Philip said, 'I was wrong, it appears. Giles is implacable.'

'I did write. But he won't come now. And the snow has made it impossible, anyway,' Rosa said sadly.

'You did your best, my heart. Don't be sad. There's so much to be happy about. It's less than a week now, then I won't have to say goodnight at your door.' He bent his head. Then lifted it as a sound of coughing came up the stairs. He looked at Rosabelle and said ruefully, 'Sisters! Poor Emily is afflicted with her cough again. If she doesn't see about it soon, I will! Goodnight, my love.'

'You haven't long to wait now, Philip, dear,' said Emily behind them. 'Someone has to see that you behave—we can't have Rosa falling by the wayside at this late stage!'

'Sometimes, Emily, you go too far! I was merely kissing, yes, kissing my betrothed goodnight. And with three of you all sleeping in the same bedroom, seduction would be well nigh impossible! I know my limitations.'

'Spare your bride's blushes and go to bed! Goodnight, Philip, dear.' She kissed him and, raising an eyebrow at Rosabelle, went on into the bedroom.

Philip kissed Rosabelle tenderly and dragged himself away. The house grew quiet again.

Annabelle slowly mounted the stairs. It was all just as

she had pictured it exactly one year ago. The stairs were
wound with holly and ivy, and there was mistletoe in the
hall. Tonight there had been the sounds of footsteps and
suppressed laughter on the landing as the others had bade
each other goodnight, and now here at the top of the
stairs she could hear whispers and the rustle of silk and
taffeta. Even the scents of perfume and lavender, honey
and beeswax were as she had imagined them.

But hall and stairs were empty of any tall, dark-haired
beau to be King to her Queen of the Revels. There was
still no one to come in through the door, to tell her how
lovely she looked, to invite her to a ball or some other
revelry in the neighbourhood. And now there never
would be. Her own foolish, self-willed behaviour had
seen to that. She turned slowly towards the bedchamber...

There was suddenly a thunderous knocking at the
door. Becky and John Bostock came hurrying through
from the kitchen. When they saw Annabelle at the top
of the stairs Becky paused and asked, 'What shall I do,
Miss Belle?'

'You'd better open it, Becky. It's late, but it's no night
to leave a traveller outside.'

Annabelle waited halfway down the stairs, her heart
in her mouth as Becky opened the door, and she heard
a deep voice say, 'Miss Kelland?'

\*   \*   \*   \*   \*

# ANNABELLE

# *Chapter One*

*London—May 1819*

The carriage turned left into Park Lane at a spanking pace. Goss was doing what he could to make up for lost time. Annabelle Kelland held on to the strap and shut her eyes, but as soon as the carriage straightened its course she opened them again. This was an exciting moment, and she did not want to miss any part of it. The road was bustling with vehicles and people of every sort—gentlemen in curricles, on horseback, ladies in phaetons and barouches, street vendors with baskets and carts…the noise was deafening to ears accustomed to quiet country lanes. She was in London at last!

She gazed out at the busy, colourful scene. For these last few minutes she could still allow herself to be Annabelle Kelland, Rosabelle Ordway's identical twin, hardly able to contain her excitement at visiting London

for the first time in her life. Just a few minutes longer.
For, when the carriage finally drew up at Lady Ordway's
house in Upper Brook Street, Annabelle Kelland would
disappear and Lady Ordway's quiet daughter-in-law,
Rosabelle, would emerge from the carriage—young Mrs
Stephen Ordway, widowed but a year ago, returning to
London after spending a month in Berkshire with her
family.

Annabelle sat back against the cushions and tried to
look calm. If she was to convince the people in Upper
Brook Street that she was indeed her sister, then she
would have to keep a tight rein on her feelings. No excessive curiosity, no amazement at the sights of the great
city. Her sister Rosabelle had lived in London for the
past sixteen years, ever since Lady Ordway, who was
her godmother, had unofficially adopted her and brought
her here to live. Rosabelle had ended up marrying the
son of the house, and, as Lady Ordway's daughter-in-
law, she must have become very familiar with fashionable life in London. There was nothing new or particularly intriguing for *her* in the Polite World going about
its business.

So, for the next four or five weeks, while Rosabelle
continued her convalescence in the tranquillity of
Berkshire, independent, country-bred Annabelle would
have to adopt her sister's graceful manners and quiet
ways... She was confident that she could do it, though
it wouldn't be easy. But—she leant forward again and
gazed out of the carriage window—just for these last few
moments she would be herself, Annabelle Kelland still,
peering out uninhibitedly at the lively scene before her,
admiring the fashionable crowds as they paraded in Hyde
Park.

Another smart turn, this time to the right, a trot

through a street lined with large houses…they had almost arrived! The carriage drew to a halt before one of the larger houses, and even before it stopped Goss had leapt out and was opening the door for her. This, then, was the Ordway residence in Upper Brook Street. The charade was about to begin…

Goss was looking worried as he helped her out, and kept throwing anxious glances at the windows.

'What is it, Goss?'

'Nothing, ma'am. Nothing at all. I expect the Colonel is inside.'

'The Colonel?'

'Colonel Stanton, ma'am. He's…he's a bit of a stickler for punctuality.'

'Indeed? An admirable quality,' Annabelle said as she went up the steps. Then she forgot Goss and concentrated on the task before her. Rosabelle's careful coaching was about to have its first test. The stately fellow coming towards her must be Lady Ordway's butler. She hesitated for only a second, then took a deep breath and moved forward.

'Good evening, Whitcroft. What a lovely day it has been!'

'Good evening, Mrs Ordway. Indeed it has. I trust you had a pleasant journey?' The butler's wrinkled face was wreathed in smiles, and Annabelle relaxed a little. The first hurdle had been successfully cleared. Whitcroft had been with the family for years—and had known Rosabelle since she had first come to London. To be accepted by him so unquestioningly was very encouraging.

She smiled back and said, 'Very pleasant, thank you. How is Lady Ordway?'

'Better, ma'am. Her ladyship is expecting you.'

Annabelle walked through the door, and gazed round her as if glad to be back. Yes, it was all as she had pictured. A spacious hall, paved in marble, with a handsome staircase winding its way up on the left. To the right a door, surrounded with a beautifully carved case. The dining room. In the shadows beyond the stairs the library. And at the top of the stairs the drawing room. Lady Ordway's room was another flight up… She turned to go up to it, but had only ascended a step or two when a voice came from along the hall.

'Whitcroft, get Goss for me, will you? Before he goes to the stables with the carriage. I want a word with him.'

The voice was brisk, but deep and attractive. The speaker had just emerged from the library. He was in shadow, but as he came forward and paused to speak to the butler, Annabelle stopped and caught her breath. A handsome man in his thirties, tall, loose-limbed, clean-shaven, his black hair cut fashionably short… Discipline and determination were evident in the firm mouth and the strong line of the jaw, but it was a good face, with plenty of humour and intelligence in it.

Was this…*could* this be the infamous Giles Stanton? The monster whose brutally unsympathetic attitude to Rosabelle had caused her breakdown? Whose harsh insistence that she was to return to London today had resulted in Annabelle's offer to come in her sister's place? Surely not!

Rosabelle's account of him had led her to picture a middle-aged Colonel in the Duke of Wellington's service—a rigid disciplinarian, coldly issuing his orders and his criticisms, bullying poor Rosabelle till her nerves had been reduced to tatters… She had been quite certain he would have a leathery, weatherbeaten face, a soldier's face, complete with grey side-whiskers and a military moustache. She hadn't imagined anything like this!

It was fortunate that the gentleman's attention was on Whitcroft, for otherwise he must surely have wondered what was wrong with her. But she was quite unable to move. Fascinated, her hand on the newel post, one foot on the first stair, her other on the second, she stared at this elegant man of fashion, impeccably dressed for the evening. You couldn't say he was a dandy, though he was obviously a man of wealth. His beautifully fitted coat lay smoothly over the broad shoulders, but the cut was plain, and though his linen was snowy white, there was an absence of any fuss and frills, a pleasing lack of ostentation. And she had to say that he didn't appear to be a tyrant at first sight—his manner to Whitcroft was authoritative, but easy, and that voice was very attractive...

Whitcroft went out and Giles Stanton turned his attention to Annabelle. In spite of her raised position their eyes were on a level. Hazel eyes, a curious mixture of tawny gold and green...

'Good evening, Rosabelle. I thought you'd be here before this. I sent the carriage early enough.'

The voice had changed—no warmth or flexibility in it for her.

'What's wrong? Have you left your tongue in Berkshire?' Annabelle swallowed and tried to think of something to say, but he sighed impatiently and went on without waiting. 'When you've finished staring at me as if I'd grown two heads, you had better visit Aunt Laura. She too has been expecting you for hours. Where the devil have you been?'

Annabelle suddenly came to her senses. Now that sounded *much* more like the creature of her imagination.

For all his pleasing appearance she had not been so far out, after all! Overcoming a slight feeling of disappointment she surveyed him more calmly. So this was Giles Stanton, Stephen's cousin and heir, now in control of the enormous Ordway fortune. What a very ill-mannered way to greet his cousin's widow, newly returned after a month in the country! Resisting the temptation to reply in kind, she took a deep breath and said sweetly, 'Good evening, Giles. Thank you—I had a pleasant journey, and feel remarkably fresh. I enjoyed my stay at Temperley enormously. How are you?'

Hazel eyes looked at her coldly. 'We'll go through the niceties of conversation later—I have an appointment in ten minutes. Where *is* Goss?'

'May I have a word with you before you see Goss?' When he looked as if he might refuse, she added firmly, 'Please.'

'Very well.' He led the way to the room at the back— he didn't believe in wasting time, that was obvious. Though he was dressed to go out for the evening, the table was scattered with papers which he must have been studying until the carriage arrived. He ushered her in, then turned and waited. What a pity the expression on his face was so very disagreeable! Such a pity... Annabelle pulled herself together.

'If you are about to blame Goss for not being here earlier, you would be unjust.'

'What on earth do you mean? Goss had the express commission to see that you arrived in good time. He set off more than early enough this morning. You are an hour or more overdue. Of course he's to blame!'

His tone of impatient dismissal irritated her. 'I think your experiences in the Army may have prepared you ill for normal travel, Giles. This was not a military expedition, nor was Goss overseeing a baggage train! He did his best to do as you had…commanded. I am sure he is not an unkind man, but he was so anxious not to fail you, that he would have brought me to London—a journey of over forty miles—with no opportunity for rest or comfort on the way.'

'That cannot be so. I allowed plenty of time for stops!'

'That must be a matter of opinion. Five minutes or so to change the horses may be an estimable aim in Army life, but I assure you, it is not the norm in civilised society. Certainly not for me. Goss told me what you had ordered, but I insisted on adequate time for refreshment at every stop. He could do nothing about it.'

For the life of her Annabelle could not resist a slight note of satisfaction creeping in to her tone. Once Goss had told her of 'the Colonel's' orders, she had taken pleasure in spending much longer than necessary at the inns, determined to prove that 'the Colonel' could not order *her* about as he chose!

The satisfaction did not escape Giles's notice. His eyes narrowed, then his expression grew even more forbidding. Annabelle raised her chin and stared back at him bravely, but she was secretly puzzled by his reaction to her. He was not just simply annoyed. He quite clearly disliked his cousin's widow, but *why*? Rosabelle was such a gentle, inoffensive creature… Sooner or later, Annabelle promised herself, she would find out what lay behind this antagonism—and then she would make him pay for his treatment of her twin. He was still looking at her, as if debating whether to pursue the matter, but he eventually turned towards the door, simply saying as he went, 'You'd better see Aunt Laura.'

Annabelle stood her ground. 'Goss is not to blame!'

'Very well, very well. Let me deal with my servant in

my own manner, if you please. You may spend as long
as you like with Aunt Laura—I shall be out for the rest
of the evening.'

'Thank you, Giles,' said Annabelle. At the irony in
her voice he turned and she suffered another inspection
from those cold, keen hazel eyes. But once again he decided to say nothing, and simply ushered her out. A few
minutes later, as she was ascending the stairs, she heard
Goss's anxious voice in the hall, followed by a brisk
reply. She permitted herself a small smile at his words.

'Nonsense, Goss. You did surprisingly well. I had forgotten the allowances we have to make for the ladies.
You'd better make sure the horses are seen to, I expect
you've been pushing them. And now I'll have to hurry—
the Duke doesn't like to be kept waiting any more than
I do.'

Annabelle opened the door of what she hoped was
Lady Ordway's bedchamber and went in. Heavy curtains
were half-pulled across the window and the room was in
semi-darkness, and she waited for a moment, letting her
eyes accustom themselves to the dim light. The atmosphere was stifling. A maidservant was remonstrating
with a figure in a chair by the window, but was being
ignored. Lady Ordway was getting up, arms stretched out
in welcome.

'Rosa! You're back! My darling girl!'

'Aunt Laura!' Annabelle hesitated, for the first time
feeling some qualms about her imposture. Her sister's
mother-in-law had changed almost beyond recognition
in the years since she had last seen her. It was cruel to
deceive this frail, elderly woman, who was clearly so
deeply moved at the thought of seeing her beloved
daughter-in-law again. But she must do so, just for a few

moments. To tell her the truth without warning would be equally cruel. She walked over to the window and gently embraced Lady Ordway. After a moment she was released, and the invalid settled back into her chair. Annabelle found she was being closely surveyed.

'You are looking well, my dear. Temperley has been good for you. Have you dined?'

'Not yet, though I had something on the way. I only arrived five minutes ago.'

'I know. I heard the carriage. I expect you would like to change after the journey, but we could have something to eat here together afterwards. Wilson will arrange it, won't you, Wilson?'

'Of course, my lady. Welcome back, Miss Rosabelle.' With a smile and a curtsy the maid disappeared.

There was a short silence then Lady Ordway said carefully, 'Do you know where your room is, my dear?'

'Yes, I... Aunt Laura! What do you mean? Of course I do—unless you've changed it.'

'Ah, yes. I suppose Rosa would have taught you all about the house and servants. Tell me—she...she isn't still ill, is she?'

Annabelle regarded Lady Ordway in amazement. 'You know! So soon? How?'

'You are so like her, Anna! But I knew the moment you touched me. How could I possibly not know? Rosa has been a daughter to me for the last sixteen years. We have always been very close—ever since I brought her here after your mother's death. And...and this last year has brought us even closer. Do tell me. Rosa *is* getting better, isn't she?'

'She's doing very well. But it was much too soon for her to come back. I'd say she needs another month at least. She was so...fragile when she arrived—we were very worried about her. But Temperley is doing her so much good—it's peaceful there, and Becky spoils her shamefully!'

'I've worried about her, too. I...I wouldn't blame her if she never wanted to see this house again.'

'No, no! You mustn't say that. Rosa loves you. Indeed, she was so concerned for you that I had to work very hard to persuade her to stay in Berkshire and let me come in her place. She has written to you to explain.' Annabelle passed a letter to Lady Ordway, who opened it eagerly.

Annabelle smiled sympathetically and went on, 'Shall I leave you to read it, while I change? I feel rather travel-worn.'

'Thank you, my dear. And after you've changed you shall come back to dine with me so we can talk. Wilson will see that one of the new maids is sent to help you. Wilson will arrange it all—I rely on her for everything. And she is the soul of discretion. Off you go, my dear. Half an hour?'

'I'll be back as soon as I can. And...Lady Ordway...'

'Yes?'

'I'll do my best to be a substitute for Rosa.'

'Be yourself. That will be enough. Half an hour.'

Annabelle thought for a moment, then walked confidently along the landing to her room. She found Wilson already there.

'Your valises are here, Miss Rosabelle. Lily will be along in a minute or two, and she'll unpack them. She's new, but she seems to know what she's about, which is more than can be said for most of the young ones nowadays. She might suit you. I've had one of the dresses you left here freshly ironed. It's hanging in the closet. Now, if you'll excuse me, I'll see to her ladyship.'

'Wilson, how is Lady Ordway really? She still looks ill.'

'Oh, no! She is much better than she was. She was a little depressed after you went away, Miss Rosabelle. But the Colonel...I mean the master, has spent a lot of time with her—he's been very kind.'

'He has?'

'Oh, yes. And truly, Miss Rosabelle, she is a lot stronger. But she...she needs to be taken out of herself.'

'We'll have to see what can be done.'

'I'm sure your return has done her good already, ma'am.'

'Thank you, Wilson.'

The new maid appeared as Wilson was leaving, and with her aid Annabelle changed the clothes she had travelled in for a pretty muslin dress in palest lilac. Lily was not a chatterer and Annabelle had plenty of time for reflection. It seemed to her that her stay in London could bring benefit to more than Rosabelle and herself. She thought that Lady Ordway had been immured for far too long in that dim, stuffy room, with nothing to think of but the sadnesses of the past. Fresh company and new thoughts might rouse her a little. Rosabelle had possibly been over-protective of her. It was a year since Stephen had died, and his mother should now be persuaded to take a greater part in the world. What better reason than that Annabelle wished to see something of London Society during her month in London?

When Annabelle presented herself for dinner she saw that a table had been set up for them in the middle of Lady Ordway's room.

'This is really very pleasant,' said Lady Ordway. 'I've been eating from a tray, either in bed or in my chair for so long.'

'You haven't begun dining downstairs yet?'

'I…I haven't managed to face it yet, Anna. I don't know if I ever shall.'

Annabelle eyed Lady Ordway. The last years had taken their toll, but she was still a pretty woman. 'I'm sure you will in time. And now I'm here, I'll help you. By the time Rosabelle comes back, you will both be ready to face the world again, I promise you.'

'I failed her so badly, Anna. I wouldn't blame her if she never came back.'

'I assure you, Rosabelle would be here this very moment if I hadn't persuaded her to stay in Berkshire.'

'But, Anna, I don't quite understand. It's very pleasant to have company, and I am delighted to see you again after all these years, but…why did Rosa feel it necessary to send you in her place? Why the deception? I am sure that Giles would have let her stay longer had she explained.'

'Rosa was quite sure he wouldn't! In fact, he said he would fetch her himself if she didn't come back today. She didn't think he would accept me as a substitute, either, so…we decided that I should pretend to be her.'

'But I hardly believe…' Lady Ordway paused for thought. 'He can be a little overbearing, I suppose…he always has such a clear idea of what he wants done, and he gets impatient with delay. I think he frightens Rosabelle. She's such a gentle creature.'

'And he's a bully!'

'No, no, my dear. You mustn't believe that! It's just that he's been so overworked this past year—he hasn't had time for niceties.'

Annabelle took time to reply to this. She would have rather said that Giles Stanton's attitude to Rosabelle revealed a chilling lack of humanity. Before being allowed

to go to Berkshire, her poor sister had been harassed and
bullied until she had given a promise to return exactly
one month later. Giles had made it clear that, unless she
did, he would refuse to pay Stephen's debts, and that she
and Lady Ordway would consequently be faced with
penury! Lack of nicety, indeed! He might have been
bluffing, she supposed, but to someone in her sister's
state it had been sheer cruelty!

However, though Annabelle was sorely tempted, she
kept her thoughts to herself. It was obvious that
Rosabelle had not told her mother-in-law of Giles
Stanton's threats. And it was not for Annabelle to tell
her, either. So she didn't pursue the matter, but said instead, 'This sole is delicious. Is Mrs Brook still here? I
understand you have some new servants.'

'Yes. Wilson, Whitcroft and Mrs Brook are all that
are left of our old staff. All the others went after…after
Stephen died. But Giles has recently engaged a new
housekeeper, and three new maids.'

'Personally?' asked Annabelle, surprised. 'I should
have thought that was hardly an occupation for "the
Colonel"! It should have been Rosa's responsibility, if,
as I understand it, she is to run the household for him.'

'He used an agency. I have to say that they seem very
satisfactory. And dear Giles is so considerate of her.'

'Considerate! Of Rosa?'

'Yes. I am sure he wanted to save her the trouble of
having to set about engaging servants the minute she got
back. And managing with such a small staff as we had
was very difficult.'

'All the same,' said Annabelle, the light of battle in
her eye, 'it would have been more tactful if Giles had
waited till Rosa's return. It was very high-handed of
him.'

Lady Ordway regarded her with a smile. 'You haven't changed, Anna. You were always ready to do battle on Rosa's behalf. And I won't deny that Giles can be high-handed. It comes of having a successful career in the Army. But in this case I'm sure he meant it for the best.'

Annabelle was by no means so sure. The dislike in Giles's eyes had been very obvious. 'You don't think that…?' she began delicately. 'Might Rosa not have felt it showed some lack of trust in her judgement?'

Lady Ordway sighed and said slowly, 'It's difficult to say—I suppose it might. Especially as she is so unsure of herself. Anna, what has Rosa told you? About…about Stephen…and our life here?'

'She said she had given her word to you to say nothing to anyone about Stephen himself. And she didn't. But all the same, it is clear to me that she has been under stress for a long time. She could hardly avoid revealing the difficulties you were both in during the last twelve months. And that included some of her own problems with Giles Stanton.'

'She kept it all from me, you know. I suppose she thought I was too ill. I thought he was simply being…'

'High-handed.'

'Exactly.'

It was clear that Lady Ordway still had a high regard for her nephew—and, if what Wilson had said was true, he had indeed been very kind to her. So Annabelle said casually, 'It might well have been that. Are you very disappointed not to see Rosa?'

'A little. But I am delighted to see you—especially if it means that Rosa will be properly cured before she comes back. I recommended a longer stay, you know. I even suggested this switch between you myself, though

I confess I was not entirely serious!' Lady Ordway smiled. 'But it isn't as if you have never done it before.'

Annabelle grinned, then looked guilty. 'But that was when we were children. And it was only meant to tease. We've never done it in earnest before.'

'No. Are you proposing to sustain your role until Rosa returns?'

'You mean not to tell ''the Colonel''? I…I would prefer not to. But it has to depend on you, Lady Ordway. I couldn't do it without your help.'

Annabelle waited in suspense while Lady Ordway considered. She was quite determined to fight for her sister's interests. And, if necessary, she was even prepared to open Lady Ordway's eyes to Giles Stanton's true character. But to her relief there was no need for such drastic measures.

After a pause Lady Ordway said slowly, 'I think we shall keep it to ourselves, Anna. I am fond of Giles, and he has always been very kind to me. But he is a touch autocratic…he certainly doesn't like to be crossed. And he has always been somewhat critical of Rosa, even when she was a child. From what you said, it seems to have got worse, though no one ever talks about it now.'

'Why *should* he be critical of Rosa? I thought they had never met before he came back from France last year.'

'They hadn't. In the old days Giles stayed with us during the school holidays at exactly the same time as Rosa was spending the summer down at Temperley with you and your father. He never saw her then. And after that he was out of the country for ten years, all over Europe with the Army—Spain, Portugal, France, Vienna… He never even saw Rosa and Stephen after they were married.' Lady Ordway turned her head away.

'But he was always fond of Stephen, and Stephen...and Stephen idolised him.'

Annabelle put a sympathetic hand on Lady Ordway's arm. 'Don't talk of it if it upsets you—I'm here to help you forget. But just think! If I'm given a chance I might even manage to persuade Giles to change his opinion of Rosa. You know she would never stand up for herself. Could you...could you regard deceiving Giles as a kind of game? A challenge? Could you find it amusing?'

'Do you know, I think I could!' said Lady Ordway, cheering up a little. 'And then there would be no risk of his sending you back and demanding Rosa's return. Yes! I think I could!'

'Good! Then that is what we shall do. You, my dear Lady Ordway, are about to enjoy yourself.'

'Am I?' Lady Ordway smiled tremulously at Annabelle. 'Then welcome, my dear. You're very good to do this for your sister.'

'Don't credit me with too much virtue, Lady Ordway—'

'You'd better call me ''Aunt Laura'', or you'll soon be discovered,' said Lady Ordway, entering into the spirit of things. 'And I must remember to call you ''Rosa'' in public.'

'Very well...Aunt Laura! But I'm looking forward to seeing London while I am here. It's an exciting adventure for me! I'm not just helping Rosa, you know.'

'You will be careful with Giles, won't you, Anna?' said Lady Ordway with a sudden return to her former manner.

'In what way?'

'There are things I don't wish him to find out... You must be very careful.'

Annabelle was puzzled, but she did her best to reassure her hostess of her discretion, and then talked of other things. Quite soon she had her hostess laughing at her description of her ignorance of the rules of Society, and her lack of social graces.

'Surely not, surely not! It cannot be as bad as that. Even in Berkshire they must know more than that!' Then Lady Ordway pulled herself together and said, 'But just to make sure, we shall start a course tomorrow on how to behave, Anna, my dear. We can't have poor Rosa accused of forgetting all I taught her.'

'It won't tire you?' said Annabelle, pleased that Lady Ordway was taking such an interest, but surprised that she thought it so important. They would not, after all, be mixing so very much in society. And it was only for one month!

'Of course not! I shall enjoy it. And if Giles sticks to his intention of entertaining more, you will need to know what to do.'

'Entertaining more?' echoed Annabelle.

'Yes. That's why he has engaged all the new staff. And more are due later this week. Now that he is permanently in London he feels obliged to invite his friends here.'

'Permanently in London?' Annabelle stared. 'Permanently in London? You mean, from now? But Rosa said…Giles is surely going to France for the next month? That was why she had to come back today—to be company for you!'

'He has changed his plans. You, my dear, are going to see a great deal both of him, and of London society.' She looked at the appalled expression on Annabelle's face. 'Isn't that what you wanted?'

# Chapter Two

'Not...' Annabelle swallowed. 'Not quite. It's true that I wanted to see London. But I'm not sure I would have embarked on this adventure quite so gaily if I had known I should have to perform in front of Giles for a whole month! I thought we should be alone for most of the time.'

'Oh, I'm sure you'll manage, Anna! Come, my dear! This is not like you!'

'But...but I don't understand! If Giles is to be here all the time, why does he need Rosa?'

'He wants her to act as his hostess. I am not yet well enough.' She looked at Annabelle's stormy face. 'Don't be angry with him, Anna. He may be taking the opportunity to repay his friends' hospitality, but he is really staying in London for our sakes.'

'How very kind of him!' said Annabelle, without conviction. 'How is that?'

Lady Ordway remained patient. 'Giles has arranged to

stay in London chiefly because he wishes to get on with sorting out our affairs. Ordway affairs, I should say. It was urgently necessary. Stephen...Stephen left them in some disorder. And between that and the tasks remaining from his duties with Wellington, I don't believe he has stopped working since he arrived here. Rosa and I owe him a lot.'

Annabelle hardly heard her. The news that Giles Stanton was to remain in London in the foreseeable future was most unwelcome. She and Rosabelle had plotted their exchange on the basis that Giles was to be away, that he and Annabelle would hardly meet. 'He's really going to be here all the time? Here at the house, as well?'

'He has rooms in Mount Street, but he hardly ever uses them.' Lady Ordway looked surprised at the expression on Annabelle's face. 'After all, Anna, the house and most of the things in it are now his. He could have insisted that I remove elsewhere, and it is extremely kind of him to allow us to continue living here at all!'

'Kind of him! It would hardly have added to his credit in London,' said Annabelle sharply, 'if he had refused to give you both a home. Indeed, I don't see how he could have done it! It's not as if he had a wife or family of his own to house.'

She was in shock. Pretending to be Rosabelle, living quietly in London with Lady Ordway for most of the time, while Giles Stanton was safely away in Paris was one thing. But it was quite another to act as the man's hostess, to entertain the *ton* in spite of her lack of experience, to behave suitably at all times—all under the coldly critical gaze of those eagle eyes... Could she manage it?

'Aunt Laura, I'm not at all sure I can do this, after all!'

'Anna, you must! If Rosa has been as ill as you say, how would she manage? Oh, Anna, please do it, my dear—for your sister's sake!' She looked pleadingly at Annabelle. 'I know it is a lot to ask, but please say you will carry on.'

'Dearest Aunt Laura, I think I shall have to! I can't imagine that Rosa would cope, either. But it's far from what I imagined my stay in London would be. And I have few social graces.'

'I am quite certain you will manage very well,' said Lady Ordway. 'And there are so many ways in which I could help you. Remember, Rosa was very young when she married Stephen, and after the first year they never entertained a great deal. No one will expect you to manage without help.'

'But I'm not even half as…as graceful as Rosa, Aunt Laura! She seems to know by instinct how one behaves. I didn't even mix with my neighbours in Berkshire more than I had to, and it has been hinted more than once that my manners leave a lot to be desired. I've always gone my own way. I suppose I never had anyone to argue with me—'

'That father of yours has a lot to answer for!' Lady Ordway spoke with unusual severity. 'I represented to him several times the desirability of a Season in London for you, but he always put his own comfort before anyone else's convenience. But don't despair. You're a bright, intelligent girl, every bit as charming as my Rosa. With a bit of training from me, and a few lessons in deportment and dancing and so on, you'll do. We'll tell Giles your social skills need a little polishing up after being unused for so long.'

'But surely Rosa went to all sorts of balls and parties! I imagined her having a wonderful time in London.'

Lady Ordway had been talking with animation, her manner alert and eager. But now she sank back, a closed expression on her face. Annabelle hurried on, 'Not this last year, of course. But before that…' Her voice trailed away as Lady Ordway shook her head.

'It…it wasn't possible,' she said. 'Rosa and I did not go a great deal into society. Visits to a few friends, the occasional evening at Almack's. We saw very little of balls and parties.'

Annabelle was mystified. Why was the subject so painful? Anxious not to let her hostess fall back into apathy again, she said, 'I'm sure you could teach me a lot, all the same. I don't even know how to dance the quadrille, let alone the waltz!'

'Now that is something I can do! I haven't danced for years, but I remember all the steps. Perhaps we could engage a dancing master! I'll ask Wilson—she knows everything. Annabelle, we shall enjoy ourselves—you'll see!'

If Annabelle had been in a better frame of mind she would have rejoiced at the improvement in Lady Ordway's spirits. It was quite clear to her that her hostess had only needed some stimulus—such as her arrival in London—to emerge from the state of apathy and invalidism she had indulged in for so long. So she encouraged Lady Ordway in the plans she made for her education, and tried to keep any further doubts to herself.

They talked till quite late, but when Annabelle finally went to bed she found herself unable to sleep. She spent half the night wondering how she could possibly take her sister's place for the next month. When her eyes did eventually close her dreams were haunted by visions of herself committing one social error after another, before being unmasked as a fraud before the shocked eyes of half of London, including the Prince Regent himself.

She woke unrefreshed. The room was completely dark and the house seemed to be in silence. Then, as her eyes became adjusted, she saw that there was a narrow chink of light over to her left. Shuttered windows. She got up and gingerly walked over to them. A slight fumbling with curtains and catches and light came flooding into the room. It was bright daylight outside, and by craning her neck she could see sunlight on the trees in Grosvenor Square. She turned and surveyed the room. It was not as large as her bedchamber at home, though the ceiling was higher, but it was very comfortably furnished in the modern style. A closet opened off it, and walking over to it, she found that it was full of dresses, shawls, shoes, pelisses, hats and every sort of accessory. Most of them looked as if they had not been worn for some time, pushed to the back behind a collection of clothes in more sombre colours. Rosabelle had been in mourning for the past year, of course.

She went back into the room. Used as she was to the noises of country life coming in through the windows, this London house seemed unnaturally silent. What time could it be? She peered at a dainty French clock on the mantelpiece. Ten o'clock! Ten! How had she overslept so? What must they be thinking of her! She gazed round. A pretty little washstand stood against the wall and there was still some water in the jug. Annabelle hastily splashed her face and dried it, then dressed herself in a simple dress from the back of the closet—a pale green walking dress with a matching jacket of green velvet. Then she hurried out of the room. She paused outside Lady Ordway's door, but hearing nothing she went on down the stairs and into the dining room. The room was empty, the table and sideboards bare. How strange! A scullery maid was on her knees, washing the marble squares of the entrance hall.

'Oh, ma'am! Pardon, ma'am! I...I...'

'It's all right. Where...where is Colonel Stanton?'

''E went out, ma'am. Ridin'. He allus does at this time o' the mornin'.'

'I see.' Annabelle paused. She would like some air and exercise herself. 'Can you open the door for me?'

'Open the door, ma'am?' The little maid's jaw dropped in astonishment. 'Were you...were you thinking of going out? At this hour?'

'Well, yes, I am. It looks like a beautiful morning.'

It was plain that the girl thought she had gone mad, but she did as she was bid, staring all the while. Annabelle went out into the morning air and walked briskly towards Grosvenor Square. She went round the square twice, watched by various footmen, delivery boys and street vendors, who stopped in their tracks to stare at her. Annabelle supposed it was because she was out without a groom or footman. Even in Berkshire it was more usual for a young lady to be accompanied, and when the new footmen appeared she must remember to ask one of them to accompany her.

'Rosabelle!'

A horse and rider came up alongside her, the big bay curvetting and pulling at the reins as he was drawn to a sharp halt. Giles dismounted.

'What the *devil* are you up to now?'

Annabelle stared. What had she done? Surely the simple absence of a footman was not responsible for this blistering tone?

'Good morning, Giles,' she said carefully. 'I'm taking some air. It's a beautiful morning, don't you think?'

Giles took a step towards her. 'Do you know what time it is?'

'It must be after half past ten o'clock. I slept late.'

'You slept—' Giles took a look at the grinning crowd which was beginning to gather round. 'You'd better come home with me. Here, you!' he called to one of the grooms among the crowd. 'Take my horse round to the stables. Sergeant Goss will deal with her.' He tossed him a coin. Then, taking Annabelle's arm he led her back towards Upper Brook Street.

'You're walking too quickly, Giles.'

'I want you back where I can talk to you without an audience.'

Annabelle was still casting around in her mind for a clue to what had caused his annoyance, but she was beginning to become somewhat indignant herself at this cavalier treatment.

'You're hurting me, Giles. Let go of my arm, if you please!' He ignored her, and grimly continued his march. Annabelle put her weight back on her heels and halted. She was now seriously angry.

'Your military life is showing again, Giles! I am not a prisoner of war. I will return to my home at a suitable pace, and if you wish to speak to me there, I shall be pleased to listen to you—as long as you are civil. I will not be…be frogmarched along the pavement, nor will I be ignored!'

'Your holiday appears to have given you some spirit at least,' he said. 'Whatever it may have done in other respects. Very well. May I request you, ma'am, to accompany me to what is, for the moment, your home. And may I also ask to speak to you over the breakfast table?'

'You may,' said Annabelle with a queenly dip of her head, fastidiously removing her arm from his grasp. To her surprise, this gesture seemed to amuse him, and he gave an involuntary grin. Annabelle was astounded at the difference it made to his face. Humour and intelligence were once more to the fore as his expression relaxed. He was not only very handsome—he was extremely attractive!

But he soon relapsed into his former manner. As they entered the house he said peremptorily, 'In the breakfast room. In ten minutes.' Annabelle looked at him in silence. He sighed. 'Rosabelle, would you do me the pleasure of having breakfast with me? In ten minutes? Please.'

She corrected him. 'Quarter of an hour,' she said, then added formally, 'Thank you, Giles. I should be delighted.'

Giles's eyes followed her as she went up the stairs. There was a puzzled frown on his face.

In fifteen minutes to the dot Annabelle presented herself in the dining room where the table was now laid. The room was empty of servants, and Annabelle guessed that Giles had dismissed them. He was already sitting at the table, a newspaper spread out in front of him, but he looked up when she came in.

'At least you're punctual,' he said.

'Sergeant Goss told me you were a stickler for it. He didn't mention any other virtues—such as courtesy, for example.'

'I have always found empty politenesses difficult. But…' He rose to his feet, gave a slight bow and said with exaggerated care, 'Good morning, Rosabelle. Do you wish me to help you to some food? A little toast, perhaps? Some honey?'

Annabelle repressed a smile. 'Thank you,' she said demurely, 'but I can help myself.' She went to the sideboard and took a moderately generous portion of bread and butter, together with some honey. Giles eyed it as she sat down.

'You appear to have a better appetite. You used to pick at your food.' Annabelle looked at her plate. Rosabelle had never taken as much as this even at Temperley.

'The country air has done wonders for me in many ways, Giles,' she said airily.

'I think it has. Even to keeping country hours.' Annabelle looked up at this remark. 'You must own that before you went to Temperley you would never have been seen outside your bedchamber before noon, let alone outside the house! Are you about to claim you had forgotten town hours? Or were you trying to demonstrate what a reformed character you are? No longer vain and idle, but a virtuous early riser? It doesn't impress me.' He gave a scornful smile. 'A rather cheap trick, don't you think, Rosabelle? And one which merely exposed you to the ridicule of servants and tradesmen. Did you enjoy being gawped at?'

Annabelle had grown pale during this attack, and she had difficulty in suppressing an angry response. She may have made a foolish error, one which Giles would naturally not understand, nor was it one she could explain to him. But his tone and words were insulting. Rosabelle had never in her life been either vain or idle. She rose to her feet.

'I find I have no appetite, after all,' she said in a stifled voice. 'You must excuse me.' She walked to the door.

'I haven't finished.'

'If you wish to speak to me about the arrangements you are making for the house and its management, I shall talk to you when you have finished breakfast. Meanwhile I shall see if Aunt Laura is awake.'

He got up and strode after her. 'You will not upset Aunt Laura, Rosabelle. She is making good recovery at the moment. I will not have any setbacks.'

Annabelle looked at him scornfully. 'I suppose you think I would run to her with complaints? Aunt Laura has never been burdened with tales of our private quarrels, Giles, and never will be from me. But if, as you say, she is recovering and taking more of an interest in the world, then she will soon see for herself how matters are between us—unless you curb your sour, ungracious tongue. Where shall I see you? In the library?'

'In the library.' He went back to the table, his brows drawn once more in a heavy frown.

Annabelle was fuming as she went upstairs. Giles was impossible! How poor Rosabelle must have suffered under this barrage of criticism and harsh words! No wonder she had been in such a state—she had a nature which, above all, needed love and encouragement to flourish. Gentle, vulnerable as she was, she would have no defence against Giles Stanton's attacks. Her charm, intelligence, humour, even her self-esteem would all shrivel in the chilly atmosphere of his disapproval. How fortunate it was that, however much she and her sister resembled one another in appearance, their characters were so very different! Annabelle was neither gentle, nor so easily cast down! She smiled grimly. The prospect of foxing Giles Stanton, of eventually teaching him a lesson, was becoming more attractive by the minute. It wouldn't be

easy. He was no fool. If she was to avoid suspicion, she
must do more than learn the ways of society in two or
three secret lessons—she would have to learn to disguise
her own strong will and her readiness to do battle, which
was so unlike her sister's desperate need to live in peace.
But, she swore, she would do all of it if it killed her!

When Annabelle entered Lady Ordway's bedchamber
she found her awake, with Wilson in attendance.

'Good morning, my dear. Did you sleep well?'

'Thank you, Aunt Laura. And you?'

'Well enough. Anna, my dear, I've told Wilson our
secret. She will keep it to herself. And we might need
her help.'

Wilson was still regarding Annabelle as if she couldn't
believe what she saw. She pulled herself together and
said, 'I'd be pleased to help in any way I can, ma'am.
I'm sure a rest in the country is just what Miss Rosabelle
needs. But my goodness, Miss Kelland! You *are* like
your sister!'

'In looks, perhaps. Not so much in other ways. But I
have an urgent question for you both. What is wrong
with my going out this morning?'

Lady Ordway looked surprised. 'Nothing whatsoever!
Do you wish Wilson to accompany you—or Lily? The
new footmen aren't coming till later—'

'No, you misunderstand me, Aunt Laura! I went out
this morning—'

'Already?' Lady Ordway and Wilson exchanged
glances. 'Who accompanied you?'

'I went alone.'

'Oh, dear!' Lady Ordway seemed unable to continue,
so Annabelle looked at the maid.

'I'm sure you had your reasons, ma'am—'

'You'd better get used to calling her Miss Rosabelle, Wilson!'

'Miss Rosabelle. It's just that I've never known of a lady going out before noon, or even one o'clock. It's not often you see any gentlemen, either, before that hour. I can't imagine Miss Rosabelle, the real Miss Rosabelle, doing such a thing.'

'But by that time half the day is gone!' cried Annabelle. 'What lie-a-beds you all are!'

'The servants are up and about, ma'am. And the tradesmen. But ladies and gentlemen never.'

'So that's why…'

'Did anyone see you, Anna?' asked Lady Ordway apprehensively.

'Servants and tradesmen. And Giles. Now then, Wilson! Colonel Stanton was out and about. What do you say to that?'

'Gentlemen, particularly gentlemen who have been in the Army, ma'am, sometimes exercise their horses in Hyde Park at an early hour.'

'What did he say to you, Anna?'

'He was surprised,' said Annabelle with masterly understatement. 'And he was kind enough to escort me back to the house. I was totally unaware that I was offending in any way, so I was not best pleased.'

'Oh, dear. The sooner we start our classes the better, I think. Wilson, see about my breakfast, will you? I shall get up as soon as I can.'

Annabelle welcomed this sign of enthusiasm in Lady Ordway, but she had to say, 'Er…Giles and I are having a discussion in a few minutes, Aunt Laura.'

'About this morning?'

'Not if I can avoid it. I think he wishes to inform me about his plans. I had better see him, don't you think?'

'Oh, yes! We mustn't keep him waiting. He has so much to do. We can have our lesson this afternoon, Anna dear. I'll try to make some notes. I'm sure I shall forget something vital. Oh, this is just like the old days when Rosabelle was a young girl! Come along, Wilson. My breakfast!'

Annabelle went down to the library better prepared than she had been for anything Giles Stanton might bring up about her morning excursion. To her surprise he did not refer to it again, but was quite businesslike. In fact, the meeting began quite well, with what was almost an apology from him.

'I have engaged several servants while you were in Berkshire. I admit that it would have been more fitting to wait for your return, but things here were getting desperate. The lack of a good housekeeper was very marked, and I could hardly engage a competent housekeeper and then expect her to work entirely without maidservants to support her.'

'Of course not, Giles,' said Annabelle meekly. 'Indeed, it would be quite hard for anyone to manage.'

He gave her a sharp look, then said, 'It is possible that I was overhasty in my judgement of your contribution to the household. It is true that your absence was felt more than once.'

'You mean I was not vain and idle *all* the time?'

He said stiffly, 'No. In fact, I think Aunt Laura and I have reason to be grateful to you for your management of the house in the past year.'

'Why, thank you!' said Annabelle, delighted to have wrung this acknowledgement from him. However, her pleasure was soon destroyed, and the atmosphere took a turn for the worse from then on.

'That is not to say that I have changed my opinion of you entirely, Rosabelle. I still find it difficult to forgive your behaviour towards my cousin.'

'Some day you might tell me exactly what it is you accuse me of, Giles. And at the same time you might show me what evidence you think you have for it.'

He gave her a searingly contemptuous look. 'Don't try your games on me! You must know what you've done— I don't need to tell you. As for evidence—you've already seen it. There was evidence enough for even the most objective reader in Stephen's diary. Or have you conveniently forgotten about that?'

The memory of her sister's bewildered distress as she had talked of the letters and the diary, her desperate denials of any wrongdoing, gave Annabelle the courage to face him calmly. 'I should like to see them, all the same. And the letters you said you received from him.'

'So that you can pick them to pieces?'

'No. Merely so that I can defend myself. Or are we in a wartime court-martial situation here? No argument for the defence allowed?'

There was a pause. Then Giles said, 'I can't let you have Stephen's papers at the moment. I'm working on them. There's still an enormous amount of confusion, and it would take more time than I can spare to separate a few odd sheets from the rest. I am still trying to see if I can rescue any of my aunt's personal fortune from the mess.' He looked at her sharply. 'I'm still sure you could help me if you chose. Or do you persist in your refusal?'

'I tell you, I *can't* help you. I don't know what happened to any of the money.'

Giles got up. 'Stephen, presumably with your help, not only spent all the income—a considerable annual sum— from the trust fund his father set up, he also appears to have persuaded his mother to part with most of her money, too. What did the two of you spend it on?'

Annabelle thought it best to say nothing. She was sure that Rosabelle had no idea, but it was wiser not to enter into any discussion of such a dangerous topic. Giles made a gesture of impatience,

'You see? I am absolutely certain you could help me if you would, Rosabelle, but you persist in remaining silent. Why? I don't believe I am being unreasonable. I've paid off the most pressing of Stephen's debts, I've secured this house and set up a small annuity for my aunt—all out of my uncle's estate—'

'Which Stephen would have inherited if he had lived long enough. Let me remind you of that, since you appear to have forgotten it! Just three more years and it would all have been his, income, capital, this house... everything.'

'But not for long. The Ordway fortune would soon have gone the way of the rest, if you and Stephen had had your way with it. Between you, you would have got rid of the lot!'

'Perhaps you think it's fortunate that he died when he did?' said Annabelle sharply. She spoke without thinking, enraged by his insistence on Rosabelle's guilt. But the effect of her words on him was electric. He strode over, took her by the arms and shook her, his face contorted with anger.

'You little...! I loved my cousin! Loved him! Which is more than you ever did, you self-seeking opportunist! How *dare* you suggest that I wanted Stephen dead? By God, if it weren't for Aunt Laura, I swear I'd throw you out today, bag and baggage!' He thrust her away from him and walked over to the window, where he stood, clearly fighting to control his feelings. Annabelle was

shocked at his violence, but she was ashamed, too. Her
words had been ill chosen. She had certainly not meant
to imply that Giles rejoiced in Stephen's death.

After a moment's silence, she said, 'I should not have
said what I did, Giles. Please forgive me.'

'No, you should not,' he replied sombrely, without
turning round. 'I never imagined I would inherit the
Ordway fortune, nor did I want or need it. Stephen was
so much younger than I was.' He paused, then went on,
'He was still a child at the time of my uncle's death;
there had to be trustees then. But the estate should have
gone to him when he was twenty-one. I tried to dissuade
my uncle from putting those conditions into his will—I
fought against it right up to his death, but I couldn't
move him. Sir John was adamant. Stephen had either to
have a son, or to wait till he was twenty-five. Before that
he could live on the income from the trust which had
been set up for him, but not touch the principal. I never
understood why. And now my cousin is dead, and I am
beset with unanswered questions, enigmas, mysteries…and chaos.'

He turned towards her, standing stiffly upright like a
man expecting a blow. His face was very pale. 'Rosabelle, I have to know! Will you tell me this at least? I
have begun to suspect that…that Stephen committed sui-
cide? Am I right?' He came away from the window
again, and stood over her. They were so close that their
eyes were only inches apart. Shocked beyond measure,
transfixed by that piercing gaze, she couldn't utter a
word.

'Tell me, damn you!'

Annabelle was totally unprepared for anything like
this. When Stephen Ordway had died, she and her father
had been informed that there had been an accident, that

he had fallen down some steps and broken his neck. And
during her stay at Temperley Rosabelle had said nothing
about her husband's death. There had certainly never
been the slightest hint that Stephen had killed himself.

She drew back a little—Giles stood waiting, watching
her, too close for comfort. She must say something!

'Why should you think that?' she asked carefully.

# Chapter Three

'Damn it, why do you always have to prevaricate! You're just like all the rest of your sex!' The pain behind Giles's angry outburst was all too clear. Annabelle tried to answer him as honestly and as patiently as she could.

'I...I don't wish to prevaricate. I...I wasn't there when Stephen fell. I just don't understand why you should think such a thing.'

He turned away abruptly, as if to reject her sympathy, and walked about the room. After a while he said wearily, 'Like everything else, there's a mystery about it. I've...I've been making enquiries—oh, you needn't worry! I've been discreet.' He threw a scornful look in her direction. 'Apart from his doctor, you and Aunt Laura were the only ones allowed near Stephen towards the end, and though I've asked Cottrell he refuses to comment.' He was back in front of her. 'Did my cousin really fall down those steps? Or did he throw himself down? It's quite possible. Quite understandable. The poor fellow was overloaded with trouble—his debts, an unfaithful wife—'

'I…I don't know,' said poor Annabelle. These were deeper waters than she had anticipated when she had so blithely embarked on her impersonation of Rosabelle. Of one thing she was completely certain. It was quite out of the question that Rosabelle had ever betrayed her husband—such disloyalty would have been utterly against her nature. Yet…in another respect she knew Giles to be right. Rosabelle had not loved Stephen as a wife should. She had married him to please her godmother, and had lived to regret it.

'One thing I can assure you of, Giles,' she said steadily. 'Stephen may have had debts, but he did *not* have an unfaithful wife!'

Giles ignored this. 'If Stephen's death was a straight-forward accident, why all the mystery?'

'You must ask Aunt Laura that, not me,' she said. 'I can't discuss it with you. I gave my word to Aunt Laura not to discuss Stephen with anyone.'

She shifted uneasily under Giles's brooding regard, but stood her ground.

'You are, of course, aware that I could not possibly approach Aunt Laura on such a matter,' he said finally. 'She loved my cousin too much. But don't place any dependence on my not finding out what happened— eventually. And then, by God, you'll answer for it.'

'Condemned and sentenced without a hearing. Is that it?'

'I've given you your chance, Rosabelle.'

Annabelle was about to argue again, but then the fu-tility of it struck her. His present prejudice was like a brick wall. She reined in her temper and said as calmly as she could, 'Giles, are you sure you want to do this?

Aunt Laura is just beginning to live again. Do you really want to revive all the pain, all the distress for her? I honestly don't know whether Stephen killed himself or not. But what good will it do if you establish—somehow—that he did? It won't bring him back. And Aunt Laura will almost certainly suffer another setback.'

'I suppose that would suit you very well!'

Good resolutions faded at the bitterness and contempt in his voice. She said angrily, 'You're impossible! I think it would be better for all of us if I went back to Temperley for good!'

'Oh, no! As I said before you went to Berkshire, you owe something to the Ordway family, Rosabelle Kelland, and you're going to repay that debt at least! God knows why, but Aunt Laura is devoted to you—'

'And I love her, too, Giles! Never forget that!'

'So you'll stay in London and earn your keep. When she is fully restored to health and spirits, then you can talk of escape to Temperley.'

'And where are we going to live till that happy time?'

He looked surprised. 'Here, of course!'

'With a constant threat of eviction over our heads, if I don't obey you? Of being reduced to penury through Stephen's debts? That will hardly be conducive to our peace of mind, will it? You see, I too remember your words before I left for Berkshire!'

'Those debts are paid in full. That was done shortly after you left London.'

Annabelle gazed at him in disbelief.

'Oh, you may look amazed, but did you really believe that I would willingly cause Aunt Laura any further anxiety? Whatever happens, her future is secure. And I suppose that means that yours is, too. Your financial future,

that is. And the house is available to you both for as
long as you're likely to want it.'

'Even if you marry?'

'I don't envisage marrying for some time—if ever.'
His face was closed.

Annabelle suddenly felt exhausted. So many different
emotions in such a short space of time—anger, frustration, pity, and now, incredible though it seemed, gratitude! She roused herself to say, 'Giles, little though you
may believe me, I am grateful for what you've done for
Aunt Laura. And…and me.'

'I could hardly have done less.'

'I know you dislike me. There is little I can do about
it, except to hope that with time you will see how unjust
you have been. Meanwhile…'

'Meanwhile we shall have to rub along as best we can.
Is that what you want to say?'

'Yes. If I am not to return to Temperley then there's
nothing else to be done.'

'I suppose not.' He became businesslike again. 'I've
been waiting for your return to leave London myself for
a few days. It won't be for long, however, and when I
return I shall want to start entertaining—I owe a great
deal of hospitality. I shall require you to act as my hostess.'

'Do we have servants enough?'

'Not quite. I have asked the agency to send round a
couple of footmen. Whitcroft can deal with them. He
might think a third is necessary. If so, you must see to
it. And the new housekeeper will want to engage more
help in the house and kitchen. You'll have to talk to her
about it. Apart from that, you'll keep Aunt Laura company.'

'Yes, sir! Straight away, sir!' said Annabelle, with a

salute. '*I require you to… You must… You'll have to… You will keep…* Do you ever request anyone politely? Or has Upper Brook Street become an Army barracks?'

'I'm sorry,' he said stiffly. 'I told you, I haven't the patience for empty courtesies. When I travel over rough ground I spend as little time on it as possible. And the ground has recently been very rough indeed. But I should, indeed, be grateful for your help.'

Annabelle could now see that he looked bone-weary himself. 'I suppose that will do,' she said philosophically. 'And I shall give you all the help I can. If only to prove I am not what you think me.'

'That will be difficult,' he said with a return to his former grim manner. 'But we shall call a truce, for the moment.'

Annabelle escaped with a sense of profound relief, and hastened up to Lady Ordway's room to share the news. With Giles away they had some time when they could work on her deficiencies as a social hostess without a need for concealment.

'But this is very good news!' said Lady Ordway. 'And I have more. Wilson has found us a dancing instructor, who will come tomorrow. And she has heard that Mrs Thelwell—a most respected member of the *ton*, but living in very reduced circumstances—might be willing to coach you in social behaviour.'

'I should have thought you were more than capable of that yourself, Aunt Laura!'

'But I get tired, my dear. And we have other work to do. I intend to see that you have some new and beautiful dresses to dazzle the *ton*. I used to love buying them for Rosabelle in the old days. I believe Madame Fanchon is still highly regarded—'

'But I saw a closet full of dresses this morning in Rosabelle's room—surely we could make do?'

'That is one of the things you will have to learn, Annabelle! One does not "make do" when mixing with the *ton*! Goodness me, girl! Don't you want some pretty new dresses?'

'Yes, but…how will we pay for them?'

'Leave that to me! Giles has restored my income quite considerably, and I shall delight in spending it on clothes. I shall order some for myself, too. No more objections, if you please!'

Annabelle had to give in. In truth she could see that the prospect of preparing for her pseudo-goddaughter's re-entry into Society was giving Lady Ordway a great deal of pleasure.

From then on Annabelle underwent an intensive course in learning to be a lady of society. Ridiculous though some of the rules seemed to her, she meekly worked to learn them, and since she was an intelligent girl she was soon reasonably conversant with them. She learned to subdue her own stride to a graceful mincing walk, she became versed in the exact depth of a nod, bow or curtsey to give to different levels of acquaintance, she acquired a range of subjects suitable for conversations at table, at routs and balls, for afternoon calls. She was taught the names of those members of society who were approved, and those whom she must avoid.

'Of course, it is much too early, I am sure, for you to be considering remarriage, Mrs Ordway,' said Mrs Thelwell. 'But well prepared is well armed, and it doesn't do any harm to know who would do.' And she proceeded to give Annabelle a surprisingly comprehensive list of eligible bachelors and widowers. To

Annabelle's amusement, Philip Winbolt was one of
them. But when she mentioned him to Mrs Thelwell, the
response was discouraging.

'Ah, yes, Lord Winbolt's grandson. A charming young
man, and a most desirable match. But he seldom comes
to London, except when he visits his grandfather in
Arlington Street. He inherited Shearings, his uncle's estate in Berkshire, and spends most of his time there. He
is not a lover of town life. I doubt you will see him
enough to become properly acquainted with him.'

Annabelle hid a smile. She was already very well acquainted with Philip Winbolt. The Shearings estate bordered on that of the Kellands', and the Winbolts were
their closest neighbours. Philip Winbolt had been a frequent visitor to Temperley since his arrival in Berkshire,
and Becky, the Kellands' housekeeper, had been convinced that he came looking for a wife. Annabelle had
not been interested. Mr Winbolt was not to her taste—
he was far too polite, too much the gentleman. More
Rosabelle's style, perhaps… She wondered briefly what
Rosabelle would make of him. And what Mr Winbolt
would make of Rosabelle. And whether he would notice
the difference… He would certainly be far too polite to
comment if he did!

Annabelle also took advantage of Giles's absence to
inspect the household arrangements, discussing with the
new housekeeper how they could be improved. The task
was not difficult. She did not doubt her ability to manage
the household in Upper Brook Street after her long experience in managing Temperley for her father. There
were a few practices and customs that were different, but
she quickly mastered these, and was soon confident that

the domestic side of her life in London would present no problems.

Her social life was a different matter, but even there she found enjoyment. Mrs Thelwell was a hard taskmistress, but a delight to her pupil. The lady was so dedicated, so serious, so convinced that the only object for any young woman must be to acquire a rich and eligible man—young or, in her eyes, preferably old.

'For you must know, my dear, that older men are so much more reliable in their affections. And never forget, a man of mature years has had time to gather the fruits of his success. Why, look at Lord Osborne—his mansion in Portman Square is a veritable treasure house of elegant furniture, statues, pictures and I don't know what else besides. Now, *he* is *devoted* to his young wife. He never lets her out of his sight.'

Something in Annabelle's expression caused Mrs Thelwell to add hastily, 'And there are others…I cannot quite recall at the moment… Oh dear, you will think me a sad scatterbrain.'

'My dear Mrs Thelwell, you have been a mine of information and instruction! I cannot begin to thank you enough. I am truly not thinking of acquiring a husband for some time yet, but the rest of what you have taught me is invaluable. I now feel so much more fitted to face society.'

'But, Mrs Ordway! You are lovely enough to disarm any criticism. And I am sure society will be delighted with you, once they know you for yourself.'

This seemed a somewhat cryptic observation to Annabelle. 'Know me for myself? How else should they know me?'

Mrs Thelwell who, for all her apologies and claims to being a scatterbrain, was usually a highly composed creature, looked discomfited. 'Forgive me, I spoke without thinking.'

Annabelle was not satisfied. 'If I am to enter society with confidence again, Mrs Thelwell, I must know what is being said or thought about me.'

Mrs Thelwell hesitated, then said finally, 'It's not about *you*!' She lowered her voice. 'I have no desire to distress you, Mrs Ordway, and I would not dream of saying anything in front of Lady Ordway, but as you have insisted… You did not mix in society a great deal when your husband was alive, so it does not surprise me that you are unaware of what was being said. Mr Ordway, the late Mr Ordway, was not…not…' She was clearly at a loss.

'Quite the thing? Would have been on your list of people to avoid?'

'Er…well, let us say rather that he was not regarded with universal approbation.'

'I see.'

'I hope I have not distressed you. I am sure if he had lived he would have overcome society's prejudices in time. But it was not to be. His accident…' She paused, but when Annabelle did not respond, she went on, 'You need have no fear for yourself, my dear ma'am. I prophesy that you will be a great success.'

Mrs Thelwell was still looking anxious. Annabelle was grateful for the warning she had been given, and had no wish to upset her companion. So she merely smiled. 'If that is indeed the case, then much of it will be due to your efforts. Thank you again, Mrs Thelwell. This past week has been most enjoyable.'

Lady Ordway came in at that moment, followed by Wilson, who was laden with boxes.

'Good evening, Mrs Thelwell. Rosa, my dear, look!

The dresses have arrived from Fanchon. She's a dear
creature. She must have worked all hours to get these
done in the time.'

In the subsequent flurry of activity, unwrapping, ex-
claiming, trying on, Mrs Thelwell's words were pushed
to the back of Annabelle's mind. But that night she lay
awake, thinking of Stephen Ordway and her sister's life
with him. She was not as surprised as she might have
been by Mrs Thelwell's words. Neither she nor Becky
had taken to Stephen Ordway on the one occasion he
had paid them a visit, not long after he and Rosabelle
had married. Golden hair, bright blue eyes, slender,
graceful build—he looked handsome enough, and at first
they were impressed by his surface charm.

But as time wore on he had become bored in the country, and petulantly impatient with Rosabelle when she
had wanted to visit old friends and show him her favourite haunts. He had even begun to make fun of people
the twins had known and respected for years, and his
scorn for country bumpkins had soon begun to show
through. No one had been sorry when the Ordways' visit
had come to an end. There had never been another, and
Annabelle had never been invited to Upper Brook Street.
Rosabelle wrote regularly, but after that sole visit she
had seemed to distance herself from her family in
Berkshire.

Stephen was now dead, but he still apparently had the
power to cause distress to those he had left behind—
Lady Ordway, Rosabelle, even Giles Stanton. Giles
Stanton. A curious man. Was he a villain? Or was he
someone who still thought of Stephen as a boy, an innocent younger cousin who had idolised him, and who
now needed to be avenged? Had Giles, too, been taken
in by the angelic looks, the apparent charm? From all

accounts, he had not seen much of his cousin in later years…

Just as Annabelle was drifting off to sleep, a vision of herself just ten days ago, about to leave Temperley for London, drifted into her mind. She had been laughing, assuring Rosabelle that all would go well with their changeover. She had almost got to the door when Rosabelle, clearly on impulse, had clutched her arm and whispered, *'I gave my word to Aunt Laura that I wouldn't tell anyone about Stephen, but I can't let you go without warning you! He had some strange friends. Don't take any risks.'*

Her sister had been desperately anxious that she should take the words seriously. But what had she meant by 'strange friends'? And why had she thought a warning necessary—so necessary that she had been prepared to talk about her husband in spite of her promise to his mother? The incident was odd, but it had left an impression.

Annabelle sighed and turned over in the bed yet again. What had started out as a lighthearted exercise in deception, merely in order to give her sister more time in the country, was proving to be much, much more complicated. But…but if Rosabelle could be re-established in the eyes of London society, then this visit would have done more good than she could have hoped. So much depended on the next few weeks!

To Annabelle's relief Giles's business kept him out of London for longer than he had planned, and he was away for well over a week. When he did arrive back it was early in the morning and he looked travel-stained and weary. Annabelle was up. She was still unused to town hours, and though she did not go out, she was always awake and active from about eight o'clock onwards. She was in the drawing room when she heard the bustle at the door, and came out to see what it was.

'Giles! You're back!'

'I do believe I am,' he said sourly. 'I had hoped to get to my room and have a wash and shave before anyone saw me. What are you doing up?'

Annabelle took a breath. 'Was the journey very fatiguing, Giles? It looks as if it was. Shall I send for something to eat for you?'

'I had some coffee when I got off the coach. It was vile.'

'Then you go upstairs and I'll send Sergeant Goss to you, and I'll see Mrs Brooks about some food.' Giles hesitated. 'Go on,' said Annabelle firmly. ''How long do you need? Half an hour?'

'Twenty minutes,' he said with a slight grin. Then he frowned again. 'Why *are* you up?'

'I can't sleep when it is so bright outside. I still haven't managed to shake off country hours. And when there is so much to be done here…'

'Still trying to impress, Rosabelle?' he asked as he started up the stairs.

'What a futile exercise that would be,' Annabelle snapped. Just for a moment she had felt sorry for the man. She was a fool!

He came down after twenty minutes looking brighter, and regarded the substantial breakfast laid out in the dining room. 'Are you not joining me?' he asked in surprise, gazing at the single setting.

'I might. If you can be civil,' she said.

He took a deep breath. 'I'll try. Now sit down and join me.'

They sat down. 'Do you wish to tell me what you've been doing?' Annabelle asked.

'Nothing to any purpose, though I've left a few irons in the fire...' The servant was dismissed with a nod and Giles waited until they were alone. Then he looked at her thoughtfully. 'I'd like to know—'

'Know what?'

'What goes on in that lovely head of yours.'

'If you are about to start being unpleasant again, I shall leave the table and get on with what I was doing before you came.'

'No, don't go!' he said. 'Let me tell you what I was doing. I've been investigating a couple of references in Stephen's diary.' Annabelle stiffened, but though he noted it he made no comment. 'About a man called Da Costa.' He paused. 'You don't know the name?'

'No, I've never heard of him.'

'First I went to a tavern, a wretched hole near Woolhampton on the Bath Road.'

Annabelle dropped her knife. 'But that's not far from Temperley!' she said.

'I hadn't thought of that. Is it a coincidence?' said Giles as he picked up the knife and gave her a clean one.

There was something in his manner which was making her uneasy. 'What else could it be?' she said.

'I don't know. Why aren't you eating?'

'Because I'm listening to you, and waiting for you to get on with it!' said Annabelle, irritated. 'I don't like cat-and-mouse games.'

'Now why should I be playing cat and mouse?'

'I have no idea, but I wish you would stop.'

Giles sat down again. 'Very well, I will! I went to this inn and asked about Da Costa. The landlord knew him.

He was most unwilling to talk, but I persuaded him in
the end.'

'What did you do?' asked Annabelle coldly. 'Burn the
soles of his feet?'

'No, just bribed him.'

'And?'

'The landlord told me that Da Costa was in the habit
of meeting someone else there.' Giles was now watching
her very closely. 'A gentleman called Selder.'

Annabelle waited. Giles continued to watch her
steadily. Eventually she said, 'So? Did he say why they
met?'

'Oh, you're good!' said Giles. 'You're very good.
Your stay in Berkshire has done wonders for your ability
to dissemble. The last time I mentioned Selder's name
you jumped a foot.'

'What do you mean? I've never heard the name before—' Annabelle stopped short. 'When...when was
that,' she asked.

'You're now claiming you've forgotten? That's going
a bit far, don't you think? It was just after I came back
to England. When I found Stephen's diaries. But I knew
about the affair before that—I've told you before.
Stephen had already written to me about it.' He had been
bent towards her, but he now sat back and regarded her
cynically. 'Why don't you spare me this play-acting,
Rosabelle? We both know that Selder was your lover.'

Annabelle jumped up, turning her chair over in the
process. 'That's it! I've had enough!' She leaned over
the table and glared at him. 'I am telling you for the last
time, *Colonel*, that I was *never*— n-e-v-e-r—*never* unfaithful to Stephen. If Stephen says so in these diaries
you keep refusing to show me, then he was lying—or
mad. I have never had any sort of lover. Do you hear me?'

'It would be difficult not to,' he said unpleasantly. 'You're shouting like a fishwife.'

'Heaven give me patience,' said Annabelle in exasperation. 'What am I supposed to do? Accept everything you throw at me without a word in my own defence? Sit down meekly and say that I'm sorry, I'll never do it again?'

'Since Stephen is dead that would be difficult, don't you agree? But it would probably mean as much as anything else you might say. And why do you keep asking to see the diaries? I showed you the relevant pages before Easter.'

'Did you, indeed? Well, I want to see them again. Now!'

'I really cannot imagine what you hope to gain, Rosabelle. But I'll fetch them. I'll meet you in the library.' He got up, picked up her chair and went out. Annabelle sank back into the chair. She was trembling. She had come within a hair's breadth of betraying herself! Giles must have tackled Rosabelle about Selder before Easter. Oh, why, in Heaven's name, hadn't Rosabelle told her more? But a moment's reflection told her that she was being foolish. Of course she knew why Rosabelle hadn't. Rosabelle had given her word to Lady Ordway that she would say nothing either about her marriage or about the events leading up to Stephen's death. Distressed and ill though she had been, she would not break that promise, either to her sister, or to anyone else—not even to defend herself. Rosabelle was incapable of betraying anyone, least of all her husband, and if any evidence of her absolute integrity was needed, it was this refusal to talk.

Annabelle could not criticise such loyalty. But the result was that she felt she was fighting Giles Stanton with one hand tied behind her back. And with this sort of opponent she needed all her wits and every other assistance she could get. Would the diaries be of any help? They might reveal something that Giles had missed, though it was unlikely—he had obviously studied them carefully. But it was necessary to see them, all the same. She got up and made her way to the library.

Giles was laying out a pathetic collection of papers and torn, dog-eared notebooks.

'How can you claim to understand these…scribbles?' asked Annabelle, after she had studied them for a few minutes. 'Half of them aren't legible, and the rest don't make sense!'

'That's what you said last time.'

'Thank goodness for that!' thought Annabelle, and said aloud, 'It doesn't make it any less true.'

'Let me show you. Here…and here… As you see, he is quite explicit about Selder and yourself.'

Annabelle cast her eyes over them, then turned a pale, shocked face towards him. 'I…I don't understand some of the words. But I can guess their meaning. I…I…how could anyone mix my name up in this…this filth!'

'You must excuse me. But I didn't force the diaries on you. You demanded to see them.'

'But, Giles! You can't really be taking these…these obscenities seriously! They're evidence only of the disturbed state in which they were written!'

'And whose fault was that?' Annabelle was still shocked. She looked at him briefly, then set her face and was silent. She had said she would not defend herself again. Giles made an ironic gesture of acknowledgment and went over to the window. There was a pause, during which Annabelle bundled the diaries together, put them back in their box, and closed the lid firmly on them. If Rosabelle's husband, and later Giles, had subjected her to this sort of accusation, it was even less surprising that she had eventually collapsed. Annabelle was feeling sick herself. But she must pull herself together, and continue the fight to clear Rosabelle's name!

'I…I find it very difficult to understand, Giles, why you should be so adamant, so rigidly determined to believe the worst,' she began, speaking to his unyielding back. 'I don't believe that you really listen to anything I say to defend myself. Why is that?'

Giles turned round. His face was in shadow. 'I never met you when you were a girl,' he said, almost conversationally. 'Whenever I stayed with the Ordways you were down at Temperley, spending the summer with your father and sister. Aunt Laura was always saying what a perfect daughter you were, how loving, how gentle—how glad she was that she had agreed to foster you. Even then, Stephen distrusted you.'

'B…but how? Why?'

'He thought you had wormed your way into his mother's affections at his expense.'

'That is rubbish!'

'Is it? Stephen believed it to be so. And the terms of his father's will didn't help. He was…humiliated by the thought that he wouldn't be allowed to inherit before he was twenty-five. At twelve or thirteen that must have seemed a lifetime away. His father's rejection of him must have made him all the more possessive of his mother. So I suppose the more she spoiled you, the more isolated he felt.'

'But Aunt Laura adored Stephen!'

'I know she did, and I told him so. But he wouldn't listen to me. He was convinced you were trying to come between them. And I have to say that from his accounts of the arts you employed, the tricks you got up to, it could well have been true.'

Annabelle thought for a moment, wondering how to deal with this. For her, it was simply more evidence of Stephen's duplicity. But Giles would not think so. She said slowly, 'You never questioned what he was telling you? You never suspected that you might be being manipulated?'

'A child of that age? That's absurd! I had known him from babyhood! He was a delightful little chap—open, frank, honest. He was never very strong, but he was full of pluck. Not an ounce of guile in him! Don't try to defend yourself by casting doubts on Stephen, Rosabelle. From beginning to end you were the cause of the deepest unhappiness in my cousin.'

'That he was unhappy I have no doubt. But, believe me, it was not because of anything I did. Aunt Laura loved all her family—that's the way she is. But Stephen was her only son and she worshipped him. She gave him everything!'

'Even a wife he didn't want?'

# Chapter Four

Annabelle was shocked again and showed it. 'What are you saying now? That I trapped Stephen into marriage?'

'Stephen was certain that Aunt Laura more or less forced him to marry you because it was the only way she could make your future secure. You had no fortune of your own, and the Ordway money was too well tied up. If you can bear to read more of Stephen's writings, you can read his letters to me. It's all there.'

Annabelle felt a rising tide of anger and frustration. It was so plausible! Had she not known her sister as well as she did, she might even have believed this rubbish herself! But she controlled her feelings. Giles's accusations were unwelcome, but they were at last giving her something tangible to work on. At last she knew the reason why his dislike of Rosabelle went so deep. But flat denials would not be enough. Giles remembered only the delicate, charming little boy he had known in the past, and had believed his cousin's tales.

'These…ravings—' she pointed to the box of diaries
'—if Stephen was so indifferent to me, why was he so
distraught when he writes about the affair with Selder?'

Giles paused. Blinded by his deeply ingrained prejudice against his cousin's wife, this was obviously something he had not considered. 'Perhaps he loved you more
than he realised. Or perhaps he saw that the chances of
having the son he needed were in danger.'

Annabelle put her head in her hands. It was aching.
For a few minutes neither of them spoke.

Then Giles said, 'I warn you, Rosabelle, I mean to
find out the truth. About Stephen, why and how he died,
and where his money went. And about Selder.'

'And I am not afraid of that. As long as what you find
out *is* the truth, and not a set of prejudices and lies.'

'At least you have more spirit that I credited you
with.'

'Thank you. I suppose you mean it as a compliment.
I was ill before Easter, Giles, and your bullying made it
much worse. But I believe I can stand up to you now,
and I will.' She pointed to the diaries. 'You can put these
away again. I do not regard them as evidence of anything
at all, and the house is tainted by their presence. Though
I have done nothing to deserve it, I still feel…ashamed
that my name is associated with such filth. They would
best be burnt.'

His eyes showed a reluctant admiration. 'If I were not
already so convinced of your guilt, I could almost believe you sincere.'

Annabelle said with more than a touch of irony, 'I
don't know whether to thank you for that or not.
But…believing me guilty, do you wish me to continue
to run this house?'

'Oh, I do! I want you where I can see you. And I will

not deny that you are needed here. As long as you do not upset Aunt Laura, you will stay.'

Annabelle bit back a retort. Time and patience, she told herself. Time and patience!

Giles went on, 'And now, if you'll excuse me, I shall seek her out. She might even be up already.'

Annabelle looked at the time. It was only eleven o'clock. She would have sworn it was well past noon. These revelations and battles with Giles certainly made the time pass, though as a cure for boredom they were somewhat extreme!

Following Giles's return to London, preparations went swiftly ahead for a reception, to be followed by several evening parties. Though he made no further reference to their conversation in the library, Annabelle was aware that Giles was keeping a careful watch on her. Let him! It had taken a few days to overcome the feelings of disgust aroused by the diaries, but she had managed it. Now, pleased with the success of her domestic arrangements, confident of her ability to move in the best circles without making mistakes, and aware that she had one of the prettiest collections of dresses in London, Annabelle's mind was more easy. She had nothing to hide, nothing to be ashamed of...except when she remembered that she had everything to hide! She was, in fact, not at all the woman Giles Stanton thought her to be. Not Rosabelle Ordway, but Annabelle Kelland, doing her best in difficult circumstances. When she permitted herself to think of it, the thought of his rage and contempt if that piece of outrageous chicanery ever came to light kept her awake at night, and gave her nightmares when she slept.

But during the day she managed to concentrate on her

role as Rosabelle, Stephen Ordway's widow, newly out of mourning and about to re-enter society.

On the night of the reception she took more care over her appearance than ever in her life before. Annabelle Kelland had dressed carelessly, negligently almost. But Rosabelle Ordway, real or counterfeit, dressed as the genuine article—a member of London's highest society, about to entertain some of the foremost names in social, diplomatic and military circles.

No one could have faulted Lady Ordway's choice of gown for her. In deference to her recent emergence from mourning the dress was white. But it was far from being the sort of artless creation worn by girls in their teens making their debut in Society. The stiff folds of *peau de soie* gleamed in the candlelight, and the touches of crystal and gold silk in the trimmings echoed the sparkle of her eyes and the rich, dark gold of her hair. It was a highly sophisticated creation by one of London's most skilled dressmakers. Excitement had brought a delicate colour to Annabelle's cheeks and deepened the blue of her eyes. And Lady Ordway had produced a gold, pearl and crystal filigree necklace which completed an exquisite picture.

'My dear girl,' cried Lady Ordway when she saw her. 'You look even more lovely than I had imagined!'

'Pray tell me more, Aunt Laura! I need all the confidence I can muster! And may I say how splendid you look yourself?'

After much coaxing by Annabelle, and a special request from Giles, Lady Ordway had agreed to attend the reception. 'Giles asked in such a particularly pleasant manner that I should come, dearest Anna. I do think you are having an effect on him.'

Annabelle merely smiled, but she had no illusions. Giles had not changed his attitude to her.

This was made clear when she finally entered the white-and-gold drawing room. It was a room which she particularly liked. When she had first arrived it had been full of knick-knacks and gewgaws on all sorts of small tables and stands, and displayed in cases round the walls. The room was ornate in itself—the fireplace alone was an intricately carved masterpiece of rioting cherubs and garlands—and was better left uncluttered. She had recently seen to it that most of the cases and stands, together with their contents, had all been removed and put away in an attic. Now the beauty of the room's proportions, the decorated ceiling and silk wall-coverings, the candles in the delicate crystal chandeliers and gilded girandoles, were reflected clearly and without distraction over and over again in the huge mirrors on either side. The effect was as stunning as she had hoped.

Giles was standing by the empty fireplace, which was now filled with flowers. He was looking moodily at the carved surround, tracing the curls of one of the cherubs with his finger.

'Ah! There you are, Giles!' said Lady Ordway. 'Do turn round! We are both here.'

He turned, and the colour in Annabelle's cheeks grew slightly deeper as he took in her appearance. For a moment his eyes widened, and there was something in his gaze…admiration, certainly, but there was more than that. Warmth, feeling… She had no time to analyse either it, or her own response. It disappeared immediately, to be replaced with his usual, cold regard. Then he switched his attention to Lady Ordway, and smiled down at her.

'This is a great occasion, Aunt Laura.'

'Oh, yes! I don't know who isn't coming, dearest Giles. It has been nothing but acceptances. I had dared to hope for the *ton*—but the house has never before seen such a distinguished collection of ambassadors and attachés. And the service people…'

'That is not what I meant. It's a great day now that you have come down to join us again. I hope it's the forerunner of many such occasions. And I thank you for making the effort.'

'It was no trouble at all! Wilson helped, of course. But Rosabelle here has been such a darling girl—helping me to choose my dress, and the jewels to go with it. But don't you think that gold necklace looks well against her dress, Giles? And doesn't she look a dream?'

'Lady Ordway has been good enough to lend her necklace to me for the evening,' said Annabelle stiffly, as Giles's eyes rested on it.

'My mother had one like it,' he replied. 'I was wondering what had happened to it.'

'So she did! Your dear grandpapa gave her one when she married your papa, and I admired it so much that he had another made for me when I married his son. I had quite forgot! What did happen to it, I wonder? Oh!'

Lady Ordway looked distressed as Giles said harshly, 'I expect it went along with the rest to her… successor, ma'am. Though I cannot imagine it is to my beloved stepmother's taste.' Lady Ordway put her hand on his arm, and Giles forced a smile. 'But such things are best forgotten. I have no wish to spoil your evening. Come, I see Whitcroft is trying to catch your eye.'

'Dearest Giles!' Lady Ordway gave him an affectionate smile and moved away to speak to the butler. She was out of earshot. Giles turned his attention to Annabelle.

'Tell me,' he said. 'What have you done with Stephen's snuff boxes and the rest of his things?'

'They're in the attic,' Annabelle said calmly. 'I thought they were better out of the way.'

His mouth twisted in an unpleasant smile. 'Of course,' he said. 'Of course you would, Rosabelle. They were Stephen's treasures—he spent years collecting them.'

'Giles, please!' said Annabelle. In spite of herself her voice wavered. Her nerves were already so tightly stretched that she could not bear it if he started to attack her now, however discreetly. 'Can we not have a truce— for tonight, at least? It will do you no good if your acting hostess disappears before the evening has even begun.'

He looked at her fingers, twisting and turning on the filigree posy holder she carried, and said stiffly, 'I'm sorry. I'll try to avoid controversy. For tonight, at least.'

'I'll have the things brought back tomorrow, if that is your wish.'

'No. As a matter of fact, I like the room without them.'

For the rest of the evening Giles's behaviour was impeccable. The huge room soon filled with a chattering, laughing throng, and he moved among them with ease. Annabelle was astonished at his polished charm. Was this the man she had accused of not knowing what to do in civilised society? How mistaken she had been!

She herself was soon surrounded by numbers of people, all wishing to make the acquaintance of the lovely Mrs Ordway. Lady Ordway stayed firmly at her side, keeping her on the right lines when the conversation became difficult or obscure, but, ironically enough, it was Giles himself who actually rescued her from an awkward situation.

She had been caught by an obviously important guest,

a distinguished-looking gentleman, covered in orders and decorations. Aunt Laura was too far away to be appealed to, and the conversation was getting a little strained, as Annabelle talked her way through a delicate web of references to people and events about which she knew nothing. It would have helped, she thought bitterly, if she had the remotest idea who the gentleman was! He obviously expected her to know him and was beginning to look somewhat puzzled at young Mrs Ordway's evident distraction. To Annabelle's enormous relief, Giles joined them just in time.

'I had thought you were in Vienna still, Duke.'

'No, m'boy. I came back. M'work is done there. I hear Wellington's finished in France, as well.'

'Yes, Europe seems to be prepared to manage without us, thank God!' Giles turned politely to Annabelle, who was still trying to look as if she knew who her companion was. 'I expect you know that His Grace was in Vienna when I was there, Rosabelle.'

'Just been tellin' her. Best adjutant Wellington ever had.'

'You flatter me, Duke. But…may I take my cousin away from you? There's a group of the old campaigners over there who are demanding to be introduced.'

'I thought I recognised them! ''Old campaigners'' indeed. Not one of 'em is over forty! Well, my dear, I suppose I'll have to let you go. But you'd better take care with those ''old campaigners'', 'pon my word, you had! Their campaigns haven't always been on the field of action!' He gave a deep chuckle, then moved away and Rosabelle could breathe again. For once she did not object to Giles's peremptory tone.

'This way, Rosabelle.' He took her arm, and as they made their way through the crowded room he said, 'I must congratulate you on the success of the arrangements. You must be pleased with your efforts.'

'I shall be—but not before it is all successfully over, Giles.' Taken by surprise, she smiled at him. His hold on her arm tightened momentarily, and his face softened. But then, once again, the moment vanished. The barrier came down and his handsome face lost all its expression. At least, thought Annabelle, suffering an unaccountably sharp disappointment, he could hardly look at her with his usual dislike in the middle of a room full of guests!

Giles's friends were fellow officers, none of whom had met Rosabelle before. They laughed, admired, flirted a little, and she, free of the dread of failing to recognise someone she 'knew', was able to relax and respond. They all warmly congratulated Giles on his lovely cousin, and begged him to bring her to the balls and routs which were taking place nearly every day in London in the Season.

'We shall see,' said Giles. 'I suppose we can hardly avoid one or two of them.'

'What a frown, Giles, old fellow!' said a dashing Major, with just such whiskers as Annabelle had expected to see on Giles. 'Don't be such a dog in the manger. And why is it that we have never met this enchanting lady before?'

Looking at Giles's expression, which was growing more forbidding by the minute, Annabelle said swiftly, 'Major Dabney, you must know that Giles has been away for much of the past year. And I…have been living a very retired life since…since my husband died. I have only just started to mix in Society once more.'

This gave them all a moment's pause. But then Major Dabney said, 'I hope you will permit Society to see a little more of you, Mrs Ordway. If Giles finds himself unable to escort you, I should be delighted to offer my services.'

'And I!'

'And I!' The chorus was almost universal.

'Thank you. You are all very kind. And if I should need anyone I shall be sure to remember you. Now you must excuse me. I see my godmother beckoning to me.' With a charming smile to all of them she escaped while Giles was still able to be civil to them. He really was a dog in the manger, she thought rebelliously.

The reception was a triumph. Everyone said so. People came and went throughout the evening, but the rooms were always crowded, and there was the sort of animated hum in the air which betokens success. Lady Ordway took it very well, and though she was still in bed when Annabelle saw her the next morning, she seemed none the worse for the experience.

'My dear! You must be so pleased. I knew you could do it. Look!'

Lady Ordway's bed was covered in cards and letters. 'People have been so kind. They seem genuinely pleased to see me up and about.' Her eyes filled with tears. 'I was afraid…'

'Dearest Aunt Laura,' said Annabelle quickly. 'You must put the past behind you! You must know that people have very short memories—even in the country, yesterday's sensation is quickly replaced by the next. And how much truer must that be in London! I am certain that you would be very kindly received wherever you went.'

'This is your doing. I would never have roused myself without your encouragement, Anna. Thank you, my dear.'

'Nonsense! And it isn't Rosabelle you should thank, but Giles. He was the instigator.' She gave Lady Ordway a warning glance. Giles was on his way upstairs. He came in with a face of thunder, his arms full of flowers.

'I took these from Whitcroft as I came up. There's one for you, Aunt Laura. The rest are for Rosabelle.'

'Why do you always call her Rosabelle, Giles? Why not Rosa, as I do?'

'I've never considered the matter,' he said. 'What shall I do with the flowers? Rosabelle appears to have a brand new batch of admirers.'

'Yes, she has!' said Lady Ordway, happily. 'And the dear girl deserves every bit of admiration. She looked absolutely beautiful, don't you agree, Giles?'

'Exquisite,' he said tonelessly. 'And we are all impressed by her ability to charm. I would not have suspected it before last night.'

'Giles!'

'I think Giles means that he is grateful to me for exerting myself on his behalf,' said Annabelle, smiling sweetly in his direction. 'After all, they were all his guests, most of them friends of his. I am sure he wanted me to make them feel welcome.'

'Indeed! And Dabney, Pettifer and Wainwright obviously felt *very* welcome.' He looked at the cards on the flowers. 'Their requests for further acquaintance are most pressing. But I am surprised not to see the Duke of Armagh's card among them. He is a well-known connoisseur of beauty.'

'Why, thank you, Giles!' The sweetness of Annabelle's smile did not diminish. So that was the distinguished gentleman's name! She went on, 'The Duke was very kind, but out of my league, I believe. However, I find your other friends *very* amiable. Surprisingly so.

Or is it a case of the attraction of opposites? I'll take the flowers, Giles. They should be put in water. They are too beautiful in themselves to suffer for their donors' lack of tact in sending them.'

'Lack of tact? Whatever do you mean?' asked Lady Ordway.

'I'll leave Giles to explain, Aunt Laura. Perhaps he'd have preferred it if the bouquets had been sent to him!' was Annabelle's parting shot as she went out of the room to find the housekeeper.

When Annabelle returned Lady Ordway was alone. Her face was troubled.

'I should have thought Giles would be pleased at last night's success,' she said. 'But something seems to have put him in a bad mood. It was the business of the necklace, I suppose. I had quite forgotten that my sister-in-law had been given one just like it. It must have been passed on to Giles's stepmother, and he hates to be reminded of her. Though why he should take his ill humour out on you, I cannot imagine.'

'Can't you? He thinks I'm Rosabelle.'

'You mean, this…coolness towards her is as strong as ever? He is still prejudiced against her? I had hoped that would fade with time.'

'I'm sure it will soon,' said Annabelle with determination. It occurred to her that this was an opportunity to talk to Aunt Laura about Stephen, Giles and Rosabelle. 'Is Giles intending to come back?' she asked. 'Or have we time to talk a little?'

'He's gone out for a ride. I think he intends to call in at Tattersall's. He was talking of buying another mare.'

'Good. Aunt Laura, can't you tell me *anything* which will help me to understand Giles? I know you are fond of him, and he is good to you. *Why* has he this prejudice against Rosa? Is it…is it something to do with Stephen? I know so little about Rosa's husband.'

Lady Ordway plucked at the sheets nervously. She suddenly looked much older. 'I don't want to talk about Stephen, Anna. Please don't ask me to!'

Annabelle was disappointed but tried not to show it. 'I don't want you to do anything that distresses you, Aunt Laura.' She put her hand on Lady Ordway's arm. 'We won't talk about Stephen. But can't you give me a hint of what it is that causes Giles to be so…so unfair to Rosa? He seems to be reasonable enough with everyone else.'

Lady Ordway sighed. 'I love Giles, and I love Rosa. It's such a pity he can't forget the past. Rosa is such a kind, good girl, she deserves better. But Giles was prejudiced against her from the beginning. He never met her in the old days, of course, but he seemed to think that Rosa did her best to come between me and my son. He even tried to warn me about it!'

'He said as much the other day…I told him that it was nonsense.'

'Of course it was nonsense! But then he was predisposed to be suspicious—'

'Of Rosa? But why?'

Lady Ordway sighed again. 'Not just Rosa. Of any personable young woman, Anna.'

'Oh, come! He's a grown man with a successful career already behind him. You don't manage to become a Colonel in the Guards at his age without considerable force of character. Are you trying to tell me that Giles Stanton is *frightened* of women? I would find that very difficult to believe. He certainly doesn't give that impression.'

'He's not frightened of them. I said he was inclined

to be suspicious of them. And it's perhaps not so surprising. He learned not to trust one woman when he was
still very young.'

Annabelle hesitated. 'This is to do with the necklace,
isn't it? And Giles's stepmother, perhaps?'

Lady Ordway hesitated. 'I suppose that now Giles is
back in London, the scandalmongers are bound to talk
again...' She paused here for so long that Annabelle had
to prompt her.

'What happened, Aunt Laura?'

'Giles was deeply attached to his parents, particularly
his mother, my husband's sister, Margaret. He was dev-
astated when she died. It was very sudden, and he was
only ten or eleven at the time.'

'That's sad. He was old enough to realise what he had
lost. Rosa and I hardly remember our mama—we were
still so young.'

'Yes, my dear. And that is sad, too. Your mama was
the most enchanting creature I ever knew. You are both
very like her, though Rosabelle is quieter. But at least
your papa genuinely mourned your mother.'

'He still does. Though I could wish... Never mind.
What are you saying? That Lord Stanton did not mourn
his wife's death?'

'Before my sister-in-law had been dead three months,
Giles's father remarried. A young woman half his age,
who, it appears, was his mistress. She was a real
beauty—as beautiful as you and Rosa—and she could
wind Lord Stanton round her little finger. He was quite
besotted. But...she had little else to commend her, as
Lord Stanton soon discovered. Her house parties became
notorious, and his father was eventually forced to send
Giles away. That's why the boy spent his summers with
us. Since then, Venetia Stanton's name has become a

byword for every kind of extravagant and shameless behaviour. She eventually left her husband, but not before she had ruined him. He now lives in retirement on his estate, and sees no one.'

'Not even Giles?'

'Giles goes to Avenell quite often, but Lord Stanton is in a sad way. He hardly speaks to his son. He resents him.'

'Resents him? Why?'

'Because when Giles discovered that his father was unable to keep up the mortgage payments on his lands, he stepped in and bought them up.'

'How could he do that? Or is it since he inherited the Ordway fortune?'

'Oh, no! At least, not if you mean the money my husband left. The Ordways were all fabulously rich, and Giles's mother was an heiress in her own right. When she died Giles inherited the best part of her fortune, though I believe he has spent a good deal of it on his rescue of the Stanton lands.'

'I see. It's a dreadful story. But it happened twenty years ago. Since his mother died Giles has seen the world and mixed with all sorts of people, good and bad. Why has he not been able to put it behind him? It's absurd that he should blame all women for the sins of one!'

'I don't suppose he does. And if he ever met someone who was strong enough to overcome his prejudice he would make a wonderful husband. He is rich, handsome, and he can be very kind.' Lady Ordway gave Annabelle a mischievous look. 'Perhaps you're the one? You appear to have the spirit for it.'

'I think that is most unlikely, if not impossible! Even if I wished to be, I start with the serious disadvantage of deceiving him. If the masquerade ever came to light, can

you imagine what he would say? It would confirm all
his worst opinions of women in general, and Rosabelle
and me in particular! No, I don't think there is any
chance of a match between Giles Stanton and me! And
think of the quarrels we should have! I am no doormat,
you know!'

'That much I had noticed, my dear,' murmured Lady
Ordway.

Annabelle was kept too busy in the days that followed
the reception to ponder very often on what Lady Ordway
had said. A state of armed neutrality seemed to exist
between Giles and herself, and they both worked in rel-
ative harmony to maintain the standard of entertainment
set on that first night. She was completely unaware of
his state of confusion about her.

Giles Stanton numbered many distinguished people
among his friends and acquaintances—diplomats, military personnel, naval officers—people he had known in
Spain and Portugal, in Vienna, Brussels and Paris. After
the Duke of Wellington's return to England and the end
of the Allied Occupation of France many of them had
taken up residence in London, and it was now Giles's
intention to return the generous hospitality he had enjoyed for years as a bachelor at loose in the great cities
of Europe. The house in Upper Brook Street was eminently suited to such occasions, and as soon as the family's year of mourning after Stephen Ordway's death had
ended he had wasted no time in setting things in motion.

But in deciding to entertain such eminent and sophisticated guests he had taken something of a gamble.
Though his aunt was now slowly improving, she was not
yet ready to take over the reins of the household. And

Rosabelle Ordway had been an unknown quantity. He had not been at all impressed by what he had seen of her before Easter—thin, pale, nervy, apparently ill at ease in company, and far too easily reduced to tears. He might have forgiven her for all of this, if he had believed for one moment that she missed Stephen. But it was clear she did not.

She may have attempted to convince Giles that she had remained faithful to her husband—and what a vain exercise that had been with the evidence of Stephen's letters so vividly in his mind!—but she had never pretended that she had truly loved his cousin, or that she was sorry he was dead. Her one saving grace in Giles's view was her indisputable devotion to Aunt Laura.

He had been puzzled by her. This…colourless nonentity was a far cry from the seductress portrayed in the letters. He had even sometimes thought she must be playing a part, though for what purpose he could not determine. He was not a man to be softened by milksop manners and pathetic looks, and it had not been her tears which had moved him into letting her visit her family at Easter. It would have been too unreasonable not to allow her to go.

But he had not thought twice about insisting on her return at the given time, in spite of the change in his plans. He wanted her in London for purely selfish reasons. More than one lady had indicated her willingness to act as a proxy hostess until Lady Ordway was well again, and that was something Giles wished to avoid at all costs. Give a woman a hold over you and you could be stuck with her for life! At least he would be safe with his cousin's widow—he knew her for what she was.

But two weeks after the reception he sat in the library, ignoring the papers spread out in front of him, and coming to the conclusion that he was now more perplexed than ever by Rosabelle Ordway. A month or two ago he would have sworn she was an idle, broken butterfly, incapable of coping with a large household and a demanding social life. He had allowed for it. With a competent housekeeper, a good cook—and Rosabelle as a nominal hostess, kept well in the background—he would manage well enough. Though he could hardly hope to compete with the high standards of entertainment set by his friends, he had hoped for a modest degree of success.

However, it had recently been borne in on him that Rosabelle was, in fact, extremely capable at running the house, and that her skills and energy in organising entertainment of almost any kind were considerable. She had a trick of individuality, making something special of the smallest event, of casting a mantle of novelty over the most mundane occasion. He now discovered that evening invitations to the house in Upper Brook Street were among the most sought after in London. And as for Rosabelle staying in the background…he had difficulty in keeping up with her!

With all this success, Giles wondered why he was not happier. His friends were envious of his cook, impressed with the standard of comfort and elegance in the house, and they all raved about his cousin's lovely widow. It was astonishing, he told himself bitterly, quite astounding, what a pair of dark blue eyes and an enchanting smile could achieve. Such a woman had no need of intelligence or wit. She had only to sit there and look at a man, and before he knew it he was under her spell…

# Chapter Five

Giles pushed his chair back impatiently and got up. He knew he was not being completely just. Rosabelle was quite often quiet, almost subdued, especially when she was with people of the *ton*. Was she wary of what members of London society were saying of her? But she was neither stupid nor passive. She could be lively, she was frequently witty, and could hold her own in the most demanding conversations, particularly with his old friends—those who had lived abroad for most of their careers. Even on topics she could know little about, she was able to listen and respond intelligently. And though her battles with him were bitter, she nearly always gave as good as she got. But lively or quiet, witty or subdued, the result was always the same—they all sought her out. Was this what Stephen had not been able to face? Rosabelle's popularity with the gentlemen?

Giles threw himself back into his chair, frowning heavily. She *must* have been playing a part when they had first met, six months ago. One month's holiday in Berkshire could not have brought about such a change. And she was certainly lying when she swore she had not had an affair with Selder! She knew the name very well, even though she had attempted to deny it. He had not forgotten her dismay and horror when he had first mentioned Selder's name to her—before she had been to Berkshire and recouped her forces.

But a few days ago, when he had sprung it on her after his return from Bristol, he would have sworn she had never heard it before! What a consummate piece of acting that had been! Did she really think, however, that he was stupid enough to be taken in by an air of innocent enquiry, dark blue eyes wide, delicate chin lifted in that way she had when waiting for a response… It was a very pretty chin, even when it was lifted even higher in challenge, a refusal to back down…

Damn it! She was a liar and a cheat, however popular she might be with those who didn't know her. He was really looking forward to the day when he had finally solved the mystery surrounding Stephen's life and Stephen's death. No evasions, no denials would avail her then. She would have to admit her guilt once and for all. And then…? Giles pushed the problem of what he would do with her then to the back of his mind.

He was grateful when Whitcroft came in and interrupted his thoughts.

'A Major Dabney to see you, sir. And Goss brought this from the Receiving Office.' He handed Giles a letter.

'Show Major Dabney in, Whitcroft. You'd better fetch some wine.'

The letter was from Charlie Fortescue, and looked as if it might be interesting. It was to be hoped so. After his session with the innkeeper at Woolhampton he had visited Charlie in Bristol, and had spent five fruitless days there making enquiries about Da Costa, and searching the docks and taverns. But he had failed to find any trace of the man. Perhaps this letter would have something—Charlie had promised to enquire further… He was casting a rapid glance at it when Whitcroft showed Major Dabney in.

'Good morning, Dabs! Come and sit down, why don't you? Whitcroft is just about to fetch something from the cellar.'

'Er…well, if it's all the same to you I'd as soon have some ale. Jolly thirsty! Been ridin' in the Park.'

'I'll join you.' Giles nodded to Whitcroft, who disappeared. 'This is a bit early in the morning for you, isn't it?'

'Well, I wanted to talk to you, old chap. Thing is, I was tellin' Mrs Ordway t'other evenin' how pleasant it is in the Park early in the morning—'

'How would you know? You're never up before eleven!'

'I never mentioned *dawn*, dear fellow. Eleven o'clock or noon was what I meant.'

'Go on.'

'And she happened to say how she envied me.'

'Did she, indeed!'

'I was a touch flabbergasted, I can tell you. I've never met a lady yet who wanted to know anything about the outside world before about one o'clock. But apparently Mrs Ordway's an exception. She finds it hard to lie abed when it's so light, she says. Thing is, would you object if I was to invite her to take a turn round the Park one morning? Thought I'd better ask.'

Giles's first impulse was to refuse, but he restrained himself. He really had no reason to. Dabney was a per-

fectly eligible member of society, he was reasonably
rich, and he knew how to behave. Rosabelle would be
safe with him. It was unconventional, perhaps, for a lady
to be out riding so early in the morning, but Rosabelle
was no debutante. She was, or had been, a married
woman, and there was nothing questionable in her riding
round the park with an escort. Perhaps the question ought
to be whether Dabney, whom he liked, would be safe
with his cousin's widow! Eventually he said, 'Go ahead
and ask her.'

'Thanks, Gil. Didn't think you'd mind.'

Whitcroft came in with two tankards, which the gentlemen quaffed in companionable silence. Then Dabney
said with a gesture at the letter, 'I hope I didn't interrupt
your work. The Beau still keeping you busy? You seem
to do nothing else nowadays. I thought you'd sold out!'

'This? Oh, this isn't work. It's the reply to an enquiry
I made in Bristol. About a chap called Da Costa. I'm
trying to find out a bit more about Stephen's activities
before he died, but I don't think this can have much to
do with them.'

'Ordway's activities, eh? Er…got very far, Gil?'

'Not yet, but it's early days. Why? Do you know anything about them?' Giles asked in surprise.

'No, no! Nothing at all. Never knew your cousin.'

'I didn't think you would have. He was much younger
than either of us.'

'Heard of him, though.' Major Dabney stopped.

'And?'

'You been about the town much, Gil? Since you came
back from France?'

'Not yet, but I'm planning to. What is all this about,
Dabs? It's not like you to be cryptic.'

Major Dabney looked uncomfortable. 'Thing is…'

'Well?'

'I don't want to interfere, Gil, but…it might be better to leave well alone. No sense in stirring things up.'

Giles sat up and looked coldly at his friend. 'Explain!'

'It isn't all that easy! I just thought you might be wiser not to delve too deeply into your late cousin's activities.'

There was a pause, during which Major Dabney avoided Giles's gaze. 'What do you mean by that?' asked Giles softly.

'It's no use using that tone, Gil! It might scare the junior staff, but it don't frighten me! I've known you too long.'

'So?'

'This is damned awkward! I've no wish to offend you, old chap, but the long and short of it is, that, from what I've heard, your cousin ain't too well thought of in London! Some of his activities won't stand close investigation. He mixed with a rum crowd.'

Giles eyed his friend thoughtfully. Then he said, 'Have you by any chance been talking to Stephen's widow?'

'Mrs Ordway?' Major Dabney looked at Giles in astonishment. 'Good God, what do you take me for? I wouldn't mention it to *her*, 'pon my word, I wouldn't! Not at all the sort of thing to do! Bound to distress her.'

'Well, where did you hear it?'

'As a matter of fact I wouldn't know where I heard it first. It…it's fairly common knowledge. But I shouldn't worry. Unless you go poking around in it, it'll die down. Eventually.'

'Is Stephen the only victim of the gossip? What about the rest of the family?'

'Who would that be? You? Lady Ordway? Don't be a fool, Gil!'

'What about…Mrs Ordway?'

Major Dabney stared at Giles. 'What the devil's got into you, Gil? Of course not! Most people seem to think she's well rid of him!' He looked at Giles's set face, and said in a softer tone, 'Sorry if you don't like it, old chap. I know you were quite fond of him and all that, but that's what they say. And everyone I've spoken to is jolly pleased to see Mrs Ordway in society again.'

'I'm sure,' said Giles. 'She livens it up no end.'

Major Dabney looked slightly puzzled at his tone, but ended by saying, 'She certainly does. Lovely woman. A star. So, it's all right if I ask her, then?'

'Ask her what?'

'To ride in the Park!'

'Of course. I'm not her guardian.'

'Er…is she up?'

'I'm sure she is. I'll ask Whitcroft to find her for you.' He pulled the bell rope by the fireplace, then came back. The two men waited in a slightly uneasy silence for Whitcroft to appear.

Just before he came the Major said awkwardly, 'I hope you didn't mind my mentioning what's bein' said about your cousin, Gil.'

'Not at all. You weren't very specific, though. Does that mean that rumour is vague?'

'Er…no. But I've said all I'm going to say. Just wanted to warn you. Didn't want you to get into difficulties.'

'You're quite right, Dabs. Thanks.'

Whitcroft came in to say that Mrs Ordway was in the drawing room and Major Dabney went out. Giles picked up the letter again, and tried to concentrate on it.


Dear Gil,

There is absolutely no need to thank us, we were very pleased to see you…

The sound of laughter came through the door. Dabney had left the damned thing open in his eagerness to present his invitation to Rosabelle. He had plenty of address—Rosabelle would probably accept it... Giles went to the door and shut it. It was nothing to him what she did. He picked up the letter again.

I've had an encounter with another of the Excise Officers. He was out of Bristol when you were here...

Rosabelle knew that he went out every morning. They had met on that first day after her return. If she was so anxious to go riding why hadn't she mentioned it to him? Something could have been arranged... Giles looked down at the paper in his hand and sat down at his desk. Charlie Fortescue's writing was like a spider trail across the paper! It made it very difficult to concentrate...

...but has now returned. I talked to him at some length...

Perhaps she wasn't all that taken with riding! Perhaps it was just an excuse to have some time with Dabney. It must add to a woman's consequence to have a handsome chap like Dabney escorting her everywhere. An officer, too.

A most interesting chat...

Pettifer, too, had been here the other day to see if she would go to the theatre. And Wainwright had been quite cast down when she had had to refuse his offer of a drive out to Kensington. All those sensible men, good officers, falling over themselves to please her! What fools men were! Giles gave a snort of contempt and returned to his letter.

> and I think you'll be surprised at what I have learnt about your friend…

Not all of her beaux were officers, of course. Monteith had called yesterday to arrange to take her to Kew… Supercilious type. The son of an Earl. Aunt Laura had been in a flutter… And there was another whose name he couldn't recall… That damned woman had them all twisted round her little finger…! Giles got up impatiently and took the letter over to the window. The light would be better here, and he could perhaps read it without distraction.

> Da Costa has been known to my contact for some years. He has been involved with a good few things in his time, but it is suspected that, for the past few years, he has been working on pirate ships…

Giles's attention was at last securely caught. Piracy! He sat down on the window seat and read more carefully…

> There's a thriving trade for these villains in and around Bristol. They fit up here, and then, with information supplied by spies in the shipping trade, they prey upon merchant ships, concentrating on the more profitable cargoes, chiefly in the Mediterranean. One such, *Le Faucon*, operated by a Frenchman called

Legrand, was sunk off Algiers last autumn, but
there are always others. My friend believes Da
Costa brings information to the ships. He would be
very interested in anything you can tell him.

Sara and I hope that your plans to entertain
London are going well. We may take you up on
that invitation to visit you, but not yet…etc, etc…

The letter continued for a page more, but there was
nothing relevant to his enquiries… More sounds of
laughter penetrated from the hall. Dabney brayed like a
horse! He must be leaving. Good! But what had
Rosabelle said to him? Giles got up and went out into
the hall.

Dabney had hold of Rosabelle's hand and they were
smiling. But when Rosabelle saw Giles her smile faded
and she drew back.

'Dabs, I forgot to ask you—'

'Good morning, Giles,' said Rosabelle clearly.

'Good morning. I hear you are still unable to get used
to town hours. Why didn't you say?'

Rosabelle gave him a speaking look, then said, 'Major
Dabney has found a solution. I gather you don't object?'

'Of course not. Why should I object?'

'Why, indeed?' She turned to Dabney. 'The day after
tomorrow, then? I'll consult Goss about a horse.'

'I could bring one along,' said Major Dabney eagerly.
'I have the prettiest little mare. You cannot imagine—'

'Don't put yourself out, Dabs. Absolutely no need for
it,' said Giles, overriding the Major's protests. 'The stables are full of horses badly needing some exercise. I'll
see to it.'

'Right! I'll take my leave, then. Wait! What was it you wanted to ask me, Gil?'

Giles looked blank, then said, 'Oh, yes. Is Nicholson back yet, do you know?'

'He's not due for another three weeks. I thought I told you that the other day?'

'So you did! I'd forgotten. Right.'

The Major shook his head and said, 'I told you all that work wouldn't do you any good, Gil. Get some fresh air yourself. The day after tomorrow, Mrs Ordway. Eleven o'clock! Gil!' He saluted them both and strode off.

Giles walked back towards the library deep in thought. At the door he stopped and looked back. Rosabelle was about to go upstairs again.

'Rosabelle!' He walked back. 'I'd like to make sure the mare I have in mind for you will do. Have you ridden much in London?'

'Er...not a great deal. But I've ridden a lot down at Temperley.'

'Open fields and country lanes. Not the same thing at all. Can you be ready to go out in half an hour?'

'Where?'

'Riding in the Park, of course!' He repressed a smile at her obvious desire to ride battling with that independent spirit of hers, and decided to make it easier for her. 'Rosabelle, if you are free for an hour this morning, I should like very much to take you riding. Would you come? Please.'

She looked at him suspiciously. 'Why?'

'It's a pleasant morning. I feel like fresh air. And I should like to make sure that you will be safe with Dabney.' When she still looked sceptical, he added irritably, 'And I think it would look better in the eyes of the world if your first excursion into Hyde Park was with a member of the family!'

Her face cleared. 'Ah, that sounds more like it. Half an hour?'

'Half an hour. I'll go and see Goss.' Giles walked away, satisfied. He had done his duty by the family, he told himself. And it wouldn't do her any harm to see the sort of person she might meet at this hour in Hyde Park.

Annabelle went up the stairs with a light step. The prospect of some exercise and fresh air was very attractive. But did Rosabelle possess a riding habit? And would her sister's boots, supposing there were any, fit her? To her relief, at the back of the closet was a dark green riding dress and some tan boots which fitted perfectly. The dress was just a fraction tight, but was perfectly wearable. Rosabelle must have been quite young when she had last worn it—it had obviously lain in the closet for years.

Lily found a white lace-edged kerchief, which she tied into something like a man's cravat, allowing her to leave the dress open at the neck. Tan leather gloves, and a dark green hat with a small plume completed the outfit. After a quick check in the looking glass Annabelle was satisfied that she would do, though she had a fleeting regret for the new and very stylish habit she had left behind at Temperley. She went downstairs with two minutes to spare. Giles was waiting in the hall.

'I will say this for you. You are more punctual than most women of my acquaintance,' was his greeting.

'Heavens! A compliment! A real one.'

'Real?'

'One of the first things I was told about you was that
you believed in punctuality.'

'Who told you that?' he asked as he escorted her outside, where Goss was waiting with the horses.

'Why, Sergeant Goss here.'

'Goss wasn't with me when I arrived at Christmas.'

Annabelle kept her head. 'I meant the first thing
Sergeant Goss told me, when I came back from
Temperley,' she said fluently, then hurried on, 'Have we
at last found a virtue I possess? Punctuality. It's not a
very noble one, but I suppose it will do.'

Goss handed her up and they set off along Upper
Brook Street towards the Park.

'You're wrong,' Giles said. 'Punctuality is a very important virtue. In wartime it can be vital.'

'I can well believe that to be so. Giles, I should like
to hear of your adventures in the Peninsula. Spain has
always held my imagination.'

They negotiated the crossing into the Park. 'They
weren't adventures, Rosabelle, as in a romance. Men
died in them.'

'I'm sorry,' she said quickly. 'You are right to rebuke
me. I didn't think before I spoke.'

He looked at her downcast face and said more kindly,
'I lost some good friends out in Spain, but for all that
there were adventures which we all enjoyed—times
when we laughed, and times when we were simply glad
to be alive with a good horse under us, and the plains
of Estramadura before us.'

'What is Spain really like?'

'You cannot imagine how different it is from England.
The countryside is harsh, unyielding, with no shade or
hill to break the monotony. It can be unbelievably hot
in summer, and men can die of the cold in winter there.

But it has its own, stark beauty—vast skies and endless horizons.' Giles was lost in thought for a moment. Then he looked back at her and said with a smile, 'But there were many times when I longed for a more temperate climate, green grass, lazy rivers, the dales and moors of England...'

'You never came back to England during that time?'

'No.' His face closed up. 'No, I didn't. I chose not to.'

The ghost of Stephen...and someone else?...floated between them. A hazy picture of a beautiful woman wearing a necklace of crystal, gold and pearls, a woman who had taken his mother's place, disgraced it, then cast it carelessly aside. Giles was frowning, and Annabelle, reluctant to let the unusual mood of camaraderie go, cast around in her mind to find something to say.

'Lord Monteith is of the opinion—' she began. Her choice was clearly an unfortunate one. He interrupted her.

'I heard him airing his opinion on the wars in the Peninsula the other night. He must have been all of fifteen and at school when Talavera was fought and men died by the hundred. Spare me the inanities of such a supercilious ass!' Giles's tone was savage. 'Why are we riding at such a funereal pace? The horses need more than this to get the fidgets out of them.' His bay jerked forward at his master's urging and set off at a gallop.

One did not gallop in the Park, it was simply not done. Annabelle knew that very well—it was one of the many rules Mrs Thelwell had carefully instilled. But, after a second's pause, she let her horse have its head and followed Giles's example. It was glorious!

By the time they drew up they were at the far end of the Park. Giles was standing by his horse, adjusting one of the girths, when Annabelle reined in. He went to help her dismount.

'That was wonderful, Giles!' she laughed, as she leapt gracefully down. 'That bay of yours is a magnificent animal, but this mare is superb! She goes like the wind. I should love to try her out on a proper stretch of ground.' She looked up at him ruefully, the laughter lingering in her eyes. 'But not here! Society will disown me if I ever gallop like that again here. I must look a wreck!'

Giles looked at cheeks flushed with excitement and exercise, eyes sparkling with enjoyment, the sheer vitality of the woman before him. His hands were still at her waist... With an effort he drew away.

'I'm afraid your hair is coming down, Rosabelle. Do you wish to fix it?' he said coldly.

The pleasure slowly drained out of her face. 'Of course. Thank you.' She turned away from him and raised her arms to take off her hat, hooking it on to the saddle. She was still panting after the gallop, and it was easy to see the rise and fall of her bosom in the closely fitting riding habit. He had always thought of her as slight, but she was, in fact, a very shapely woman... He gazed in fascination as she bent her head and started to coil her hair. It slipped through her fingers like molten gold...

'Why are you staring so, Giles? I'm sorry if my appearance offends you, but it is entirely your fault. If you had told me we were going for a gallop, I would have made sure my hair was more secure. I suppose you will now call me a hoyden.'

'I...no, I will not call you a hoyden.' Giles was forcing himself to speak calmly. He was shocked at the feelings roused when his hands had been round her waist, and again at the sight of Rosabelle twisting her rope of hair. They were not the sort he had ever felt for a respectable woman before. Not in his life. This sudden desire to take her into his arms, to let that dark golden hair flow over him, to loosen the delicate lace at her throat and kiss the hollow thus revealed…

She had her back to him. He put his hand out to pull her towards him… The big bay horse sidled away and pulled at the rein. By the time he had brought it under control again she had finished tidying herself and was looking cool, neat, remote even. But the lace at her throat was still rising and falling more rapidly than usual, and one small tendril of hair was still curling round her ear… He looked away, angry with himself and her. His horse's movement had saved him from making a disastrous mistake—the damned animal had more sense than its master!

'Shall we go back?' he said abruptly.

'Of course,' she said.

Once again he helped her as she mounted, but this time she was silent. They rode back towards the gate. Giles was working hard to bring his feelings into line, full of scorn for his own weakness. How could he account for that sudden, almost overwhelming desire to make love to Rosabelle Ordway, there on the spot? He had always prided himself before on his cool approach to such matters.

There were women to whom one made love—charming, sophisticated beauties who surrounded Wellington and his officers—to whom love was a game, who knew how to please a man in return, of course, for certain favours, without any thought of long-term commitment.

And then there were what one might call respectable women, women with pretensions to virtue.

A sensible man avoided the slightest romantic involvement with any of these, for before you knew it she was talking of wedding bells and trousseaux and you were caught. Caught in a lottery where the chances were heavily weighted against you. Caught as his father had been. As Stephen had been. Women of virtue! He smiled grimly. Rosabelle Ordway, a woman of virtue? What a fool he was! How could he have forgotten, even for one moment, Stephen's anguished letters?

He stole a glance at her. She was looking withdrawn, sad almost. The flush in her cheeks had died down, her breathing was more even. You might say she was the perfect picture of a young society matron about to take a short, sedate ride in the Park! The trappings of respectability were there, certainly. Her behaviour in public was impeccable, and even in his own circles she had so far won approval from all sides—and that included the most rigidly hidebound sticks in the War Office. Charming she might be, original she certainly was, but she never overstepped the mark in public.

But she *must* be playing a part! Stephen had written of his wife in terms which could never be applied to a respectable woman. He had known the wanton in Rosabelle Ordway. And Selder, he must suppose, had known it, too. How long would it take before Dabney, Wainwright, or one of the others…? No! The smooth pace of Giles's horse faltered as he tightened his grasp on the reins. That was too much! That idea was one he could not even begin to tolerate. He found he was struggling once again to bring his feelings into order. What the devil was wrong with him? Why was he unable to believe that Rosabelle Ordway would run true to form?

The problem was that he was finding it increasingly difficult to reconcile the woman he was getting to know with the picture drawn by Stephen in those damned letters. He was as big a fool as all the rest!

Goss was waiting for them at the gate to the Park. When they were within sight of him, Giles said curtly, 'I see no reason why you should not go with Major Dabney tomorrow morning. But I don't advise going as far as we did today. Keep to the more frequented paths.'

She looked at him mockingly. 'Major Dabney has a greater sense of propriety than you, Giles. I don't imagine for one moment that we will go above a slow trot, or out of Rotten Row.'

'As well for him, perhaps.' She looked at him, clearly puzzled by his tone, but said nothing. When they reached the house, Giles watched as Goss took charge of Rosabelle's horse and was rewarded with a charming smile. She couldn't resist trying to enchant everyone! Absolutely everyone!

Annabelle went up to her room to change. She felt…strange, unsettled. Why had she been so tinglingly aware of Giles's hands on her waist? Why the sensation of shivers running down her spine when she met his eyes…? It wasn't the first time by any means that a gentleman had helped her thus from a horse, so why, this time, had she felt so breathless, as if she was on the threshold of something…something unimaginably exciting? His hands had tightened as he held her. Had he seen the effort it had cost her not to put her arms round his neck?

She had done her utmost to hide the feelings he had aroused, but had he been aware of them all the same? Was that why he had been so curt, so cold? He was quite right, of course. No decent woman would even think such things. The trouble was, these new and powerful emotions had taken her completely by surprise. She had never experienced anything like them before. Was she a wanton? And later, when she had turned away to avoid his eyes, had concentrated on tidying herself as quickly and as neatly as possible, had he thought she was deliberately flaunting her hair before him?

No one had ever before regarded her with such stony disapproval. She had deserved it. How could she be so shameless! She must make quite certain that such a thing never, never happened again!

Her resolution was not put to the test in the days that followed. Giles seemed to be avoiding her, and once again Annabelle felt deeply shamed that he thought it necessary. However, she maintained her air of calm, and when they did meet managed to treat him politely, but at a distance. She rode out most days with one or other of her cavaliers, and in the evenings entertained at Upper Brook Street, or went out with Lady Ordway. They were frequently escorted by Giles, but though she seldom lacked partners she was never invited to dance with him, and their conversations were limited to banalities. During the day he spent a great deal of his time in the library, or out and about, presumably with his friends.

For the rest she rejoiced to see Lady Ordway growing happier and more active with every day that passed, and she herself was still fresh enough to town life to take pleasure in the endless round of soirées, balls, concerts, and all the rest. She had become adept at appearing to understand a comment or observation without having the slightest notion of what was meant, and had learned to switch effortlessly to safer topics before any discrepancies became obvious. In fact, this constant challenge to her wits added secret spice to Annabelle's social life. Otherwise, deprived of her verbal battles with Giles, she might eventually have become bored with the frivolities which made up the London Season.

# *Chapter Six*

Annabelle was growing anxious about the length of her stay in the city, and said so to Lady Ordway.

'Good gracious, Anna! Is it so long since you came here? I am surprised. How time has flown!'

'That's one of the most pleasing things you could have said to me, Aunt Laura! It proves that you really are better. Can it be that you are even enjoying yourself?'

'Well, I am! More than I have for years. You and Giles have both been so kind, and my old friends have made me so welcome. But I suppose you are pining for Temperley?'

'No, not exactly... But I can't be Rosa forever. You wouldn't wish me to, I'm sure.'

'No, that's true. I miss Rosa. But I should miss you, too!'

Annabelle started to laugh. 'You can't have both of us. I don't think Papa would like that, and just think how

London would regard us. They'd think they were seeing double!'

'Well, they would be, wouldn't they?' Lady Ordway joined in Annabelle's laughter. But after a few minutes they both became sober again.

'I have to say, Anna, that I cannot at the moment see how you and Rosa could possibly change places. Giles would be bound to suspect something if you suddenly insisted on going to Temperley again so soon.'

'I agree. And even if we managed that, I can already foresee some difficulties Rosa's re-entry into society will create. It wasn't easy for me to take her place, but I had one advantage. She had been seen but seldom in public during her year of mourning, and society had rather forgotten exactly what she looked like, how she spoke and behaved. But the *ton* have seen so much of me in recent weeks that it would be much more difficult now to deceive anyone.'

'Especially Giles.'

'Especially Giles. In fact…in fact, I'm beginning to be of the opinion that *that* might be impossible. He's very astute. Sooner or later one of us will be required to confess the plot to him.'

Lady Ordway sighed. 'Oh, dear! I hadn't foreseen all this…'

'Nor had I,' said Annabelle ruefully. 'It's all his fault, of course. If only he had gone to France as he promised, instead of entertaining half of Europe here!'

'But…I thought you were enjoying yourself?'

'I am! I love it in London.'

'Rosa seems to be loving it at Temperley… Perhaps she would like a little longer there? There's a Mr Winbolt…'

'Philip Winbolt? She has met him?'

'Yes. I had a letter today. She can't say much, of course, but I gather she was rather impressed by him. Do you know him, Anna?'

'Yes, I do. Well, well! Rosabelle and Mr Winbolt…'

'Did you like him? Do you think he and Rosabelle might suit?'

'I found him over-solicitous. He seemed to think that every woman of his acquaintance was a delicate creature, needing his protection and help. You can imagine how I felt about that, after years of running Temperley single-handed! But Rosabelle is different… Do you know, Aunt Laura, I rather think they might be an ideal pair! And if Rosabelle was attracted to him, it would be a very good match for her. Mrs Thelwell considers him extremely eligible. '

'Then he must be. I don't know how she gathers her information, but I've never known her to be wrong!'

'If it did come to anything… How would you…what would your feelings be?'

'I know what you are thinking. My poor Stephen. But…I know now that Rosabelle was too young when she married him. I've known it for a long time. It was just…I persuaded her into it because I thought it might change him. But it was a disastrous mistake.'

'Change him? How?'

'To be…to be…' Lady Ordway's lips trembled and she shook her head. 'No! It's no use, Anna. I can't tell you. But I have bitterly regretted that marriage. Though I loved Rosa so much, I ended up trying to make use of her. I nearly ruined her life. If she could find happiness with someone else—someone who would love her the way she deserves—then I would be the happiest woman in London, I think.'

'Well, then,' said Annabelle briskly, anxious to turn

Lady Ordway's mind into a more cheerful direction, 'it can't do any harm to leave matters as they are for a week or two. Meanwhile, we must put our minds to the problem of effecting an exchange when the time is ripe! Perhaps when the season finishes?'

Just a few days later Lady Ordway came in from an afternoon drive in a state of eager excitement. She said triumphantly, 'Anna! I have the answer to our problem! I have just been talking to Mrs Arbuthnot, and she has the highest opinion of the waters at Bath. They have done her no end of good, she says.'

'And?'

'We could go there! Giles had talked of going to his estates in the North at the end of the season, but I am sure I can persuade him to take us to Bath instead. And the Bath Road passes within a few miles of Temperley.'

'But if we stayed at Temperley, Giles would meet Rosabelle there! And as soon as he saw us together he would know instantly what we had done. It wouldn't work, Aunt Laura.'

'Wait! Giles and I would not go to Temperley. I have some very good friends at Reading whom I haven't seen for years. We would stay with them and you—'

'—would pay a visit to Temperley, ostensibly to see my father... I see!'

'And after a day or so Rosa would join Giles and me at Reading, and the three of us would carry on to Bath!' Lady Ordway sat back, looking very pleased with herself. 'Is that not a good plan?'

'An excellent one! It would mean that Rosa's return to London would be postponed as well. Society will have a chance to forget me. But...what reason can we give for your not coming to Temperley with me? The house is big enough for twenty visitors.'

'Your papa is an invalid, Anna! We could not possibly foist ourselves on him. Besides, I should really like to see the Chamberlaynes again.'

'Very good. The next most important question is— can you persuade Giles to take you to Bath?'

'I'm sure I could. He's so very kind. The difficulty will be to find him at home for long enough to bring the question up! He spends so much time out of the house nowadays.'

Annabelle bit her lip. She too had noticed that Giles was seldom at home, and thought she knew the reason for it. Odious, conceited man! Did he not realise how much she regretted that moment of weakness in the Park? How small the danger was that she would repeat it? There was really not the slightest necessity for him to spend so much time with his friends!

But later that night, as she lay in bed, Annabelle asked herself why she was not more pleased at Lady Ordway's ingenious plan. Her task was accomplished. Rosabelle had enjoyed an untrammelled month—more!—in the peace of Temperley, and she had seen more than she could ever have imagined of London and its Society. If the Bath project succeeded, Rosabelle Ordway would return later in the year to London, and Annabelle Kelland would settle down again to her busy but quiet life at Temperley.

It might take Rosabelle a while to accustom herself to the life in society again, but she would manage. And if the affair with Philip Winbolt was serious, he would visit her there. She did not doubt for a minute that if Mr Winbolt truly fell in love with her sister, he would forgive her for her deception. He was as gentle and as understanding as Rosabelle herself. With Mr Winbolt to protect her and to believe in her, what would it matter if Giles remained unconvinced of her innocence?

It was all very satisfactory, so why was there this pain somewhere inside her? What did it matter to her—this conviction that Giles would quite certainly never forgive her for deceiving him? That it would only confirm his jaundiced view of women in general, and of Annabelle Kelland in particular? Annabelle reviewed his character defects in detail. She rehearsed in her mind the insults, the harsh orders, the unreasonableness of his behaviour... But nothing seemed to chase away this feeling of sharp regret that she would soon never see him again.

Giles was not seeing his friends as often as Annabelle believed. He was busy seeking out people who had known Stephen Ordway. He told himself that his aim was to prove Dabney's view of Stephen totally mistaken. And if he should discover more about Rosabelle Ordway in the process, then well and good! But, as time went on, he began to realise that any attempt to prove Dabney wrong was vain. Instead, he grew more and more troubled at the picture of Stephen which was emerging.

His cousin *had* mixed with one of the most unsavoury sets in London Society. His word, his honour, his integrity *had* been compromised time and time again. And while no one knew, or no one would say, what he and his friends had been up to, they all condemned him without hesitation. When Giles suggested that he might have been weak, foolish, easily led, the world agreed with him. But one man, who had been close to Stephen in the old days, added that though he had always been weak and foolish, he had also been a liar and a cheat.

'You're wasting your time on that cousin of yours! He

wasn't worth it! Oh, he could charm the skin off a cat, when he was in the mood, but it was all show. Look, Gil, I was at school with the fellow, and I know. What's more, I'm not afraid to tell you—not like some of these others. Believe me, Stephen Ordway was a bad lot from the day he was born. A manipulator and a liar.'

Giles rejected this, of course, immediately. This was not the Stephen he knew. But in the end he had to admit that Dabney's advice had been sound. He had stirred things up which would have been better left alone.

However, he found he could not leave it there. Stephen was dead, beyond the reach of harm or censure, but his widow still lived. What part had Rosabelle Ordway played in all this? In all his researches, there had not been the slightest hint of criticism directed against her. But then, he had never heard any mention of Selder's name, either. It was evident that the pair had kept their activities very discreet. Giles was convinced that there must be someone in London who knew more about Selder, and he set about trying to find whoever it was.

His quest took him into curious byways, and among those who lived in the twilight of London's underworld. He learned one or two names of men who had been part of Stephen's circle, even came to recognise one or two— a blond giant called Fraser, and a small, stocky man called Burrows. But he never heard a whisper of the name of Selder.

Lady Ordway eventually managed to broach the question of a visit to Bath with her nephew.

'I am much improved in health, dearest Giles, but Dr Cotterell has persuaded me that a short visit to one of the watering places would be beneficial. To Bath, say.'

'Then you must go to one. Indeed, it would suit me very well to take you.'

'It would?'

'I had intended, as you know, to go north, at the end of June—I've even started to make some arrangements. But I had been wondering what to do about the house here. I don't like the idea of leaving you in London without someone to keep an eye on you. Especially in the heat of the summer months. But if you and Rosabelle were to spend a few weeks in Buxton, then I could escort you there. You would be quite safe there while I pay a visit to my father at Avenell, which is only a dozen or so miles away. Then I could later join you, and escort you back again.'

'Buxton!'

'Yes, why not? The facilities there are first class. The waters are considered to be as good as any in England, and the Crescent is very handsome, with two or three excellent hotels and apartments.'

'It's such a long way away!'

'A mere sixty miles further than Bath! Have you ever seen anything of Derbyshire, Aunt Laura? It's very beautiful, I assure you.'

'I visited Avenell once—just after your uncle and I were married. I remember that the journey seemed endless!'

'We could take it in easy stages. Several friends of mine live on the route, and they would be delighted to welcome you. Or there are one or two excellent inns I have come to know, too.'

'Mm...I...I wondered if we might go to Bath, Giles? The beauties of Nature are all very well, and I'm sure your friends are delightful, but I prefer life in a city. Bath is such a *civilised* place, and there would be amusement

for Rosa, too. The Assembly Rooms there are a great
deal more fashionable that anywhere so far north as
Buxton could be. Who has ever heard of Buxton?'

'I thought it was the waters you were anxious to take,
Aunt Laura? But...' Giles looked at Annabelle. 'I suppose it is your wish to go to Bath?'

'Yes,' she said bravely, putting up her chin. 'I've always heard that it's a beautiful city, and that the shops
and entertainments there are quite outstanding. Buxton
could hardly compete.'

'Frivolity and fashion. Is that all you think of?'

'Giles! I would prefer to go to Bath, too. Rosa was
merely supporting me.'

'Was she? Well, I suppose I could go north later—in
the autumn. I'll think about it, Aunt Laura. I'll have to
ask my agent if there's any pressing business at Avenell
first.'

'Yes, do, dearest Giles! I am persuaded that everyone
at Avenell Hall could do very well without you till the
autumn.'

'We could always go without you, Giles,' said
Annabelle with a mocking look. 'We should be safe
enough with a suitable number of grooms and servants.
We could then indulge our love of frivolity and fashion
without denying you your chance of worth and achieve-
ment at your country seat.'

Giles looked at her blandly. 'I wouldn't hear of it. We
shall all three go either to Bath—or to Buxton.'

The two women exchanged a glance. Their beautiful
scheme was in danger of going sadly awry!

A day or two after this debate Giles took them to the
theatre. It was intended to be an evening of harmless
amusement, one of many such. But this particular visit

resulted in a sequence of events which was to have a far-reaching effect on several lives.

As they took their places in the auditorium Giles stiffened. His eyes were fixed on three people sitting in the box opposite theirs, and Annabelle wondered what could possibly interest him in such an ill-assorted group. On the left was a generously proportioned lady in black, looking around with good-humoured self-assurance. Her plump face was thickly powdered, and it was very clear that her sable hair owed more to art than to nature.

On the right was another lady on the shady side of forty, equally heavily made up and with hair as spuriously golden as her friend's was black. She wore a low-cut red dress and a great deal of jewellery—several rings and necklaces, and a long string of milk-white pearls wound extravagantly among the brassy curls. Between these two sat a young man in his late twenties.

Annabelle could hardly believe her eyes. He was almost too handsome to be real—more like a statue out of classical antiquity! Tall, broad-shouldered with classically perfect features and lint white hair—what on earth could he be doing with the two harpies?

Annabelle raised her opera glasses to her eyes…and gave a gasp as she caught a glimpse of one of the necklaces worn by the woman in red…

'Give me those!' Giles said sharply. He held them to his eyes, then gave an exclamation of disgust and turned to Lady Ordway. 'Would you please excuse me, Aunt Laura? The play is one I have seen before, and there is something else I really ought to be doing at this moment. I shall return before it is over and wait for you in the anteroom. Winterton is in the next box—I'm sure he would accompany you downstairs.' He was very pale.

Lady Ordway looked at the woman in the box opposite, and nodded. 'Of course we shall be perfectly all right, Giles,' she said. 'We shall see you after the play.'

Giles bowed, thrust Annabelle's glasses back into her hand, and disappeared.

'Poor boy!' said Lady Ordway, shaking her head. 'That dreadful, dreadful woman!'

Annabelle fingered the necklace round her own neck. 'Who is she, Aunt Laura? Is it…is it Giles's stepmother? The necklace she's wearing is the same as this, isn't it?'

'Yes,' said Lady Ordway bitterly. 'That's Venetia Stanton. And she's wearing Margaret Stanton's necklace. But not only that. The pearls in that…trollop's hair— they too belonged to Margaret. She inherited them from my mother-in-law, who had them from her mother.'

'It's a lovely string of pearls.'

'They are worth a king's ransom! So large and so perfectly matched. But that isn't the point, Anna. Margaret Stanton and her mother Emily before her were both decent, well-bred gentlewomen. The value of those pearls goes far beyond their intrinsic worth—they represent pride in family and reputation. And to see them flaunted in that shockingly vulgar manner… I do not blame Giles's revulsion!'

'Who are her friends?'

'The woman in black was Nellie Marsden before she married a German aristocrat. A camp follower. Now she's the Baroness Leibmann.'

'Is that the Baron sitting between them?'

'Good Lord, no! He's eighty if he's a day! No one ever sees him. I don't know who the Adonis in the box is, I haven't seen him before.'

At the end of the play Annabelle and Lady Ordway made their way, escorted by Lord Winterton, down to the anteroom. But there was such a crush on the stairs that Annabelle was separated from the two older people. She could see the feathers on Lady Ordway's headdress waving on the other side of the staircase, and at the bottom of the stairs she tried to cross over to rejoin them. But the tide of people was too strong, and she merely succeeded in losing her fan, as it was torn from her in the mêlée. A strong arm swept her to one side into a safe corner, and a minute later her fan was returned.

'Ma'am?'

'Why, thank you! You are very kind, sir!' said Annabelle with a slightly nervous smile.

The gentleman smiled back, and though he was not precisely handsome, Annabelle thought how charming he was. She started to smile more widely. But then, quite unaccountably, she found herself trembling, chilled to the bone as if she was suffering a sudden attack of ague. Her skin crawled as he spoke again.

'Why, Rosabelle!' he said. 'What a piece of good fortune! I've been hoping to see you.' He cast a glance up the staircase. 'But this isn't the place. We'll meet again before long.'

Then, before she could say anything, he disappeared into the crowd. Annabelle leaned against the wall. What was the matter with her? The crowd had pushed her, but there had been no real danger. Why this sudden reaction? It couldn't have been the gentleman who had rescued her fan—she had never seen him before in her life. Yet...who was he, and what had he meant? He knew her twin, so much was certain, but she could not somehow imagine Rosabelle making a friend of him. A second shiver ran up her spine. Annabelle passed a hand over her forehead—was she sickening for something? The room was hot, but she felt chilled... She nearly jumped out of her skin when a hand descended on her shoulder. Turning, she found Lady Stanton peering at her throat.

'Look, Fraser!' the lady cried. 'It's the girl with my necklace!' The woman's fingers stretched out like talons to touch it. Annabelle's head swam as a waft of perfume threatened to overpower her, and Venetia Stanton's heavily powdered face was thrust close to hers.

'Who the devil are you, my dear?' demanded Lady Stanton. 'And what are you doing with a copy of my necklace? Don't tell me that my toad of a stepson has a *petite amie* at last! Did *he* have it made for you?'

Annabelle felt sick. 'I beg your pardon,' she said as clearly and as coldly as she could. 'You must excuse me.' She tried to get round the side of the group. The tall, fair man was in her path.

'Let me pass, sir!' cried Annabelle, frantically. She had never before felt so trapped and ill. Suddenly Giles was there at her side, and she turned towards him gratefully, clutching his arm. The man called Fraser instantly stood aside and bowed.

'I'm sorry if I frightened you, ma'am,' he said. 'I had no intention of doing so, believe me.'

His tone was indifferent, with a touch of surprise, and Annabelle felt slightly ashamed at her panic. She nodded stiffly and he turned away.

'Are you ready to join us again?' Giles's tone was curt. Annabelle became conscious that she was still holding his arm more tightly than necessary, and with a murmured excuse she released him. Her knees were weak, as if she had just been through some deadly peril, and she was by no means certain she could walk. Berating herself for her stupidity, she took a step towards Lady Ordway, who was standing over by the door.

But Lady Stanton had not finished with them. 'What, no greeting for your own stepmama, Giles?' she called shrilly. 'How uncivil of you!'

Without even a glance at her Giles replied, 'I do not owe you any civility, ma'am. Excuse me.' Lady Stanton let out her breath in a long hiss at this set-down, but Giles ignored it. With a frown he took Annabelle's arm and skilfully steered her through the crowds. A carriage was waiting for them and he saw both ladies into it, treating Annabelle, who still shivered occasionally, with gentle consideration, patiently parrying Lady Ordway's anxious questions.

This was a side of Giles Annabelle had not seen before, and she was disarmed by it. If only he could be like this all the time, she thought wistfully. She felt safe, cherished. In the darkness of the carriage she smiled wryly to herself. She had scorned Philip Winbolt for the very qualities that Giles was now displaying. Why was it so different?

It was still quite early when they reached Upper Brook Street, but Lady Ordway announced that she was very tired, and was going to bed. The evening had not been without its difficulties.

'And if you take my advice, Rosa, you will do the same. You look quite worn out. Thank you for taking us to the theatre, Giles. The play was delightful, though…' She decided not to finish the sentence, bade them both goodnight cheerfully enough and then went upstairs. Giles raised an eyebrow at Annabelle.

'Are you too tired, too? Or would you have a glass of wine or ratafia with me? It might help you to sleep.'

This was an unexpected gesture. Since the ride in Hyde Park Giles had been careful to keep his distance. What was in his mind? Whatever it was, it would surely be wiser to follow Lady Ordway's example and go straight to bed! She cast wisdom aside and said, 'I…I'd like a glass of wine, Giles. And some *pleasant* conversation!'

He laughed and escorted Annabelle into the drawing room. Whitcroft brought the wine, poured out two glasses, then left the decanter on a table by the sofa. Giles stood in his favourite place in front of the fireplace.

'You're looking better,' he said. 'I thought for a moment you were going to faint in the theatre. I was afraid I should not reach you in time. Was it the crush? The lack of air?'

'I don't think so. I am not normally affected by such things. No, it was more like a passing attack of fever. It has quite gone now.'

'I saw you drop your fan—that was when I started to make my way to you. Who was the man who returned it, do you know?'

'The dark gentleman?' Annabelle repressed a shiver, and spoke without thinking. 'I've never seen him before.'

Giles regarded her for a moment in silence. 'Strange!' he said, and drank some wine. 'Did…my stepmother say anything to upset you?'

Annabelle looked blankly at him, and he went on stiffly, 'I thought Aunt Laura would have told you who she was. The woman in red in the box opposite. I saw her talking to you just before I reached you.'

'Aunt Laura did tell me—I'm sorry, Giles, I was wool-gathering. No, she didn't frighten me, though I…I didn't like her. She asked about this necklace. She…thought you might have given it to me.'

'I see. Well, whatever the cause, I'm sorry I left you to fend for yourself. I shouldn't have done it. I should have stayed with you in the box.' He turned and put both hands on the mantelpiece, looking blindly down at the garlanded cherubs. 'It's just that…I cannot bear to look at her. Especially when…'

'Yes, I know,' said Annabelle softly. She rose and came over to the fireplace. 'Aunt Laura told me the story, Giles. I'm sorry.' She put her hand on his arm.

He stared at it in silence. Annabelle, suddenly confused and embarrassed, worried lest he should think this an unmaidenly advance, jerked it away.

'No! Don't go! Rosabelle…' He pulled her back and took her into his arms. She looked into his eyes, and what she saw there made her heart thump. She suddenly felt breathless.

'Don't go!' he said again slowly, and bent his head. His lips touched hers in a featherlight kiss. Annabelle felt more shivers running down her spine, and her knees felt as if they might give way beneath her, but this time the sensations were entirely pleasurable. She moved closer, grasping his shoulders for support. Giles tightened his hold and kissed her again, more firmly. A ripple of feeling ran through her veins, unlike anything she had before experienced.

She found herself responding, tentatively at first, then, as the strange new feelings increased, more eagerly. For a glorious moment she was lost in a swirl of sensation, eyes shut, her body pliant and yielding. But it did not last long. Reason soon returned and she was suddenly nervous. This was uncharted, alien territory for her, and she did not trust it.

'Giles,' she murmured, putting her hand between them and pushing him away. He caught the hand and took it to his lips. Annabelle watched, fascinated, as he turned it and kissed the centre of her palm. She gave a little cry

of delight, and he laughed and pulled her back to him.
He started to kiss her again, and this time Annabelle was
half lifted off her feet as he swept her into a passionately
deep embrace, muttering her name, his lips on her eyes,
her hair, then back to her lips… For longer than she later
cared to remember she responded with a fervour equal
to his, but when he started to urge her towards the sofa,
her fears returned.

'No, Giles!' she panted, and using all the resolution
she could muster she dragged herself away from him.
She became aware that her hair was halfway down her
back, her dress was crushed and in disorder, and her lips
felt bruised and sore. As sanity returned, as her sense of
fitness, of outraged propriety gradually overcame the tumult of her emotions, she felt deeply ashamed. She
turned away from him and bent her head. 'This is not
right! It cannot be right! You…you despise me already,
I know, but I am not a wanton, whatever you may think.'

Giles was equally roused. He was breathing rather fast,
and his hands were trembling. It was almost as if he had
not heard her words. He stepped towards her and, taking
her hand back in his, pulled her roughly towards him,
trapping her in one arm, while he forced her chin up
with his other hand, bending his head over hers…

'No!' cried Annabelle again, and gave him a sharp,
hard push. He paused, but instead of letting her go, he
held her away from him, staring at her with a dazed
expression in his eyes. Then slowly the wonder died, and
a curiously cynical smile took its place. He released her,
and turned away, back to the fireplace. For a moment or
two there was silence in the room.

Then he said evenly, 'Forgive me! I…I forgot myself.
God damn it, Rosabelle, what are you? I thought I knew

all the tricks women can employ, but you have me mystified.'

She was shocked, and her face showed it.

His voice was harshly impatient as he exclaimed, 'Oh, for God's sake, don't look at me with the eyes of a hurt child! That was no child's behaviour just now.'

'I...' Annabelle swallowed painfully. 'I was not play-acting, Giles. I am aware that I behaved badly, that I should have put a stop to...to our lovemaking long before I did. Indeed, it should never have begun! But...but I don't know what came over me! I had never felt such a strong...such a strong attraction before—never even knew such...such a thing existed. And...and it took me by surprise.'

'Oh come, Rosabelle! Don't try my credulity too far!'

'You may disbelieve me if you wish, Giles. But I assure you, it was a...a new experience.' She stopped and swallowed again. 'Putting an end to it was one of the hardest things I have ever done. But I had to. For my own sake and yours.'

'How extremely noble of you!'

'Please...! If it had gone any further, we would both have regretted it. There are too many barriers between us for love to flourish.'

'Love! My dear girl!' His scornful tone made it clear what he thought of love, and she flinched.

But after a moment she continued steadily, 'You know I am right. Thinking what you do about me, you would surely have despised yourself later for succumbing to the impulse, the weakness of the moment. And...' she faltered, then went on firmly, 'And for me at least, only love, sincere and lasting love, could excuse such behaviour. I am ashamed of myself.' She lifted her chin and regarded him proudly. 'But I employed no tricks. Forgive me, if it seemed to you that I did.'

# Chapter Seven

Giles found her honesty curiously convincing, and was disarmed by it. Others in similar circumstances would have burst into dramatic tears, indulged in furious accusations of an attempt to seduce them, gathering up a cloak of outraged virtue around them—conveniently forgetting their own eager responses just a moment before. But Rosabelle Ordway had rejected such histrionics, and he was impressed. No other woman of his acquaintance would have been so frank about her own feelings.

'Perhaps I was wrong to accuse you of tricks. My excuse is that I, too, was…taken by surprise.' He stopped as he realised how true this was. It was not normally part of his nature to be so carried away, so lost to the world around him. He frowned and went on, 'This was not what I intended when I invited you to a glass of wine. I saw that you were distressed at the theatre. I meant only to comfort you, to soothe your lacerated nerves. But then you offered me comfort instead…'

Annabelle could see that he was genuinely disturbed by what had happened and decided to accept what he had said—it was, after all, an apology of sorts. Her own feelings were still in turmoil, and she wanted nothing more than to escape to her room before she betrayed more than she wished. She nodded, not meeting his eyes and turned towards the door.

'No, don't go yet!' he said. 'You haven't finished your wine. And there's something more. Something I must ask you. Please stay.' The words were abrupt, but this was a plea rather than a command. She hesitated, then came slowly back and sat on one of the chairs.

'Thank you.' He brought her glass over, put it beside her, and then went back to the fireplace. He stood for a moment, obviously marshalling his thoughts.

'Rosabelle, it is true that I had certain prejudices before we ever met which have given me a jaundiced view of you—a view which seemed at the time to be perfectly justified.' He stopped. Annabelle held her breath—was Rosabelle about to be vindicated?

Giles went on, 'I told you, I believe, that I intended to find out more about Stephen's life and death. And I have recently been searching London for people who knew him.' His face grew sombre. 'It hasn't been pleasant. It has gradually been borne in on me that the boy I knew…the boy I thought I knew…existed only in my imagination. I may have made a mistake in believing everything he told me without question. It is possible that the faults in your marriage to Stephen were not on one side only.' He paused, obviously waiting for her to respond. But Annabelle was not ready to say anything. If Giles had been talking to people who had known his cousin, then he probably knew far more about Stephen and his marriage than she did!

He gave a sigh and went on, 'I can see that it will take time for you to believe me sincere. And I don't blame you. If I have been wrong, I must have hurt you badly in the past. But—at the risk of offending you yet again—can you really tell me nothing of Selder? He is the stumbling block to every enquiry I have made. Don't shake your head, Rosabelle! Believe me, I am not at the moment pursuing the question of an affair between the two of you. Even if that were the case, I am prepared to accept that, however wrong it may have been, you may have been seeking consolation for the failure of your marriage.'

Annabelle remained silent. Giles had always been so convinced of Rosabelle's guilt that it would be a waste of breath to deny the existence of any affair. But his next words surprised her.

'I have even begun to ask myself whether your involvement with Selder might have been a figment of Stephen's disordered imagination… No, don't say anything—I know you have always denied its existence. But let us put that to one side for the moment… It is only one piece—a very important piece, but one of many— of the puzzle surrounding Stephen's relationship with Selder. To solve the whole I need to know more about Selder himself. So far he is a figure in the shadows, a cipher. Can't you tell me *anything* about him?'

For the first time since coming to London, Annabelle wished passionately that she had never embarked on this stupid, senseless, dangerous masquerade. Rosabelle just might have been able to respond to Giles's appeal, but she herself was totally in the dark about the man… And now what was she to do? The choice before her was stark. She could confess to Giles, on the spot, that she was Annabelle Kelland, and therefore knew absolutely nothing about Stephen, Selder, or anyone else. Or, as Rosabelle, she could apparently persist in her refusal to talk of Selder.

Giles would be disappointed, angry even. But that would be nothing compared with his anger and disillusion if she, Annabelle Kelland, told him that she had been deceiving him systematically, constantly, for the past six or seven weeks! Especially only moments after he had said he might be beginning to trust her! She simply could not face it.

'I…I cannot,' she said in a low voice. 'I know nothing of Selder. I have no idea where he can be found, or anything else about him.'

The air was filled with his sharp disappointment, but he took it better than she had thought. 'I half expected that,' he said. 'Your acquaintance with Selder must have ended some time ago. And Selder is a very elusive creature. But, if you ever find that you know something after all and feel able to confide in me, I should be very obliged to you, Rosabelle.'

'I assure you, Giles, that I will,' said Annabelle with all sincerity. 'And now I should like to say goodnight and go to bed.' He escorted her to the foot of the stairs, where he stood for a heartstopping moment, looking down at her.

'I wish I could make up my mind about you,' he said. 'Perhaps, with time, we may yet come to a better understanding?'

'I'd like that,' she said. But she spoke sadly, and he wondered why.

Annabelle was not sure how to face Giles the next day, but in the event he made it easy for her. There was no consciousness of the evening before in his manner, as he enquired if she had slept well, whether she felt more herself.

Lady Ordway answered for her. 'She certainly seems it. I was quite worried about her last night. Tell me, Rosa, will you be fit enough for the Marchants' ball? You have only to say the word and I shall send a note of apology to Countess Carteret.'

'I am quite recovered, Aunt Laura. Thank you both for your concern, but it really isn't necessary any longer. I don't know what came over me last night.' She felt colour rising in her cheeks, and, avoiding Giles's eye, she added, 'At any stage. But I am quite well again this morning.'

'That's good! Giles, have you heard from your agent yet?'

'No, Aunt Laura, but I shall in the next few days. Hathersage would have replied immediately if there had been anything urgent, so it seems highly likely that we shall be able to go to Bath. You could begin to make plans on that basis.'

'I shall tell Barker to write straight away to enquire about houses. Somewhere near the Assembly Rooms, I think…' She hurried off to write a note to their man of business. Giles and Annabelle were left alone.

'I…I must see the housekeeper…' Annabelle's voice trailed away under Giles's continued steady regard. 'Please don't look at me in that way, Giles!'

He shook his head as if to clear it. 'I don't know what the matter is with me,' he said irritably. 'I was certain that cold light of morning would bring me to see reason. But even now you are still exercising your damned enchantments, Rosabelle.'

'I have no enchantments!' she cried. 'You must abandon this nonsense, Giles! Last night was an…an aberration which we should both forget.'

'I know, I know! And I am sure it will pass. Very well.' He took a breath and became businesslike. 'If Hathersage's report is favourable, and I think it will be, we can leave London at the beginning of July. Aunt Laura tells me that you would like to visit Temperley on the way?' Annabelle nodded. The thought of Temperley and what it meant depressed her.

He went on, 'Shall I escort you there?'

Annabelle's heart gave a jump, but she managed to say casually, 'Er…you could, I suppose. But perhaps it would be better for you to stay with Aunt Laura. She hasn't seen these friends for so many years, she might need your support. I can ask my sister to send a carriage to Reading to collect me and bring me back. It isn't far.'

'I suppose you're right.' He started walking to the door. 'Have you any commissions for me in the town?'

'No, but…Giles!'

'Yes?'

'Are you… Do you plan to be at the Marchants' ball?'

'I think so, yes. But I shan't ask you to dance with me.'

'Why not?' demanded Annabelle in absurdly sharp disappointment.

Giles raised an eyebrow. 'I might find it impossible to ''abandon this nonsense'' if I found you in my arms again—during a waltz. I can't put my reason under such a strain. Not twice in one week.'

'We…could dance something else?'

'Very well. We might dance the boulanger together. Will that do?'

'If I am free for it,' Annabelle said primly.

His sudden grin flashed out. 'You will be, Rosa! You will!'

The Marchants' ball was held in Berkeley Square. It was one of the last functions of the season proper, and as such was well attended. Indeed, it would probably reach the ultimate accolade of being declared a sad crush by those who attended. The rooms were crowded almost beyond their capacity, but even so, the lovely Mrs Ordway still created a stir when she entered the ballroom. The experiences of the night of the theatre visit, far from giving Annabelle hollow eyes and pale cheeks, had added a bloom to her complexion, and deepened the sparkle in her lovely eyes. She was wearing another of Fanchon's creations, a pale blue-green silk overlaid with silver embroideries on net.

Lady Ordway had sighed when she had first seen it, and talked of water nymphs and the like, and at the ball her sentiments were fervently echoed by more than one admirer. Giles looked increasingly bored at the comparisons with mermaids, water sprites and naiads which permeated the conversation, and said roundly that he preferred on the whole to dance with a woman, not a fish. But he took good care to sign her card for the boulanger before it was quite filled up, and then added his name for a set of country dances as well.

'Aren't you going to ask her for one of the waltzes?' asked Lady Ordway, looking on with pleasure at this improvement in relations between her nephew and so-called daughter-in-law.

'No, Aunt Laura! Not in public. She will have to be satisfied with the boulanger and the country dances.' As Annabelle gasped in indignation at this high-handed approach, Lady Ordway laughed.

'But why, Giles?'

'Safer,' he said enigmatically. 'Besides, Rosa has every other dance booked. I'm lucky to have two.'

Annabelle's first partner came to claim her, and she was swept away on to the floor. From then on, apart from the boulanger Giles had booked, he saw little of her before supper, for she danced without a break. They were a lively party during the supper interval, and Giles had every opportunity to observe just how well Rosabelle Ordway could behave. He could not fault her behaviour, and once again he was cast into a most unaccustomed state of indecision. What sort of woman was this? And, more important, why did she have such a confoundedly disturbing effect on him?

After the interval several of the younger ladies disappeared to tidy themselves up. Dancing was resumed and Giles stood with the Duke of Armagh, watching the gaily dressed crowd swirling by in a waltz, while he waited for Rosabelle to reappear. He caught sight of her on the other side of the room and was just about to excuse himself and make his way across, when he saw that she was engaged in conversation with a stranger. Something about the man caught his attention. He had seen him before… But where?

'Who is that over there, do you know, Duke?' he asked his companion.

'What? Talking to Mrs Ordway? By Jove, that's Falkirk! He's back, then.'

'Falkirk?'

'Yes. He's a distant connection of the Banaghers. That's a strange affair, Stanton. He couldn't have imagined for a minute that he would ever inherit the title, but it looks very much as if he will. There's something wrong with that family—dead or dying, the lot of them, and not one of them with an heir. One or two went in the wars, of course—they're an Army family. But the rest…no surviving children. It sometimes happens. So, when old Arthur Falkirk goes, which could, I gather, be at any moment, young Julian, against all the odds, will be the fifth baron. It's to be hoped he's a bit more fertile than the rest of his family! He looks as if he might be.'

'I don't believe I've met him at all.'

'I'm surprised—he was an Army man, too. Mind you, he's always been a touch come and go, Stanton. Very elusive kind of a fellow. But perfectly sound. Plays at all the best clubs when he's in town. Actually, he usually gives this sort of do a miss, he's not much of a party beau. But perhaps, in view of the change in his circumstances, he's planning to join the marriage stakes. Eh? It's good to see him in society again—we haven't seen him for the past year or so.' He regarded the two across the room, then added, 'He's a lucky dog! Mrs Ordway seems quite taken with him.'

Falkirk shifted his stance a little, and came more clearly into view. Giles remembered where he had seen him before—at the theatre, just before Rosabelle had been taken ill. He ought to go over…

A few minutes before this exchange took place, Annabelle had just re-entered the ballroom when she heard the voice behind her.

'Rosabelle!'

She swung round, puzzled. Where had it come from?

'I hoped you'd be here.' The gentleman who had rescued her fan at the theatre came up to her and bowed over her hand. The doors leading to the garden behind him were wide open, and Annabelle suddenly felt cold. Pulling herself together she smiled. There was absolutely

no need to feel so very nervous. She had not the faintest
idea who he might be, but it was a situation she had
dealt with many times in the past. She gave the stranger
a brilliant smile.

'How…how nice to see you! I can't remember when
we last met before I saw you at the theatre. It must
be…er…let me see…' He was laughing.

'Excellent! I would never have imagined you could do
it! And with such verve. You are looking surprisingly
well. I can hardly believe the improvement in looks and
spirit!'

She must be overheated—this cool draught of air was
causing her to shiver. Or had the attack of fever returned? She had an absurdly strong impulse to seek Giles
out, to feel his protective presence once more.

'Rosabelle! You're shivering!'

There was no sympathy in his voice, no concern. He
did not even seem surprised. In fact, had it not been
absurd she would have said he was pleased! She did not
like this man.

'I…I think I am not well, sir,' she said dismissively.
'You must excuse me.'

'Of course. But before you go I'm afraid I must ask
you for a meeting elsewhere in the next few days—
somewhere where we can talk more privately, perhaps?'

'I don't think so, Mr…' Her voice died away. She
was feeling so ill that she could no longer dissemble.
'Forgive me, sir. I'm afraid I've forgotten your name.'

'What a pity!' he said. Why was there so much mockery in his voice? Or was she just imagining it? Was it a
symptom of the fever, which seemed to be growing
worse? He regarded her for a moment, then said, 'It's
Falkirk, my dear. You have my permission…indeed, my

injunction…to forget any other. My name is Julian Falkirk.'

What on earth did this strange, menacing man mean by that? Had he really said those words—or was her illness playing tricks with her imagination? But she was very happy to have an excuse not to see him again. She said brightly, 'Well, Mr Falkirk, I'm afraid it is quite impossible for us to meet again. We are very shortly leaving London for Bath, and I'm afraid…'

'It's a matter of some papers—papers you must have, which belong to me.'

'Papers?' They were standing in comparative isolation, ignored by the dancers, but now she saw Giles's tall figure threading his way towards them. Annabelle was smiling brilliantly in relief as she turned to Mr Falkirk. 'I'm sorry, Mr Falkirk! I haven't any papers. You must ask Colonel Stanton about them.' She nodded her head briefly and went to leave him.

Julian Falkirk caught her arm as she moved away. 'That won't do! You don't escape me so easily, Rosabelle. We must speak again.'

Annabelle removed her arm from his grasp. 'I've told you, sir—I cannot! I have no time before we go.'

'Then I shall have to see you in Bath! Perhaps you will have remembered about Stephen's papers by then. I do hope so.' He bowed gallantly. 'I shall look forward to Bath.'

Annabelle paid no attention. She didn't even hear what he said. Giles was now only a step away, and she turned to him gratefully, not bothering to hide her delight that he had found her. She had no idea how pale and nervous she looked.

Giles took both her hands in his. 'You're ill again!

You should not have come out tonight. Come, I'll take you home.'

'I…I think it has passed, Giles.' She looked back, but the sinister Mr Falkirk had disappeared. 'Yes, I feel much better, really I do!'

'At least come and sit down for a few minutes. We could sit in the conservatory where it is cooler.'

'Thank you.'

They wove their way through the dancers to the small winter garden which had been built on to the end of the ballroom. Here they found a table and two chairs, in public view, but obviously meant for those seeking some quiet refreshment.

'Wait here!' he said. 'I'll find a waiter. Wine?'

'No, I'd like some lemonade, please. I…I feel thirsty.'

'Are you sure you wouldn't prefer to go home? I could easily find Aunt Laura.'

'I shall soon be perfectly restored, I promise you. I don't know what came over me, but it has passed.'

Giles found a waiter who brought a glass of lemonade for Annabelle, and some wine.

'Now, tell me. Who was the man you were talking to?'

Annabelle jumped. She wished he had not reminded her of Falkirk. 'I…it was Mr Falkirk,' she said uneasily. 'I don't know him very well. I…I don't like him.'

'Wasn't it the same man who returned your fan at the theatre?'

'Yes. Yes, it was.'

'It looks as if it is Falkirk who puts you into a quake. What did he want?'

'I can't remember…'

'Didn't I hear something about papers?'

'Yes! He asked if…if I had some papers of

Stephen's… I said I hadn't anything at all, and…and told him to apply to you…' Annabelle had the strangest feeling of reluctance to discuss Mr Falkirk. However absurd it seemed it was as if the power of his personality had put a spell on her and she felt that she was courting danger by even mentioning his name. All she could think of was that she wanted to forget him as quickly as possible. 'Giles, can't we talk of something else?' she said desperately.

Music sounded in the ballroom. 'Mrs Ordway,' said Giles getting promptly to his feet. 'Would you give me the infinite pleasure of dancing with me?'

'Why, thank you, Colonel Stanton! I should be delighted.' Annabelle got up and shook out her skirts. She took Giles's proffered arm and gave him a mischievous look. 'How delightfully formal you are. And to think I once accused you of not knowing how to behave!'

'Oh, I know all the rules of good behaviour, Rosa. But you have an astonishing talent, which I have never before encountered in any other female, for tempting me to abandon them!' He looked down at her with a wicked glint in his eye, and it took all the self-discipline Annabelle possessed to ignore it and take the floor with him.

They danced in perfect harmony, their steps fitting as if they had practised for years, and Annabelle had never felt such a sense of rightness, of happiness and, curiously enough, security—though this was not something she had ever prized before. It was not that Giles held her particularly close. He was careful to keep the correct distance from her, never allowing, even in the turns, the space between them to diminish. But as he guided her confidently through the crowded ballroom, his hand at her waist was sure, and his other hand held hers in a firm grip. And, whenever their eyes met, which was often, the expression in his was, for once, warm, with a touch of humour and...something else, not so easily defined. But definitely exciting.

The waltz ended and they rejoined Lady Ordway. For the rest of the evening Giles did not leave her side except when other partners claimed her for their dances. His attentiveness clearly caused disappointment in some feminine hearts, and Annabelle was able to feel proud at being sought out, looked after, by a man she was growing increasingly to respect and admire...though these words seemed almost too cool, too rational for the unfamiliar emotions she was beginning to experience.

She lay awake that night, going over the evening in her mind, re-living the waltz with Giles and his subsequent behaviour. She spent some time examining this strange, new feeling of shared warmth, oddly mixed with something less reassuring—something exhilarating, but frightening too, as if she were about to take a step into territory hitherto unknown to her. Whatever it was, she knew she trusted Giles, relied on him in a manner she had never before allowed herself with anyone else. He had been so kind to her after her conversation with Falkirk...

Her happy musings came to a sudden halt. Why did she react with such strong dislike to that man? His very name sent shivers up her spine. She drew the bedcovers more closely round her. Giles could hardly have been serious when he suggested that talking to Falkirk had caused her mysterious attacks of fever! And yet...it was a curious coincidence...

Annabelle was suddenly wide awake. What if it was not she, but *Rosabelle* who suffered this strong reaction to Falkirk? What if it was Rosabelle's horror of him which was being transferred by some strange sympathy to her identical twin? Was that possible? They had occasionally felt each other's injuries, though not often, and only when the pain had been severe. And she had been worried about her sister long before Rosabelle had arrived, looking like death, at Temperley. That must be it! Rosabelle, for some reason or other, was terrified of Falkirk!

Annabelle tossed and turned for a long time. In a week or two she and Rosabelle would be changing back. Was she prepared to abandon her sister to the unsolved mysteries, to throw her back to deal with Falkirk alone? And more than that, could she bear to leave her growing friendship with Giles to wither away, without making the slightest attempt to persuade him that her intentions in taking Rosabelle's place had been honest, even if her actions were not? These and other disturbing reflections kept her awake till morning.

Captain Pettifer had suggested some time before that Annabelle might like to visit Vauxhall Gardens, and since she had heard a great deal about them she was eager to accept the invitation. But Lady Ordway had at first demurred.

'For you know, my dear, though Vauxhall is a charming place, a delightful experience with all those lights, and the entertainment, and I don't know what else besides—a lady has to be *careful* when she goes there. One never knows who else will be there.'

'What do you mean?'

'Well, it's not like Almack's or an entertainment at a private house. All the world will be admitted, as long as they pay the fee for entrance.'

'I'm sure Captain Pettifer will look after me, Aunt Laura.'

'But I'm not sure, either, that it's quite the thing for you to be going there alone with a young man you hardly know!'

'Rosa will be safe enough with Richard Pettifer,' Giles said tolerantly. 'But if it would make you feel happier, Aunt Laura, we could add ourselves to the party.'

'I certainly think it would be more fitting if Rosa had a chaperon. But would Captain Pettifer be pleased, Giles? And what about Rosa?'

'Well, what about Rosa?' asked Giles, turning to Annabelle.

'I have no objection, if you can arrange it, Giles,' said Annabelle innocently. 'I wouldn't wish to rouse criticism. And Captain Pettifer is your friend, surely?'

As a result of this conversation, Lady Ordway, Annabelle, Giles and Captain Pettifer found themselves being sculled across the Thames to Vauxhall the next evening towards the sounds of music emanating from Vauxhall Gardens. They were all in good spirits as they landed and were escorted to a comfortable booth near the centre, where they would be able to see the entertainments, and later, the fireworks. Altogether the evening augured well.

Soon after their arrival, music struck up in the Pavilion and Richard Pettifer was prompt to ask Annabelle to do him the honour of dancing with him. They spent an energetic half-hour, after which they returned to the booth. But Giles had apparently taken Lady Ordway for a stroll round the grounds, for it was empty. Annabelle sank down on to one of the chairs, and gratefully accepted the glass of lemonade her partner had managed to procure for her.

After a few minutes Annabelle's attention was caught by a figure in a brightly striped dress making a slightly unsteady way towards them. She was accompanied by a tall young man with white-blond hair... The latter stopped to talk to someone, but Lady Stanton carried on, and, with some dismay, Annabelle saw that she was making straight for the front of their booth.

'Why, if it isn't Giles's *petite amie*! You're not wearing your necklace tonight, dear. Why not? Oops!' The lady was quite definitely the worse for wine. Captain Pettifer stood up, looking embarrassed.

'I don't think, ma'am...'

'No, no, no! You're going to say I shouldn't be here, aren't you? But you're wrong, soldier! You sh'd treat me with respect! My name, dear fellow, is Venetia Stanton, and I am Giles's stepmama!'

'Quite! Captain Richard Pettifer, ma'am. And this lady is the widow of Colonel Stanton's late cousin, Mrs Stephen Ordway. I still don't think—'

'Well, well, well! So this is the famous Rosabelle! Oh, what a lot of trouble you caused us all, my girl!' said Lady Stanton, waving an uncertain finger. With a sense of nightmare Annabelle saw Giles and Lady Ordway approaching. At the same time the blond man came up and took Lady Stanton's arm.

'Leave me alone!' said the lady, wrenching her arm away. 'It's all right, Fraser! This is Rosabelle Ordway— did you know? I never met her, of course, in the old days. But it's all right to talk to her. She's friends with Selder again. I saw them together at the theatre just a night or two ago.'

'Venetia—'

Opposition merely made Lady Stanton more argumentative. She said more loudly, 'It's all right, I tell you! You were there, too! You must have seen them, Fraser! Don't you remember?' She smiled foolishly into Fraser's furious face, and said cajolingly, 'Don't frown like that, Fraser! They're friends again, I tell you! She was talking to Selder and they were smiling.'

Giles stopped in his tracks, his face suddenly pale.

'You must excuse me, Lady Stanton, but you are quite mistaken. I don't know anyone of that name,' said Annabelle desperately.

'What nonsense! Of course you do—' It was not quite clear to the rest of them what Fraser did then, but Lady Stanton turned round with a little cry of protest. 'Fraser!' Then her voice died, and she suddenly looked old and frightened. 'Oh God, I forgot! She's right—we've been told to forget him…I forgot, I tell you! I won't do it again, Fraser! I just forgot! I won't mention him again. I swear I won't. He doesn't exist any more.'

'It's time you went home, Venetia,' was all Fraser said. But his eyes were cold, inhuman. 'Come!'

'Wait!' Giles was standing in their way. He regarded his stepmother with ill-disguised dislike. 'When was it you saw her?' he asked grimly. 'The night before last? Talking to Selder at the theatre?'

Lady Stanton started to nod. 'That's right—'

'That's enough, Venetia!' Fraser's voice was like a whip. Giles turned on him.

'I asked a question, sir! And I'd like an answer.'

Fraser looked dangerous for a moment and Richard Pettifer stepped forward to range himself by Giles. Then, with a graceful gesture of surrender, Fraser looked at Lady Stanton and said, 'Very well. If the lady really wishes to talk to you, I won't stop her. Venetia?'

'I…I don't think I will,' she mumbled, with another scared look at Fraser. 'I'm tired. I want to go home. No, really, Giles. I…I've forgotten all about it.'

Giles took a step forward, but Richard Pettifer put a hand on his arm. 'I don't think you'll get anywhere, Gil. And you don't want to make a fuss here. The ladies…'

Giles looked as if he was about to argue, but then, with a glance at Annabelle, he said, 'I suppose you're right, And there are other ways.' He turned to Fraser. 'But I shan't let the matter drop. It's too important to me.'

'By all means do your best, sir!' said Fraser. He gave Annabelle a look from those light, inhuman eyes. 'I don't think you'll find Mrs Ordway very forthcoming, either.'

He took Lady Stanton's arm with apparent solicitude, but Annabelle saw the lady wince again. The two walked off towards the exit.

# Chapter Eight

'Who is this man that dreadful woman was talking about, Giles?' asked Lady Ordway. 'And why do you wish to find him? Is it…is it something to do with Stephen?' Her voice wavered, and she put a trembling hand on Giles's arm. 'Don't meddle with it, Giles! Leave well alone, I beg you!'

Giles took her hand and said reassuringly, 'It's only to do with some of Stephen's money, Aunt Laura. Nothing serious. We'll talk about it when we are at home. It's nothing to worry you.'

'No, but—' Lady Ordway was not reassured. She had sensed the drama which lay behind that small exchange. Her lips trembled and she grew very pale. Annabelle came out of her trance, took her arm and helped her into a chair, murmuring words of comfort.

'I'm sorry to intrude,' said Captain Pettifer. 'But I think the ladies have had a bit of a shock, Gil. Might they prefer to cut the evening short?'

'Indeed, I think my aunt would be better at home, sir,' said Annabelle gratefully.

'Giles can take me back, my dear,' said Lady Ordway. 'Pray don't spoil your own and Captain Pettifer's pleasure.'

'I think,' said Giles with great force, 'in fact, I am sure, that Rosabelle should accompany you, Aunt Laura. Richard will understand.'

'Of course, of course. I'll see to procuring a boat for us. Excuse me.' Captain Pettifer hurried away.

'Giles, I—'

'Later, Rosabelle,' said Giles. His voice was neutral, but his eyes when he turned to look at her were stony. 'Aunt Laura must be seen to first.'

The journey back to Upper Brook Street was accomplished in near silence. When they were back at the house, Captain Pettifer wasted no time in taking his leave, but not before assuring Annabelle that he hoped to make up for the night's disappointment by taking her to the theatre as soon as it could be arranged. Annabelle smiled non-committally, wished him goodnight and turned to see Lady Ordway up to her room. She delivered her into the capable hands of Wilson, who instantly prescribed bed and a sedative.

'But I must see Giles!' Lady Ordway said fretfully. 'He must stop these enquiries into Stephen's affairs at once!'

'You can talk to him tomorrow, Aunt Laura. I am sure he will listen to you. But tonight you should really settle down and rest. It will do no one any good if you are ill again.'

'Tomorrow then, 'said Lady Ordway. 'I shall see him tomorrow.'

'Good. I'll tell him.' She went to the door.

'Anna!'

'Yes, Aunt Laura?'

'Anna, come back here for a moment!' When Annabelle reached her bedside, Lady Ordway clutched her hand. 'I can see Giles is angry with you. But please don't tell him tonight that you and Rosa have changed places! Try to wait until we go to Bath. It isn't very long now.'

'But, Aunt Laura—'

Clutching her hand even more tightly, Lady Ordway said desperately, 'Please say you won't tell him. He will be in such a fury with all of us, and I don't think I could stand it, Anna. He would send you packing, I am sure. He might even refuse to have Rosa back! And I could not bear it if I had neither of you.'

Anna bent over and kissed her. 'He couldn't do that, Aunt Laura. We both love you—he couldn't keep us away!'

'But a scandal will ruin Rosa's prospects with Mr Winbolt, and I have such high hopes for them both! And if Rosa does return now, Giles will be impossible with her, and she will be ill again, and…and…' Painful tears rolled down her cheeks. 'Things have been going so well. I couldn't bear it if we went back to all the misery of last year, Anna, I really couldn't! Promise me you won't tell!'

Annabelle hesitated. Giles was certainly going to quiz her about this man Selder. How could she keep silent?

Lady Ordway was growing agitated again. She looked ten years older than she had at the beginning of the evening. Her fingers sought to hold on to the sleeve of Annabelle's jacket. 'Promise me, Anna!' Wilson moved forward anxiously and shook her head.

Annabelle could not help but respond to the desperation, the fear, the anguish in that voice. With a deep sigh she said slowly, 'I promise. Now will you try to rest?'

Lady Ordway sank back and closed her eyes. 'Thank you, my dear. Thank you.'

Annabelle went downstairs with a heavy heart. She had been mad to give her word! But what else could she have done? And there was some justice in what Lady Ordway had said. Giles *would* be furious. He *would* react badly to being told that he had been made a fool of for so long. Rosabelle, Lady Ordway and herself—all three of them would suffer the full force of his anger. Whereas, if she kept silent, he would be angry only with her. She stopped where she was on the stairs. And how very angry he would be! He must now be convinced that she had known Falkirk's real name from the beginning. For that must be it. Falkirk and Selder were one and the same man. Lady Stanton had only seen her once before—and that had been at the theatre, when Mr Falkirk had returned her fan. From a distance, their conversation must have looked friendly.

She might just have persuaded Giles that the meeting in the theatre was a casual encounter, that she truly had not known who Falkirk was. But the meeting with the man at the Marchants' ball, witnessed by Giles himself, was far more damning. There she had done her best to pretend she knew who he was, to acknowledge him as an acquaintance, if not a friend. It was really exquisitely ironic! Apart from feeling a prickling horror of the man, she had not known what he meant by anything he had said. But Giles, who had observed it, and had questioned her about it afterwards, would never believe her. He would regard her as a liar and a cheat, and her promise to Lady Ordway would stop her from defending herself with the truth. Her budding friendship with Giles was over. Annabelle was shocked at the sharp pang of regret which this caused her. She stopped again, took a deep breath, then braced herself and walked down the rest of the stairs.

Giles was waiting for her in the hall. 'How is Aunt Laura?' he asked.

'I left her in Wilson's hands. I think she will be all right. She's anxious to see you as soon as possible to-morrow.'

'I shall make a point of seeing her as soon as she is awake. Though I know what she wants—she hopes I will stop uncovering her son's disreputable past. But it's too late for that. I only wish she had told me herself... However, I can at least promise to conceal as much as I can from the rest of the world.' He took a breath, then said formally, 'I'd like to see you for a moment in the library, Rosabelle. It won't take long.' He led the way along the hall, stood to let her pass before him into the library, then came in and shut the door. To Annabelle it sounded like the door of a prison cell closing...

Giles walked past her and stood at the other end of the huge writing table. They faced each other along its length. Annabelle looked down and saw that Stephen's diaries and notebooks were scattered between them.

'There they are,' Giles began. 'A record of a young man's degradation. I had begun to believe that they might be no more than that—drug-induced fantasies, a release of spite and spleen against a world which had not given Stephen Ordway what he wanted. But in one respect they are true after all.'

'Giles, please—'

'No, Rosabelle! Spare me any further lies. I really do not want to hear any more about your relationship with Selder—or with anyone else! What I heard tonight was pretty well conclusive, and I don't think I could stomach any more. You and Stephen were well suited.'

Annabelle said in a low voice, 'Are you then abandoning your search for the truth?'

'Why should truth interest you? But since you ask, no, I am not. I shall continue my efforts to find out what happened when Stephen died. I owe something to the Ordway name. And, if necessary, I shall then bury the facts decently, for the same reason. But you…I want as little to do with you as possible!' He paused for a moment. When he continued his tone was almost conversational.

'You know, Rosabelle, you will never know how close you came to achieving your aim.'

'My aim?'

'I must suppose you intended to share in the Ordway fortune, if not through Stephen, then through me.'

'You!'

'I had begun to have some regard for you,' he went on, ignoring her exclamation. 'Not just a feeling of lust for that lovely flesh, which you were so expert in arousing. I found myself enjoying your company, respecting your wit, your intelligence…even the display of compassion you put on for my benefit. How galling it must be for you, Rosabelle, that my revered stepmother let the cat out of the bag just a little too soon.'

'Believe me—'

'Believe *you*? What a ridiculous concept! I'd as soon believe…that whore who calls herself my stepmother.'

For the first time his iron control slipped, and Annabelle saw how very angry Giles was. His voice was harsh and ugly, and after one searing look at her, he turned away as if he could not bear the sight. 'I was filled with shame tonight at the thought of what a stupid, gullible fool I had been,' he said with bitter contempt. 'God knows, the evidence was clear enough, but a smile or two, a few melting looks from a pair of blue eyes, a touch of sympathy, and there I was, just like the rest, ready to ignore it all, rushing headlong into the snare. Till tonight I had honestly thought better of myself. Till I heard that you had been, after all, one of them.'

'That is not so!' cried Annabelle passionately, roused at last by this accusation. 'Lady Stanton was mistaken!'

'You mean that Falkirk and Selder are not one and the same person?'

'No! Yes! At least…'

'Well?' he asked ironically, as her voice died.

'I was not smiling at Selder at the theatre. We are not friends.' Giles turned away with a contemptuous laugh, and even to Annabelle this sounded hopelessly feeble. She felt defeated, unable to defend herself as she wished, hobbled by her wretched promise to Lady Ordway. 'What…what do you propose to do?' she asked miserably.

'I don't know.'

'Are you…are you going to send me away?'

'Believe me, there is nothing I would like more! But I don't want to upset Aunt Laura more than I have to, and she depends on you. However hard I work to save Stephen's name, I won't be able to conceal everything, and she is bound to be distressed. You will stay with her.'

His peremptory tone roused Annabelle to rebellion. 'And what is to prevent me from walking out of this

house and returning to Temperley? Taking Aunt Laura
with me if necessary.'

'As a hostage? If you do that, Rosabelle, then I will
surely ruin you.' He said this quietly, but with such menace that she felt chilled. 'And the same is true if I learn
that you have communicated with Falkirk again. I won't
have a spy in our midst.'

'I am no spy, Giles,' said Annabelle proudly, trying
not to show how affected she was by his manner. 'I
wouldn't communicate with Mr Falkirk, even if I could.'

'Wouldn't you?' Giles gave her a cynical smile.
'Whatever you say now is a matter of indifference to
me, I'm afraid. But I meant what I said. Try to get in
touch with Falkirk again and the world will learn how
sadly it has been deceived in the lovely Mrs Ordway. So
if you have any regard for your family in Berkshire you
will pay heed.' Giles went to the door and opened it.
'Goodnight.'

As Annabelle passed him she hesitated and looked up.
It seemed impossible to her that this could be happening
after the feeling which had been aroused between them.
Surely somewhere deep inside he must *know* she was
honest, whatever the evidence? 'Giles…' she whispered.

He stared down at her cynically. Then, without warning, he put his arms round her, pulled her to him and
kissed her. The kiss was rough, bruising, without respect
or consideration. She struggled to free herself but he held
her easily, forcing her to submit…

When he finally released her Annabelle stood back.
She had lost the battle to maintain her composure. Slow,
painful tears were trickling down her cheeks. 'Why,
Giles?' she asked. 'Why?'

'For old times' sake, my dear! To get rid of the memory of other kisses of yours. When I was in danger of

becoming yet another of your poor deluded victims. But don't worry. They won't be repeated.'

'God forbid they should, Giles!' she said bitterly. 'You should be ashamed of them.'

As Annabelle went back upstairs to her room she impatiently wiped the tears off her cheeks. This was no time for weeping and wailing. Tears were a weakness she had always despised. She must pull herself together and plan what was to be done. The situation was potentially catastrophic. In a week or so, she would go to Temperley, and Rosabelle would join Lady Ordway and Giles on the trip to Bath. Giles was certain to notice the substitution very soon—he was too astute not to—and would then realise that he had been duped by the sisters.

But far from improving the situation, it would probably make it much worse. Giles would be even less inclined to give either of the sisters credit for honesty or good intentions when he realised how they had deceived him. In his eyes they would be identically lovely in looks, and identically shameful in their behaviour.

Annabelle felt perilously close to tears again at the thought that she had lost Giles's good opinion again. She walked in a daze to her room and allowed herself to be undressed and prepared for bed without really noticing what was happening. For some minutes after the maid had gone Annabelle stood quite still in the centre of the room. It wasn't, she told herself carefully, it wasn't that she was in *love* with Giles Stanton. That was out of the question, an absurd idea. How could this possibly be love? She *disliked* him! He was rude, arrogant, high-handed, authoritarian, impatient... He had judged and condemned Rosabelle and herself without a hearing, and had treated them both abominably.

She had worked hard to run his house and entertain his guests, all without a word of praise or gratitude, only censure. And then he had kissed her against her will... She tried to hold on to the disgust and revulsion she had felt towards him after those kisses, but her thoughts slid away to the memory of others on the night of the theatre visit. She had felt neither disgust nor revulsion then—she had enjoyed them. She must acknowledge the fact, if only to herself...

But she *wasn't* in love with him. She wasn't! So what did that make her? The wanton Giles thought her? It might be true. Before coming to London, she had been a complete innocent in such matters. The various hopeful young men who had called at Temperley in the past had never aroused more than a mild feeling of friendship, which quickly turned to impatience if they became too attentive. She had certainly never felt the slightest desire to behave with them as she had done with Giles. Lost in his kisses, feeling that a door to new, previously unsuspected delights was opening...

But perhaps that was just the effect that any experienced man could have on an ignorant girl...? Annabelle smiled wryly. Until Giles had kissed her she had begun to believe that she was not someone who *could* feel very deeply. She had begun to reconcile herself to the idea of leading an uneventful life at Temperley for the rest of her days, incapable of either rapture or despair! How wrong she had been!

She moved slowly over to the bed and sat down. She had experienced such a turmoil of emotion in the past week, such an intensity of feeling, that she was in danger of losing her famous ability for cool, rational judgement! She must pull herself together before it was too late. It was total folly for Annabelle Kelland even to think of falling in love with Colonel Giles Stanton, autocrat and her implacable critic. Annabelle lifted her head proudly. Fists clenched, she made herself a promise. She would retain her own self-respect, whatever Giles thought of her. And there would be no further thought of love.

Giles did not go to bed at all that night. He sat up, staring at Stephen's diaries, an ever-diminishing bottle of brandy at his elbow. He was concentrating fiercely on Stephen, Falkirk, the inn at Woolhampton, the question of piracy, Stephen's debts...anything, in fact, but the thought of Rosabelle Ordway. He must tackle Selder, or Falkirk, as he must now be called. That was absolutely vital. Then perhaps he could clear up this whole affair and start life afresh. He had always wanted to see the Americas. Perhaps he could take off for a year or two? Travelling alone was much better than...

He poured some more brandy and drank it down. Of course travelling alone was better! There were always women to provide companionship, if one needed it. They didn't have to have hair of molten gold and dark blue eyes, and a defiant, delicate chin... Hell and damnation! Giles put his glass down with such force that it broke. He stared at it, then got up, went to the window and opened the shutters.

Daylight poured into the room, dazzlingly bright daylight, and he groaned and held his head. After a minute he lifted it again and started for the door. Action was what was needed. A bath, a shave, a ride in the Park first to clear his head, then he would set about finding Falkirk. Calling for Goss, he strode out of the library and took the stairs two at a time to his bedchamber.

He spent most of the day in a search for his stepmother, finally ascertaining that she had left the protection of her latest lover and was living in Cavendish Square with her friend, the Baroness Leibmann. By the time he had discovered this Giles was jaded and in need of distraction. Thoughts of Rosabelle Ordway intruded into everything he did, and it was driving him mad! Tracking Falkirk down among the London clubs seemed a much more attractive prospect for the evening than talking to a woman he had avoided all his life.

At the very least, it would give him an excuse to spend some time in convivial, masculine company. So he collected a few of his friends and together they visited a number of the gaming clubs around St James's. At each one Giles played high and won considerable sums. It gave him no pleasure, no relief from his obsession with Rosabelle Ordway, and when Captain Wainwright congratulated him on his winnings, he was hard put to it to reply civilly.

'By Jupiter, Gil,' said his old friend, 'the cards are running your way tonight! I hope you're not in love, old chap!'

'Why the devil should you worry about that?' said Giles, somewhat disagreeably.

'Well, you know what they say—lucky at cards, unlucky in love, eh, what?' Captain Wainwright roared with laughter at his own witticism, though he failed to notice that Giles did not join in.

But at last Giles's patience was rewarded. Halfway through a game at Watier's he observed that Falkirk had appeared across the table from him. He studied his opponent with interest. Black hair, strong features, with a flashingly white smile—the man was not exactly handsome, but there was something engaging about him. He was obviously popular—several prominent members of the club greeted him cordially as they passed. He played well, but in spite of a stylishly nonchalant air, he placed his bets cautiously, always with a good eye for the odds, and with the sense to know where to stop. An interesting man—the polished charm obviously hid a clever, self-disciplined, and probably dangerous animal.

When play stopped for a while Giles made his way over to him.

'Mr Falkirk?'

Falkirk turned. Giles watched him closely. Falkirk must recognise him, must know him for Stephen's cousin, but there was nothing in the man's demeanour to indicate this.

'Yes, I'm Falkirk. But…I'm afraid you have the advantage of me, sir. Do I know you?'

'I'm Giles Stanton. I believe you knew my cousin.'

'And who might that be, Stanton?'

'Stephen Ordway. May I talk to you? There's an empty table over in the corner. We shan't be overheard there. I'll get the waiter to bring a bottle of wine.'

There was a wary look in Falkirk's eyes, but he smiled amiably enough. 'Of course. You intrigue me, sir.'

They went across to a distant corner of the room. The waiter brought a bottle of burgundy, poured some, and withdrew.

Falkirk took a sip of the wine. 'Excellent! But I'm afraid I don't know a Stephen…Ordway, did you say?'

'Now that is not worthy of you, Falkirk! I saw you.'

There was a sudden stillness in the air, and the chatter and laughter faded further into the background. Then Mr Falkirk smiled again. 'Saw me?' he asked with an air of surprise. 'You might well have. I talk to a lot of people I don't really know. Yourself, for instance. Tell me, sir, why the inquisition?'

'To be exact, I saw you talking to Mrs Ordway at the Marchants' ball the other night. I believe you mentioned some papers to her?'

'Ah, yes! The lovely Rosabelle.' He smiled again and looked discreet. 'I'm not sure I ought to discuss my conversation with her. It was…a private matter. Between the two of us. May I ask what your position is?'

'I try to guard the interests of our family. And to prevent any gossip.'

'Gossip? But surely a widow is free to talk to whom she chooses without causing comment?'

There was a short silence. Then Giles said blandly, 'If you haven't heard of my cousin, Falkirk, then how do you know he is dead?'

He was pleased to see he had made a hit. But Falkirk recovered so quickly that anyone watching him less keenly would have missed the momentary chagrin. 'I remembered him as soon as you mentioned Mrs Ordway. You must forgive my lapse, Stanton. When one is enraptured by the wife, one tends to forget the existence of the husband, don't you agree? I'm afraid I never knew him well.'

'And these papers? I believe Mrs Ordway referred you to me?'

'I see. Rosabelle has been confiding in you, has she? I am surprised.'

'No,' said Giles evenly. 'Not as much as I would like. But I'm learning. I seem to learn more every day, from various sources. Including my cousin's diaries.'

'Diaries?' Falkirk's tone was sharp. 'Stephen Ordway kept a diary?'

'Yes. I haven't deciphered them all, but they're a sad record, I'm afraid. Towards the end of his life my cousin was quite distressed, particularly by his wife's interest in a certain Mr Selder. And there are some matters in them concerning this Selder which puzzle me. I'd like to talk to him. Do you know him?'

Falkirk was prepared for this. He had regained his former relaxed manner. 'Selder? No, I don't think I do.'

'He seems to be a difficult man to trace. I would think he didn't exist except that...'

'Except what?'

'I'm sorry, I'm boring you about my family affairs, when I should be offering you help with the papers you wanted. Mrs Ordway seemed to think that they might be among my cousin's effects, though I have to say I haven't yet come across anything of that sort. Were they so very private?'

'We'll forget the papers,' Falkirk said curtly. 'I was wondering if I could help you about Selder. Can you describe him?'

'Not yet.'

'Surely Mrs Ordway...?'

'She seems to be very reluctant to talk about the fellow at all.' Giles watched as Falkirk imperceptibly relaxed. 'But I'm hoping to have a description soon,' he added affably. 'From someone who saw him quite recently at the theatre. I could pass it on to you, if you are serious about helping me.'

Something ugly showed for a moment in Falkirk's eyes. He suddenly stood up. 'Please do.'

'Thank you,' said Giles, also getting to his feet. 'Er...there's one more thing. I have no desire to offend you, Falkirk, but Mrs Ordway has asked me to convey a message. She desires me to tell you that she no longer wishes to continue with your acquaintance. She would prefer not to talk to you again.'

'Really?' This was said with a distinctly ironic tone

in the voice. 'You have indeed been taking charge,
Stanton! Still, if that is what the lady says...'

'I'm afraid she does, sir. So, if you think there are
papers of yours among my cousin's effects, I suggest you
deal with me. Believe me, I can be very discreet. Can
you tell me what they are?'

Falkirk appeared to be considering this for a moment.
Then he said with an indifference which Giles was certain was assumed, 'They are not at all important. If you
come across anything you think is mine you might pass
it over to me. I am lodged in Clarges Street. I, too, can
be discreet—you might tell Mrs Ordway that, and tell
her also that I will, of course, respect her wishes. But—'
he looked up at Giles and smiled '—allow me to give
you a word of warning. I am not usually so complaisant.
It would be most impolitic of you, or anyone else, to try
to interfere otherwise in my affairs. I don't like having
my plans upset—I'm sure you understand, Stanton.'

'May I ask what your plans are?'

'Why, to enjoy life, of course!' The smile flashed even
wider. 'I'm a very simple fellow, Stanton. All I want is
to be free to enjoy life in my own way. And, when my
cousin dies, to take my proper place in society. There
can't be much wrong with that, surely?' He bowed and
walked away. Giles watched him go. Mr Falkirk was
taking his time, nodding to someone here, exchanging
words with another there. But there was a sense of urgency about him, and the effortless grace of his previous
movements was no longer there. Though he was doing
his best to disguise it, Mr Falkirk was seriously shaken.
So much the better!

But Giles was shortly to learn just how seriously his
words had shaken Mr Falkirk, and to be shocked, horrified even, at the result. He knew Falkirk for a villain.

But he still had not quite realised how ruthless and dangerous a villain the man was…

The next day Giles presented himself at the Baroness Leibmann's house in Cavendish Square. He was confident the Baroness would receive him, for they were old acquaintances. He had known her in Holland, when she had still been Nellie Marsden, living under the protection of a minor Dutch aristocrat. It had been one of the jokes of the army when she had left him, just when he was on the point of turning her out, to marry the practically senile Baron Leibmann. Nellie always landed on her feet.

But when he arrived he found the house in confusion. Servants were running here and there, carrying clothing, silverware and other valuables, and two of them were struggling up the stairs with a huge chest.

'I'm afraid the Baroness is not receiving visitors, sir,' said the butler. 'She is very distressed.'

'Distressed? I'm sorry to hear that,' said Giles, looking with some curiosity at the bustle. 'Perhaps you would take up my card? In fact, it is Lady Stanton I have actually come to see.'

Consternation showed in the butler's face. 'That is quite impossible.'

'Impossible? Why should you say that? Come, man. Take my card to one of the ladies, Lady Stanton for preference.'

'Her ladyship…passed away yesterday, sir. Last night, in fact.'

'*What?*'

'Her ladyship is dead. Baroness Leibmann is not at home to visitors.'

'Good God! Look, here is my card. She must see me.'

The butler was about to refuse, but then glanced at

Giles's card. His eyes widened in surprise, and he looked more human. 'Colonel Stanton!'

'Lady Stanton was my stepmother. It is imperative that I see the Baroness.'

'If you will wait in the hall, sir, I'll take your card up.'

'I have a better idea,' said Giles impatiently. 'I'll take it up myself.' He brushed past the butler, and found the right room by the simple expedient of following the raucous sound of Baroness Leibmann's voice. In the panic of the moment Nellie Marsden of Stepney was in the ascendant.

'What are you doin' 'ere?' she demanded, when Giles went into the room. She was surrounded by dresses, fans, shoes, thrown all over the chairs and sofas. Open boxes and bags lay everywhere. On her lap was a large jewel case into which she was cramming jewels of every kind. Among them was a long string of pearls which Giles had last seen wound in Venetia Stanton's hair.

'I came to speak to Venetia.'

'Well, you can't! She's dead.'

'So I understand. It was surely unexpected? She looked in…perfect health when I saw her at Vauxhall the night before last.'

Nellie Marsden's busy hands were stilled for a moment. She looked up at Giles and made a visible effort for control. 'You saw her? Did you speak to her?'

'I couldn't. She was with a gentleman called Fraser, and he wouldn't permit it. What is all this, Nellie?' He gestured at the chaos around them.

'I'm leaving London. I'm needed in Germany. It's urgent.' She started putting the jewels in the box again. Giles walked over and removed the pearls.

'These were my mother's. I'll take care of them.

Nellie—' He took her face in his hands and held it still. 'Tell me what's happening,' he said urgently. 'How did Venetia come to die?'

'Oh, get out! I've no time to talk to you!' she said, shaking him off. 'I've things to do.' Giles regarded her grimly. Nellie Marsden, one of the toughest and most experienced campaigners of them all, was in a panic.

'Heart attack?'

'Who? Venetia? No.'

'Has Baron Leibmann had a heart attack?'

'Oh, 'im! No, nothing like that. He just wants to see me.'

'So, why are you so frightened? Nellie, *how did Venetia die*? I shan't go until I know.'

# Chapter Nine

Nellie didn't answer immediately. Instead she asked, almost reluctantly, 'When you saw Venetia at Vauxhall…what was it she said?'

'That she was pleased to see that Mrs Ordway and Selder—'

He stopped. The jewel box had slipped from Nellie's lap and fallen to the floor with a crash. The woman's cheeks were ashen.

'So that's it!' she whispered. Then she got down on her knees and started scrabbling the jewels together, piling them carelessly into the box again. 'I've got to go, I've got to get out of London now,' she muttered.

Giles got down beside her and put his hands on hers. 'You're not going anywhere till you tell me what I want to know,' he said harshly. Now they were so close he could smell her fear, see the terror in her eyes.

She whispered rapidly, 'Venetia was found by the watch last night. By the Chesterfield gate in Hyde Park.

She…' Nellie swallowed. 'She'd been beaten over the head. They say it must have been done by a gang of vagabonds. Her jewels had all been taken.'

'Vagabonds? Are they…are they sure?'

'Of course!' Her voice was shrill.

'Then why are you in such a panic? Tell me, Nellie!'

'Why shouldn't I be in a panic? My friend has been clubbed to death!'

'By vagabonds in the Park? I don't believe it!' He held her eyes. 'Nor do you. Did…did Selder have anything to do with this?'

'Don't!' she screamed, clearly terrified. 'Selder doesn't exist any more, I tell you! He told us, all of us. We're to forget 'e ever existed. Otherwise… Oh God, I'm so frightened!'

Giles got up and walked about the room in an effort to keep a cool head in the face of this appalling news. He turned back to the Baroness. She had collapsed in a heap on the floor and lay there moaning.

'Nellie, this won't do! Calm down!' Giles went over, helped her up and settled her on the sofa. 'What's in this glass? Brandy? Have some.'

Nellie gulped the brandy down. It didn't do much good. Her teeth were chattering and she was trembling. 'It was always the same when she'd 'ad too much wine—she couldn't hold her tongue,' she muttered. 'But 'e warned 'er. She should've kept her mouth shut!'

'You mean,' said Giles incredulously, 'Venetia was killed just because she mentioned Selder's name?'

'That's about the sum of it, yes. Fraser must've told him about it. Or someone.' Nellie seemed to come to her senses. She looked sharply up at him. 'And that's all you'll learn from me. I've no ambition to have my battered corpse found by the Watch. I'm gettin' out.'

Giles controlled himself with an effort. This was not the moment for guilt or self-recrimination, he had to learn what he could from the woman before him in the time left. It was obvious that further questioning would be useless without a powerful incentive. Would money serve? He thought not. Nellie more than likely had enough salted away, and her husband was rich. Help in saving her neck? That would be more to the point. He thought for a moment, then said, 'You're quite right. You must get away, of course. Heaven knows what Selder will do next. I can see to it, Nellie. I'll arrange for you to leave secretly for Germany tonight, if that is your wish. Selder and the others won't catch you, I promise you.'

Nellie was rightly suspicious of such a generous offer. 'What's the catch?'

'Tell me more about Selder and his band. My cousin was mixed up in it somehow and I must know what the connection was. And how and why he died.'

Nellie considered carefully. 'Tonight, you said?'

'There's a courier going to Antwerp tonight. You probably know him—Captain Foster. I can arrange for you to travel with him.'

Nellie poured herself another glass of brandy. 'Young Foster, aye? I knew 'im years ago when 'e was just a lad...' She made up her mind. 'I can't tell you much. Selder was always very close.'

'Tell me what you do know.'

'I'll tell you one thing for free!' she said with intense seriousness. 'There's nothing, not one thing, that Selder wouldn't do. I don't set myself up as a pattern of morality, but Selder...that one has no morals at all. He's a ruthless fiend. And if he don't get his way by usin' charm, then he'll use blackmail, threats, and...worse. He went out of sight when Stephen Ordway died, but he's in London again now, and very anxious we should know that he's turned 'is back on the old ways.'

'Where does he say he's been all this time?'

'Abroad, with the Army—just like yourself, Colonel. In London just for the odd leave. But if that's true, then he spent his leaves on business as well as pleasure! Selder made a fortune out of the likes of Stephen Ordway. He had a villa out in Kensington... We 'ad some rare old parties there in the old days. Wild, they were. But there were some we weren't invited to—and I wouldn't 've gone if I *had* been invited, neither. I'm not exactly what you'd call respectable, but I do draw a line at some things.'

'For example?'

'I don't want to talk about it... Look, men and women...that's one thing. A bit of fun, a lark, plenty of drink—and more. And if the punter wants to show his appreciation, that's all right by me! But...grown women weren't welcome on those special nights.'

Giles felt sick. Were there no depths to which his cousin had not sunk? Nellie went on, 'Selder wants to forget all that now. He's made 'is money, he's got another name, and he's all set to be a respectable member of the aristocracy. It's natural he should want to cut his connections with the likes of us, but I just don't like 'is way of doin' it, that's all. And you needn't ask me what 'is other name is, for I won't tell you, not if you promised me the Crown Jewels.'

Giles did not waste time trying to persuade her. He already knew Selder's other name. 'We'll call him Selder,' he said. 'Tell me this...how did my cousin die? Do you know?'

'They used a bit of persuasion on him. Too much.

They didn't mean him to die, that I do know. But 'e was always a bit of a lily, and they must 'ave 'it 'im too 'ard.'

'You mean…they beat him to death?' said Giles incredulously.

'I told you, you don't know what Selder's like! Specially when he's mad. Look, Stephen Ordway and Selder used to be very thick, till they fell out over Rosabelle. It was all right again for a while, but then there was a row which was a lot worse. A real break. Ordway found something out about Selder—something that could ruin him. And after Johnny Kingsley died 'e threatened to use it. Imagine! Threatenin' Selder! He must have been out of his mind. Anyway, that's when they tried to teach 'im a lesson, and 'e kicked the bucket. And the rest of us will go the same way if we aren't careful.'

'So Stephen didn't fall down the cellar steps, after all?' Giles asked.

Nellie shook her head. 'That was a story put about by those two poor women—his mother and his wife. They're your sort, Colonel. They put the family name and all that above everything else, too. They knew what Stephen Ordway was, and they didn't want no enquiries made.'

'And his wife was anxious to save her own reputation, no doubt.'

'Oh, no! She wasn't like that! Well, I can't say that for sure. I never knew her—but from what the others said… I do know that Selder was really mad for her for a while, though.'

Giles put this aside for later consideration. Time was moving on. 'Who were ''they''? The ones who wanted to teach Stephen a lesson. Apart from Selder.'

'I don't know. I wasn't there, was I? But I bet Fraser and Burrows were mixed up in it. They're Selder's shadows—they do 'is dirty work.'

'Who was Kingsley? Was he murdered, too?'

'Like as not. I never asked. He was a nice young gentleman—I could never understand how he got mixed up with that lot. He wasn't rich, he had to work for a livin'—at Lloyds. But I reckon the second bust-up between Stephen Ordway and Selder was something to do with him.'

'How?'

'That I really cannot tell you, 'cos I don't know. Selder, Stephen Ordway, and the others—they were the…what we called the inner circle. Venetia and I never knew what went on inside that. Men's affairs. No females allowed.' She got up and said very determinedly, 'And that's enough. I've told you all I can. Now I expect you to keep your word, Colonel. I can be ready at six this evening.'

Giles eyed her and decided that he had got all he could out of Baroness Leibmann. It was clear that, even if she knew any more, she was not going to talk about it. He promised that a carriage would be sent on the dot of six, and she would be given a pass which would see that she got to Germany without delay. He took his leave and went to the door. Then he stopped. It was no use—there was one more thing he had to know.

'Stephen and Selder fell out over Rosabelle Ordway, you said. Was it because they were having an affair?'

Nellie gave him a look that was hard to interpret. Then she said baldly, 'Yes.'

Giles was not surprised, but all the same, his heart sank like a stone. He turned to open the door.

Then Nellie went on, 'But it wasn't a quarrel over an unfaithful *wife*, Colonel.'

'What do you mean?'

'Work it out. You're not stupid.'

Giles frowned. 'You mean Stephen was in love with *Falkirk*—'

Nellie Marsden's terror returned in full force. 'Oh Gawd! 'ow do you know that? I never told you that!'

'Isn't that what you were implying?'

'No! I mean his name! I never told you 'is other name.'

'Oh, I knew that before I came here.'

'You did? Well, you'd better forget it!' said Nellie intensely. 'People who know that link tend to get sick and die, Colonel Stanton. Like Venetia. Very sick, and very dead! Why do you think I'm gettin' out?'

Giles tried to get more from her, but it was useless. Nellie was finished. She could not get rid of him quickly enough. Assuring her again that everything would be in order by six o'clock that evening, he departed.

Giles's first action when he left the house was to despatch Goss to Upper Brook Street with orders that he was not to let Mrs Ordway out of his sight until further notice. Then he went to the War Office and made arrangements for Nellie's journey. After this he paid a call on the coroner. What he learned there sickened him. Venetia Stanton had been brutally attacked and murdered, but there were no witnesses and no clues. Robbery was assumed to be the motive, and 'Murder by persons unknown' would be the verdict.

Giles did not debate for long whether to tell the coroner what he knew. What could he say? He was quite certain that Falkirk had swiftly eliminated someone he regarded as a threat to his safety, but he had no evidence of that. Conjecture and hearsay were not enough and he had given his word to Nellie that she would not be involved. He consoled himself with the thought that, if things went as he hoped, Falkirk would not long escape reckoning.

He left the coroner's office and walked through the streets of London oblivious to the crowds around him, thinking over the events of the last twenty-four hours, a prey to the bitter pangs of conscience which now attacked him. How badly he had underestimated Falkirk's capacity for speedy, ruthless action! He had, after all, been warned. To think that he had actually congratulated himself on disturbing Falkirk's complacence! Venetia may have been a poor specimen of womanhood, but she had not deserved to die that way... He walked on for some time, his face grim. Venetia's death had served one useful purpose. He wouldn't underestimate Falkirk again.

He arrived back at Upper Brook Street to find the ladies immersed in plans. The fourgon carrying some of the servants to the house in Bath, together with a load of dresses and household linens, was due to leave the next day and they were busy deciding what personal possessions they would send in advance with it. Giles left them to it. There might well be changes in store, changes which would not meet with their approval, but he needed time before he announced them.

That night he walked about his room with a heavy heart. It was now perfectly clear that the delightful boy he had known as Stephen Ordway had never existed. A liar and a cheat all his life, they had said. And Nellie had hinted at something worse—real viciousness. Had

Stephen lied and cheated about his wife? But Giles suppressed that unbidden hope before it developed. No—Venetia and Nellie had both said that Falkirk had had an affair with Rosabelle Ordway, and they had no reason to lie. The man himself hadn't troubled to deny it.

But he was now haunted by the thought that Rosabelle Ordway was an obvious target for Falkirk's ruthless policy of extermination. It was an inevitable conclusion. She was one of the few people outside Falkirk's 'inner circle' who knew that Selder and the respectable Mr Falkirk were the same person. Indeed, it was surprising that Falkirk had not already made an attempt to silence her. He was not a man to hesitate—once Venetia had been perceived as a possible danger she had been swiftly eliminated. The same could happen to Rosabelle…

Or…was she being spared for some particular reason? Was Falkirk still in love with her, perhaps? Unlikely. From all accounts he was not a man to risk all for love, yet he had risked a great deal in approaching her in such a public place as the Marchants' ball. So what other reason could there be for that? Self-interest was what motivated Falkirk, first, second and last. What could he want of Rosabelle?

Giles concentrated hard in an effort to recall Falkirk's words… *'I shall have to see you in Bath!'* he had heard him say. *'Perhaps you will have remembered about Stephen's papers by then. I do hope so.'* When he asked Rosabelle what Falkirk had wanted, she had said with apparent bewilderment, *'I can't remember… Yes! He asked if…I had some papers of Stephen's… I said I hadn't anything at all, and…and told him to apply to you… Giles, can't we talk of something else?'*

How much of what Rosabelle said was truth, and how much prevarication and lies? Did she in fact know what

Falkirk had wanted of her? Was she playing some devious game of her own? She was a fool if she was…a vision of Venetia's body suddenly filled him with horror. Rosabelle must not end like that, dear God, not Rosabelle, too! But how the hell could he protect her when he was working so much in the dark! He had absolutely no idea what was in her mind.

One thing was patent—Rosabelle Ordway was in danger. Until he knew the true extent of her involvement with Falkirk, until he could persuade her to abandon any ideas she might have about him, she must be taken somewhere out of Falkirk's reach. He dared not risk anything else—not when he had so little to work with, and two women to protect. He needed time…

Giles made several decisions that night, and in the morning they were carried out with the efficiency and despatch he had acquired during his years of command. Goss was given a list of men he was to find within twenty-four hours. They were all ex-soldiers, and now, like Goss, out of the army, and possibly looking for a bit of adventure. They all had two things in common. They were reliable, and they could be trusted to keep their mouths shut. Some would be asked to stay in London to keep Falkirk and his associates under observation.

'Falkirk is a dangerous man, Goss. He has already killed once to protect himself, and will kill again without a second thought. Make sure there are enough funds for a couple of them to travel if they have to. Falkirk may go to Bath.'

'That's where we're going, isn't it, Colonel?'

Giles shook his head. 'No. It's where Falkirk believes

we're going. But the ladies and I are making for Buxton, Goss.'

'If you'll excuse me one moment, Colonel, I'll just step outside and delay the waggon. It's just about to set off.'

'On no account! I want that fourgon to set off as planned and with as much fuss and noise as possible. Let it go!'

'Er…the ladies' luggage, sir? They won't be best pleased if they are in Buxton, and some of the servants, a lot of their clothes and all of the household items are in Bath.'

Giles nodded ruefully. 'I know. But that's a small price to pay. I want to put Falkirk off the scent. With any luck he'll assume we shall follow, and leave London himself. The servants and the goods will be looked after in Bath.'

Goss privately thought that it was the ladies who would need looking after, but he said nothing.

'Now to business again,' said Giles. 'One of the men is to set off immediately with these—a letter for Captain Daventry in Leicester, another for Avenell and a list of inns where rooms are to be engaged. Send Gregson. But not a word to anyone else—no one at all!—about any of this.'

'Right, sir! Anything else?'

'Yes. I want you to continue to keep a special eye on Mrs Ordway, even when we are travelling. That's important, Goss. Three of your men will travel with us, too—one as footman, and two as grooms. And there's one more thing. There'll be letters to be posted from here—but not for a day or two *after* we have left London. There's one to a Mrs Chamberlayne at Reading, and one for the agent in Bath. And there'll be another to Temperley.' Giles smiled grimly at the thought of the probable contents of Rosabelle Ordway's letter to her sister. She was going to be furious! But…she would be safe.

It was this thought which was the driving force behind all Giles's plans. It was perfectly true that he felt he ought to inform Lord Stanton in person that his estranged wife was dead. It was undoubtedly true that Buxton was a more convenient base than Bath for directing various schemes he had in mind for the Stanton estates. But the overriding motive, the reason for all his elaborate precautions, was this fear for Rosabelle Ordway's safety. Whether she knew what Falkirk wanted from her or not, whether she was stupidly dishonest or perilously innocent, as long as she was within Falkirk's reach, she was in danger.

Meanwhile, the ladies were leafing through guide books to Bath, reading accounts of activities in the Pump Room, and planning excursions to local places of interest. A house had been found on Sydney Street, and the Chamberlaynes had been written to—they had sent a most civil response, inviting Lady Ordway to stay not two nights, but three. Rooms had been reserved at comfortable inns on the rest of the way, and, reluctant though she was, Annabelle had written to Rosabelle to let her know that the time for the sisters to change back had at last arrived.

Then, out of the blue, Giles suddenly announced that he had changed his mind. They were to go to Buxton, after all.

'But you can't do that!' cried Annabelle desperately. 'I've written to my sister, Aunt Laura has arranged to stay with the Chamberlaynes, we've rented the house—'

'I am aware of what you have done,' said Giles, in the tone he now normally used towards her—cool, impersonal, distant. 'But the arrangements for Bath are not irreversible.'

'But I *must* go to Bath!'

'I've no doubt Bath would suit you better, Rosabelle. Buxton is a poor second to Bath, I grant you, in every respect except the qualities of its waters. It would certainly provide you with fewer opportunities to parade yourself before the eyes of an admiring and frivolous society. But since my primary concern is not to administer to your vanity, but to see that Aunt Laura has the treatment she needs, I have decided to take you both to Buxton. All the arrangements are made. We set off early tomorrow morning.'

'Tomorrow morn— But…but this is absurd! What can I possibly tell my sister? She is expecting me at Temperley at the weekend!'

'You will naturally write her a letter. I will see that it gets to her. Tell her that, since I have urgent business in Derbyshire, I have changed our plans. Come, it is not so long since you last went to Temperley. You are surely not claiming that she will miss you?'

Annabelle was speechless. It was Lady Ordway's turn. She had not been quite herself ever since the night at Vauxhall, but she did her best.

'A change in plan is quite out of the question, Giles! You forget, the fourgon with all our luggage has already left for Bath! And Lily has gone with it! What will Rosabelle do without a maid?'

'That's right!' cried Annabelle. 'We won't have a thing to wear! You must see how ridiculous you're being, Giles!'

'I'm sorry about the maidservant, but all the rest has

been taken care of. Trust me, Aunt Laura,' Giles said,
ignoring Annabelle. 'I have very good reason for my
decision. We shall take the journey in very easy stages,
and I've arranged for us to spend the weekend with
friends of mine near Charnwood Forest—that should
break the journey for you. You'll like Selina Daventry
very much, I know you will.'

Lady Ordway was by no means so sure, but she lacked
the energy to argue further and Annabelle was left to
fight her own battle. But all her arguments were in vain.

'He's impossible, quite impossible!' Annabelle said,
stormily pacing up and down in Lady Ordway's room.
'He offers us no explanation, no excuse—he simply refuses to discuss anything at all! We are to go to Buxton.
And that's the end of the matter!'

'He has always been a touch high-handed,' said Lady
Ordway weakly.

'So you have said before. But this is positively Gothic!
I could scream with fury! What are we to do?'

'I don't know, Anna dear. But he did say that his
business was urgent.'

'And you believe him? I think it's because he can't
bear to see us enjoy ourselves. He thought I was looking
forward to my stay in Bath.'

'No, no! You are not doing Giles justice! He would
not be so petty.'

A snort from Annabelle showed what she thought of
this.

'Really, Anna, I do think he has important business
with his father. He isn't even going direct to Buxton. He
plans to spend some time at Avenell beforehand.'

'Then why cannot he go to see his father, and allow
us to make our own way to Bath? Can't you ask him?'

'I couldn't do that!' Lady Ordway was really shocked.

'Giles has assured me that his reasons for taking us to Buxton are sound. We must trust his judgement.'

Without Lady Ordway's support Annabelle was powerless. In the end she was forced to bow to the inevitable, and, with no very charitable feeling towards Giles, sat down to write another letter to her sister. This was going to be even more difficult than the last one.

But as she sat at her writing table and considered the situation she grew calmer. Perhaps this delay was not so disastrous after all? It would provide time in which Rosabelle's relationship with Mr Winbolt could develop, and the more she thought about those two, the more convinced she was that they would suit each other perfectly. Any delay was surely to the good there! And her own case? Ah, there she was less sanguine. But at least she had been given a few more weeks to try. She started writing more confidently, and, in the end, the letter was in the same light-hearted vein as all her others. There was even less point at the moment in worrying Rosabelle with her own problems.

Dearest Sister

This will be as great a shock to you as it is to me. Colonel Stanton—for I cannot bring myself to call him anything else, unless it is The Monster—has decided in his wisdom that we should be better off going to Buxton! He is quite adamant.

Apparently, he intends to visit his father in the vicinity, though he has not informed me of the fact. I had to learn even that much from Aunt Laura! I suspect that this is not his only reason, however, though I cannot imagine what any other could be. He can surely hardly be serious when he hints that

my character may have something to do with his
decision! I wonder whether Aunt Laura and I made
the mistake of appearing too pleased with the notion
of going to Bath? For such a killjoy as Colonel
Stanton, the temptation to change his plans must
have been quite irresistible. But let us forget the less
pleasant aspects of life in Upper Brook Street!

The sad truth is that by the time you receive this
letter we shall be on our way north to Buxton, and
it will be impossible for me to see you for seven or
eight weeks! Words cannot express how sorry I am.
I assure you, my darling sister, I would have hired
a chaise and come alone if it had been possible, but
the change of plan was sprung on us with hardly a
day's notice, and I have been kept exceedingly
busy. Colonel Stanton is all consideration! I expect
he wanted to spare us the pain of learning too soon
that we were not to enjoy the excessive dissipations
of life in Bath! I understand that Buxton will provide me with 'fewer opportunities to parade' myself. I quote.

Since I shall not be seeing you in person for some
time, I send you my love, and best assurances that
I am happier than I may seem! Life with The
Monster in the house is at least never dull. And you
may have an easy mind about Aunt Laura. She continues to improve, and, however little I deserve it,
she seems to be very happy with

                                    Your loving Twin.

As she folded the letter Annabelle even smiled. If
Giles read it—as he probably would—it would do him
no harm to see what she thought of him!

* * *

They left London in Giles's comfortable new travelling coach at seven o'clock the morning after. It was an impressive cavalcade. Lady Ordway and Annabelle sat inside, Wilson and the new footman sat behind, and luggage was piled on the roof. One groom sat beside the coachman, and another rode postilion. Giles, accompanied by the faithful Goss, rode alongside. It was so early that the streets were deserted, and within the hour they had reached the Edgware Turnpike gate and had turned right to join the Holyhead Road at St Alban's.

Giles was as good as his word. They took the road north in very easy stages, and since the carriage was well sprung and could be opened up when it was warm, they were reasonably comfortable. They spent the second night at Woburn, and in the morning they visited the great house there. The housekeeper was very pleased to show them round, and they were all impressed with the interior furnishings and designs. But afterwards Lady Ordway refused to accompany them on a tour of the grounds, pleading that she had walked enough.

'Though I should like you to have some fresh air and exercise, my dear,' she said with a smile at Annabelle. 'Let me take the carriage back to the inn. I could have a rest there, while you and Giles walk back through the trees.'

Annabelle was not sure she wanted a tête-à-tête with Giles, and doubted he would wish for one with her. But to her surprise Giles received the suggestion kindly.

'It isn't far,' he said, seeing her hesitate. 'Not more than half-an-hour's walk.'

Annabelle eyed him suspiciously. She could not imagine that he desired her company for any pleasant reason.

Giles had something to say to her in private. But in the end, curiosity prevailed.

'Then I should like to do it,' said Annabelle. 'Thank you.'

# Chapter Ten

At first they walked in silence, taking pleasure in the fresh air, the sunshine glinting down through the massive canopy of trees overhead, and the peace of the countryside. Giles seemed to be in no hurry to begin.

Annabelle, too, was reluctant to disturb the apparent harmony, but after a while she said, 'Giles, may I ask you a question?'

'Certainly. Though I do not guarantee to answer it.'

Undeterred, she went on, 'I have no desire to spoil a very pleasant excursion, but what is in your mind, exactly?'

'In what respect?'

'I am not stupid—'

'It is some time since I last thought you were, Rosabelle.'

'I am not stupid,' she repeated, 'and I should like to know why you are taking so many precautions.'

'Precautions?'

'Or is it merely that you do not trust me out of your sight?'

'That would not be unreasonable, surely?'

'That's what I thought at first,' said Annabelle, maintaining her tranquil tone, 'when I couldn't go anywhere during the last days in town without falling over Goss. I became quite annoyed with the poor man, but when I asked him about it, he came up with a hopelessly inadequate excuse.'

'Now Goss didn't tell me that.'

'I expect he didn't wish to worry you, Giles,' Annabelle said affably. 'We all know how devoted he is. And it can't be pleasant to be asked to spy on the lady of the house.'

'He was not spying on you.'

'Well, I've come to see that. And though it seems mad, I now think you had commissioned him to protect me! Can that be so?'

He looked down at her with a hint of admiration in his eyes. 'You're certainly not stupid, Rosabelle. On the contrary.'

'I can't accept too much credit. It didn't occur to me immediately. But after that you were so...I won't say *unusually* tyrannical, but so extremely tyrannical! Not just with me—I have come to expect it from you as far as I am concerned—but with Aunt Laura, too. At first I was so incensed by your overnight decision to reverse all our arrangements and take us to Buxton that I couldn't think rationally. But then...this sudden change was *so* discourteous to the Chamberlaynes, *so* upsetting to the agent in Bath, that you must have had a very pressing reason for it. And then, when I thought again about Goss's behaviour, I came to the very odd conclusion that you were doing it for my sake.'

Giles's tone was repressive as he replied, 'I'm afraid you're flattering yourself. There were other considerations.'

'I am relieved to hear it! Knowing your opinion of me, I was completely puzzled as to why you were prepared to go to such lengths to look after me. I wondered if you had gone mad. Er…would you mind telling me why you think I need protection?'

Giles walked on in silence for some time. Then he said, 'This conversation must remain between ourselves, Rosabelle. I do not want Aunt Laura to be disturbed by it. Do I have your word on that?'

Annabelle gave him a twisted smile. 'If you think it worth having.'

'When Aunt Laura is concerned I do not doubt your good intentions. And what I am about to tell you might upset and frighten her.'

'Then you have my assurance that I won't say anything.'

'Good!' He seemed not to know how to continue. Annabelle waited. This line of communication which had opened up after days of silence was so slender, so fragile, that she dared not risk breaking it.

At last he said abruptly, 'Your friend Falkirk is a very dangerous man, Rosabelle. Did you know that?'

Annabelle recalled the irrational feelings of terror the man had aroused in her on the two occasions they had met. That they had been communicated by some strange empathy from her twin, she had no doubt. She said gravely, 'He is not my friend, Giles. He never was. And I have always thought him dangerous.'

He stared at her so intensely that she grew uncomfortable. 'That is true,' she said at last. 'Though I know that you do not believe me.'

'I wish I could!'

'Giles, this journey to Buxton will prove very tedious if we cannot come to some sort of a truce. I know your position, you think you know mine. Only time and circumstances can change either. But if we are to spend twice or three times as long on the road as we need—'

'Why do you say that?'

'It's obvious we shall, if you carry on avoiding the post houses, and insist on using your own horses all the way. For some reason you wish us to travel to Buxton without being followed or traced. And I suspect the new grooms are there to look after more than the horses...' She gave him a straight look, then said, 'It's Falkirk, isn't it? He is the reason for all these measures.'

'My stepmother is dead, Rosabelle.'

Annabelle stopped and stared at him in shock. 'Lady Stanton? But...how?'

'She was murdered. I think Falkirk was responsible.'

'Murdered? But, no! That cannot be! Falkirk can't...'

'I am as certain as I can be that he got rid of her because she knew too much! And you...you are in the same danger. For God's sake, Rosabelle, don't try to defend him! Even you might find that difficult.'

Annabelle was distraught. 'I was not trying to defend him in the least! Oh, why won't you trust me?' She turned her face away.

Giles watched her in brooding silence. At last she managed to speak again.

'I...I am grateful to you for telling me about your stepmother. It must be painful for you to speak of her. I am sorry. Tell me what causes you to think I am in danger.'

'Because you know the link between Falkirk and Selder.'

'So do you!'

'Falkirk doesn't know that. Not for sure. Besides, I am well able to look after myself.'

'But why does it matter?'

'Oh, come! We have both agreed you're not stupid. Falkirk is a respectable member of the *ton*, accepted everywhere and ambitious for more. When his cousin dies, Falkirk will be Lord Banagher. Any association with the name of Selder would ruin him, if it came to light. Selder was the leader of a gang of villains of the lowest possible sort, up to every conceivable vice. Murder was the least of their crimes. And Stephen was one of them. Don't try to tell me you didn't know!'

She looked at him blankly, and Giles thought for a moment she was going to faint. He took her arm, but she removed it.

'I...I need to sit for a moment. Excuse me.' She was deathly white. Slowly she went over to a seat nearby and sat down. For a moment she had forgotten he was there. 'I didn't know,' she whispered. 'I really...didn't...know. Why didn't she tell me?' Then she buried her face in her hands.

The impulse to take her into his arms, cradle her, comfort her, until the look of horror disappeared from her face, and some vestige of colour came back to her cheeks, was almost overwhelming... But Giles remained where he was, his face devoid of expression. He was far from convinced that Rosabelle Ordway was as innocent as she claimed, and until he was, he would not give in to these irrational and dangerous feelings. However, it was perfectly possible she had not known the full extent of Selder's villainy. Nellie Marsden had said as much.

After a minute or two he said gently, 'I'm sorry if I shocked you, Rosabelle. I see now that Stephen must have kept most of his activities concealed from both of you. I doubt that Aunt Laura could have told you anything more than you already knew.'

Annabelle looked up at him, wondering for a moment what he was talking about. Then she realised with relief that he had misinterpreted her unguarded exclamation. He had taken 'Why didn't she tell me?' to refer to Aunt Laura. She resisted a strong impulse to tell him the truth there and then. It would be stupid to say or do anything irrevocable while she was still so shaken. She got up, and strove to speak naturally.

'Forgive me. I'm better now. It was a shock. Shall we…shall we carry on?'

'Take my arm.'

'No. Thank you. I am well able to walk without assistance.'

It was Giles's turn to be tentative. 'Rosabelle, an opportunity to talk in confidence like this may not occur often. May we talk it over a little more?'

'Yes, yes. Of course!' said Annabelle, bracing herself.

'The papers Falkirk mentioned at the Marchants' ball…he seems to regard them as important. Do you really know nothing about them?'

Annabelle didn't know what to say. She knew nothing herself, of course, but Rosa might! 'I…I can't remember, Giles,' she said in the end.

But her hesitation had been noted, and Giles's manner grew cooler. 'A pity,' he said. 'It might have helped me.'

'Giles, why *are* we going to Buxton? Would it not have been better to try to expose Falkirk for what he is, instead of running away?'

'I'll stop him somehow or other, never fear. Indeed, I have set things in motion in London… But I have other considerations—you and Aunt Laura, for one. Your life, and perhaps that of Aunt Laura, would be too great a price to pay for the satisfaction of tackling Falkirk face to face at the moment.'

'You really think our lives are at risk?'

'Falkirk is ruthless. And frightened. That's a dangerous combination.'

She nodded and fell silent.

Giles went on, 'Also, I want to destroy Falkirk, if I can, without exposing the true extent of Stephen's villainy. Not only for Aunt Laura's sake—my mother was an Ordway, too, don't forget, and I must do what I can to protect their name. And...I am also going north to see my father.'

'You wish to tell him yourself about your stepmother?'

'That, yes. And...it's time I made my peace with him. After all, Venetia was the chief source of dissension between us.'

'Was she? Aunt Laura said that he resented your acquisition of the family lands, after he had...sold them.'

'So she has talked to you, has she? It's certainly true that you cannot trust a woman to keep her mouth shut!'

'Giles! Aunt Laura told me some of the story in an effort to excuse your conduct.'

'My conduct?'

'Yes—she attributed your general ill-humour and overbearing ways, not to mention your distrust of women, to the unfortunate experiences in your family.'

'Whereas we know that my distrust of women has recently been more than justified. Is that not so, Rosabelle?'

Annabelle sighed in exasperation. 'How long do you think we shall spend on this visit to Buxton?' she demanded.

'Seven or eight weeks, all told. Why?'

'I'd like to make a suggestion. You say my life is in danger. That isn't a pleasant thought, and the journey is bound to be somewhat nerve-racking, whatever precautions you take. But life is going to be even more unpleasant for us all, if we snap at each other all the way to Buxton and back! Can we not come to some sort of accommodation, just for two months? A kind of truce—however insincere? I would endeavour not to do anything to provoke you, and you in your turn would have to try to avoid being quite so critical of me. Let us, just for a short time, be kind to one another, Giles. Or, if being kind is impossible, then at least we could try to be civil! What do you say?'

He looked doubtful.

'I'm not asking you actually to like me, or…anything else,' said Annabelle, faint colour rising in her cheeks. 'I know you don't. This is not an effort to persuade you to change your mind about me. It is merely an attempt to make the journey easier for all of us.'

'I suppose you're right,' he said at last. He turned to her, and she would have sworn there was a look of genuine regret in his eyes. 'I cannot say that I trust you, Rosabelle, much as I would like to. The evidence against you is still too overwhelming. But—' He held out his hand. 'Yes, I will agree to your truce.'

They shook hands, and then resumed their walk.

The weather remained kind, and the travellers continued to enjoy their leisurely journey through the English Midlands, particularly as there was not the slightest sign of any interest in their progress. Giles was as good as his word, and he and Annabelle had many lively, but perfectly friendly, conversations with each other. The inns where they stayed were modest, but comfortable, and in the evenings they went for walks, or talked, or played cards. The shadows of deception and danger, lack of trust, and all the rest were firmly kept in the background.

Eventually they turned through the walls of a pleasant country estate, where they were to spend a couple of nights.

'I must say, I had never expected the journey to pass so pleasantly,' said Lady Ordway, as they drove up the drive to the Daventry home. 'Though I have yet to see natural beauties to rival the architecture of Bath, Giles.'

'You shall, Aunt Laura, you shall. Only have patience. These Midland counties are not impressive, I agree, but Derbyshire will astonish you with its beauty.'

Lady Ordway was not moved. 'I visited Avenell when you were a baby, Giles. I know what Derbyshire is like.'

'Then you have to agree with me. It is of all places the most beautiful I have ever seen.'

'You are not being partial, by any chance, are you, Giles?' laughed Annabelle.

'How could you suggest it? But look—we are expected.'

What seemed to be a vast crowd of people was waiting on the steps of the Daventry home. They were greeted enthusiastically by all of them. After a few minutes of confusion, Annabelle finally managed to sort out Captain Daventry, his wife Selina, his mother Mrs Daventry senior, and five children. Captain Daventry bore Giles and the children away to the stables, and the four ladies mounted the steps to the front door.

'We are so pleased to have you here, Mrs Ordway,' said Selina Daventry. 'We see Giles three or four times a year, but this is the first time he has brought someone with him. I gather you are on the way to Avenell?'

'We're actually making for Buxton—Lady Ordway is to take the waters there, but I think we are to visit Avenell on the way.'

'Really?' said Mrs Daventry. 'I'm very glad indeed to hear that.'

They went into the big saloon and sat down. The two ladies of the house were obviously very interested in their guests, and it became clear that Giles was a great favourite with them. He was young James Edward's godfather.

'I cannot tell you how kind he is to the child—to all the children, in fact,' Mrs Daventry said.

The senior Mrs Daventry broke in. 'Mirry and Lucy are twins, Mrs Ordway,' she said. 'Colonel Stanton has told us that you have a twin sister, too?'

'Yes,' said Annabelle. 'Though we haven't lived together since we were six years old.'

'How very sad! Why was that?'

'My mother died, and—'

'I badly needed a daughter, Mrs Daventry,' Lady Ordway intervened. 'So I begged Mr Kelland to let me bring Rosabelle up in London, and he agreed, on condition that I let her spend the summer months each year with her sister in Berkshire.'

'I think my father was quite glad to be relieved of one of us. And it has worked out very well.'

Perhaps sensing that the subject was a difficult one for her guests, though not, of course, even remotely guessing why, Mrs Daventry had the good manners not to ask any more questions. Instead she suggested that she should take them to their rooms. 'Take as long as you need to refresh yourselves after the journey,' she said gaily.

'Captain Daventry and Colonel Stanton will be some time yet, if I know them! James has recently acquired a couple of very handsome hunters.'

'Have they known each other long?' asked Annabelle.

'Ever since they both joined the army. But James sold out after Waterloo. His father wished him to take over the management of the estate, and I have to say that I was very happy that he did! Of course, Giles went on to further glories. We are very proud of him.'

While Lady Ordway sat in the saloon with Mrs Daventry's mother-in-law, the rest of the family took Giles and Annabelle on a short tour of the estate. Annabelle found herself walking with Captain Daventry, and the two boys, and she was so absorbed in what they were telling her that she was surprised to find they had outstripped the rest of the party. With a laugh, they stopped and sat down on a fallen tree trunk to wait. The two little girls came running up, each clutching a bunch of flowers, which grew in profusion in the hedgerows.

'Mrs Ordway, these are for you, we picked them our own selves! Aren't they pretty?'

'I think they're very pretty. Mmm…and they have such a nice smell, too! Thank you. It's a long time since I had such a delightful bouquet. I shall ask your mama if I may put them in my bedroom. Do you think we could find a few fern leaves to put with them? For greenery.'

The two little girls towed her away, assuring her that they knew just where to find such ferns. The rest of the party followed them more slowly, until the boys suddenly took to galloping down the hill. Giles and the Daventrys were left alone.

'What a delightful girl! Oh, forgive me! I should have said young woman. But when you told us of your cousin's wife I had imagined someone more sophisticated, Giles.'

Giles's eyes followed Annabelle as she went back down the path with the twins. They had each taken a hand, and the three of them were laughing and chattering as if they had known each other forever. When would he begin to fathom the contradictions in Rosabelle Ordway's character?

'She…she has a happy knack of fitting in wherever she goes, Selina.'

'That is certainly true!' Captain Daventry said. 'She was very interested in what we are planning to do with the farms here.' He looked guilty as his wife gave an exasperated groan.

'James! You promised me you wouldn't!' She turned to Giles. 'He will keep boring our poor guests with his wretched ideas, Giles. He gets carried away when he talks of his plans—he simply cannot see that changes in farming methods can't possibly be an interesting topic of conversation for town-bred visitors. I'll have to explain to Mrs Ordway as soon as I have an opportunity.'

'Well, I don't think you need worry, Selina! She was far from being bored! Indeed, she made one or two very pertinent observations.'

'That only increases my admiration for her manners, James! How could she possibly be interested?' She laughed and shook her head at her husband. Then she turned to Giles. 'Tell me, Giles, are Major Dabney and Captain Wainwright well? And has Richard Pettifer's aunt finally declared him her heir yet?'

The talk turned to other matters.


But later that evening the subject came up again.

'So you're making for Avenell?' Captain Daventry

said. 'Do you plan to stay there long?'

A shadow came over Giles's face. 'No—three or four days at the most. I…I have to see my father. And then I need to take a little time to see how the estate is faring.'

'Are we to stay with Lord Stanton, Giles?'

'I…I'm not quite sure, Aunt Laura. I've reserved some rooms at an excellent inn nearby. You would be very comfortable there. My father may not be well enough to receive visitors.' Giles's tone was restricted. The Daventrys, fully conversant with the situation between their friend and his father, hastened to change the subject.

'Mrs Ordway, I hear that my dreadful husband has been teasing you with his views on farming,' cried Selina Daventry. 'You must forgive him. Since he left the Army he has taken with enthusiasm to being what he calls a modern landowner. He is really quite a rational creature, but on this subject he is sadly blind. He forgets that ladies of the *ton* are neither interested nor informed on such matters.'

'I've told you, Selina. You are quite out. Mrs Ordway displayed an astonishing grasp of our problems.'

'Oh?' said Giles, turning to Annabelle. 'Is this a new talent, Rosabelle? Where on earth have you learned about farming? Who has been teaching you?'

'I…I… You forget, Giles. In my youth I spent every summer down at Temperley.'

'Children's games?'

'No, indeed! Annabelle ran the estate from a very early age, and, like Captain Daventry here, was eager to convey her knowledge to anyone who would listen.' She turned to her host. 'My father is an invalid and was happy to delegate the running of Temperley to my sister.

She takes a keen interest in the land. I'm sure she would enjoy talking to you, Captain Daventry. You would have a lot in common.'

'A gel! Running an estate!' cried the older Mrs Daventry. 'How odd!'

'I suppose it is, ma'am. But I think Annabelle is happy to do it.'

'She must be an able teacher,' said Captain Daventry with a smile. 'But then you are twins, are you not? So perhaps there is an extra line of sympathy between you.' His wife interrupted him.

'Are you very alike? I was rather disappointed when I found that our two are not.'

Annabelle hesitated. This was a dangerous moment. But Lady Ordway came to her rescue. 'There are similarities of appearance perhaps, but they are not at all alike otherwise. They have led such very different lives. I pride myself that Rosabelle is the prettier, but you might call me over-partial, I suppose. Annabelle has always led such an outdoor life—she was sadly brown when I was last at Temperley. Tell me, Mrs Daventry, is this delicious dessert made with your own fruits?'

The moment passed and Annabelle breathed again. The rest of the visit passed without incident, and when the time came for them to leave she did so with regret. She had developed a fondness for the Daventry family, but doubted very much that she would ever see them again.

They had all enjoyed their visit to the Daventrys, and a more relaxed atmosphere could be felt as they continued northwards. Giles's manner towards Annabelle was very nearly affable. Even Lady Ordway was impressed with the scenery before Matlock—the glens, the rippling, sparkling river, the rocks towering above them—and Annabelle was enraptured. They spent a very comfortable night in Bakewell, and set off in good spirits on the last stage of their journey. However, as they drove into the courtyard of a charming inn, not far from Avenell, a shadow fell over the company.

It was a beautiful afternoon, and the ladies had till then been very content with their day. But ever since midday, Giles had been growing steadily more taciturn. By the time they drew up at the inn, his face was grimmer than ever. Annabelle badly wanted to reassure him, give him support for the unpleasant task before him, but she dared not. Instead she concentrated on the scenery and did her best to distract him. She met with little success.

Lady Ordway whispered, 'Try not to worry, Anna. Giles was very short with you just now, I know, but he cannot be looking forward to this visit to his father. Their estrangement must give him pain.'

Annabelle did not know how to reply. She knew, more than Lady Ordway, how difficult it was going to be at Avenell. There was no easy way for Giles to break the news about his stepmother's death, whatever Lord Stanton's reaction might be. She knew, too, that she must say nothing of it to Lady Ordway. It was for Giles to tell her. She sighed and said, 'We must just wait until we see him tomorrow, Aunt Laura.'

After Giles had seen them comfortably settled in their rooms, he rode off to Avenell. Annabelle stood at her window and watched him go—he looked like a man riding to a wake. Then she turned back sadly into the room.

As the walls and towers of Avenell came into view Giles's heart grew ever heavier. It was the scene of so many happy childhood memories, all overshadowed by the nightmare of what had followed, when his stepmother had usurped his beloved mother's place. And now he had come to tell his father that the usurper was dead. The drive rose steeply from the road and Giles dismounted as usual and left his horse at the lodge. He walked up the winding carriageway, through hedges and trees, deep in thought.

As a child he had felt bewildered, hurt at the change in his life. He had regarded himself as an exile, forced to live among comparative strangers while his father filled his home with strangers. Later, when he was old enough to understand what had happened, he had become contemptuous of his father's doting fondness for Venetia Stanton. With increasing frustration, unable to do anything to prevent it, he had been forced to hear of the dissipation of Stanton wealth, the mortgage and loss of Stanton lands, to see his mother's jewellery given away—all to keep this woman happy and at his father's side. He had felt no sympathy, only scorn for an ailing old man left alone when the money, and Venetia, were gone.

Looking back now, Giles realised that Lord Stanton had long since regretted that catastrophic marriage, but Stanton arrogance and Stanton pride had prevented him from admitting it. It had not been surprising that his father had responded to his criticisms not with regret, but with fury, and that father and son had fallen out, comprehensively. The world was mistaken when it attributed Lord Stanton's resentment to Giles's efforts to buy back and own the Stanton lands his father had so stupidly lost. The roots of their estrangement lay in those unfilial expressions of contempt, in the arrogant lack of tolerance shown by his only son.

Older now, and wiser, Giles understood for the first time how his father had felt. He now knew what it was to despise a woman for what she had done in the past, what she was likely to do in the future, to know her to be a liar and a cheat, but still, in spite of everything, to remain fascinated. Since meeting Rosabelle Ordway he had been drawn himself into this honey-trap. He had seen Rosabelle enchanting the Daventrys, cultivating the children, pretending to take an interest in poor Daventry's schemes, laughing with Selina…

He had watched her apparently artless delight in the beauties of nature on their journey, her solicitude for his aunt. He could remember the sincerity in those deep blue eyes as she swore she had no idea who Selder was… And in spite of all he knew about her, he still had to exercise the greatest possible control not to seek her out, to coax her to smile at him, talk to him, laugh with him. In danger of such a spell himself, he could at last understand his father's infatuation with Venetia Stanton, and feel ashamed that he had been so unforgiving.

He had reached the gatehouse, its ancient tower guarding the entrance to Avenell. He paused, then strode across the courtyard to the massive oak door which opened on to the Great Hall.

He was met at the door by an elderly valet who, on the few occasions such services were required, acted as both footman and butler.

'Good evening, Howells. How are you?'

'Very fit, master Giles, very fit. Lord Stanton is waiting in the little parlour. If I may mention it, we've been looking forward all day to this moment.'

Giles permitted himself an ironic smile. 'You're kind to say so. Is my father well, too?'

'Fair. But he hasn't his old strength. He doesn't stir much out of his chair nowadays.'

'I need to talk to him. Is he well enough for that?'

Howells stopped and gave Giles a worried look.

'He's well enough for a talk. It…it… Forgive me, master Giles, but is that all it would be? The last time…'

'I know, I know. The last time I tried to have a talk with him there was an almighty row, and we parted on very bad terms. You needn't be so careful in mentioning it, Howells. God knows, the shouting was so immoderate that most of Derbyshire must have known the Stantons had fallen out again! Very embarrassing for all concerned.'

'It's not that. After you left, he was really ill, master Giles. Very distressed was Lord Stanton. And he's not getting any younger. I'm not sure that another…talk like the last would be good for him.'

'I intend this one to be different, Howells.'

'I'm very glad to hear you say so.' Howells led the way into a small passage and opened a door to the side. 'We've put you in your old set of rooms, sir. Would you like anything to eat?'

'Not now, though I might have something later. But a tankard of ale wouldn't come amiss. I'll have it in the little parlour with my father. I'll only be a minute or two.'

'Very well, sir. I'll be waiting for you.'

Minutes later Giles entered the passageway leading to Lord Stanton's rooms to find Howells waiting there, as he had promised. Howells opened the door to the little parlour, went in and said quietly,

'Colonel Stanton, my lord.'

# Chapter Eleven

Giles bent his head as he entered. The Stantons were a tall race, and the Tudor members of the family who had redesigned the south range had forgotten to allow for it. But the low door led into a beautiful room. It was spacious—'little' only by comparison with Avenell's state reception rooms—and panelled throughout in silver-grey wood. At the end of the room surprisingly large mullioned windows overlooked the terraces falling down to the valley below. Giles could remember hearing, on summer evenings in the past when the windows had been open, the sound of water swirling round the boulders in the river, and splashing against its banks. But now the windows were shut, and though it was still quite light outside, the curtains were half drawn against the evening sun. There was a large wing chair by the fireplace, and a table by it.

'Since you're here, you'd better come in, hadn't you?

You've taken your time. We've been expecting you this past hour or more.'

'I'm sorry, sir. I had to see that Lady Ordway and her daughter-in-law were comfortably settled.'

'They're at the Stanton Arms, I suppose.'

'Yes.'

'Hmm.'

Howells came in with a tankard of ale and some wine for his master, which he put on the table. He poured the wine, then left the room, giving Giles a significant look as he went. The interruption gave Giles time to marshal his thoughts. The sight of his father, a gaunt figure huddled in his chair, dark eyes sunk deep in their sockets, had affected him more than he was willing to admit.

'How are you, sir? Howells seemed to think you were not altogether the thing.'

'Howells is an old woman. You needn't concern yourself about me, sir. I don't suppose for a minute you're here to enquire about my health. You've more important things to see to, no doubt.'

'No, Father. This time I've come to see you. I'd like to talk to you.'

'Hmm. Would you? I'm not sure I'm fit enough for that.'

Giles took a breath and said resolutely, 'Father, things have happened recently which…which have caused me to think again about the past. I…I have come to regret some of the things that I have said and done. I'd like you to forgive me for them.'

Lord Stanton sat up and stared at his son. 'Well, I'm damned! This is a change of heart! What the devil has caused this turnaround?'

'Several things. But before we go any further, I have…' Giles paused. He could not in all honesty call his news bad. 'I have some news for you, which I hope will not be too much of a shock. Venetia has died.'

'Who?'

'Venetia, Father. Your ex-wife.'

'Has she, indeed?' Lord Stanton sat in silence for several minutes, a number of expressions chasing one another across his face—a frown, a look of sadness, and finally one of relief. 'So she's gone. I suppose you've come to congratulate me on my loss.'

'No. Though I'd be a hypocrite if I expressed any sorrow for it,' Giles responded, silently conscious all the same of regret for the manner in which Venetia had died.

'Hmm.' There was a slight pause while Lord Stanton looked away. Still not looking at his son, he said eventually, 'You're right, of course. I lost my head over her and regretted it ever after. I was a fool.'

'You may have been a fool, sir, but it was at least a human failing. I was far too critical of your behaviour. I forgot the respect I owed you. And I should have understood your situation better.'

Giles kept his gaze steady, as his father shot him a fierce look, as if suspecting him of irony. Then Lord Stanton looked away again. 'How could you?' he said. 'You were a child.'

'I meant later. I didn't think ill of you when I was a child. I loved you and I loved my home, and I was deeply unhappy when you sent me away. Especially as at the time I couldn't understand why.'

Another fierce look, then a rueful nod, as if to acknowledge the justice of Giles's remark. 'The thing was, Giles…oh, damn it, I discovered I'd made a mistake very soon. Of course I did! But I wasn't going to acknowledge it. I was determined to live with it. And that meant countenancing her friends and putting up with their ways. But

I wasn't going to have you corrupted by them. I *had* to send you away.'

'I understand that now.'

'You do? Hmm.'

'And I'd like us to bury the past. It seems a suitable moment to do it. Could you do that, Father? Will you forgive my harsh words the last time we met?'

His father was clearly having a struggle with Stanton pride. 'So you admit you were at fault, do you?' he said gruffly.

'I do. Freely.'

'You were damned impertinent, sir. Not just on that occasion, either.'

'I was angry. But I shouldn't have expressed myself so immoderately.' Giles met Lord Stanton's glare this time with a hint of affectionate amusement. 'We both have a temper, sir.'

'Very well, very well. I daresay there were faults on both sides. How long are you staying?'

Taking this to mean that his apology was accepted, Giles sat down and relaxed.

'As I told you in my letter, I'm escorting Aunt Laura to Buxton.'

'Hmm. And she's at present at the Stanton Arms? With her boy's widow?'

'Yes. I thought it might be too much for the household here…'

'I've never heard such nonsense! Bring them to Avenell! Howells is perfectly capable of seeing that they're comfortably accommodated. That woman— what's her name? Dunnock! She can sort out the rooms tomorrow. Glad of something to do, I daresay. Tell her to get some help in if she needs it.'

To Giles's astonishment, Lord Stanton's eyes had suddenly brightened, his voice was clearer and stronger, and he was sitting upright, impatience and energy in every line. The elderly invalid had vanished. Was that all it had needed to cause this transformation? A reconciliation with his son? Giles was moved, suddenly overcome by a feeling of humility, which was as rare as it was unexpected. He took a moment to recover his normal voice.

Then he said mildly, 'There's quite a party of us. Aunt Laura has her own maid and manservant. We travelled in my own carriage, and with our own horses, so there's a coachman and two grooms. And Goss, of course.'

'Good God! What a household! Too high in the instep to travel like ordinary mortals, eh? Post horses not good enough for you?'

'It wasn't that, sir. But that's a tale for tomorrow.'

'Well, Avenell's big enough, heaven knows. Tell Howells. He'll deal with it all.'

'It's very good of you, Father.'

'Nonsense! It's a poor day for Avenell when the guests of the Stantons have to put up at the local inn! Fetch them tomorrow as soon as the ladies are up.'

'Thank you, sir. I will. Now, tell me truly, how you are?'

Giles and his father talked in unusual harmony for some time. Lord Stanton had clearly long wished for a reconciliation, but was too stiff-necked ever to have asked for one before it was offered. But now that barrier was overcome, father and son both felt the need to make up for lost time. More wine and ale were called for, and it was late before Giles finally bade his father goodnight. He left him planning how to entertain his guests, and harrassing poor Howells by issuing all sorts of conflicting orders.

* * *

When Giles set off from Avenell the morning was bright and fresh and glimpses of sunlight sparkling on water could be caught between the lush foliage on the river bank. He paused before riding down into the valley and gazed about him. He was surrounded by a land-scape—his landscape—of sun and shadows, hills, moorland and meadows, rocks and rivers—green and grey, purple and brown. It stretched for miles in every direction, gleaming in the morning sunlight. He listened with contentment to the sound of water rushing down from the hills in a thousand tiny waterfalls, forcing its way through narrow channels, past huge rocks, rippling over the pebbles of the river bed.

For so many years he had returned here with feelings of loss and resentment, an alien in his own country. Even ownership of the land had not brought back a sense of belonging. He had sought compensation, won rewards on foreign soils, but they had only ever at best been a poor substitute for Derbyshire and Avenell. Now, his estrangement from his father ended, things had changed—miraculously so—and once again he felt he belonged. Nothing could blunt this feeling of joy, of satisfaction in this reunion with his roots, and in his happiness he was ready to reconsider his other problems with a more open mind. Chief among them was the question of his feelings towards Rosabelle Ordway.

At Woburn Rosabelle had asked him for a truce, and he had agreed to it. It would have been inconvenient, to say the least, if they had continued their journey in an atmosphere of open antipathy and distrust. But till now, though he had adopted a more friendly attitude, he had not actually felt more kindly towards her. She had remained the woman who had betrayed his cousin and had lied outright to protect herself afterwards. He had still

suspected her of setting out quite deliberately to attract
him, and, though he had kept it well hidden, he had still
resented her power over him, despised himself for his
own weakness.

But suddenly such thoughts seemed unworthy.
Rosabelle Ordway might be the villain he had thought
her—but this morning it suddenly seemed less likely. All
his instincts were against it. The full story of her association with Falkirk had yet to be revealed, and there
might well be an explanation which could clear her. One
thing was certain. Rosabelle Ordway seemed to have
reached a part of him which no other woman ever had.
Surely that must mean something? Perhaps he should
trust his instincts after all?

But then a small cloud crossed the sun, and Giles gave
a frown. He had seen a good few men go to the wall
because they followed their instincts rather than their
heads, his father for one of them. Damn all women! Life
would be so much less complicated without them.
Perhaps, until the Falkirk business was resolved, it would
be wiser not to let Rosabelle Ordway gain the complete
hold on his life and his emotions that instinct told him
she could. But he could surely allow himself to enjoy
her company without any grave danger, couldn't he?

Lady Ordway and Annabelle had got up early, too.
The inn was right on the river and Lady Ordway had not
been able to sleep for the noise made by the water.

'I never have been a devotee of the countryside, Anna.
I find it very noisy. Town life always suited me very
well.'

'Aunt Laura! The world goes into the country for
peace and solitude! How can you say it is noisy?'

'The world is mistaken, Anna dear. That river is ex-

tremely loud! And I'll swear that forty or fifty birds
never stopped shouting to each other outside my window
this morning. For a while I even thought one of the cows
was in the bedchamber with me! I do so wish we had
gone to Bath!'

'But even from the little I've seen of it, Derbyshire is
beautiful!' Annabelle looked out of the window. 'Ah!
Here's Giles. I wonder how he got on?'

'He looks remarkably cheerful.'

As Giles came in through the arch, he looked up and
saw them, and his face lit up in a smile. Annabelle's
heart turned over. If only, she thought, oh, if only he
would always look at me like that! For a moment she
was lost in a dream where she and Giles... Reality took
over, however, and with a wry look, she followed Lady
Ordway sedately down to the coffee room.

'Good morning, Giles. Did you sleep well?'

'Very well, Aunt Laura.' They exchanged greetings—'the niceties of polite conversation', thought
Annabelle ironically—and then Giles issued an invitation
from his father to stay at Avenell for the next day or
two.

'How kind,' said Lady Ordway. 'Er...how far is
Avenell from the river, Giles?'

'Quite a way above it. But I thought you'd been there
before?'

'Once. A very long time ago. I can't remember much
about it.'

'Avenell stands on a hillside a hundred and fifty feet
or more above the river valley. Why do you want to
know?'

'Aunt Laura was kept awake all night by the sounds
of the river, Giles,' said Annabelle, her eyes full of
amusement. 'She finds the country very noisy.'

'I shall see you are put in one of the rooms at the back, Aunt Laura,' promised Giles. He grew grave. 'But there's something I have to tell you before we leave for Avenell. Shall we go into the garden?'

As they walked along the paths of a pretty little garden at the back, Giles gave Lady Ordway the news of Venetia Stanton's death, though without any unnecessary detail.

'But, Giles,' she protested, 'we cannot possibly intrude on Lord Stanton at this time!'

'He wants you to come. Say you will, Aunt Laura! Your rooms in Buxton are not yet available—they have been reserved from the weekend. It would please my father—and me—immensely, if you would agree to spend the rest of the week at Avenell. I think you must know what an act of hypocrisy it would be for him to pretend he is distressed at Venetia's death. They were divorced some years ago, as you know. And…it would mean a lot to me.'

Lady Ordway was eventually persuaded to consent, and they set off about an hour later. Though the steep winding drive up to Avenell gave her some qualms, and though she was not at all happy when the carriage rumbled over the ancient drawbridge, they arrived perfectly sound at the door of the Great Hall.

Lord Stanton was at the door to greet them.

'My dear Lady Ordway,' he said. 'Laura! This is a delightful honour. It must be twenty-five years since we last met.'

'More than that, Lord Stanton. It was not long after I married Sir John.' She allowed herself to be ushered in and gazed round doubtfully. 'Avenell hasn't changed…

This hall is so large! All that stone! It must be impossible to heat—and the draughts…'

'We only use the Great Hall on state occasions, Laura. The South Wing is very cosy. Come, I'll conduct you myself to meet Mrs Dunnock. Howells has gone to see to the disposition of your staff and luggage. All of it.'

'All of it! It's barely enough to keep us decently clothed! As for the sheets and other things… Giles sent the van off to Bath, Lionel!'

'Did he, indeed? I wonder why? Well, you won't need household stuff at Avenell, Laura. And I believe some boxes arrived for you here yesterday. Mrs Dunnock will show you to your rooms, and then we'll meet in the Little Parlour. You'll find that more to your taste.'

'I remember it. A sadly low ceiling. But the views were quite nice. If you like the country, that is…' Her voice died as Lord Stanton escorted her out of the Hall and along the passage.

Annabelle and Giles were left alone in the Great Hall.

'She's tired, Giles,' said Annabelle. 'She didn't sleep last night, and though you've looked after our comfort on the journey wonderfully well, it has taken a lot out of her. She really needs to stay in one place for more than a few days.'

He smiled at her. 'Don't worry. I'm not offended, and neither is my father.'

'You've…you're on better terms with him again?'

'I can't think why I waited so long. Venetia's death provided me with an excuse… No, excuse isn't the right word. Gave me the impetus. But I shouldn't have needed one.'

'I think relationships with one's parents are often difficult. My own father ignores my existence most of the time.'

'That's not altogether surprising, is it?'

'I beg your pardon?'

'Well, surely you've lived with Aunt Laura for most of your life? You don't see him often.'

'What? Oh, no! No, I don't. Er…perhaps I should see what is happening to Aunt Laura?'

'I expect you'd like to see your room, too. I hope you like the sound of running water, Rosabelle. I expect they've given you the Blue Bedchamber, and that overlooks the river.'

The subject of Annabelle's father was forgotten, much to her relief. Though she did not claim, even to herself, that she had been honest with Giles, she had always tried to avoid telling him an outright lie. Sooner or later she was bound to be faced with the problem, but the longer that moment could be postponed the happier she would be. Perhaps at Buxton, when they were settled for some weeks, she could find a way of ending the imposture and telling him the full truth at last. But not yet. Not here at Avenell.

The day after their arrival Giles rode over to Buxton to take a look at the rooms which had been reserved for them and to have a talk with Gregson, who was waiting there until they came. He came back just in time for dinner. Mrs Dunnock, excited by the opportunity to show her mettle to these London visitors, had produced an excellent meal, and, to accompany it, Howells had brought up some very good wines from the cellar.

But after the table had been cleared for dessert, and the company was sitting replete and relaxed, Giles informed them that Buxton was suffering from an outbreak of summer influenza.

Lord Stanton said instantly, 'You must stay here till the worst of the epidemic is over, Laura.'

'We couldn't so impose on you!'

'Don't be foolish—I'd enjoy your company. And I can't allow you to expose yourself and that lovely young creature to infection! No, I insist. Another two weeks— the worst of it will have passed by then.'

Lady Ordway looked helplessly at Annabelle.

'I think it's extremely kind of Lord Stanton to invite us to stay longer, Aunt Laura. He's right. It would be foolish to risk catching such a very unpleasant disease, when you have come all this way for your health! The waters of Buxton will keep. And you couldn't ask for a more beautiful place to stay.'

'You like Avenell, d'ye?' asked Lord Stanton, enormously pleased with these words.

Annabelle, already after one day at her ease with him, smiled. 'I have no great experience of the world, sir. Till now I have only known Berkshire—and London, of course—but I can safely say that I have never seen a place which suits me more. Berkshire is beautiful, but it has nothing to compare with the splendour of Derbyshire. A gentle domestic cat compared with a mountain lion.'

'D'ye hear that, Giles? You seem to prefer Europe. Laura, I know, is more at home in London. But this young lady has more taste than the lot of you put together!' He shot a sly glance at them both. 'Except that she seems to have a liking for you!'

Annabelle gasped, but Giles was already speaking. Smiling lazily, he said, 'Father, I hate to disillusion you, but the young lady in question has been in Derbyshire for not much more than three days, and the road from Matlock to Avenell has so far been her sole experience

of the county. I think we should pay tribute to her charming manners and desire to please, rather than her judgement.'

Annabelle responded with energy, 'I was perfectly sincere in my praise! But in spite of my natural desire to
please Lord Stanton, I cannot allow his partiality for his
son to blind him.' She turned to her host. 'Though I am
grateful to Colonel Stanton for his help and support in
the last months, I must confess that I have not found it
at all easy to like him. His life in the Army has encouraged an unfortunate tendency to order people about,
which I find far from pleasing!'

'Rosa!' Lady Ordway was scandalised, but Annabelle
stood her ground.

'I hope you will forgive my plain speaking, sir.'

'Of course I do! And I know exactly what you mean.
A touch arrogant, is he?'

'High-handed, certainly.'

Lord Stanton was enjoying this exchange. 'But you're
obviously a girl of spirit. You don't let yourself be over-
borne, I hope?'

'I try not to. But it can be very difficult for a mere
female—'

'A mere female?' asked Giles. 'You underrate yourself, Rosabelle.'

Lady Ordway intervened. 'Lord Stanton, I don't know
what you will be thinking of my goddaughter. She is not
usually so forgetful of her manners. Giles has been very
kind to us both. He is a dear boy.'

Having made her position clear to anyone who cared
to notice, Annabelle was now prepared to enjoy herself.
'A "dear boy" was not how you thought of him when
he changed our minds for us at a moment's notice and
hauled us off to Buxton, Aunt Laura. Or am I wrong?'

'No…not exactly. Though he has since made up for it a little—he has at least seen to it that our boxes were diverted here to Avenell, though the rest of the things went on to Bath in the fourgon. I don't think I have yet thanked you for that, Giles,' she said, turning to him with a smile.

'Thanked him! When the confusion was all his doing! Really, Aunt Laura!'

Lord Stanton frowned. 'You must have had good reason for all this, Giles? I don't believe you're as arbitrary as this tale would suggest.'

Annabelle now regretted where her careless words had led her. Giles might not wish to tell his father the whole of what lay behind the change of plan. He would certainly not want to frighten Aunt Laura with it.

'I…I will allow that it was reasonable, sir. He had some… sad news which he wished to convey to you personally, I believe?'

'Ah, yes. Venetia. Quite true. Hmm. We will grant that he is a good son, Mrs Ordway.'

'Since we are all speaking frankly, I will contest that,' Giles said. 'But I intend to be a better one in the future, sir.'

'Very good, very good. Now, what plans do you have for entertaining the ladies, Giles?'

'You see me demoralised, sir. I hardly dare suggest a thing for fear of being called high-handed or arrogant,' Giles said with a perfectly straight face.

'How delightful to hear it!' said Annabelle sweetly. 'Well then, Giles, in that case, I shall take shameful advantage of this rare state of yours and, if Aunt Laura agrees, I shall ask you to take us to see more of your wonderful countryside. I shall then be able to converse

with enough authority on Derbyshire and its attractions
to satisfy even you.'

'I should be very pleased to show you anything you
would like to see. Aunt Laura?'

'Yes. That would be very agreeable.'

'We shall all go,' said Lord Stanton. 'And I know
exactly the place to make for. There's an excellent inn
at Bradshaw—you remember it, Giles? The landlady
there worked in our kitchens when she was a girl, and
she's an excellent cook. We'll have a day's tour of the
countryside, and stop for something to eat at the King's
Head. How would you like that?'

It was settled that they should go on a tour of the
district the day after next. Lady Ordway felt she would
like time to settle in at Avenell before venturing on any
expeditions.

The company broke up. Annabelle and Lady Ordway
were led through a warren of rooms by one of the maids,
who was to take Lily's place during Annabelle's stay at
Avenell. She had a strong Derbyshire accent, but turned
out to be deft and helpful. After she had gone Annabelle
stood at the window in her wrapper, listening to the
sound of the river, and looking out over the hills to the
moorland beyond. She took a deep breath. Whatever
Giles may say, she felt an affinity with this land, such
as she had never before experienced. She was enchanted
by the serene beauties of its valleys, or dales as they
were called, but there was more to it than that.
Something about the restless energy of its rivers and
streams, the uncompromising strength of its rocks challenged her, appealed to the rebel in her. She was eager
to know more of it.

There was a tap at the door. She went over and opened it.

'Giles! Is something wrong?'

'No, no! I just thought you might prefer to have this tonight. When I was in Buxton today I called at the Receiving Office and collected several letters which were waiting there. I've only just managed to look through them. This one is for you. I believe it's from your sister. Goodnight, Rosabelle.'

'I'm very obliged, Giles. It was kind of you to bring it.'

'So I'm not as bad as you painted me tonight?'

A smile broke over Annabelle's face and lit her eyes with mischief. 'Not always, Giles. I even manage to like you sometimes. Goodnight.' She shut the door.

The candles burned low as Annabelle sat at the table reading her sister's letter. It made distressful reading. Rosabelle was perplexed and unhappy. Her relationship with Philip Winbolt had developed even more quickly than Lady Ordway had hoped, and, though Mr Winbolt had not exactly declared himself, he had made it clear that he was strongly attracted to her. And she knew herself to be in love, truly, deeply in love, for the first time in her life. But the gentleman was under the impression that she was Annabelle, of course. Though she had found it very hard, Rosabelle had been forced to put a stop to his overtures before they went too far.

At this point Annabelle lifted her eyes from the letter and slowly shook her head in despair. How could they have imagined, the two of them, that a simple exchange of places—just to give Rosabelle extra time for recovery—would lead to such heartache, not just for one, but for both! They had been foolishly irresponsible, and now they were paying the price. She took up the letter again...

The situation between Rosabelle and Mr Winbolt had come to a head on the very day that Annabelle's letter had arrived, telling her of the plan to go to Bath. Ashamed and unhappy, Rosabelle had seen the letter as a welcome release. She would go to Bath with her god-mother, and hope that she would in time manage to forget Philip Winbolt. But now...! The decision to go to Buxton had changed everything. It would be impossible to keep the situation in limbo for seven or even eight weeks! She would simply not be able to sustain it!

Annabelle's heart gave a leap. If Rosabelle wanted her permission to reveal everything, she would give it without a second's hesitation. She wanted nothing more than to confess her real identity to Giles, while there was still time to repair the inevitable damage and perhaps to go on to a better understanding with him... She read on eagerly.

But to her intense disappointment this was not what Rosabelle wanted. On the contrary. She had consulted their father, and his advice had been to continue to see the Winbolts as before, without yet revealing her true identity. He had suggested that she should give Philip Winbolt time to get to know her so well that, when she eventually confessed her deception, he would understand and forgive her. And this was what she had decided to do. But if Mr Winbolt was to believe in her basic hon-esty, then it was obviously vital that the changeover should remain a secret until Rosabelle herself told him the truth. It would be disastrous if he heard it from any other source. The letter ended with a disguised, but none-theless passionate, plea to her sister to do nothing which might jeopardise this plan.

Annabelle slowly folded the letter and put it away. In other words, she had to remain Rosabelle Ordway until her sister's situation had been cleared up. She must! Rosabelle's happiness was at stake. In the last few weeks she had learned so much more about the life Rosabelle had led with Stephen Ordway, how unhappy she had been. How could she possibly refuse to help her now? From her knowledge of Philip Winbolt he was sure to forgive gentle, vulnerable Rosabelle, once he knew her. She sighed. Clarification of her own situation with Giles would just have to wait... And, to look on the bright side, perhaps Giles, too, would understand and forgive Annabelle, once he knew her properly...

# Chapter Twelve

The day of the expedition dawned bright and sunny. Lord Stanton's own barouche was harnessed up, and laden with the impedimenta which its owner thought necessary for the comfort and convenience of his guests. Lady Ordway was to travel in the barouche with Lord Stanton, but there had been a certain amount of discussion as to how Annabelle would go.

'Mrs Ordway will ride, of course,' said Lord Stanton decidedly. 'It's the only way to see the countryside to advantage.'

'It's quite a long round trip, Father,' said Giles. 'And Rosabelle is not accustomed to country riding. She is a town girl at heart.'

'Oh, no, I should love to ride!' Annabelle exclaimed. 'How fortunate that I have brought my riding dress with me!'

'It's not a canter in the Park, Rosabelle! It's hard

country, and you would spend a good part of the day in the saddle.' Giles was quite firm. 'I really don't think—'

'If you do not wish me to accompany you, then there is no more to be said, Giles.' Annabelle looked at him with reproachful blue eyes. 'But after leading us all to believe that you were prepared to do anything we asked, I am disappointed…'

He looked as if he was about to deny her, but then he smiled and shrugged his shoulders. 'If you are determined to suffer, how can I refuse? I should be delighted to escort you.' He added kindly, 'You could always ride home in the carriage, if it proves too much for you.'

Annabelle thanked him meekly, secretly swearing to herself she would ride all the way there and all the way back, if it killed her! She caught Giles's gaze and lifted her chin defiantly. From the grin on his face he had guessed what she had been thinking.

It was settled that Lord Stanton's carriage would take the road to the village of Bradshaw, while Giles, Annabelle and a groom would ride over the moors. The two parties would meet in the King's Head, where Lord Stanton had already ordered a meal for them.

'You could show Mrs Ordway Blackhole cavern on the way, Giles. But you must promise not to hide from her!'

Giles laughed, and his father explained that he had taken Giles as a child to the cavern some miles before Bradshaw, and the boy had completely disappeared.

'Disappeared?' exclaimed Lady Ordway. 'But did you not keep a strict eye on him?'

'He wasn't out of my sight for more than thirty seconds, Laura! But don't worry—the little devil wasn't in any danger. He had slipped behind a crack in the rock and was hiding from us. He was completely invisible.

He came out a few minutes later roaring with laughter. The only damage he suffered was the thrashing I gave him for the fright he had given us.'

'One of the few times—in my childhood—that I remember your being really angry with me, sir,' said Giles ruefully. 'We were usually good friends.'

'I was furious that you had frightened your mother so. You were the apple of her eye.' Lord Stanton paused, lost in thought. Then he sighed. 'Yes…you're right, Giles. Those were happy times… And so is today. So, Mrs Ordway, don't stand any nonsense from this villain.'

'I won't, Lord Stanton. I'll get him to show me the crack first, and then I shall know where to look if he disappears. Though I might just leave him there! He's not the apple of *my* eye!'

'I think that is most unhandsome of you, Rosabelle. After I have given in to you on all points, too.'

The party set off in laughter and mutual good humour.

Annabelle and Giles reached Blackhole cavern after one of the most enjoyable rides she had ever known. They managed to keep up a fair pace, except when Annabelle stopped to exclaim over the view, or paused for a breath of the clean, invigorating moorland air.

'It's like nothing I've ever seen or imagined, Giles! Those weird shapes on the hills in the distance. What are they?'

'They're rocks eroded by the wind.'

'Sculpted by the wind, rather. Like strange, contorted monuments erected by a race of giants. And the sweep of the moors all round—beautiful! I could stay here forever!'

'I doubt that. You're seeing the moors today in sunshine—at their kindliest. They can be cruel, and very dangerous. I'd rather contend with a battalion of crack French troops than these moors in bad weather. But, as you say, on a day like today they are...magnificent.' He looked round with an expression of supreme contentment. To Annabelle he looked completely one with this powerful, beautiful landscape, and a sudden feeling of desire ran through her veins so strongly, that she had to restrain herself from touching him. She was shocked and confused by its force, and turned her face away, pretending to look at the hills in the other direction.

'Rosabelle, if we are to see the cavern before meeting the others, we must move more quickly.'

'What? Oh, yes! Lead on!'

If Giles found her more silent on the rest of the ride, he made no comment.

They reached the cavern in good time, in spite of Giles's warnings, and, leaving their horses in the care of the groom, they walked up a steep path to its mouth. Here they paid their fee, and followed the guide—an elderly, craggy man who talked in a dialect which sounded very strange to Annabelle's ears—into the hillside.

In truth, Blackhole cavern was an awesome place. Flares had been placed at each bend, and anywhere where the going was insecure, and the smoke from them curled upwards towards an invisible roof, veiled in a mysterious swathe of darkness. Their guide went on ahead, his flambeau gleaming on the wet surfaces of the cavern, the uneven flickering from its flames reflecting a thousand twinkling stars in the rocks around. At one point Giles took Annabelle's hand to help her down a slippery descent, and afterwards kept it in his. Once again she was astonished at her unruly body's response to his touch. She wanted to take the hand to her cheek, feel its warmth against her mouth… Shocked, she almost snatched her hand away, but controlled the impulse. Giles might well wonder what was wrong, and, on a more ordinary human level, she was grateful for the warmth of the contact. The cavern was impressively awesome, and she felt threatened by its dank atmosphere, stifled, even, by the pall of darkness pressing in on them from every direction…

Then they turned a corner and Annabelle stopped short, confronted by a fantastic sight. Numerous flares had been installed here, and their light was caught by a hundred…two hundred…more than she could count… luminous white shapes, chandeliers, long, cathedral-like structures, hanging down in graceful clusters.

'Giles!' breathed Annabelle. 'What *are* they?'

'Stalactites, mistress.' The guide had evidently mastered the word for the benefit of visitors and was proud of it.

'Stal-stalactites? Made by magic?'

'Nothing so sensational. Constant dropping of water over limestone, Rosabelle.'

'It's an amazing sight,' she breathed. 'Icicles of stone. What a strange, wonderful country this is, Giles! The monuments on the hillside, and now these… You have no need of art galleries—Nature does it all for you.' She gazed at the stalactites for a long while. There were hundreds of them, in all sizes, disappearing into the darkness at the back of the chamber. She shivered.

'You're cold!'

'I suppose I am. But it's not just that. I…I think I prefer to be above ground, Giles.'

'Then we shall go back. Come!' He shouted to the guide, and the little party set off back to the open air.

Not far from the entrance, where the daylight made things more visible, Giles said softly, 'Wait a moment. Look!'

He went over to the wall of the cavern and put his hand behind a fold in the rock. Annabelle followed. There was a small niche where Giles had put his hand, invisible to the casual observer.

'So that's where you hid?'

He nodded. 'I doubt I could get in now, though!' he added with a smile.

'For Heaven's sake, don't try, Giles! You would surely get stuck, even if you succeeded.'

The guide had missed them. He came back, apologising for having wandered on without them.

'I was just checkin' the gate. It's kept open in summer, but I like to check it now and then, just to see it's in workin' order. We 'ave to be careful, like! Look!' He took them beyond the narrow throat of the cavern just before the exit and showed them a rod set into the wall. He unhooked it and a metal gate, rather like a portcullis, descended from above, closing the cavern behind them. 'It's gradely, isn't it? The Duke 'ad that put there. We shut it in winter—we doan't want gypsies or the like winterin' 'ere.'

They showed suitable admiration for the Duke's arrangements, then Giles paid their fee, adding a small douceur. With relief, Annabelle breathed in the sunshine and sweet, fresh air.

'I'm sorry, Rosabelle. I wouldn't have taken you down there if I had known it would have such an effect.'

'No, no! I'm very glad you did! An extraordinary sight!' She took another deep breath, then smiled apologetically. 'You'll have to forgive me, Giles. I am a poor creature, and ashamed of myself. But thank you for taking me. I would not have missed it for the world.'

They walked down to the horses. Once again Giles seemed to find it necessary to support her with a hand under her elbow as they trod over the rougher places on the path. Annabelle was grateful. She had not had such a long ride since leaving Temperley, and the unaccustomed exercise, followed by the experiences in the cavern, had used up her reserves. Time enough later to keep a distance between them. For the moment, she enjoyed the feeling of Giles's protective hand under her arm.

Lord Stanton and Lady Ordway were waiting for them at the inn. 'There you are!' cried Lord Stanton. 'Our good landlady was only waiting till you came to serve our dinner—there's spatchcocked eel, cold fowl, mutton chops, pigeon, gooseberry pie, cheese cake, tarts, custards—'

'Stop, stop!' Annabelle protested, as the buxom landlady showed them into the parlour which had been set aside for them. She surveyed the feast laid out for them. 'I thought I was hungry, but I shall never do justice to such a splendid repast!'

'I shall. Mrs Gantry, how do you go on? I'll swear you're handsomer than ever!'

'Get away with you, master Giles! Pay your compliments to them as deserves them! And who is this young lady, might I ask?' She regarded Annabelle with a benevolent eye, clearly hoping that she was Master Giles's young lady.

'Hmm,' said Lord Stanton. 'You're off the mark, Bessie. This is Mrs Ordway, Lady Ordway's daughter-in-law.' Mrs Gantry was disappointed, but curtsied and assured Mrs Ordway with undiminished good humour that she was very welcome.

After the meal Lady Ordway announced her intention of taking a short rest. The landlady had put a bedchamber at her disposal, and she intended to spend an hour or so on the bed before they set off for Avenell again. Lord Stanton approved of the idea, and said that he would stay in the tap room and exchange a few words with Tom Gantry. Giles looked at Annabelle.

'Would you like to rest, Rosabelle?'

'No, thank you. But I am perfectly capable of keeping myself amused if you wish to be with your father.'

'Well, Giles?' asked Lord Stanton. 'Do you wish to listen to Tom and me chatting over old times, talking of people you never knew? Or…do you think you should look after your guest?'

Giles gave his father a level look. 'I think you'd be easier without me, sir. Tom is not a fan of the reforms I've introduced at High Kimber. I'm sure you'd be more comfortable making gloomy forecasts about the probable outcome, without my presence to bring reason into the argument.'

'Go along with you, Giles. Enjoy a pretty girl's company, and forget us fogies. We don't like change, that's our trouble. Off with you!'

'Would you like a walk, Rosabelle? The path along the stream is comparatively shady.'

'Yes, I should. But can we not walk up to the moor?'

'Of course. I am at your disposal, as you said. But…without daring to dictate to you in the slightest…' He said this gravely, but with a twinkle in his eye that made Annabelle laugh. 'May I point out that there is little or no shade up there, and the sun is still high? I know your intrepid spirit too well to suppose you will drive back in the barouche, and this means that you have a long, energetic ride back. You might prefer to conserve your strength for that. The stream here would be a more restful walk—it isn't one of your placid Berkshire meanderers, but I think you'd like it. But…I merely place the facts before you. You must make up your own mind, of course.'

'Giles, you worry me. I hardly recognise you in this guise!' Annabelle laughed up at him. 'But I would not wish you to think me deaf to reasonable persuasion. I'd like to see your stream.'

They walked in companionable silence through the garden at the back of the inn, past dogs and chickens somnolent in the afternoon sun. A wicket gate opened on to the footpath which led down to the stream. Giles was right. There was shade here, and a cool, refreshing breeze.

'Giles, where or what is High Kimber?'

'It's a small estate a few miles across the moor from here. Tom Gantry was a gamekeeper and general factotum there when he was younger.'

'Stanton land?'

'Yes,' he said curtly. Then, more amiably, 'I'm sorry. Yes, it belongs to the Stanton estates. It was out of our hands for some years, but I managed to get it back. It's not an important part, though. The land there is not much use—some sheep, a few cattle. Before he…got rid of it, my father used it chiefly as a…a retreat, I suppose. There's some fishing, and shooting on the moors. The house is comfortable, but quite small.'

'So what are you doing that meets with such disapproval?'

'Trying different breeds of sheep. Getting rid of the

cattle. Don't worry, my father and Tom will enjoy their chat, but they know things were not doing well at High Kimber. It's so remote that no one bothered with it until we took it over again. But the country round about is glorious.'

'I should like to see it.'

Giles's expression had been rather forbidding, but now it softened. 'Is there any corner of Derbyshire you would *not* like to see?' he asked with a smile.

'I suppose not. I love it all so far. It's so different from Berkshire.'

'And even more different from London.'

'What? Oh, yes!' The mention of London had brought a feeling of constraint into the conversation, and there was a pause. Then she went on, 'It seems so remote now—London Society, the balls, the receptions, and all the rest. Unreal.'

'And you now feel you'd like to reform. To live a more useful life?' There was more than a touch of scepticism in his voice. After a morning of such mutual enjoyment and harmony this took Annabelle by surprise, and she was hurt.

'I'm not certain that you're in a position to judge what my life has been, Giles,' she said steadily. 'I assure you it has been useful at times. And though I am far from claiming that I am perfect, I see no need for any drastic reform.' She moved away from him and stood on the edge of the bank, looking down into the water. 'Are there trout in this stream?'

'Rosabelle, if only—'

'You could believe me? Trust me?' She looked up at him, meeting his eyes frankly and fearlessly. 'Why don't you try, Giles? What have you to lose? You were wrong about Stephen. Perhaps you've been wrong about me, too.'

'How can I be? How can you justify your denial that you knew Falkirk?'

'Oh, no! That's not what I meant. I'm suggesting you have *faith*, Giles. Not that you should have your doubts explained away. What value would there be in an explanation, however convincing it might be? Unless you have confidence in me as a person, you could never be *sure* it was the truth.'

'You ask a lot, Rosabelle.'

'I don't deny that.' Annabelle held her breath, as they walked on in silence. Was it possible that she could persuade Giles to listen to her?

'I don't know what to think about you,' he said almost angrily. 'I've never before known anyone who has confused me more. When it comes down to it, things like "trust" and "faith" are matters for instinct, not reason. But with you my instinct is so very much at war with my reason.' He stopped abruptly, as if he regretted having said so much. Then he shrugged and went on, 'The evidence, which you seem to treat so lightly, is damnably convincing.'

'So it is.' Annabelle's tone was neutral, though her heart sank. She had failed.

'But when I see you with my father, with the Daventrys, with my friends...I can't understand how anyone so loving, so concerned for others, could be the woman I first thought you. A schemer, an unfaithful wife, Falkirk's mistress, a greedy opportunist...'

'Pray go no further, Giles! You are making my head swell with your compliments!' Annabelle said bitterly.

'I tell you, I now find it impossible to believe you have been such a woman! My instinct tells me that much, if nothing else. I believe you are telling me the truth when you say that you were never unfaithful to Stephen.'

'Giles! I…'

'But there is obviously a great deal more which you are hiding from me. And that is where my instinct advises me not to trust you.'

Annabelle felt a curious mixture of delight and disappointment at Giles's words. That he no longer believed Rosabelle to have been unfaithful was a huge step forward, but he was perfectly right not to trust her in everything. And when he did discover the truth, it was by no means certain that he would find it possible to forgive her. She was very serious as she said, 'Giles, I swear you will know the truth in time, and my hope is that you will understand. But I cannot tell you the whole yet.'

He looked disappointed. 'So trust is to be one way only?'

'My secrets involve someone else. Otherwise I would tell you instantly.'

He nodded. 'You sound as if you sincerely mean it. In that case I will try to manage without. It won't be easy.'

'I imagine not. I…I am sincere in my feelings for you, Giles.'

'Are you?' he asked with a return of his glinting, teasing smile. 'What a pity! You regard me as a tyrant, an unfeeling despot, rude, overbearing, arrogant… Is that enough?'

'You forgot "high-handed".'

'Ah, yes.' He took her hand. 'Do you really think so badly of me, Rosabelle?'

'Not…not always.' As usual, his touch was confusing her, making it difficult for her to think, even to breathe!

He was lifting her chin with one finger, forcing her to look at him.

'Tell me one thing,' he said. 'When this is all over, when Falkirk has been dealt with and Stephen's unhappy story is buried with him, when the truth is at last out between us...' He paused.

'Yes?' Her voice was hardly more than a whisper.

'Could you like me better?'

'I...I think so.'

'Good!' He bent and kissed her, very gently. 'I'll wait till then. Meanwhile...we shall be friends. Real friends, not just enemies in a truce. What do you say?'

With an effort Annabelle pulled herself out of the dream his words had called up. 'I'd like that. And I swear you won't be sorry, Giles.'

The excursion to Bradshaw was the first of several equally delightful days spent in exploring the countryside. Lady Ordway accompanied them to Chatsworth, Haddon Hall, and the town of Bakewell, but she was not interested in spending time on the moors and in the dales. Giles and Annabelle were free to ride almost anywhere they chose, accompanied only by a groom. The original two weeks passed in a flash. Lord Stanton declared that their sojourn at Avenell was doing them far more good than any waters Buxton could provide, and pressed them to stay longer. Avenell was proving a pleasanter place than Lady Ordway had remembered, and though she demurred, she was easily overruled.

'Avenell is at its best in this weather, Aunt Laura. Why don't you enjoy it?' said Giles. 'I plan to go to London for a while at the end of August, and I could escort you to Buxton just before I leave.'

'London?' said Annabelle sharply.

'There are people I have to see, Rosabelle. But I won't be away for longer than I can help. And you'll have Gregson and the other two to look after you.'

So it was decided. Giles and Annabelle were free again to roam the moors in perfect weather and perfect harmony. They spent one whole day at High Kimber, and Annabelle was entranced by it. The house was old— as old as Temperley—but built to withstand the harsh climate, the icy winds, the hail and rain which, she was told, winter brought to the moors.

'And not only winter. You've been fortunate, Rosabelle. The weather has been so fine that you haven't any notion of what the moors can be like in a storm— even in summer. In that respect it's like Spain. A man can die of exposure if he's caught out on the moor for long.'

Giles talked to Annabelle freely of his experiences in Spain and elsewhere with the Army. She became surprisingly well acquainted with the foibles and virtues of the great of Europe—including even the great Duke himself. On one occasion she accused Giles of not liking him. It was towards the end of the fortnight and they had ridden up to the moors once again.

'Like him? I've never considered whether I like him or not. He's short-tempered, pig-headed, unreasonable, high-handed—all of the things you've called me—and more. But I would trust him more than any other man alive to pull us out of a mess—as he did at Waterloo. He's the greatest man I shall ever meet.'

'I should love to meet him. Though I am very much beneath his notice, I know.'

Giles gave a crack of laughter. 'He would make straight for you, Rosabelle! The Beau has a connoisseur's eye for the ladies. A beauty like you would be a prime target.'

'The Beau? Is that what you call him?'

'Not in his hearing.'

'I find it hard to believe he would even look at me! In competition with all the great ladies of Europe? You exaggerate, Giles!'

He grew serious. 'I think you're the loveliest thing I've ever seen. Even when you were ill and unhappy last Christmas I thought you had possibilities. But now...' He looked up at her. She was standing on a rock, the better to view the scenery. The wind was teasing her hair and blowing her riding habit against her body, outlining long, slender thighs and a tiny waist. The effort of climbing the rocks up to her vantage point had given colour to her cheeks, and an extra sparkle to her dark blue eyes.

'Rosa!' He held up his arms, and she laughed and bent down to be lifted off her rock and into his arms. For a moment they looked at one another.

'The groom,' she murmured.

'He can't see us. He's down behind the hill with the horses.' Giles's voice was uneven. 'Rosa, I promised myself I wouldn't kiss you again before everything was clear between us.'

'But I didn't promise not to kiss you, Giles,' Annabelle said softly. She put her arms round his neck and pulled his head down to hers...

After a minute or two Giles lifted his head enough to murmur, 'Rosabelle, my lovely rose...'

Annabelle felt a cold shiver run down her spine. Giles, misinterpreting her reaction, held her more closely, and started kissing her again. She responded to his caresses eagerly, in a feverish effort to drown her fears. But some of the magic had gone, and after another minute Giles said firmly, 'This will not do. This is not the way.' He put her gently, reluctantly, from him. 'After I come back from London—'

'Giles, are you going to London to find Falkirk?'

'To see what has been happening, yes.'

'Oh, Giles, take care! I couldn't bear it if... Take care!'

'Don't worry Rosabelle. I shall come back within ten days to Buxton, I promise. And if you are not already submerged in invitations to the balls and concerts there, I shall take delight in escorting you. But we won't have the freedom we have enjoyed here.'

'Nor could we anywhere else! Our London friends would be shocked at how much time we have spent alone together. I'm not sure that even Aunt Laura is aware of how much. It would be considered most improper by the *ton*.'

'Most reprehensible, I agree. Have you felt threatened by it?'

'Not in the slightest.' She looked at him shyly. 'I have enjoyed getting to know your country...and you, Giles.'

'Thank you. But it isn't over yet, Rosa. There are years more to come—once we have rid ourselves of the...burdens of the past.'

Annabelle was as anxious as Giles to bring an end to the deceits and burdens of the past, but the weeks at Avenell had been so idyllic that she left with regret. Who knew whether she would ever see Avenell again? One person was convinced she would. Lord Stanton had watched the growing friendship between his son and his younger guest with complete approval.

'I won't bid you too hearty a farewell, Mrs Ordway. You're welcome to come at any time. But I expect Giles

will see to that, and I would be happy to see him do so.
It's time he settled down.'

'But, Lord Stanton, there's nothing—'

He chuckled. 'Roses all over your cheeks! I've embarrassed you! But time will tell whether I'm right or
not. Meanwhile—I might even pay a visit to Buxton. I've
a fancy to see Laura Ordway's face when she is drinking
those waters!'

The carriage was loaded, the grooms sprang away
from the horses and they were off on the last stage of
their journey.

The healthful properties of the water at Buxton were
known to the Romans, but it had been a fairly obscure
place in the north of England until just forty-odd years
before. Then the fifth Duke of Devonshire, husband of
the exquisitely lovely Georgiana, had commissioned one
of his architects to design an ambitious group of buildings to house visitors to a modern watering place. This
was the Crescent, and, as the carriage carrying the party
from Avenell drew to a halt in front of their hotel, even
Lady Ordway paid tribute to the success of his designs.

The Assembly Room and other public rooms were to
be found in the Great Hotel, which stood at the eastern
end of the graceful curve of stone. At the western end
was another hotel, the St Ann's, which was almost as
large. And in the centre of the Crescent were five sets
of comfortable lodging houses. An arcade of shops under
a covered walkway linked the two hotels.

Giles had reserved a suite of rooms in the St Ann's
Hotel. 'I thought it would be quieter for you here, Aunt
Laura. St Ann's Well is close by, too.'

'The rooms are very handsome, Giles. Thank you. I

dare say it is not more than five minutes' walk to the Great Hotel.'

'Less than that,' said Giles.

'Or possibly much more—there are some delightful shops, I see, on the way,' Annabelle remarked with a smile at Lady Ordway.

Indeed, Buxton proved to be much more pleasant a place to stay than Lady Ordway had feared. The new buildings were commodious and comfortable, the shops in the Arcade could satisfy the most demanding tastes, and the company, though not quite as worldly and sophisticated as that to be found in London, Brighton or Bath, was sufficiently interesting to keep Lady Ordway happy. The day after they arrived Giles took them to the Great Hotel and introduced them to the Master of the Rooms. Under this worthy's benevolent eye they entered their names in the Subscription Book, and were introduced to a number of ladies and gentlemen, all of whom, as Lady Ordway later remarked, seemed to have a surprising elegance of mind, and dress.

'For you know, Giles, that I was very doubtful of what we should find here by way of company. I am very favourably impressed.'

Annabelle had been reading the Rules of the Ballroom. 'There are balls every Wednesday, Aunt Laura, and on Mondays and Fridays you can play cards—though I believe there's a card room, as well, isn't there, Giles?'

'Yes, there is. But I'm afraid that you'll have to ask the Master to introduce you to suitable partners for the next ball. I'm off to London as soon as I am sure you are comfortably settled.'

'Giles!'

'I'm sorry, Aunt Laura. I have urgent business there,

but it shouldn't take too long.' He looked at Annabelle. 'I'll be back as quickly as I can.' But then he stopped. It was impossible to say anything more. Agreeable as Buxton was, it was too busy a place for anything but the briefest of private conversations. The freedom they had enjoyed on the moors was a thing of the past.

It was ironic that when their place of retreat was eventually betrayed to Falkirk, it was done quite unconsciously. And by someone with every reason to wish them well.

# Chapter Thirteen

When Giles reached London he set about gathering information—though the city was very thin of society. Old Lord Banagher was holding on to life by a thread, and Falkirk must be expecting to hear that he had succeeded to the title at any moment. Gossip had it that the new Lord Banagher would waste no time in seeking a wife and settling down to enjoy his elevated position.

There was also news of Selder. One of Giles's old friends worked in the Navy Office and had been investigating Kingsley.

'I'm sorry, Gil. I know Kingsley was one of your cousin's closest friends, but he almost certainly killed himself because he knew he was about to be found out. He was giving information about shipping to a man called Selder—you've heard the name?'

'Yes, I have.' Giles hesitated, then said, 'I'm about to make an accusation which I cannot yet prove.'

'Dangerous work.'

'I'm sure it will go no further. Freddy, what would you say if I told you that Selder is another name for Julian Falkirk?'

'Falkirk!' But, after this first astonished exclamation, Commander Halton fell silent. Then he said, 'You know, Gil, it wouldn't surprise me at all. It would fit in with one or two other things we've heard. Yes, Falkirk might well be the man, though, like everything else in this damned case, neither you nor I can prove anything. If, as I understand, Falkirk is about to move up in the world, you'd need impeccable evidence. He's acquired some powerful friends.'

'What sort of evidence?'

'Unimpeachable witnesses willing to swear to the link between Falkirk and Selder. And something which linked either, or both, to criminal activity. Preferably written. Good enough for a court of law, anyway. Listen, I'd be delighted to hear from you if you learn anything else. My friends would be more than grateful if we could nail the fellow. Everything seems to have gone quiet at the moment, so there's no chance of catching anyone red-handed.'

A letter to Giles from Charlie Fortescue gave a possible explanation for this lack of activity.

Dear Gil,

I have a small item of news for you. Da Costa has been found, but I'm afraid he will not be the source of information we had hoped for. He appears to have had a fatal disagreement with some of his friends here in Bristol. His body was fished out of the harbour two nights ago. If I hear any more I'll let you know.

I hope your other enquiries are meeting with more success than this.

Yours, Charlie

Falkirk didn't leave anything to chance, thought Giles grimly. Venetia, Stephen and Da Costa—all eliminated. Possibly Kingsley, too. And Rosabelle? No, that was one death that Giles was not going to allow. Not while there was breath left in his body. He suddenly felt he could stay in the city no longer. He must get back to her, see that she was safe.

When Giles arrived in Buxton, the first person he encountered after a tediously slow journey was Gregson.

'Any sign of untoward interest in the ladies, Gregson?'

'None at all, sir. But they are generally admired. Very popular we are, sir.'

'Oh?'

'Her ladyship has made one or two friends among the gentry here—there's a sprinkling of older tabb— I mean older ladies, Colonel Stanton, sir. And Mrs Ordway is all the go with the younger ones. Out most days, she's been. I've had my work cut out to keep an eye on her.'

'I wouldn't have thought there'd be that many young men at Buxton.'

'Oh, it's not that many, Colonel! Just the one.'

Giles stopped. 'Indeed? Who's that?'

'Lord Monteith, sir. Very taken with Mrs Ordway, he is.'

'That young puppy!' The exclamation was out before

Giles could stop it. But well aware of the impropriety of discussing such matters with Gregson, he went on with a frown, 'I'm glad to hear she has been kept amused. Is Lady Ordway well?'

Gregson failed to notice the warning signals. 'I don't think she likes the waters much, sir. But she's pleased as Punch at Mrs Ordway's success. Hearing wedding bells, I imagine.'

'Wedding bells? What rubbish is this? What the devil are you thinking of, Gregson? Don't let me hear any more damned stupid gossip about your betters!'

'Sir!' Gregson drew himself upright and looked suitably rebuked. Still frowning, Giles strode into the hotel and went up to his room.

'So that's the way of it!' said Gregson to himself. 'Well, well!'

By the time Giles entered the Assembly Room dancing had already begun. He had no eyes for the stately Corinthian columns, the handsome marble fireplaces, the magnificent ceiling decorated in the style of Mr Adam, though the room was generally accepted as one of the Crescent's chief splendours. What he saw was Lord Monteith leading Mrs Ordway down the room, with an air of triumph, while the rest of the world, it seemed to him, looked on in approval. Giles joined his aunt at the side of the ballroom and grimly prepared to wait for the end of the set.

'Giles! We had quite given you up! How nice to see you!' said Lady Ordway. 'Rosabelle is dancing with Lord Monteith. Such a handsome couple.' She looked fondly at the two on the floor. 'I must tell you that I have great hopes. He has been most particular in his attentions.'

Giles's eyes followed hers, admiring Rosabelle's graceful movements. 'And what about the lady?'

'Rosabelle? Well, Giles, it would be an excellent match, would it not? And she seems quite taken with him. Look at her!'

Giles's first reaction was one of angry protest, but then he looked again at the couple, and started to grin. Rosabelle was the very picture of a polite young lady enjoying herself at a ball, exchanging snippets of conversation with her partner, and accepting his obvious admiration with becoming modesty. Though it was understandable that the company at Buxton should be deceived by her expression of smiling interest, it did not deceive him for one instant. The poor girl was bored beyond measure.

Much cheered, Giles looked and wondered at his aunt's blindness. How could anyone who knew Rosabelle fail to see the signs, the total absence of everything which made her special? Her enchanting, heart-warmingly spontaneous smile, the confiding tilt of her head when she was intrigued, the eager readiness to take up the conversation again when the movement of the dance had interrupted it...

He relaxed and enquired of his aunt how she was enjoying life in the watering place, complimenting her on the obvious benefits of her regime.

'The waters must be doing me some good, Giles, for they are perfectly horrid to taste! But the climate here is excellent! Even on the hottest day there is always a breath of air—I suppose it is because Buxton lies so high.'

'I'm glad to hear it, Aunt Laura. Ah! The end of that interminable dance.'

Lord Monteith was leading Rosabelle off the floor. He

was still talking to her, and she still maintained her air of courteous interest. But when she saw Giles she stopped dead, and the enchanting smile he had remembered illuminated her lovely face.

'Giles!'

If Giles had suffered the slightest pang of jealousy on hearing of Lord Monteith's pursuit of Rosabelle, it evaporated without trace in the spontaneous warmth of that smile. She recovered herself immediately, however, and continued so calmly with civil enquiries about his journey that, had he not known her better, he might have thought he had imagined it. Certainly Lady Ordway and Lord Monteith had not noticed anything. The latter spoke as soon as there was a gap in the conversation. He asked with the air of a man who was sure of his reply.

'Mrs Ordway, may I have the pleasure of the supper dance?'

'I'm afraid not, Monteith. Mrs Ordway should pay some attention to the head of the family, now that I have returned. Duty before pleasure, you know.'

Giles's words could not have been better chosen to appeal to this dutiful young man. Lord Monteith nodded, bowed, and excused himself, promising to approach Mrs Ordway later.

'Really, Giles! How dare you dispose of my beau in that cavalier way! As if I owed you any duty!'

'No, but I recognise mine to you! And rescuing you from that pompous young ass is the least I could do. Do you care to dance?'

'You don't deserve that I should!'

'Good! I should much prefer to talk. Shall we sit down? I could fetch you both something to drink. What would you like, Aunt Laura?'

Lady Ordway was staring at Giles rather strangely, as

if a new and startling idea had just occurred to her. 'I...I...think I shall have a word with Lady Skelmersholme, Giles. She is on her own at the moment. I am delighted to see you back. But I can talk to you tomorrow, after all. Excuse me.'

She moved away, nodding to this acquaintance and that as she went.

'Would you like to sit down, Rosabelle? Or shall we take a turn outside?'

'Please, I should love to walk! It's very hot in the room.'

'I think the weather must be changing. There's a sultry feel to the air.'

Giles and Annabelle went down the wide staircase and out across the gravelled forecourt to the Slopes beyond. They were not alone. The heat of the rooms had tempted others to take the air, and the Slopes were dotted with ladies in their pale ball gowns and gentlemen in evening dress. They strolled up the grassy incline. Annabelle was happy to remain silent, enjoying the faint breeze and the sounds of music which drifted across from the open windows of the Assembly Room.

'Aunt Laura looks well,' said Giles.

'She is enjoying herself.'

'And you? Have you been enjoying yourself, Rosabelle?'

'Of course.'

'If I may say so, you looked rather bored when I first saw you.'

'You may not say anything of the kind! I was not in the slightest bored! This is mere prejudice against Lord Monteith, who is a most estimable gentleman.'

'Oh, Rosabelle! You may deceive the rest, but you cannot deceive me.'

Her eyes flew to his, then dropped. 'I…Lord Monteith has been very kind while you have been away.'

'So I hear. I'm afraid you have been raising false hopes in the young man's breast.'

'What makes you think they are false?'

'You won't marry Monteith.' Once again her eyes flew up to meet his. What she saw there caused the delicate colour to rise in her cheeks. 'Not while I am alive,' he added, casually.

'Really, Giles! You always think you have the ordering of everything! Allow me to tell you that Lord Monteith is the epitome of every girl's dream—rich, eligible, personable…'

'But not for you. I know you too well.'

'Wha…what do you mean?'

'Tell me, if you can, that I'm wrong.'

'I shan't choose to tell you anything. But I shall soon begin to wish you had not come back if you are going to tease me. How was London?'

'Pretty empty. I saw some friends. Falkirk had not as yet come back from Bath.' He eyed her carefully. 'Rosabelle, how many people have you written to since being here?'

'Only my sister. Why do you ask?'

'I was wondering how Monteith knew you were here.'

Her tone was cooler as she said, 'I am aware that your opinion of me is low. But I do not write to gentlemen I hardly know, Giles. Lord Monteith is here with his great-aunt. We met by chance.'

'Good. Let us hope there's no one in London he would be likely to tell. What about your sister?'

'My sister?' As usual, Annabelle grew wary when her sister was mentioned. 'What about her?'

'Will she tell anyone where you are?'

'It's most unlikely. She lives very quietly at Temperley. Unless she says something to Mr Winbolt.'

'Winbolt?'

'Yes, m— her neighbour in Berkshire.'

'It's not a common name. Is that Philip Winbolt? Of the Second Dragoons? With a grandfather in Arlington Street?'

'I don't know about his army career, but he has a grandfather in Arlington Street, yes. Do you know him?'

'I should say I do! A great fellow. Gentleman Jack, we used to call him.'

'Really? Why was that? Was he…was he rather too much of a gentleman, then?' asked Annabelle carefully.

'As polite and neat a fellow as you ever met. You wouldn't think he would willingly offend a soul. But give him a horse, put a sword in his hand and an enemy to fight—my God, what a transformation! Rides like a whirlwind and fights like a demon. There isn't anyone I'd rather have by my side in a fix. Well, well, well. Gentleman Jack in Berkshire, eh? Your sister knows him, you say?'

'He's…he's a neighbour.'

'What did you think of him? You met him when you were at Temperley, surely?'

'Er…the Winbolts were away for the whole of the time. My sister seems to approve of him.'

'Very popular with the ladies, was Philip. But discreet. He won't talk. And if he did meet Falkirk in London, he'd have the chap's measure in no time. I think we're safe there.'

* * *

Annabelle forgot to mention Philip's sister, Emily, who was also in Rosabelle's confidence. And she could not possibly have known that Philip would take his sister to London at the point when Falkirk was scouring the capital for information about Rosabelle Ordway's present whereabouts, nor that Emily would be introduced to the future Lord Banagher, and find him a charming man, who shared her interest in the theatre. And that, in the course of their conversation, she would mention, quite harmlessly, that her friend's sister, Mrs Ordway, was taking the waters at Buxton.

But the result was dramatic.

Giles had hardly been back a week when Gregson told him that a stranger from London, a tall, good-looking fellow with blond hair, had arrived in Buxton and was making enquiries about a Mrs Rosabelle Ordway. Gregson, a lad Giles had always said was born to be hanged, had feigned ignorance, but had most obligingly offered to find out where the lady was staying and promised to bring the information the next day to the gentleman's hotel, the White Hart. This seemed to suit the newcomer—he seemed strangely reluctant to be seen abroad himself, and didn't seem to object to the delay. He was waiting for a friend to arrive, he said.

Within an hour of receiving this information, Giles had completed his arrangements. A surprised Annabelle and an absolutely outraged Lady Ordway had been bundled out of the hotel, and urged into Giles's travelling coach. Servants and luggage were bundled off, too. Annabelle noticed that not only were Goss and Gregson in close attendance, but two grooms were riding alongside. Giles was leaving nothing to chance.

'But, Giles, it is too bad of you! I don't understand!

I don't understand at all! Where are you taking us? And why did you refuse to tell us before this?'

'To Avenell, Aunt Laura. To stay with my father again. And I didn't want anyone in the hotel to overhear.'

Annabelle looked at Giles with a slight frown. 'Falkirk?'

'Fraser is in Buxton. Somehow or other Falkirk has learned where we are.'

'Giles, before we go another mile I insist on knowing what is going on!' said Lady Ordway. She sounded most unusually angry. 'What do you mean by saying I shall be safe and comfortable? I was perfectly safe and comfortable at Buxton!'

Giles looked at a loss, but Annabelle nodded her head at him. 'It is better that you tell Aunt Laura, Giles. Being kept in the dark is far more nerve-racking than the truth, however unpalatable.'

'The hotel at Buxton was too public a place to be safe, Aunt Laura. Avenell was once a fortress, and it can be so again.'

'But why on earth should we need a fortress?'

Picking his words with care, Giles told his aunt of the serious threat Falkirk represented to Rosabelle's safety. 'Apart from two men who are his closest associates, Rosabelle is the one person left alive who can identify Falkirk with Selder, the man who, among other things, murdered Stephen. I have men looking for evidence to incriminate Falkirk, but until then Rosabelle must be kept safe.'

'But that's impossible! I think it is time I told—'

'Please don't bring Annabelle into this, Aunt Laura!' said Annabelle desperately. 'I know you feel she ought to be told, but we cannot at the moment consult her. I have every confidence in Giles. Leave Annabelle in peace at Temperley. You know she has other things on her mind.' She turned to Giles. 'I should have told you this when we were speaking of your friend, Mr Winbolt, Giles. My sister and Mr Winbolt are in a fair way to making a match of it.'

In spite of his worries Giles was intrigued. 'Gentleman Jack in love? And with your sister, Annabelle?'

'Exactly!' said Annabelle with a meaning look at Lady Ordway.

'When this is over, Rosabelle, I insist on meeting the lady! I'd like to see the girl who has caught Philip Winbolt at last.'

Annabelle smiled at him with the strange sadness Giles had noticed once before. 'You shall, Giles, you shall!' she said.

'Good God, what is all this?' was Lord Stanton's greeting as the two coaches with four outriders drew up outside the Great Hall. Giles had sent one of the grooms on ahead to warn his father, but his message had been brief. 'One two, three, four... Giles, what the devil is going on? Come in, come in, Laura, and you too, my dear Mrs Ordway! What a time to be arriving, you must be worn out. Come in!'

In the short time given him Howells had done wonders. The ladies' bedchambers had already been prepared, and a tray of refreshments was waiting on the table in the Little Parlour. Lady Ordway sank down on to a conveniently placed chair.

'Lionel, you must forgive us. I don't perfectly understand why we have come here in such haste, but I am sure it must be highly inconvenient.'

'You are talking nonsense, Laura! I am delighted to

see you back here, though I am even more in the dark than you are! Where is that boy of mine? Howells, go and find Master Giles.'

'I'm here, Father.' Giles came in with the air of a man who has accomplished as much as he can.

'Tell me what this is all about. Don't think I'm not pleased to see you all again—I'm delighted! It was damned dull after you'd gone to Buxton, and in fact you've saved me the effort of joining you all there in a day or two. But what's this army you've brought with you, Giles? It's worthy of a prince of the blood at least! Delusions of grandeur, my boy! You'd better send some of them to the inn—there aren't enough decent rooms over the stables here.'

'They are soldiers. Or at least ex-soldiers, well used to discomfort. And they can't go to the inn, because they're here to do a job.'

'What the devil is all this, Giles?'

'And it's really all so unnecessary. If only Giles knew…' began Lady Ordway.

'Aunt Laura, I think we ought to leave Giles to explain the situation to Lord Stanton, don't you? I expect you'd like to change after the journey. Please excuse us, Lord Stanton. You are very kind to make us so welcome.'

Annabelle swept Lady Ordway off to her room without allowing her to say any more. They found Wilson unpacking her mistress's bags, sniffing at the manner in which the clothes had been bundled up.

'I shall have to give several of your dresses a good press, my lady. Such a rush we were in!'

'Of course you couldn't pack properly, Wilson. We left in an indecent hurry, and I know who should bear the blame! Annabelle, you have twice interrupted me when I was about to tell Giles the truth, but it cannot go

on. I can't let him continue to take all these absurd precautions to protect you, when they are not at all necessary! You must tell him you are not Rosa! He will be
angry, I know, but not half so angry as he will be if you
leave it much longer.'

'I can't, Aunt Laura! And you must keep quiet, too!
Not for my sake, but for Rosa's. Philip Winbolt isn't
merely one of Giles's acquaintances—they are old com-
rades in arms, and great friends! If Giles discovers that
his friend is being deceived, what is he most likely to
do?'

After a moment Lady Ordway said slowly, 'He would
write and tell him so.'

'Exactly! Now read this letter. I didn't show it to you
before—it is too unhappy and I didn't want to distress
you.' Annabelle handed Lady Ordway Rosabelle's desperate plea to keep up the deception for a little longer.

'My poor Rosa!' said Lady Ordway, wiping her eye.
'Oh, Annabelle, what a fix we are in! Why did I ever let
you talk me into it?'

'I meant it for the best! But, Aunt Laura, I know Philip
Winbolt. If Rosa is given her chance, I am sure he will
forgive her. Rosa will have her happy end, you'll see. It
will just take a little time.'

'Are you sure?'

'I am quite certain. And you'll like Mr Winbolt. He
is perfect for her.'

'Well, then, I suppose…'

'And what is Colonel Stanton going to say?' asked
Wilson grimly.

'Colonel Stanton has nothing to say to anyone! Miss
Rosa and Mr Winbolt can settle their future without
him!' said Annabelle sharply.

'But what about your future, Anna!' wailed Lady

Ordway. 'I had begun to think… Oh, it is too bad!' She started to weep again.

'Don't cry, dearest Aunt Laura. I'm sure I could make Giles understand. Eventually. And if I don't…' Annabelle stopped.

Lady Ordway lifted her head and started to look more cheerful. 'There are other fish in the sea! That's quite true! Anna, that's very true! Lord Monteith was extremely attentive. And he is even more eligible than Giles. He'll be a Viscount one day.' This thought seemed to provide real consolation. She went on; 'I cannot like deceiving Lord Stanton while we are his guests, but I will say nothing more. It would be wonderful if Rosa could be really happy again. And, as you say, Giles is not the only possible husband for you.'

Annabelle was so shocked at her reaction to these words that she was silenced. She stared at Lady Ordway without really seeing her, all her energy concentrated on the effort not to burst out with an angry contradiction.

'Good. I'm glad,' she said at last. 'Excuse me, Aunt Laura. I…I think I'll go and tidy myself up. We left in such a hurry… Excuse me.'

She made her escape.

But once back in her own room Annabelle dismissed the maid who had been waiting for her, sat down at the dressing table and stared into the looking glass. Lady Ordway's words had removed a veil from something she had really known all along. Aunt Laura was wrong. Giles Stanton *was* the only possible husband for her! What she felt for him went far beyond friendship, or physical attraction, or any of the other excuses she had found for hiding the truth from herself. She had indisputably fallen irrevocably in love with the man. Marriage to anyone else was out of the question. She gave a deep sigh of despair. What a senseless piece of idiocy! How could she have been so stupid?

She stared at the reflection in the looking glass. She could hardly believe she was looking at herself. Sad and pale, a lost, vulnerable look about the eyes…surely this was Rosabelle! The lips twisted in a wry grin. If it were, there would be no problem! Oh, how could this have happened? She had been immune to love for so long, so complacent in her ignorance of its irrational powers— how absurdly ironic that she should eventually fall in love with the man who had been so ready to condemn her sister! She had sworn to make him pay for it, but it now looked as if she was to be the one who would pay.

Rosabelle Ordway was not the liar and cheat he had thought her, but Annabelle Kelland was! He could despise her with some justification—and certainly never love her back. She watched a tear roll down the cheek of the face in the mirror… But then she lifted her chin defiantly. She was not Rosabelle Ordway, she was Annabelle Kelland and that stood for something, too. Annabelle was not going to give in without a battle!

She was sure that Giles felt something for her—otherwise why go to all this trouble to protect her? What if she told Giles before the matter went any further, while she was still at Avenell? He could hardly throw her out, and with time she might persuade him…but there was Rosa to think of…

She would write to Rosabelle! Perhaps her sister's affairs had progressed to the point where the secret could come out… That was it! She would write to Rosabelle immediately.

But after the letter was written and sealed, and Lord

Stanton had franked it for her, Giles refused to let her dispatch it.

'Rosabelle, it would be madness to write from here!'

'It's to my sister, Giles! I must tell her where I am—she'll be worried! It must go!'

'I'm afraid I can't allow it. I don't know how Falkirk knew we were in Buxton, but I suspect your correspondence had something to do with it. No, the letter will have to wait till I have heard from London. It won't be long now. Trust me!'

A few days later she was sitting in the garden admiring the view when he came in search of her. She watched his lithe figure striding along the terrace against the background of Avenell's massive grey stone walls, and she once again felt the kinship between man and surroundings. This was undoubtedly Giles's heritage. There was an unconscious pride, arrogance almost, in his movements, and she could feel the presence of generations of Stantons walking along the walls with him. But the Stantons appeared to be marching into battle.

'What the devil do you mean by this?' Giles demanded as he reached her.

The sun was in Annabelle's eyes as she looked up. 'What is it?' she asked.

'A letter, Rosabelle! A letter you gave to Gregson to post in Bakewell!'

'That's my letter!' Annabelle jumped up and snatched it from him. 'How dare you take it!'

'You're lucky I didn't tear it up, you little vixen! What do you mean by going behind my back to one of my own men?'

'You said yesterday that Fraser must have gone back to London. There's surely no danger now. And since I

couldn't get word to my sister any other way, I had to
ask Gregson to take it. If you had been more reasonable—'

'Reasonable! God give me patience! Don't you realise
that Falkirk has other men working for him? Fraser is
bound to have left someone behind in case we turn up
again! And I'd be willing to wager a considerable
amount that his deputy has already conscripted half a
dozen men or more to find out where we've gone. It
won't be long before they do—Avenell is, after all, an
obvious place to look—but there's no sense in making
them a present of the information! You're a fool,
Rosabelle!'

Annabelle was by now as angry as Giles. 'I suppose
you pay Gregson to go running to you with reports on
everything I do!' she said icily.

'Have you paid the slightest attention to what I've
said? Of course Gregson reports to me. All my men are
under orders to tell me everything. And you needn't look
at me with that basilisk stare—perhaps you've forgotten
that it's all for your benefit.'

'For *my* benefit? That's a joke! You're enjoying yourself enormously, Giles! Back to war. Heroes, all of you!
Well, I'm not one of your men, and I'm not under your
command, and I shall do as I please!'

'Try it! You'll find you won't get very far, my girl.
And if you were one of my men you'd learn that it's
wiser not to cross me!'

'You're a bully, Giles! I always suspected it, and now
I know it for a fact.'

'Bully or not, I want no more of your childishly stupid
obstinacy. You can send your letter when I'm satisfied
the danger is over. Not before.'

He strode off again before she could find suitable

words to reply. She was fuming. The fact that she loved him did not blind her to his faults. He was an arrogant, high-handed oaf, and she wouldn't be able to live with herself if she allowed him to get the better of her. That letter had to go!

It took a few days for Annabelle to form a plan to outwit Giles, and another few before circumstances were favourable. But the day finally came when Giles had to go to High Kimber to see to some business there, and took Goss and Gregson with him. As soon as they were safely away Annabelle dressed in her riding habit, put her precious, franked letter in her side pocket, and went in search of another of Giles's men.

'Good morning, Challing! I'd like you to do something for me, if you please.'

'Can't be done, Mrs Ordway, ma'am. Colonel's orders,' said Challing promptly.

'Whatever do you think I am going to say? I wouldn't dream of asking you to disobey Colonel Stanton's orders. What a notion! No, it's just that I was thinking I would exercise my horse—within the park, of course. On the front lawn. I have Lord Stanton's permission, and if you were with me there could hardly be any danger, I think.'

'Well, er…'

'Good! Let's get the horses.'

They cantered and trotted happily enough for some time, Challing ever watchful. At last, when his attention was elsewhere, Annabelle's hat, encouraged by a jab from her whip, went sailing off in a breath of wind and landed on the ground. Hearing her cry of dismay, Challing leapt from his horse and ran after it. Annabelle gave both horses a crack of the whip and they galloped off down the lawn towards the fence. The mare took the

fence easily, the brown cob less so. A few more yards
and the cob gave up. Annabelle and the mare went racing
off towards the drive at the bottom. Before poor Challing
had even caught his mount, she was on the road to
Bakewell. All she had to do now was to get her letter to
the Receiving Office, ready for the London coach.

# Chapter Fourteen

It was market day in Bakewell, and the town was full of people, stalls and carts. The Receiving Office, she knew, was on the other side of the square, and, feeling rather noticeable on her horse without a groom or a hat, she dismounted, and tied the mare to a post outside one of the inns. Then she turned to make her way through the crowds who swarmed around her, jostling and pushing. Suddenly she felt herself being caught and dragged behind the back of one of the booths. When she opened her mouth to scream a handkerchief was thrust over her mouth.

For a moment she struggled, then a voice said in her ear, 'If you move an inch more you'll get this knife between your ribs.'

Convinced that her last moments had come, Annabelle stiffened. She would not give in without a fight. But the voice went on, 'I won't kill you unless I have to. But you'd be surprised, Mrs Ordway, at how very easy it is, if you know your job, to slide a knife into just the right place. And I'm an expert. I hope you understand? Nod, if you do.'

Annabelle nodded.

'Good. Now, you're going to walk with me to the carriage. I'll remove the handkerchief, but, if you want to live, you won't make the slightest sound.' His arm was still tight round her and she could feel the point of the knife against her side. A second man put a cloak round her shoulders and removed the rag. She took several deep breaths as they moved into the open square.

'Make way there, make way!' her captor called. 'Can't you see the lady is feeling faint? Make way!'

Annabelle could hardly believe what was happening. The sun still shone, the crowds still chattered and laughed all around them, but she was inexorably led to a closed carriage which was waiting on the edge of the square. When they reached it, she was pushed inside. The door was shut and the carriage moved off. Annabelle felt stifled.

'Please,' she whispered. 'Please…let go of me! I need some air.'

'Let her go, Burrows,' said the other man. 'She can't do anything now.'

Burrows shrugged and released Annabelle. She sank back against the squabs and closed her eyes, fighting to overcome a deadly faintness. The carriage rolled on.

'Cor! What a piece o' luck, Burrows! How did you know she'd come to Bakewell?'

'I was on the watch. Fraser said she'd be at Avenell.'

Cautiously Annabelle opened her eyes and gazed at her captors. They could not have presented a greater contrast. Burrows was short and stocky with dark hair and close-set eyes. The man opposite had a long melancholy face. She would remember both of them. When she looked back she saw that Burrows's eyes were on her.

'What do you want of me?'

'I don't want anything!' he said. 'I was told to find you, that's all.'

'Not to…kill me?'

'No. You'd be dead if I had.'

'Then why?'

'Fraser wants to talk to you.'

'Do you know why?'

'You have something he's been told to find.'

Annabelle was about to argue with him, but again decided to hold her tongue. It might be that this was the reason she had not already suffered the same fate as Venetia Stanton. Not yet, at least. She sat back to consider her situation. That it was perilous she had no doubt. Falkirk and his gang were ruthless, so much was certain. It would be some time before Giles heard of her disappearance, though she was sure he would come looking for her as soon as he did.

But until he found her she was on her own. She rejected the thought that he might not find her at all. So what should she do? She decided that all she could do for the moment was try to find out where they were taking her. And, giving the impression of being even more passive and helpless than she actually felt, she lay back with her eyes half closed…

The air was sultry, and it became very hot in the carriage. Burrows opened one of the blinds. Annabelle guessed they were travelling in a northwesterly direction—certainly what shadows she saw suggested this. After what seemed like an age her vigilance was rewarded. They turned off at a place she thought she recognised. If she was right the road would begin to rise…

Sure enough, the pace slowed down and the surface became rougher. The air was still heavy, but a few degrees cooler.

They were high up on the moors. Suddenly, in the distance she caught sight of the strangely shaped stones she had seen on that first ride with Giles—and many times since. They were on the road to Bradshaw! In her excitement she had grown less cautious. When Burrows saw her looking out, he promptly drew down the blind. Annabelle bit her lip. She had been careless. It was vital he shouldn't know that she knew where they were.

'Where are you taking me?' she asked, letting her voice tremble. 'It all looks so strange and desolate! Where are we?'

'Never you mind. Is there anything to eat, Cartwright?'

So the other man was called Cartwright. Something else to note.

Some sort of sausage and bread was produced, and a flagon of ale. Annabelle had no liking for it, but forced herself to eat and drink a little. She needed to keep her strength up.

After another age the carriage came to a stop and Cartwright opened the door.

'For God's sake! Are you sure this is the place?' he exclaimed. Burrows pushed Annabelle before him into Cartwright's arms.

'It'll do till Fraser gets back. No one's going to look for her here! The farm is deserted, and the fellow who looks after the cavern is away.'

'I wouldn't look for the devil himself here. A godforsaken country, this is.'

Annabelle looked around, taking care not to seem other than tired and dispirited. She had been right! The

carriage was standing in front of the set of semi-derelict
buildings at Blackhole cavern. The cavern itself was only
a hundred yards away. And High Kimber was just six
miles distant across the moor…

'Ah, there you are! Well met.' Burrows was greeting
a third man who had just ridden up. 'See to the horses,
will you! They can have an hour's rest, then I shall take
the carriage to Buxton. You can keep Cartwright company—he's scared.'

'I am not! I just don't like the place.'

'Never mind that, get the girl into the house. I'll bring
the rest of the things in. Make sure you tie her up!'

'Oh, come on, Burrows, there's no need for that!
Where would she run to up here?'

Burrows shrugged his shoulders. 'As you please.'

Annabelle allowed herself to be hustled into the house,
her mind busy with plans. There were now two points
in her favour—she was free to run, and she knew where
she was. How could she turn them to her advantage? She
needed a horse…and time.

They had something else to eat, then Burrows and the
driver of the carriage got up to go. 'I'll be back in the
morning with Fraser. Don't damage our prize,
Cartwright. She's to be delivered whole. You'd better
see what you can do about the window, though. It looks
as if there might be a storm before long. Till tomorrow,
then.'

Burrows and the coachman went out, and some time
later Annabelle heard the sound of the carriage being
driven off. She wondered what time it was. The light
was fading, but that might be because of the clouds
which were massing towards the west, covering the sun.

'I'd better look for something to cover the window.

We don't want our sleeping beauty's bedchamber to get wet, do we?' said the newcomer with a leer.

Cartwright said laconically, 'Touch her and you're a dead man tomorrow. She's prime meat, she is. Reserved for the chief.'

'Come on, then. Come and help me get this window sorted.'

Cartwright cast a glance at Annabelle. She was sitting on the ground, her back to the wall, the very picture of hopeless dejection.

'There might be something round the back…'

Annabelle got softly to her feet. She crept to the window and saw the men busy with a pile of ancient wood and what looked like old cloths. Picking up her skirts, she ran to the door, then scrambled desperately up the path towards the cavern. She heard shouts behind her and looked back. Cartwright and the other man were at the bottom of the slope. She was discovered. Waving her arms, she gave a terrified scream and plunged past the narrow throat into Blackhole cavern. But once out of sight her demeanour changed surprisingly. She moved purposefully along the side of the cavern feeling for the small irregularity which would tell her she had reached her goal…

When the men came storming through Annabelle was safely hidden in Giles's niche. 'The girl's a fool! There's no way out, and she could kill herself in here!' Cartwright was worried. His voice sent echoes all round.

'Are you sure? There's nothing at the other end?'

'There can't be! It goes into the hillside—doesn't it?'

'Well, she's not here, and, if there's no way out, then she must be further down. Come on!'

'Wait!'

Annabelle's heart gave a leap. She held her breath.

'What is it?'

'Go slowly! We don't want her slipping past us. You go on ahead and I'll follow.'

Breathing as shallowly as she could, Annabelle waited while the sounds of the men's footsteps faded into the depths of the cavern. She counted ten to make sure, then crept out of her shelter and made for the gate. Her hands were shaking so much that it took precious minutes to unfasten the hook, but she managed it, and the gate shut with an impressive clang. By the time the men came running back, Annabelle was at the bottom of the path, and racing for the stable. Here she saddled up the third man's horse and galloped off.

After a while she slowed the horse down. There was no sense in risking a fall in strange country, and though it was still only afternoon, heavy clouds in front of the sun were darkening the sky. The light was very poor. She was safe enough. The men would not get out of the cavern till someone came to release them, and High Kimber was a mere six miles away. All she had to do was to head in the right direction and hope that the storm would hold off till she reached it.

After half an hour Annabelle began to realise that a ride in full daylight with Giles leading the way had prepared her ill for the journey she was now attempting. The path was elusive, crossed with sheep tracks and old drainage ditches. Snatches of rain were making it slippy. Boulders could be avoided easily enough, but there were smaller stones and rocks which were difficult to see in the half-light, and she was often forced to dismount. But she kept the horse's nose pointed in the direction of High Kimber and plodded on, comforting herself with the thought that every step took her further away from danger.

Then the storm, which had been rumbling for some time, suddenly broke overhead with a spectacular flash of lightning, followed immediately by a loud clap of thunder. Annabelle's horse reared up in terror, so suddenly that she had no time to save herself. She fell, hitting her head on something hard…

It was the rain which brought her round. She lay for a moment, thankful for its refreshing coolness on her aching head. Then, as consciousness returned, she stirred and made an effort to sit up, but as soon as she put her hand to the ground an excruciating pain shot up her right arm. Sick and dizzy, she paused before attempting anything further. But she soon began to realise that she was in some danger. The rain was no longer a friend, it was fairly beating down, no longer refreshingly cool, but soaking through her riding habit, heavy and chilling.

She must stand up. There was no sign of the horse, but a cluster of rocks could just be seen through the curtain of rain. If she could get to those she might find some shelter for a while. With infinite care she took first one step then another, supporting her injured right arm with her left. By the time she had reached the rocks she was exhausted. She sank down and huddled under an outcrop, grateful for shelter from the storm, however slight.

Here she sat in a daze, forcing herself to think, in spite of the throbbing of her head and the pain in her arm. She was very cold. She dared not stay here for very long. Giles had said that many had died of exposure on the moors, and she could believe it. Though the thought of setting off again into the full force of the storm appalled her, she knew she must… This would not do! Annabelle Kelland was made of sterner stuff than this.

Slowly, painfully, taking one step at a time she made her way along the path. She knew another fall would finish her, so she looked for and found a stick and, holding it in her left hand, used it to test the ground ahead. There was no idea of time, nor any thought to spare for her aches and pains. Her whole being was concentrated on progressing towards High Kimber.

After a while the rain eased, then stopped and the evening sun came out again. The going became easier, and the path started to descend. Surprisingly, this was more difficult to manage, and each jolt as she dug her stick into the ground for support sent more pain shooting through her head and arm. She was barely conscious by the time she reached a farmhouse on the edge of the moor, and only vaguely heard the barking of the dogs as she went up to its door.

'Well, dang me! Whatever's this? A gipsy, by God! Get off with you, before I let the dogs loose!' said an angry voice. Annabelle could just make out a substantial form outlined in the doorway against the light of a kitchen fire.

'Please!' Annabelle croaked. 'High Kimber.'

'What is it, Pa?' Another figure joined the first. A child's voice.

'A gipsy woman.'

'Let me see… That's not a gipsy, Pa! Look at her dress—it's soaked through, but it's a decent riding habit. She's hurt! Let her in!'

The farmer took hold of Annabelle's arm as she staggered. The pain was so intense that she fainted.

The first thing she became aware of was the smell of lavender, scenting the sheets in which she lay. She opened her eyes. Giles's face hovered over hers.

'I wish you *were* here!' she said fretfully.

'I am. What did you think I was? A hallucination? I assure you I am not.'

'How did you find me? Where am I?'

'Burton sent for me. I've brought you to High Kimber.'

'That's good,' Annabelle said. His face drifted away again. 'No!' she cried in panic. 'Don't go away! Please don't leave me!'

'I won't go, I promise.' His voice, deep, calm, firm, penetrated the shadows surrounding her. 'Don't be afraid, Rosabelle. I shall stay with you.'

The next time she became conscious she could hear Giles in discussion with someone else.

'I cannot advise it,' said the stranger's voice. 'I understand the difficulties, but she really ought not to be moved again.'

'In that case we shall make do. I can have her mother-in-law fetched tomorrow, and my housekeeper will soon be back for tonight. Are you going to set her arm now?'

'The sooner the better. In case there are…complications.'

'Complications? What do you mean?'

The doctor came to the bed and saw that Annabelle's eyes were open. 'Mrs Ordway, you have broken your arm just above the wrist. The break is not a bad one, but it must be set. Do you feel you could allow me to set it?'

Annabelle looked at Giles, who nodded. 'Do it!' she whispered. 'Giles will help me.'

'Drink this first. You'll feel better,' said Giles, putting

a glass to her lips. The liquid was bitter and she would have rejected it, but Giles held her firmly until it was all gone. Then he and the doctor waited quietly until Annabelle gave a sleepy smile.

'Much better,' she said vaguely.

The laudanum was not quite strong enough to dull all the pain that followed, though it helped. But by the time the doctor drew back and said, 'Excellent!' Annabelle had had enough. She was still clutching Giles's hand desperately when the time came for the doctor to leave, and Goss was fetched to see him out.

'Thank you,' she said, her voice a mere thread of sound.

'I'll call again tomorrow, Mrs Ordway. I can't stay now—I was only in the neighbourhood to deal with an accident at Beckin, and I must get back there. Sleep as much as you can.' His voice dropped. 'If she is restless, tell Mrs Brough to give her some of this. There's more than she will need there, but it's better to be safe. I'm not sure what time I'll come tomorrow.'

'Thank you.'

The doctor went and they were alone.

'Giles.'

'Yes?'

'I was so stupid.'

'I know. Challing caught me just before I was about to set off back to Avenell. Then Burton came. Falkirk found you, I take it.'

'It was a man called Burrows, but they talked about Fraser, too. They took me to Blackhole cavern. Wasn't that strange?'

'Very.'

'I'm sorry, Giles.'

'Try not to talk, Rosabelle. You can tell me another time what happened.'

He sat quietly, waiting for the drug to take effect again, only removing his hand when her fingers relaxed. Goss came silently back into the room and waited by the door.

Giles went over to him. 'Where the devil is Mrs Brough?'

'I don't know, sir. Gregson went some time ago. They ought to be back by now. But it's a terrible night.'

'Try to see what's happening, Goss. I'll stay here.'

It was some time before Goss returned, and when he did his expression was gloomy. He waited at the door till Giles joined him outside.

'Bad news, Colonel. The storm has washed away most of the bridges. There's floods all round. No one will get here tonight.'

'What about Doctor Bryne?'

'He must have just got across before the Kimber bridge went. I didn't see any sign of his gig.'

'Hell and damnation! You mean we're stranded?'

'Yes, sir. Sorry, sir.'

'Why the devil did Mrs Brough have to visit her daughter tonight of all the nights in the year? I shouldn't have let her go.'

'It seemed reasonable at the time, Colonel. You planning to go back to Avenell and stay with Lord Stanton for a while, like.'

'Yes. Well, Goss, it looks as if we're on our own for the present. Let us hope that the complications Doctor Bryne mentioned don't materialise. Tonight at least.'

'What might they be?'

'He didn't say, but I suspect fever. Mrs Ordway was very wet and cold for a good while. If she came across the moor… It seems incredible, but that's what she said she did. It's very exposed up there.' Giles was silent for a moment. 'Check our food supplies, Goss. I know you're a dab at catering. Mrs Ordway may feel like something when she wakes—and I wouldn't mind a bite myself. Burton might have some milk and a few eggs if there isn't enough here.'

'Excuse me, sir, but mightn't it be a good idea to get the farmer's wife to come for the night?'

'It would be an excellent idea if he had one, Goss. But Mrs Burton died two years ago, and so far Burton has not replaced her.'

'I see. Difficult. Right, sir! So it's back to Spanish days, aye, sir?'

'It looks as if we might be grateful for the things we learned there if we're stranded for long, my old friend!'

Both he and Goss ate their fill before the invalid woke, and it was as well. Far from wanting anything to eat, she was in a high fever, tossing and turning in spite of the splint on her lower arm. It needed both Goss and Giles to hold her while Giles administered the draught the doctor had left behind, and even then she was still very restless for some time. She eventually fell into another heavy sleep. The two men looked at one another grimly.

'Complications,' said Giles. Goss said nothing, but set about tidying the sick room while his master sat in thought. 'We might have an hour or two before Mrs Ordway wakes again, but she will need someone with her all the time. It ought to be a woman, but that's impossible. Damn Mrs Brough! Help me to fetch the big armchair in from next door. We'll put it over in the corner by the window. I can sit in that.'

This they did, and Goss fetched some cushions and blankets. 'What the devil are those for, Goss?'

'You might find you can snatch a few winks, Colonel.'

'I don't want to sleep, damn you!'

'Beg your pardon, sir, but we don't know yet what we're in for. Mrs Ordway don't look too clever to me. What if the others don't get through tomorrow? You're going to need all the rest you can get.'

'Of course they'll get through! They have to! Doctor Bryne, too!'

'You haven't seen the rivers, sir.'

Goss's gloomy forebodings were to be fully justified. Another storm the same night put an end to any hopes of the flood waters subsiding.

But by morning the state of the rivers was the least of Giles's worries. There was no doubt in his mind that Rosabelle was dangerously ill. She couldn't stop shivering, though her skin was dry and hot. She was delirious, too, frantically calling out her own name, together with her sister's or that of Lady Ordway. Then she would cry out for him in a cracked, dry voice, which no drink could soothe. She was clearly in distress, complaining of pains in her head, bringing her arms up to hold it, and crying out when the broken arm protested.

He gave her as much as he dared of the doctor's draught, bathed her forehead, talked to her gently, soothing and comforting her as much as he could. It was a hard, long night. In the morning Goss was sent out to view the state of the rivers and came back with no good news. They were, if anything, higher than ever. He brought with him a couple of chickens and some eggs, however, and later in the morning produced a warm broth which he proposed to feed to Mrs Ordway.

'Leave her to me, Colonel. There's a plate of eggs for you in the dining room, and Mr Burton handed in a loaf of bread and some butter from his farm. There's some milk, as well. You need to have a wash and shave and a bit of a rest. Mrs Ordway will be safe enough with me—I'm an old hand at nursing, you know that.'

Giles went without much ado—he knew Goss's skills better than most. But he could not stay away long. Before Goss had managed to persuade Annabelle to take more than a mouthful of the broth he was back again, anxiously feeling her pulse and bathing the burning forehead. For the rest of the day he hardly left the room, tending the invalid with a skill and a patience which would have astonished anyone other than his friends from the Spanish wars.

The next day was no better, nor the next. He and Goss developed a routine, taking it in turns to sit with the patient, though Giles spent longer with her, and Goss did the cooking. On the fourth day there was a slight improvement in the weather, and on the fifth they were able to reach the next farm across a corner of the moor, and to get a message sent out to Avenell. The farmer's wife, though busy herself, agreed to come in for a few hours during the day to do some nursing.

But the roads remained too dangerous, and the moor too treacherous to go any further. Another day brought Gregson, but before he could go back to Avenell with news of the invalid, the rain started again and the river was impossible for anyone to cross. It was perhaps as well, for the news would not have been good. The fever had hardly abated in the six days since it had first started. Goss was looking worried and Giles himself was almost desperate.

In the evening Goss brought in a lamp and set it over by the window next to the armchair. 'How is Mrs Ordway, sir?'

'I don't know, Goss. I don't know! She's so still! Oh God, Goss! I've been in many a tight corner before, but never one like this. I feel so damned helpless!'

Goss nodded, then said, 'I'll sit here for a bit, sir, shall I? How about a bit of fresh air for yourself before it's dark?'

'No, I'll stay here. You go.'

'I don't think I will, sir, if you don't mind. I'll stay within call.' Goss made sure that water, medicine, some barley water and the lamp were within reach, then went quietly out. Giles stood by the bed. Annabelle was flushed again, turning her head restlessly from side to side.

'Giles,' she murmured. 'Giles.'

'I'm here. What do you want? Are you in pain?'

'No. Goss gave me something… But I'm so hot… Giles…I didn't mean it.'

'What didn't you mean, my Rosabelle?'

'I'm not your Rosabelle!' Suddenly she was struggling to sit up, and though Giles tried to make her lie down again, she clung to him with her good hand and wouldn't let him go. Her eyes bright with fever, she said hoarsely, 'I'm not your Rosabelle, I don't want to be Rosabelle any more! She's a liar and a cheat and you'll never forgive her. Never.' Giles put his arm round her and held her close. He could feel the heat of her body burning through the thick calico of the nightgown they had found for her.

'Hush, Rosa, my love. Forget the past. We're different people now from what we were. It will sort itself out, you'll see. But you must stay quiet and rest!'

'Will it? Will it?'

'Of course it will!'

'I don't believe you!' she cried. 'I've lost you and it's all my fault. Stupid, stupid me!' Her head turned away from him against his chest and she started sobbing. Nothing he could do would console her. But when he tried to lay her back against the pillows and cover her up she put her hand out again.

'Don't go! Stay by me! Don't hate me, Giles, stay with me just a bit longer.'

'Rosa, I—'

'*Please*, Giles!' He felt her pulse—it was racing, and her breathing was rapid and shallow. She was trembling violently.

'Let me bathe your face and hands. You're very hot.'

'No! I'm cold, and I want you to keep me warm!'

Giles gave in. He lay down on the covers beside her and carefully took her into his arms, smoothing her hair from her forehead, and holding her like a child close to him. The attack lasted for a while longer, then she grew still. Eventually she gave a sigh of contentment.

'That's better,' she said. 'That's…better…'

## Chapter Fifteen

When Giles woke the next morning he wondered where he was for the moment. It wasn't the first time he had woken up with a woman in his bed, but never before with a barrier of bedclothes between them. What the devil…? Then he remembered. He looked at Rosabelle. She was breathing regularly, and her skin was cool and moist. Her hair was a dark tangle of gold on the pillow, and Mrs Brough's nightgown, made for a more ample figure, had slipped from her shoulder to reveal the soft curves of her bosom. Giles felt somewhat light-headed himself. He bent to kiss the hollow which lay so enticingly between her breasts… When he raised his head, he saw that Rosabelle was awake. He felt himself flushing dark red, and pulled the edges of the nightgown together.

'I…I…forgive me!'

'Dear Giles. For what? Saving my life?'

'I didn't mean…'

'I know you didn't.' She took hold of his hand and

held it to her cheek. 'And if I weren't so stupidly feeble I'd show you that I forgive you. But I can hear Goss coming and I think you should be somewhere else when he comes in.'

Giles jumped off the bed, and by the time Goss entered he was in the chair by the window. Goss took one quick glance at the hollow in the covers on the bed and then studiously avoided it with his eyes.

'Good morning, Colonel. Breakfast is ready. How is Mrs Ordway?'

'I think I'm almost myself again, Goss. Have I been a great nuisance?'

'Good morning, ma'am. Not at all, ma'am. A privilege to serve you. I can see you're better. Would you like some breakfast?'

'I think I would. In fact, I am starving! But I should like to get up first. Could you send Mrs Brough in?'

'Well, now. I'm afraid Mrs Brough ain't here, ma'am. There's only the Colonel and myself until the woman comes in from the farm.'

'What? But who…?' Annabelle went scarlet. Without a word Giles got to his feet and lifted her off the bed. He wrapped her in a blanket, and carried her to the dressing room. He told her to wait, then went out and returned in a minute or two with a towel and a clean nightgown.

'Will you be safe on your own?'

'Thank you, yes. Giles?'

'Yes?'

'What happened to Mrs Brough?'

'She hasn't been able to get here. We've been cut off by floods.'

'I see. Who…who has been looking after me?'

'One of the farmers' wives.'

'All the time?'

'No. Goss and I have done a small amount. But don't worry. I've behaved impeccably. Till this morning.' He went and Annabelle looked round her. Warm water had been put into a washbasin on the stand, and a towel was waiting beside it. A commode chair was nearby. It took some time to get used to managing with only one hand, but she succeeded, and in twenty minutes she was ready again. She took a step to the door, and nearly fell. In answer to her call, Giles came to carry her through to the bedchamber. In her absence someone had changed the bedlinen. Her eyes filled with tears.

'How kind you both are!' she said.

He smiled down at her. 'Come, Rosabelle! This won't do. Tears were allowed when you were not yourself, but now you have recovered your wits and must behave sensibly.'

'Er…how long was I out of my wits, Giles?'

'It's nearly a week now. The longest week of my life.'

'It must have been. I can think of few things more tedious. I'm sorry, Giles.'

He settled her down on the bed and drew the clothes up around her. 'It wasn't exactly tedious. Well, now. Breakfast? Mrs Whatever comes in about half an hour. She has to attend to her own chores first.'

After another day the river was low enough for Mrs Brough to return, and for Gregson to ride back to Avenell. There was no excuse now for the unusual arrangements which had been in force while they had been completely cut off, and Giles's visits to the sick room were strictly conventional. On one of them he produced a tattered, indecipherable rag of paper.

'It's yours, I believe. The famous letter. Mrs Brough found it in the pocket of your riding dress. I'm afraid you'll have to write it again, Rosabelle.' He handed it to her. 'Was it so important? You nearly died for it.'

'No…it wasn't important,' said Annabelle, smoothing it out mechanically.

'So it was just that you couldn't bear what you saw as my arrogance. Is that it? If so, I'm sorry. More sorry than I can well say.'

'Don't! It wasn't that. Not…not exactly. It's true that I wanted to tell my sister that I was safe, but there was something else. Something I needed to ask her.'

'Rosa, I've had my suspicions for some time. If I ask you something, will you tell me the truth?'

Annabelle stared at him. If Giles challenged her here and now, she would have to tell him, whatever it meant to Rosabelle. She nodded.

'Is your sister Annabelle at the root of your reluctance to confide in me? I've decided that she is the only person you would defend at such expense to yourself. Am I right? Annabelle is somehow involved with Selder, and you are protecting her.'

'Wha…what makes you think that?'

'One of Selder's contacts was at Woolhampton. You remarked yourself how near it was to Temperley. Annabelle could have met him in Berkshire. You have sworn to me that you did not have an affair with Selder, and I am absolutely convinced of your integrity, your basic honesty. But there is *something* about him which you know and are concealing. It must concern your sister.'

'Giles, I…'

'You know, if Annabelle *is* involved, I would find it difficult to forgive her. She has caused you so much trouble.'

'My sister is innocent, Giles!'

'Is she? I hope so. Philip Winbolt is a good friend of mine. We neither of us enjoy being deceived.'

'No. No, of course you don't. That's very natural,' Annabelle said wanly. 'Giles, my head is aching…I can't think very clearly at the moment. Would you excuse me? You will have your answer soon, I promise.'

'I'm a brute, hectoring you like this. You're still very weak. I'm sorry. Tomorrow we shall go back to Avenell—I've thought of a way we can manage it. Rest now. The journey will make some demands on you. We'll discuss your family affairs when you're stronger.' He took her hand and kissed it, then went out.

Annabelle walked to the bed, threw herself down on it and buried her head in the pillows. She was filled with black despair. There was to be no happy end, not for herself, and not for poor Rosabelle. Bitter tears soaked the pillow, and sobs racked her slender body…

'Why, Mrs Ordway, whatever's wrong? My poor lady! Colonel Stanton, Colonel Stanton!' Mrs Brough hurried out of the room, and came back with Giles.

'Rosabelle! My dearest girl! Oh, God!' He came to the bed and tried to take Annabelle in his arms.

'Leave me alone!' she cried wildly. 'Leave me alone!'

'Mrs Brough, fetch some of Doctor Bryne's draught, if you please. Mrs Ordway is ill again.'

With a doubtful look at her master the housekeeper went away.

'Rosabelle! Listen to me! You must be calm. This is not doing you any good at all. Forget what we talked about if that is what has upset you. We won't mention it again. Only be calm, my love!'

Mrs Brough came back with the medicine.

'Here, drink this,' he said. 'It will make you feel better.'

'I don't want your medicines! I want to be well, to go back to London! To Temperley!'

'You can't go anywhere till you are strong enough. You've been very ill, Rosa. Dangerously ill. Now be a good girl and take the sedative.'

'Give it to me, Colonel Stanton. I'll see she drinks it.' Mrs Brough took the glass from Giles. 'Don't worry, sir!' she added as she looked at his face. 'Mrs Ordway will be as right as rain soon. She's bound to have these fits of depression for a while. She must take it slowly, that's all. You can't hurry these things.'

'No,' he said heavily. 'No, I was a fool. But I'd like to get her back closer to civilisation, Mrs Brough.'

'So you shall, so you shall, sir. But perhaps not to-morrow.'

In the event it was another two days before Doctor Bryne agreed to let Annabelle make the journey to Avenell, and then only because Giles insisted. Every care was taken, but when she was finally put to bed in Avenell she was exhausted.

'Rosa! What happened to you? Oh, look at her—she's a wraith.' Lady Ordway hovered anxiously as Giles carried her in.

'Aunt Laura, it's so…so comforting to see you…' Annabelle's voice wavered, and Giles intervened.

'She needs as much rest as possible. I'll get my father's doctor to have a look at her tomorrow, but Doctor Bryne said rest was the most important part of the cure. Rest and good food.'

Rest and good food was what Annabelle had in plenty in the next few weeks. Mrs Dunnock produced no end of tempting dishes, and Lord Stanton brought some delicacy or other every time he visited her. The weather, having had its fling, smiled on them, and the countryside glowed red and gold in the autumnal sunshine. As she grew stronger Annabelle spent a little time each day in the garden, and fell in love all over again with Avenell and the country round it. Giles treated her with gentle consideration, never once putting pressure on her or referring to their conversation about her sister. It was Annabelle who finally broached the subject.

'Giles, I still owe you an explanation.'

'It can wait, Rosa.'

'I want to go to Temperley soon. I must talk to my sister. Then...then I'd like you to meet her. I think you'll understand then what it was all about.'

'I have some news for you. Falkirk seems to have made the acquaintance of the Winbolts. He has been to Shearings. It seems he went to Emily Winbolt's birthday party a few weeks ago.'

'Falkirk!'

'Yes. But he's back in London now.'

'I must go back!' said Annabelle, getting agitated. 'I must see my sister.'

'I'll take you and Aunt Laura back to London as soon as the doctor says you may go. It won't be long now. Everything is in readiness.'

'Please, Giles, please make it soon!'

He took her hands and held them in a warm clasp. 'I will. I have every reason to clear this affair up as soon as possible. Then...'

'We shall have no secrets,' said Annabelle, trying to keep the sadness out of her voice.

The journey southwards, though not as leisurely as the one to the north, had to be taken in easier stages than Annabelle wished. She was desperate to see Rosabelle.

It was no longer a simple matter of ending their charade. If Falkirk knew the Winbolts, then her sister was in exactly the same danger from him as she herself had been—and with more reason! She was not an easy travelling companion. She resisted all the efforts of Giles and Lady Ordway to keep their travelling stages short, and sat in fretful silence when the state of the roads forced them into a more moderate pace.

Her companions made allowance for the fact that she was still weaker than she would admit from her illness and bore with her patiently. But on the last day, when they were expecting to reach Temperley by nightfall, early November fog in the Thames Valley reduced their progress to a snail's pace.

'I'm afraid we are going to have to stop for the night here,' said Giles, as they crawled into Wallingford.

This was the last straw for poor Annabelle. 'No!' she cried. 'It's not yet three o'clock! We can still get to Temperley.'

'Look outside, Rosa! The fog is thicker than ever. I am not going to risk being stranded for the night in some Godforsaken village, with no respectable inn, or anywhere to put the horses. Wallingford has the merit of providing at least two comfortable places to stay.'

'But I must get to Temperley! We've already wasted so much time. You promised!'

Lady Ordway intervened. 'Rosa dear, you are being unreasonable. I am sure Giles is right. And I confess, I am quite weary myself. This fog is very enervating.'

Annabelle looked at her and was ashamed. Wrapped up in her own problems, she had failed to notice how exhausted Lady Ordway was. 'I'm sorry, Aunt Laura. Of course we shall put up for the night here. But I warn you, I shall want to set off in very good time tomorrow!'

'At dawn, if you insist,' said Giles. 'And if the weather permits.'

But when she went into Lady Ordway's bedchamber the next morning she was greeted with bad news.

'Her ladyship had a very bad night, Miss Rosabelle,' said Wilson. 'She isn't fit to travel.'

'Be quiet, Wilson! I'm sorry, Anna,' said Lady Ordway weakly. 'I shall be perfectly well in a little while. I won't keep you back, I promise.'

'Aunt Laura, I am ashamed of myself. There's no question of your getting up before you feel well enough! Does Giles know?'

'Not yet.'

'Then I shall tell him.' Annabelle went to seek Giles.

When she told him the news, he looked serious. 'Another delay. And I wouldn't place any reliance on the weather. The mist may well fall again. It is most unfortunate.'

'Do you have to be so pessimistic?' cried Annabelle, distraught. 'Yes, it is unfortunate, to say the least! But what can we do? However badly I want to see my sister, I cannot risk Aunt Laura's health. I'll let you know as soon as Wilson and I can judge it is safe to travel.' She hurried away again before disgracing herself by bursting into tears.

A few minutes later Giles appeared outside Lady Ordway's room. 'Rosabelle, may I speak to you?' Annabelle came out of the room, shutting the door quietly behind her. 'How is Aunt Laura?'

'She's asleep. Apparently she was awake most of the night, and Wilson thinks sleep may be all she needs. With any luck we should be able to set off in two or three hours.'

'I have a better idea. You and Goss could ride on ahead to Temperley, and I shall bring Aunt Laura as soon as she is ready to leave.'

'But I can't leave Aunt Laura!'

'Wilson and I are perfectly capable. There hasn't been a sign of Falkirk or anyone else since we left the north, so I think it would be quite safe as long as you have Goss as an escort. He's very resourceful.'

Annabelle looked at him doubtfully. She was strongly tempted. Not only would she arrive earlier at Temperley, but the scheme had another, unexpected, advantage, which Giles could not appreciate. She would be able to talk to Rosabelle before he met them together for the first time.

'Thank you, Giles. I'll do as you suggest.'

'But...' He smiled ruefully. 'You will take care? You are not yet fully yourself, you know. I don't want all my good work undone.'

Annabelle was overcome with a sudden rush of feeling. She loved this man so much. Why was she so desperate to reach Temperley and all that that meant? 'Giles,' she whispered. 'Oh, Giles!'

He put his arms round her. 'You'll be safe with Goss,' he said. 'I wouldn't risk it if I thought there was any danger.'

'It's not that. I...I just want you to know how...how grateful I am.'

'Grateful?' he asked, smiling down at her. 'Is that all? I'm not looking for gratitude, Rosabelle.'

Annabelle took his face in her hands. 'Have faith in me, Giles. Have faith. Please.' She kissed him. The kiss deepened, and would have been deeper still but for a chambermaid who came hurrying round the corner of the stairs and stopped dead when she saw them.

'Oh! 'Scuse me, sir, 'scuse me, ma'am!' She disappeared.

Covered in confusion, Annabelle muttered something about changing and whisked herself into her room.

Within quarter of an hour she and Goss were trotting off along the road southwards in the direction of Temperley.

But at Temperley they met with a severe setback. After the first excited greetings Becky told Annabelle that her sister was not there, but in London.

'In London! Oh, no! It can't be so!' cried Annabelle in despair.

'Well, I'm afraid it is. Miss Rosa was in such a tumult, Miss Belle. Mr Winbolt just swept her off her feet. Here one day and gone the next. She was worried about you, though. Why didn't you write?'

'Never mind that now, Becky. What am I to do?'

'Your papa is here, Miss Belle.'

'I haven't time to see him now. I'll have to leave you again. Get John to saddle up some fresh horses. Becky, you'll hear everything in due course, but for now just do as I tell you! There isn't a moment to lose.'

Annabelle sought out Goss, who was on his way back from the stables. 'Goss, we've got to go back. I must intercept Colonel Stanton. My sister is in London. There is no point in his coming here.'

Goss took some persuading that it was not better to stay where they were to wait for the rest of the party. 'The Colonel would want me to make sure you didn't wear yourself out, ma'am, beggin' your pardon,' he said stiffly.

'I can't sit still, Goss! If we are to reach London tonight we must not waste a moment before finding

Colonel Stanton and the rest of the party! Please do as I say!' Though still unreconciled, Goss went all the same to find John and the horses, and soon, without any further delay, they were retracing their steps to the accompaniment of his *sotto voce* remarks.

When Giles and Lady Ordway eventually arrived at Temperley they were disconcerted to find that they were not expected.

'Miss Belle was here earlier in the day, my lady, but she never said anything about your ladyship and Colonel Stanton. In fact, she hardly said anything at all. She was in a terrible state when she heard that her sister was in London with Mr Winbolt, and left straight away. I thought she had gone to find you, but perhaps she went to London?'

Giles was looking very grim. 'You may be sure of it.' He turned to Lady Ordway. 'I must follow her, of course. Do you mind if I leave you here, Aunt Laura?'

'No, of course not, Giles. I have Mrs Bostock to look after me, and Wilson will help. Tell me, Mrs Bostock, is your master well enough to receive visitors?'

'Of course, my lady! And I'll see about a room for your ladyship straight away.'

Lady Ordway looked anxiously at Giles. 'What has happened to Rosabelle, Giles?'

'I expect she decided to make for London, as Mrs Bostock suggested. Try not to worry, Aunt Laura. I'll find her. And Goss is with her, don't forget. If I leave straight away, I might even catch up with her. Will you make my excuses to Mr Kelland?'

Calling Gregson, he wasted no more time on ceremony, but set off in pursuit.

\* \* \*

Not long after leaving Temperley, Annabelle and Goss became aware that they were being followed.

'It's probably nothing, Mrs Ordway, but we won't take any risks. Don't slow down, not for anything. Keep going.'

Annabelle snatched a quick look behind. The figure was gaining.

'Faster, Mrs Ordway! And keep low in the saddle! Faster!' Goss drew a pistol from the holster at his side as they galloped on at a breakneck speed. They seemed to be making some headway, but as they joined the road at the end of Harden Lane another horse and rider appeared. Was it rescue or more threat? As they drew rapidly nearer Annabelle instinctively started to pull up.

'No, Mrs Ordway! Don't slow down...' But Goss was forced to rein in, too. He fired back towards their pursuer, but as they both turned and made to take up their former pace, the rider in front joined in. There was a shot, a cry from Goss and he fell to the ground. Annabelle wheeled round and chased back to where he lay. Goss was clutching his side, but he gasped, 'For God's sake, don't stop, Mrs Ordway. Get away while you can!'

It was too late. The first man was upon them, and the second came riding up immediately after. Annabelle dug her spurs into her horse. It reared, then galloped madly off towards the high road. For a moment it looked as if the ruse might succeed. The two men, taken by surprise, were slow to give chase. But they soon recovered and their powerful horses quickly overtook Annabelle's mount. There was a struggle, then all three riders came to a halt. Annabelle recognised one of the men. It was Cartwright—he had been in the coach at Bakewell.

'Fraser will crow,' said the other. 'He said they'd

come back to Berkshire. And lo and behold, here they are!'

'Don't waste time,' said Cartwright. 'This is a public place. Take her to the carriage. And this time we'll make sure she doesn't get away! Tie her up.'

They pulled her from the horse and started to bind her wrists. Aware that protest would be useless she bore it stoically, though the pressure on her newly healed arm was exquisitely painful. But when they started to lead her away, she could not keep silent.

'What about Goss?' she cried.

'Who's he?'

'My groom. You can't leave him there to die!'

'Can't we? Who's goin' to stop us? You?'

'But…but he'll bleed to death!'

'What a shame,' said Cartwright. 'We'll send a wreath. Come on!'

'You mustn't leave him, I won't let you. I won't go!' Annabelle kicked and shouted with all her might. Someone must hear her, they must! Goss must not be left. For a short while they tried to hold her by force, but when she still screamed and scratched, Cartwright swore, then hit her on the head. While she was still dizzy with the pain they tied her feet together and put a gag over her mouth. Then the other man, the bigger of the two, hoisted her up like a sack, and threw her over the saddle. Annabelle was not aware of anything that followed. She was unconscious.

She became dimly aware of sounds of the high road, the toll gates, the inns, other travellers. Once or twice the motion of the carriage stopped and she guessed the horses were being changed. She had no idea of the time, though the light seemed to be fading more quickly than she would have expected. Later she saw that the fog of the previous night had returned. After what seemed like an eternity the carriage rolled in through some gates which clanged shut behind them, and came to a halt. She was carried in to a building which smelt of stale beer and worse, and deposited on a settle in the corner of a dingy room.

'She looks pretty sick.' It was Cartwright's voice. 'The bruise looks nasty, too. I hope Fraser doesn't think we've been too rough.'

'Not him. As long as she can talk that'll be enough. And what else were we to do? She's a wildcat, that one. Look at my hand! And I'll swear my shins are black and blue.'

'All the same, I'll get something for her to lie on.' Cartwright went away and came back with a rough blanket. 'Hold her up a minute.'

'Water!' croaked Annabelle.

'There's some in the old bar,' ordered Cartwright, who seemed to be in charge. 'Get it!' He held a pewter drinking vessel to her lips and she drank thirstily. The water was surprisingly fresh. Then he put a bowl of water down beside her, and untied her hands and feet. 'You can drink that if you need any more. We're going now, but Fraser's coming later. If you'll take my advice you won't try any tricks on Fraser. We've treated you like a baby compared with what he would do. We only hurt by way of business. He enjoys it.'

They left her, and Annabelle was left to her own dismal thoughts. She had no idea where she might be, though she suspected it was somewhere in London. Her physical state was pathetic—her head was throbbing, she still felt very dizzy, and there was a distinct possibility that she might be sick. She looked round. The room was lit by an evil-smelling lamp in the corner. Its dim light revealed a heavy iron door and bare stone walls, though the room appeared to be dry and free of rats. Opposite her was a barred window. She got up and walked over to it.

The window looked out on to a yard surrounded by high walls, dimly visible in the fog. No possibility of escape there even if she were able to attempt it. She went back to her makeshift bed and sank down, with nothing to do but ponder her situation. She prayed desperately that Goss had been found before it was too late. She wondered where Giles was and what he was doing. She asked herself if she would ever have a chance to tell him how much she loved him? And how sorry she was? The chance seemed at present to be remote.

Weak tears rolled down her cheeks, but she wiped them away fiercely. Fraser was not going to find her like this! She wet her handkerchief and wiped her face. The cold water refreshed her, and brought a return of her natural spirit. Whatever her situation, she could do nothing about it at the moment. It would be wise to conserve her energies for what was to come. She made what preparations she could, lay down and composed herself for sleep.

Meanwhile, Giles was riding as fast as he dared to London. The fog came down just beyond Hounslow Heath, but his pace barely faltered. Gregson, riding behind him, sent up many fervent prayers for their safe arrival, though with little real hope. But they pressed on, and towards nine o'clock they finally came to a halt in Arlington Street. Gregson waited with the horses while Giles hammered on the door. As soon as it was opened he stepped past the footman and went into the hall.

'I wish to speak to Mr Winbolt. The affair is urgent,'
he said curtly to the butler. 'Colonel Stanton.'

'The family are still at dinner, sir.'

'It doesn't matter. Tell your master I am here, damn
you!'

The servant was shocked, but assessed the situation
pretty well. 'Very well, Colonel. I will see what I can
do.' He made for a door on the right. Giles heard voices,
and he was prepared to swear that one of them was
Rosabelle's! He pushed past the butler.

'Excuse me for breaking in on you like this, Philip—'
He stopped dead. A pleasant scene met his gaze—three
young people round the top end of a large mahogany
dining table, the remains of a meal, candlelight reflecting
on the richly coloured wood, the silver and glassware.
Giles had eyes for none of this. On Philip Winbolt's right
sat Rosabelle.

For a moment he was light-headed with joy. All the
way to London he had held back his fears, forced himself
to concentrate on the road before him, pushed to the back
of his mind pictures of Rosabelle in Falkirk's power, the
horror at what Falkirk might do to her. The relief at
seeing her here, safe in London, was almost overpow-
ering, and he, who had faced battalions of the enemy
without a tremor, who had defied death in a dozen different countries, was as weak as a woman at the sight of
her. It was no longer possible to deceive himself about
his feelings for Rosabelle Ordway. She was everything
to him!

His first impulse was to take her in his arms and hold
her, just to hold her until the tumult of his feelings died
down, till he was convinced that she was truly here, and
truly safe. But then before he realised what was happening his relief turned to a fury which was as violent as it

was sudden. How dare she subject him—and the others—to such fear, such unmanly weakness? How could she be so thoughtless, so cruel!

'Rosabelle! So you *are* here! What the devil do you think you've been doing?' He took hold of her, beside himself with rage, uncertain whether he wanted to shake her, or kiss her senseless. Then he became aware that Philip was beside him, had put a restraining hand on him, was trying to tell him that Rosabelle was betrothed to him, Philip Winbolt!

Giles began to feel that he had gone mad. He had somehow strayed into a lunatic asylum, and was the latest inmate. And now Rosabelle was speaking and he couldn't make any sense of it.

'Are you saying that you've brought my sister to London, Giles? Oh, how could you? After all my warnings and letters…'

Warnings, letters? Reproaches because he had brought her sister to London? What the hell did she mean? He hadn't even seen her sister! And what was this nonsense about a betrothal? It was Annabelle Kelland who was to marry Philip. Rosabelle was his! He appealed to her to tell Winbolt the truth. But Rosabelle remained silent, staring at him as if she had been struck dumb, as if he was a madman.

They must be drunk! That was it! He began again, patiently explaining, to go over the events of the last six months. Rosabelle might be mad or incapable, but Philip would listen sensibly. But Philip's face grew graver and graver. And Rosabelle appeared to be perfectly sober. A nameless fear started to grow in Giles. There was some mystery here to which he did not have the key. But when Philip Winbolt finally spoke it was all made horribly, hideously clear.

'Giles, I…I don't know how to tell you this. I can see that you have been as deceived as I was. You obviously don't know that the Kelland sisters are identical twins. This—' he took Rosabelle's hand '—this is Rosabelle Ordway, who changed places with her sister at Easter, and has been in Berkshire and London ever since. The lady with you in the North was Annabelle Kelland.'

Giles looked blankly at his friend. What nonsense was this? Of course this was Rosabelle! His Rosabelle. But then, as he looked more closely, the woman standing by Philip Winbolt was suddenly no longer so familiar. She might be Rosabelle's double, but there was something, a faint air, an aura, which told him that this was not the woman he loved. And, for the first time, the truth began to penetrate. The woman at present standing next to Philip was indeed Stephen's widow, the woman he had met on first coming to London. She was not the Rosabelle he had known for the last six months, the Rosabelle he had fallen so desperately in love with.

He stared unseeingly at them all while his tired brain absorbed what he had been told. Twins, yes. He had known that. But identical twins? No, that had never been mentioned, not by anyone. Not even Aunt Laura, though she must have known. They had all used the startling likeness to trick him. With bitter recognition he realised that his 'Rosabelle' did not exist. Had never existed. Annabelle Kelland had played him like a fish. It was ironic, truly, bitterly ironic, that all the suspicions, all his instinctive distrust of her, which had taken so long to overcome, had always been justified, right from the beginning.

# Chapter Sixteen

For a moment he was filled with an intensely corroding sense of disillusion which blotted out every other feeling. Annabelle Kelland was false, as her sister had been false, as his stepmother had been false, as all the women he had ever known had been false. But then, as the shock faded, fear took its place. If this woman before him was not the one who had left Wallingford that morning to go to Temperley...

*'But in that case, where is Annabelle now?'* he demanded.

They all started as the butler came into the room. 'Forgive me, sir, but there's an individual at the back demanding to see Colonel Stanton. I thought it best to let you know straight away. He has ridden from Berkshire, sir.'

'Bring him in, Maynard.'

They waited tensely to see what this arrival might mean.

'John Bostock!' All three recognised the exhausted man who now entered the room.

'Colonel Stanton, sir, they found Goss, your man. He's been wounded. He says that he and Miss Belle were set upon shortly after they left Temperley by two men. They shot Goss and…and they carried Miss Belle off with them.'

'Falkirk's work!'

Philip Winbolt said, 'Maynard, fetch Stokes and Jenkins. Hurry! Where are you going, Giles! Wait! This needs planning.'

'You don't realise, Winbolt. Falkirk is quite ruthless. There isn't a moment to lose. I must find her.'

'Where would you begin to look?'

'I have men in London, who've been keeping a watch on Falkirk. They might have some news… Gregson knows where they can be found. Bostock, you're done in. Find Gregson for me—he'll be in the stables. Then find somewhere you can rest.'

'Go to the kitchens, Bostock,' said Philip. 'They'll give you something there.'

'Bostock!' said Giles. 'Tell me first. Is…is Goss badly hurt?'

'He'll live, sir.'

'Thank God! Right, tell Gregson to come here, then go to the kitchen.'

'Beg your pardon, sir. But if Miss Annabelle is in danger I'd rather be up and about.'

'Get some food into you first, Bostock! It may be a long night.'

Emily got up from the table and said quietly, 'I'll see to him.' She took Bostock out of the room.

Gregson, Stokes and Jenkins were dispatched to find Giles's men, and while they waited Giles was made to eat something while Philip filled him in on their side of the story. But when the men eventually came their information was negative. Falkirk had not been seen in London for some days.

Giles sat down suddenly with his head in his hands.

Philip said, 'Giles, this isn't any good. Unless we alarm Falkirk unduly, I am sure Annabelle is safe for the moment.'

'But she's been in his hands since this morning! I'll go mad if I don't *do* something, Philip.'

'Remember what you told me at Badajoz? You have to know the terrain before you attack. It was good advice then, and it's good advice now. Believe me, Giles, Annabelle is safe for tonight. Though Falkirk has searched the house in Upper Brook Street, he has failed to find his papers. He's desperate to have them in his hands, and his only hope is to get Annabelle to show him where they are. She's safe for tonight.'

'But Annabelle doesn't know anything about the papers, damn you!'

'We know that. But he doesn't.'

Giles turned to Rosabelle. 'Did Stephen say *nothing* before he died?'

'He was delirious,' she said miserably 'He could only think of money. He said again and again that his bank account had failed him, after all. He said it over and over.'

'No, no!' Giles exclaimed. 'It's where he hid the papers. Why didn't I think of it before?'

'But—' said Rosabelle.

'Where?' said Philip.

'I'll show you. Tomorrow. But first we must find Falkirk. I'll swear he's somewhere in London.'

'I think I could flush him out,' said Rosabelle. 'They keep an eye on this house, I know they do. If I were to take a walk out in the open street, it's very likely Falkirk would have me followed. I feel certain that he keeps a watch on us all, and he wants both Anna and me—he said so.'

Giles was of the opinion that this was far too dangerous a plan, but he kept silent. This was for Philip to decide. To his relief Philip put his foot down, and they set themselves to finding an alternative. It was clear that Philip had been as busy as he himself had been in his pursuit of Falkirk, and he had a fleeting regret that they had not been able to coordinate their efforts before. He and Philip had always been a formidable combination.

They decided that Burrows might be the key and spent some time discussing how to set about finding him and what to do when they did. Burrows was loyal, but he might be intimidated. One thing led to another and the candles burnt low. Giles hardly noticed Rosabelle's departure for bed. After her initial offer to act as a decoy she had hardly joined in their discussions at all. She seemed quite subdued, more like the woman he had first met at Upper Brook Street—as, of course, she was. How could he have ever mistaken one sister for the other? His heart lurched as he thought of his lovely, spirited, laughing Rosabelle in Falkirk's hands. But after a moment it settled back to a steady, resentful beat. Annabelle Kelland must be rescued, of course. But after that he would forget her.

They left early the next morning, taking Gregson and Jenkins with them. Giles's men were deployed all round London, listening, looking, questioning yet again for any clue to Annabelle Kelland's whereabouts. Philip's information on Burrows proved to be sound, and they soon tracked him down. At first he was more afraid of Falkirk than he was of them, and reluctant to talk. But after a while it was gradually borne in on him that these two officers and English gentlemen could be every bit as ruthless as Falkirk, and much more inventive. Moreover, between them, they seemed to have gathered enough evidence to hang him. So in the end Burrows recognised defeat and began to talk. At the same time reports started to come in from Giles's men of a deserted tavern on the edge of town where strange things had been happening the night before.

But before any action could be taken on it, Philip's Bow Street Runner, Barnaby Stokes, came racing up to them, puffing and blowing with a message which was at first incomprehensible. When he finally managed to make himself understood, Giles was astounded and Philip was beside himself with a mixture of worry and rage. Timid little Rosabelle Ordway had ignored their advice and put herself into the lion's mouth in an effort to save her sister! She had the gall to assure them, through Barnaby Stokes, that she would bring Falkirk to Upper Brook Street within the hour.

'Why the devil didn't you stop her?' Philip asked fiercely.

'Couldn't be done, Mr Winbolt. Very obstinate, the lady was.'

'But I engaged you to guard her, damn you!'

Giles, seeing that Philip wanted nothing more than to throttle Stokes, said brusquely, 'How long ago did you leave her, Mr Stokes?'

'About forty minutes ago, Colonel.'

'Then we have no time to lose. Bring Burrows along with you. Gregson will give you a hand.'

They went through the streets of London at a pace which made no allowance for the fog which had descended once again, and were at the Upper Brook Street house within ten minutes. Here they took Burrows up to the little antechamber next to the drawing room. The man was a miserable wreck and he was unlikely to give them any more trouble.

'Gregson, take the carriage out of sight, and stay with it. Jenkins, Stokes, stay with Burrows until we call you. Understood?' Giles's voice was calm but brisk, his anxieties submerged in the need for action.

'And make sure you keep him quiet,' Philip added grimly. 'I don't mind what means you use as long as he remains conscious. We must leave the door open a crack, Giles.' Giles nodded. They needed to be able to judge the moment to strike.

They waited in silence. Presently they heard the sounds of arrival, footsteps on the stairs…

'I…I can't see!' Rosabelle's voice came clearly through the door, and both men heaved a sigh of relief.

A few murmurs, and the sound of shutters being opened. Then there was a long interval while Rosabelle obviously played for time, hesitating between one side and the other of the ornate mantelpiece. Her acting was perfect—it was impossible to guess that she really had no idea where to look. Finally they heard her say, 'I think this might be it. That cherub there. His head turns.'

Giles looked appalled. He knelt down and peered through the crack. He held up his hand in a signal to Philip. They waited.

'You have to press it in a certain way. It's no good hammering it.'

'You do it!' This was unmistakably Falkirk's voice! There was a gasp from Rosabelle and a shout of triumph from Falkirk. Giles whispered, 'Quickly, Philip! Now!'

They burst through the door and threw themselves at the two men bending in front of the mantelpiece. Giles saw that Philip was already tackling Falkirk and went for Fraser...

In later years, when their wives were not there to remonstrate, Philip and Giles were wont to reminisce about the minutes that followed with a certain amount of pride. The fight was hard and dirty. From the tactics used it would have been impossible to judge who were the virtuous and who were the villains. There were no rules, other than the need to survive, and Giles and Philip used without a qualm every trick they had learned in the lowest taverns on the waterfronts of Spain and France.

In a short while Fraser was unconscious and, with Falkirk firmly in Philip's grasp, Burrows was brought in. After one quick glance to check on Annabelle Kelland, Giles concentrated on dealing with Falkirk. He made sure the man was disarmed, drew his gun and held it steadily pointing at Falkirk's heart. 'Right, you can let him go. What's that you've got there, Jenkins?'

'A stiletto, sir.'

'I should have used that thing on you, when I had the chance,' Falkirk said viciously.

'Instead of on a woman who was bound hand and foot.' This was Rosabelle speaking. 'He held it to Anna's throat in the carriage on the way here. He drew blood.'

Giles stole another glance at Annabelle Kelland. She was holding on to her chair, white as a sheet, and he now saw there was a red mark on her throat and a large bruise on her head. He turned back with a snarl towards Falkirk, but the man had taken advantage of his momentary lapse of attention. Before Giles could stop him he

had swept something up from the floor and thrust it into
Burrows in one fluid motion. Burrows was dead before
he reached the ground, his throat pierced.

Giles hardly noticed what was happening. He was bent
over Annabelle, examining the slender thread of scarlet
at the base of her throat. She was pale and trembling. A
cold and deadly rage took hold of him. He turned on
Falkirk, and, if the others had not been there, he would
have killed him on the spot, with his bare hands.

But it was not necessary. Barnaby Stokes, suddenly a
magisterial figure, was arresting Falkirk. What the com-
bined efforts of Lloyds, the Navy Office, Giles Stanton
and all his men, Philip Winbolt and all his had failed to
do, had been accomplished for them by Falkirk himself.
Selder's previous crimes were no longer relevant. Falkirk
was being arrested for the murder of one of his own
accomplices.

Giles left them to it. He went back to where Annabelle
was being comforted by her sister. They stared at one
another in silence till Rosabelle left them and returned
to Philip.

Annabelle found it impossible to divine what Giles
might be thinking. His gaze was concerned, but impersonal, almost as if she was someone he had found hurt
in the street. She said wryly, 'I said you would meet
Annabelle soon, Giles.'

His mouth twisted, but he did not reply. She sighed
and looked towards Philip and Rosabelle. Her sister appeared to be faring no better. Philip Winbolt's voice was
as cool as she had ever heard it.

'Though what you thought you might do with only
my paper knife to protect you I cannot imagine,' he said
evenly.

Annabelle roused herself. 'Don't!' she said with such vigour that her throat hurt. Giles would have stopped her talking but she ignored him. 'She cut my ropes with it so that we could join together to keep Falkirk's coachman out of the room. You'd have been outnumbered otherwise. Don't talk to Rosabelle like that!'

'Annabelle, you must save your voice!' said Giles, putting his hand over her lips. Tears filled her eyes. His touch was so familiar, so gentle. But his eyes were as cool as Philip's voice. 'The sooner you can rest, the better.'

She pulled her face away from his hand. 'I want to know something first,' she protested. 'What and where are these wretched papers?'

She watched as Giles went over to the merry little cherub on the right hand side of the mantelpiece. He pressed something and slid it to one side. When his hand reappeared it held a slender packet of papers.

'Here,' he said. 'Stephen's bank account. He used…he used to keep his pocket money here when he was a child.' His gaze held hers as he waved the bundle in front of them all.

'But that was the very place I… Oh, heavens!' said Rosabelle.

'Exactly so,' said Philip curtly. 'You took an enormous risk, Rosa. How long do you think you would have lived after Falkirk got his papers?'

Annabelle didn't hear the rest of what he said. Giles's eyes were boring into her, accusing her… She pulled herself together.

'I shall go mad,' she said as forcefully as she could. 'I've been chased, carried off, frightened half to death, rescued, beaten on the head and imprisoned, had my throat cut—well, nearly—and all for the sake of that wretched bundle of papers. What are they?'

'You mustn't talk, Annabelle,' said Giles.

'Really? Well, silence me by telling me what I want to know.'

'It seems to be a confession signed by Kingsley.'

'Kingsley?'

'Ah! And here's a letter signed by Falkirk, thanking Kingsley for his information, and telling him it will be put to good use. He even calls himself Selder in it! Exactly what we wanted. It would have been enough to deliver Falkirk into the hands of the authorities.'

'Stephen's revenge,' said Rosabelle. Her voice was sad. 'And his death warrant.'

These were the last words Annabelle could hear. The strain of the previous twenty-four hours was catching up with her. With relief she heard the sound of a carriage arriving. She hardly noticed as Giles swung her into his arms and carried her out like a baby. She was dimly aware of a crowd of people on the doorstep, but only later was she told that this was an escort to remove Falkirk and Fraser, and take them into custody.

In all the bustle of their arrival at Arlington Street Annabelle was aware that Giles was at her side constantly. She was desperate to talk to him, but they were never alone for long enough for her to attempt to breach the impenetrable wall which had come between them. He was patient, gentle, courteous—all the things he had not been when they had first met. But she had felt closer to him then, for all the accusations and taunts, than she did now, when he was being so considerate. Before he left he came in to see her, his face still inscrutable. She wanted to shout, to rage at him, anything to breach that calm, stony facade. But the drugs she had been given were working and, halfway through an incoherent speech, she fell asleep.

When she woke the next morning her first thought was that she would see Giles. He must come again to see how she was, surely? He must listen to her, he must understand, and…if he knew how much she loved him he was sure to forgive her! Wouldn't he? She insisted on getting up. It would never do if he came and she was unable to see him. Rules of propriety might be relaxed for one day, but there would be no excuse for him to visit her bedroom a second time. She must be downstairs to receive him properly.

When she came down there was such an atmosphere of happy anticipation that she was not at all surprised to hear that Rosabelle was to marry Philip Winbolt at Christmas. Anxious not to spoil Rosabelle's joy she hid her own anxieties and exerted herself to seem cheerful and eager to join in the plans that were already being made. Only once did she falter, when Rosabelle asked her about a possible second wedding. She meant Annabelle's to Giles, of course, and the question almost overset her. She kept her composure, however, and managed to turn it off with a joke. For the rest of that day throughout all the chatter and laughter, she never once stopped listening for his arrival, but though there was much coming and going, not one of the visitors had the firm tread, the deep voice that she sought.

She went to bed that night, wondering if she would ever see Giles Stanton again.

Word soon got around that lovely young Mrs Ordway was back in London after her journey to the North, and

the next day flowers arrived from Richard Pettifer, and
Captain Wainwright, and another huge bouquet from
Major Dabney. Annabelle found it difficult to laugh
when Rosabelle, Emily and Philip teased her on her success with London Society, to keep smiling when every
card was eagerly perused for the one name which she
wanted to see, but which was never there. Lord Monteith
called, but Annabelle asked Emily to deal with him,
pleading that she was not strong enough for visitors.

Then, ironically, the caller she had longed for came
just as Lord Monteith was leaving. Fortunately, Maynard
assumed he had come to see Philip and asked him to
wait in the library while he saw Lord Monteith out. On
his return Giles asked to see Miss Kelland; with a fa-
therly smile, Maynard showed him into the small parlour
where Annabelle sat. After he had gone there was a short
silence in the room. Giles did not sit down, but gazed
round at the many floral offerings.

'Still as popular, I see. But do your admirers know
who you really are, Miss Kelland?'

'Miss Kelland, Giles?'

'I understand that is your name. Or am I wrong?
Again.'

'Giles, don't…don't be angry with me. Surely after all
we have been through, you could call me by my given
name? My true given name.'

'Very well. But, before you go any further, *Annabelle*,
I ought to warn you. I am not very interested in excuses
or expressions of contrition.'

'But I *am* sorry, Giles. And I hope you will forgive
me.'

'Well now, I do find that a trifle difficult. In fact, I
would rather forget the matter altogether and talk of
other things. Tell me, am I right in thinking your sister

and Philip Winbolt intend to marry? Have they set a date?'

'Christmas,' said Annabelle miserably. 'Giles—'

'No, *Annabelle*. I came this morning to make sure you had recovered. Nothing more.'

'But this is absurd! I was wrong, I know, to deceive you as I did, but my intentions were good! Do you mean to tell me that you are rejecting me, and everything I had to offer you, everything we have meant to each other, merely because I wanted to help my sister?'

'Everything you had to offer me! What was that? You demanded everything, *Annabelle*! And you gave me nothing.'

'What demands did I make?' she cried indignantly.

'You demanded faith. I gave that to you. You demanded trust. I gave you that, too. You had my respect. You even had something I had never bestowed on any woman before. You had my love. And what did you give in return?

'I loved you! I love you!'

'Oh, spare me that! You gave me neither respect, nor faith, nor trust. And I don't believe for a moment that you know what love is. Tell me, did you love me when you were lying through your teeth about your name, about your marriage to Stephen, your relationship with Selder? Did you respect me when you were laughing every time I called you Rosabelle? What sort of love is it that can't trust me with a secret as trivial as yours? Even when you were ill you kept it up—' He stopped.

'It wasn't trivial! I came to London convinced you were a monster! Rosabelle was ill, do you hear me? Ill! And all because of your unreasonable, cruel suspicions. I wanted to punish you for your treatment of her, your threats, the way you bullied her, reducing her to a shadow, a wraith…'

'And so you did!'

'Giles, you cannot believe that of me! That I would go to such lengths to punish you. No, you cannot believe it! You are not so ungenerous. You must have some remnant of feeling—'

'*Annabelle*, apart from relief that you have escaped without permanent injury from Falkirk and his companions, I assure you I feel nothing for you. For myself I am also relieved. I was in great danger of making a disastrous mistake. Greater danger than I have ever been in my life before.'

'By that you mean marriage to me, I suppose? You reject any thought of love I may have for you?'

'I can think of nothing more repellent. It is as I have always thought. A woman's love is a trap. Women are fickle, full of self-interest and better not taken at all seriously. In fact, the whole business is tedious.'

By now Annabelle was so angry that she forgot all her good resolutions. She had confessed her deepest feelings to this man, and he had called them repellent! She had spent months agonising over her deception of him, and in the end he had dismissed her torments as trivial. She should have been warned. A man who had treated Rosabelle so harshly would never understand, never forgive. It was a waste of time to think him capable of it.

'I am sure,' she said with dangerous calm, 'that I would not wish to cause you any further tedium.'

'Annabelle—'

'Forgive me, Colonel Stanton, if I say that I would much rather not see you again. In view of the very disobliging sentiments you have just expressed, I have no doubt that this will hardly distress you.'

'Annabelle—'

Rosabelle came into the room at that point and stopped short. She looked from one to the other and said in some embarrassment, ' I thought I'd find Philip and Emily here. Forgive me.' She made to go out.

'Pray do not feel you have to go, Rosa. Colonel Stanton was just leaving.'

'Annabelle—'

'If you do not leave this room, sir, then I will.'

'In that case, there is no more to be said. Goodbye, Miss Kelland.' He turned and gave a brief bow in Rosabelle's direction. 'Rosabelle,' and strode out.

For a moment there was complete silence in the room. Annabelle felt that if she moved or spoke she would shatter into tiny pieces, and it would be impossible to put her together again. Rosabelle tried to pacify her, but it was no use. Annabelle could not even bear to hear Giles Stanton's name. From that day on, whenever Giles Stanton's name was mentioned she simply withdrew into a private world of her own until the subject was dropped. But she could not control her dreams. Night after night, after days of cheerful activity, Annabelle would wake suddenly with her pillows wet, and tears rolling down her cheeks.

For the next few weeks Annabelle concentrated on Rosabelle's affairs and the preparations for the wedding. Having seen 'Gentleman Jack' in action, Annabelle respected him a great deal more, and if anything could cause the pain in her heart to ease a trifle it was the sight of Rosabelle's happy daze, and Philip Winbolt's devotion. She also found she had much in common with Emily Winbolt, which was as well, for the lovers tended to live in a delightful world of their own which shut out ordinary practicalities like mealtimes, appointments with mantua makers and the like. She and Emily rescued many a potential disaster, and in doing so cemented a firm friendship.

In the middle of December they all left London in an impressive convoy of carriages and wagons, and descended on Temperley. Here the activity, if anything, intensified. It had been decided that the wedding would take place on New Year's Eve, and the preparations for this, together with a traditional Christmas of the old sort which was to precede it, occupied most of Annabelle's time. She laughed and joked as gaily as the rest, teased Rosabelle and Philip, kept Lady Ordway amused, ran the household and flattered herself that she kept her constant heartache hidden from the rest of the world. Of Giles she had heard nothing.

Then one day, when they were making a list of guests, Rosabelle asked almost too casually, 'Is there…is there anyone else you would wish to invite, Anna?'

Annabelle ignored this opening. 'I don't think so,' she said, equally casually. 'You've mentioned all the local people who should come. And there certainly isn't anyone else.'

She saw Rosabelle looking at her with such concern in her eyes that she almost broke down. 'Dearest Anna, are you well?'

'Of course I am! Pray don't worry about me, Rosa. I shall soon come about.' She knew she was speaking too brusquely, but it was as much as she could do to reply at all. The longing for Giles did not seem to weaken. If anything, it seemed to grow with each day that passed. So she threw herself with even greater enthusiasm into every detail for Christmas and the wedding and tried to bury all feeling under an avalanche of work.

Giles had left London as soon as the business with Falkirk and the rest had been completed. He had to leave town, otherwise the temptation to call on the Winbolts was too strong. Before he knew it he would be begging Annabelle Kelland to forgive him, besottedly swearing devotion and all the rest of the inanities that men fall into when they are haunted by the hurt in two dark blue eyes, the particular lift of a delicately proud chin, the brightness of golden hair, barely hiding a dark bruise…and other, more intimate memories. The lines of a slender figure, tossing restlessly in the room at High Kimber, the frantic voice seeking reassurance, protection, the hands clutching him, refusing to release him… He could feel them still. They were round his heart squeezing it till it ached… Enough of that! Let Philip Winbolt choose to marry if he wished! Such folly was not for him, and to be sure of it he would remove himself from temptation and retire to Avenell.

But as a relief from his thoughts the journey was not a success. He was foolish enough to call on the Daventrys, and had difficulty in parrying their eager questions.

'So Gentleman Jack Winbolt is to marry Mrs Ordway! We were so surprised when we saw it in the *London Gazette*! He's a fortunate man—we thought her charming.'

'You've met her?'

Selina Daventry opened her eyes wide in astonishment. 'Well, of course we have! You brought her here yourself not six months ago, Giles! In fact, James and I were certain you would end up marrying her yourself. It just shows how mistaken one can be.'

Giles looked helplessly from one to the other. James and Selina were old friends of Philip's as well. It could lead to all sorts of complications if he left it. He said curtly, 'Things…aren't quite as they seem. The…the lady who was with me in July was, in fact, Mrs Ordway's identical twin, Miss Annabelle Kelland.'

The Daventrys looked astonished. 'I suppose there was a reason for this hoax,' said Captain Daventry, his voice carefully neutral.

'Oh, absolve me from blame. I was as taken in as you. But I'm sorry you were subjected to it.'

'But, Giles, how dreadful! Was it just…just a joke?'

'No, Selina. She had a reason.'

'I can think of few reasons which would justify such a deception,' said James's mother austerely.

'Miss Kelland took her sister's place in London so that Mrs Ordway could have time to recover from an illness at the family home in Berkshire.'

'Mrs Ordway seems to have recovered to some purpose if she is to marry Philip Winbolt,' said the elder Mrs Daventry, unappeased. 'He must be one of the best catches in London. But I still don't understand the need for pretence.'

Giles started to agree, then stopped. He had never before really considered Annabelle's words. Had Rosabelle really been so frightened of him? Had he been such an ogre?

'After all,' said Selina Daventry. 'It's not as if you were an ogre. If Lady Ordway needed a companion, you would surely have accepted a substitute.'

Would he? Or would he have sent Annabelle back with a flea in her ear? Demanded that Rosabelle return to London, as she had promised? Having observed the sisters' fierce loyalty to each other, he could imagine that Annabelle would not have risked it. He said slowly, 'Whatever the truth of the matter, I owe you all an apology, I know. But try not to judge Annabelle Kelland too harshly. You know how close your own twins are, Selina. Miss Kelland was doing the best she could for her sister—other considerations took second place. I…I'm sorry you were deceived, but I don't suppose you will meet her again. Don't think too badly of Miss Kelland.'

'I won't,' said Selina Daventry. 'I liked her.'

But after Giles had departed for Avenell she said to her spouse, 'Not meet her again, indeed! I'll wager what you like she'll be visiting us within the year. Probably on her bridal journey to Avenell, too!'

# *Chapter Seventeen*

Giles's journey to Derbyshire was overshadowed by memories of that other journey earlier in the year. Annabelle's voice was constantly in his ear, fragments of their conversations, the sound of her laughter, her spirited responses. It was no better when he reached Avenell. His father's greeting was warm, if a little surprised, and he exerted himself to entertain him. But Avenell, too, was full of Annabelle. He was haunted by memories—of riding about the countryside with her, her cheeks rosy with exercise, her hair blown by the wind, of her flight over the moor to High Kimber, of the desperate hours when he thought she would die, and of the courage and gaiety that were such an essential part of her.

One night they were sitting in the south dining room, the heavy curtains drawn against the biting winds outside, and a huge fire burning in the hearth.

'Well, I thought I was glad to see you, Giles, but you're no better than a wet week. What's wrong?' said

Lord Stanton eventually. 'And what have you done with that charming girl? Is she the trouble? The last time I saw you together I thought you were in a fair way to making a match of it.'

'So did I, Father,' said Giles, turning his glass round between his fingers. 'But I was wrong.'

'Refused you, did she? I'm surprised. She showed every sign of being in love.'

'Father, I'd like to tell you what happened. May I?'

Giles left nothing out, from his cruel suspicions of Rosabelle Ordway, through his slow discovery of the truth about Stephen and the final defeat of Falkirk, to the last bitter quarrel with Annabelle. By the time he had finished the only light in the room came from the fire. The candles had guttered long since.

'Hmm. A curious history. What do you propose to do now?'

'What do you mean?'

'You've told me the facts. But what do you feel? Do you still condemn Annabelle Kelland for being a woman? Oh, don't look at me like that, Giles! It seems to me that that is your chief grievance. And I'm sorry for it. I had hoped that Venetia's death and our reconciliation had wiped that particular slate clean. But you're being absurd, you know. You wouldn't love this Annabelle as you do if she wasn't a woman. And a damned attractive one.'

'She may be attractive, but she lied to me, father.'

'Her reason for doing so may not seem adequate to you. But have you considered how important it was to her to protect her sister? Surely loyalty is a rare and laudable virtue? If she can be so loyal to her sister, is it not likely that she would be as loyal to a husband.'

'Why didn't she confide in me?'

'Ah! There we have it! The canker at the heart.'

'What is that?'

'You can forgive your own lack of faith in her. What you cannot forgive is her lack of faith in you!'

'What nonsense!'

'And,' his father went on, 'you are wrong. She trusted you with her life. She gave you her love. But she couldn't, or wouldn't, risk her sister's happiness. That wasn't hers to risk. Think about it, Giles. I've made some mistakes in my life and spent many lonely years as a result. I don't want you to go the same way.'

For the next few days the debate raged furiously in Giles's mind. For so many years he had lived with the assumption that women were not to be trusted. Was he in danger of losing the one woman who could rescue him from loneliness, who could give him more happiness than he had ever imagined? Had he resented the fact that she had put her sister's happiness before his?

Then two letters arrived. One was from Rosabelle. It was an invitation to the wedding at Temperley.

I do not need to tell you how pleased we would be if you could come, Giles. And I think I may also speak for Annabelle. I sometimes worry about her. Though she is always busy and cheerful, something of her old spirit seems to have vanished. Can it be that her experiences in the north and afterwards have left a mark? Some of them were certainly unpleasant. Perhaps if you came you could help her to put them into the right perspective? Of course, if you feel you cannot, then we shall try to understand. Forgive me if I seem to be interfering in matters which do not concern me—my excuse is that Annabelle's health and happiness are a matter of deep concern for all those who love her. And Philip and I are so happy that we want the world to be happy, too…

The second was from Lady Ordway. She thanked him for his efforts on behalf of her family, and gave a vivid description of the preparations for the wedding. It ended thus:

With Rosa's permission, I have enclosed a page from one of her letters written to Anna at Avenell. Anna has forgotten she left it with me, and I have not consulted her before sending it to you. You might condemn me for this, I suppose, but I thought it might explain Anna's reticence, which must have seemed unreasonable, or even sly, to you. She is the dearest girl, Giles. Do not judge her harshly.

Giles unfolded the page. It was an affecting plea from Rosabelle for her sister's continued silence on the matter of their changed identity. Only a monster could have ignored it. He mind up his mind, and went to his father straight away.

'You were right, sir. I was at fault, and I intend to rectify it immediately. It means my leaving you alone for a month or two—unless you wish to come with me… But the journey would be too much for you at this time of year.'

'What rubbish is this? I like that Kelland girl, and I'd like to make sure that you don't make a mess of it this time! Too much for me, indeed!'

Giles could see that his father's mind was made up, so, apart from warning him that they would be travelling as quickly as circumstances permitted, he said no more.

They set off more or less straight away without attempting to inform anyone at Temperley, since he meant to be there before any mail could reach them. Unfortunately the weather did not smile on them. England was swept with a series of storms which delayed any traveller fool-hardy enough to attempt such a long journey in winter. Others gave up and took shelter in the various inns, but the Stantons pressed on gamely to London. Here they stopped briefly, then set off again along the Bath Road.

Now that Giles had made up his mind, he was deter-mined to arrive at Temperley before Christmas, and any delay was intolerable. It was a severe setback when they arrived at Reading on Christmas Eve to find that a heavy snowfall had blocked the road further west. But unde-terred, he left his father and the carriage in the care of Goss at the inn, and, taking a single bag, set off alone on foot. He trudged through the snow, hearing church bells, and snatches of song from the villages, but never meeting a soul. Once or twice he wondered if he had lost his way, but then a signpost would loom up and he would rub it clear to confirm that he was still on course.

After what seemed hours, he saw the dark bulk of Temperley ahead. One of the church clocks had struck midnight an hour or more before, and he wondered if anyone would still be up, but he took heart when he saw lights in the windows. Feeling a curious mixture of ex-haustion, apprehension, and elation, he knocked on the huge oak door. After a moment it opened cautiously to reveal the substantial figure of Mrs Bostock.

'Miss Kelland?' he asked.

'Well, I don't know, I'm sure…'

'It's all right, Becky. Let Colonel Stanton in.' Annabelle's voice. Brushing the snow from his shoul-ders, Giles stepped into the hall. The candles were still burning in the sconces, and in their light he could see greenery wound round the bannisters of a wide oak stair-case and arching over the top of the stairs. The warm, intoxicating smell of spices and apples, mulled wine and baking filled his nostrils. But he took in very little of this familiar Christmas scene. His eyes were fixed on a figure halfway up the stairs. She held a branched can-dlestick in her hand and the light gleamed in the dark gold of her hair.

'Annabelle! Oh God, I'd forgotten how lovely you are! Annabelle, I've been such a fool. Can you forgive me?'

The candlestick wavered in Annabelle's hand and Giles leapt up the stairs to take it from her. Holding it high, he put his other arm round her to steady her...

'Let me take that, Giles.' It was Philip, carefully re-moving the candlestick from his grasp. 'I don't want to interfere, but you'll manage better without.'

He could have been on the moon for all the notice taken of him. With a smile he slipped past the twined figures on the stairs and ushered the Bostocks back into the kitchen, where they set to preparing something to sustain the traveller.

'Giles! Oh, Giles, I thought you'd never come.'

'I came to my senses. And then I couldn't keep away. Say it's not too late, Annabelle.'

'I love you, Giles.'

'I don't deserve this,' he said with an unsteady laugh, as she wound her arms round his neck...

'Giles, you're soaking! You don't mean to say you've *walked*...'

'No other way to get here. I've left my father with Goss and the carriage in the inn at Reading. They'll fol-low in the morning, when it's light.'

'You're mad!'

'No, Annabelle. I'm sane. Truly in my right senses for the first time in my life. Marry me?'

'Oh yes, I will. I will!'

'There's room for another wedding at the church on New Year's Eve,' said a helpful voice above them. 'And everything's prepared.'

'The guest list will be much the same, too,' added another.

They looked up. Framed in the greenery along the landing was a motley collection of nightcaps and laughing faces. Rosabelle was smiling down at them, a grinning Emily at her side. Leaning over the balustrade on the other side was Lady Ordway, nodding benignly. Mr Kelland was emerging from his room in a magnificent brocade bedgown, and from the gallery round the corner came the tapping of Lord Winbolt's stick, and a voice demanding to know what was going on.

Philip came back into the hall. 'It's not a bad suggestion. Can it be done?'

Giles smiled complacently. 'A good soldier, Philip…'

'Is always prepared. I take it that the licence is under all those capes? If you're staying, old fellow, I think you should remove some of your outer garments. There's a bit of a puddle on the stairs.'

'Well, if that's all settled I'll be off back to bed,' said Mr Kelland. 'You can see me in the morning to ask my permission, Stanton. I might even give it.'

'And I'll be off, too. Oh, Giles, I'm so *happy* for you both,' said Lady Ordway as she went back to her room. 'Wilson! Wilson!'

Emily went off to satisfy her grandfather's curiosity, and Rosabelle passed the two on the stairs, murmuring that she would find Becky to do some mopping up. Philip went with her.

'Giles!' said Annabelle, smiling her enchanting smile. 'Oh Giles! Do you really love *me*, Annabelle?'

Giles had removed his greatcoat. He gathered her up into his arms and kissed her like a man who has been starving. 'I worship every last inch of you,' he whispered. 'And after High Kimber, I do know what I'm talking about. I've been haunted for weeks by it.'

'Giles!' Annabelle tried to look shocked, but she was too happy. A smile kept breaking through. 'Happy Christmas, Giles!'

'Happy Christmas, my heart,' he said. 'A happy, happy Christmas.'

# *Epilogue*

'Past three a clock, and a cold and frosty morning:
Past three a clock: good morrow, masters all!'

The carol singers were on their way home. Almost too happy and excited to sleep, Annabelle lay listening to their voices fading into the distance. She could hear Rosabelle and Emily breathing quietly beside her in the darkness. The curtains were not completely closed, and in the blackness outside gleamed a brilliant star. It was Christmas Day—and such a day as she had not dreamt of just twenty-four hours before. Giles was here. He had come, after all, to be with her, and in just a short week they would be married. There would be a lot to do, but this special day would be spent rejoicing, giving her family and friends a chance to get to know the man she loved so dearly. Darling, dearest Giles… Annabelle at last fell asleep.

\* \* \*

Temperley had in the past been famous for its hospitality, but this Christmas feast exceeded everything that had gone before. Half the women from the estate had been at work for weeks in the kitchens and stillrooms preparing for the celebrations, and their menfolk, too, had been drawn in to help with the heavy work. And now the house was full of bustle and happy anticipation as the maids and kitchen staff approached the climax of their labours.

In the parlour the Kellands, Ordways and Winbolts were in the middle of making their guests welcome when Annabelle came in, flushed and excited.

'Giles! Giles! Come quickly—look!'

She dragged Giles through the hall. A large sled, drawn by two sturdy horses, and jingling merrily, was drawing up at the door. In the driving seat was Goss, and behind him, swathed in furs and rugs, was Lord Stanton. Others had followed Giles out, eager to see what was causing such excitement, and the sled was soon surrounded by a laughing crowd, congratulating the new arrival on his courage in braving the weather. Lord Stanton disengaged himself and barely had time to raise an eyebrow at his son and receive a nod by way of reply before Annabelle swept him off into the house to meet her father. Giles was left with Goss.

'You're a genius, Goss! How did you find the sled?'

'Spanish ways, Colonel. I commandeered it, you might say. It cost a bit, though.'

'Never mind! I'm glad to see you both safely here! I've been getting myself engaged since I last saw you, my friend. Are you going to wish me well?'

'I can't say I'm surprised, Colonel! And yes, I do wish you every happiness, both of you. A nicer young lady than Miss Kelland you couldn't wish to meet.'

Lord Stanton was taken to his room where he took off his wrappings and was led downstairs and introduced. He received a warm welcome, though some of the less well-informed visitors wondered why he had been invited. They were to learn. After a while, Mr Kelland clapped his hands and addressed the assembly thus:

'My friends, may I have your attention?' A silence fell. 'Thank you. I am a man of few words, so you will not have long to wait for your dinner. But I must do two things. I must welcome you all…heartily…to the first true Christmas at Temperley for many a long year. And second, I have to tell you… Where are you, Rosa? And Winbolt? Come here, both of you! That my daughter Rosabelle is to marry Mr Winbolt on New Year's Day.'

'God bless us, we know that!' cried someone in the crowd. 'We've all got our wedding clothes ready and waiting!'

'But what you don't know, Will Darby,' said Mr Kelland with a triumphant smile, 'what you don't know, and what I am happy to tell you all, is that…where's that other daughter of mine? And Stanton? Come on my other side! That Annabelle, here, is to marry Colonel Stanton at the same ceremony!'

A moment of astonishment and then congratulations and cheers filled the room. The twins stood on either side of their father, each holding the hand of her betrothed, shyly acknowledging the good wishes of their friends. It was a very pretty picture. The three men were dressed in the conventional garb for the country—buff breeches, Giles in a dark green coat, Mr Kelland in black and Philip in chestnut brown. The girls, in contrast, wore vivid Christmas colours—Annabelle in red, and Rosabelle in green.

'Gad, sir!' exclaimed Lord Stanton. 'I don't think I've

ever seen a more striking sight! How the devil *do* you tell those girls apart? If one wasn't wearing red and t'other green, I'd think I was seeing double!'

Giles looked down at Annabelle, then smiled at his father.

'I can tell,' he said confidently. 'Now.'

The sound of a pipe and tabour, and a group of singers and dancers caused a diversion.

> 'The boar's head in hand bear we,
> Bedecked with bays and rosemary;
> And we pray, you masters, merry be
> And seat you in the hall!'

The company joined in the old carol and followed the dancers into the Great Hall. The huge chamber was normally divided into two by screens, put in by an earlier Kelland whose wife had complained of the impossibility of heating the place. But these had been drawn aside and a number of long tables, covered with stiff damask cloths, and decorated with ivy and boughs of evergreen, filled the space. Along the side near the kitchens were serving tables laden with tongue, game pies, plates of venison, beef and duck, jellies, fruits and syllabubs, all laid out to tempt the eye as well as the palate. Flagons of ale, lemonade, and bottles of wine invited the thirsty to partake, and as soon as they were all seated eager hands started to serve them.

Then to a roll of the drum and a shrill call from the pipe, John Bostock paraded in, carrying a boar's head on an enormous dish. Applause greeted him, applause which grew louder, then turned to laughter when they saw that, in addition to the traditional rosemary and bay,

the boar wore a bridal wreath and veil on its fearsome
head.

The feast was memorable. Lady Ordway was heard to
say to Lord Winbolt that life in the country might have
its compensations, and Lord Stanton, looking none the
worse for his journey, swore he hadn't enjoyed himself
so much in years, though he was still damned if he could
tell the difference between the Kelland twins!

'Still—as long as Giles can, I suppose it doesn't matter. He seems sure enough.'

'He does, doesn't he?' said Emily thoughtfully. 'Philip
is just the same. I wonder how they do it?' Then she
turned the subject and asked about Buxton.

But when the feasting was nearly over, and Giles and
Philip were being taken round the tables to have a word
with the guests, Emily could be seen having a private
word with Mr Kelland. He smiled indulgently and nodded, whereupon Emily collected the twins and bore them
off upstairs.

After a while a roll on the drum stopped the buzz of
conversation, and everyone looked up to see Miss
Winbolt, dressed in a tall hat and carrying a wand, standing on the half landing of the stairs.

'My Lords, Ladies and Gentlemen!' she called in an
impressively deep voice. Another drum roll. 'I beg your
indulgence for a few moments, for an ancient ceremony
which cannot be delayed! For…

By ancient law, or so they say,
Each Kelland daughter this very day
Must choose a Lord whose rule will extend
From this day forth, till Twelfth Night's end.
To rule us all, both saints and devils,

> The Lords to be called—the Kings of the Revels!
> Come, Queen in Red, who'll be your choice?
> Then, Emerald Queen, we'll hear your voice!'

Emily bowed to laughing applause, then turned and held up her wand. Annabelle and Rosabelle, looking like the very spirit of Christmas in their red and green dresses, appeared at the top of the stairs, and slowly descended. Each wore a glittering paper crown on her head, and carried a golden sceptre in her hand. Emily silenced the enthusiastic cheers from the assembled company with a wave of her wand. 'Let the Red Queen speak!'

The Red Queen raised her sceptre and pointed it at Giles. 'I command you to approach, sir!' she said. Giles had a smile in his eyes as he came up to her, kissed her hand and took his place at her side.

Then Emily bade the Emerald Queen to choose, and, to no one's surprise, she pointed her sceptre at Philip, who joined the other on the stairs, with the same ceremony, and much the same smile as Giles.

Then the Red Queen took Giles's hand and looked lovingly into his eyes.

> 'Husband-to-be, our troth is plighted.
> Swear that we'll stay forever united.
> To reign together forever more
> In accordance with our ancient lore.'

Giles hesitated. 'I've done many things in my time, but I've never been foolhardy enough to attempt impromptu verse. Still, if Mr Winbolt will help...' He raised an eyebrow at Philip. Encouraged by a nod, he cleared his throat and said, 'Let me see...' Then, after a moment's thought, he said,

'Oh loveliest lady, beauty divine!
Alas! I can never be consort of thine...'

He paused. Philip, stepping forward to take the Red
Queen by the hand, said,

'Tho' now you wear red, and in spite of your wiles,
Rosa can hoax neither Philip nor Giles...'

Giles smiled and bowed to Philip. 'Thank you, my
friend! Just what I needed!' He went on,

'That minx over there, who is now wearing green,
Is really my Anna, my heart's only queen!'

The dignity of the two Queens was quite spoiled, as
Philip and Giles, grinning broadly, unceremoniously
claimed their true brides, and the hall was swept with
more shouts of laughter and applause.

'Well, I declare!' said Lord Stanton delightedly. 'What
a pair, eh, Kelland? What a pair! What a family! All the
same, Giles, don't stand for any nonsense. You ought to
punish the girls.'

'A forfeit, a forfeit!' called someone in the crowd.

'What shall it be, Annabelle?' said Giles with a mock
frown. 'Philip, how shall we punish these brats?'

'A kiss, a kiss!' shouted someone else.

Giles gave a sweeping bow. 'Just what I was about to
suggest myself, Will Darby. Thank you!'

With a laugh and a blush Annabelle and Rosabelle
submitted gracefully to their fate. It was difficult to judge
who was enjoying the 'punishment' more—the brides,
the bridegrooms or the assembled company. But the ap-

plause finally died away, and the lovers drew apart as music was heard outside.

'It's the wassailers again,' said Annabelle. 'Listen!' They listened for a moment, and then softly joined in the chorus.

> Love and joy come to you,
> And to you your wassail too,
> And God bless you, and send you
> A Happy New Year,
> And send you
> A HAPPY NEW YEAR!

\* \* \* \* \*

## Harlequin Romance®

**D**elightful

**A**ffectionate

**R**omantic

**E**motional

**T**ender

**O**riginal

**D**aring

**R**iveting

**E**nchanting

**A**dventurous

**M**oving

Harlequin Romance—the
series that has it all!

HROM-G

# HARLEQUIN®
## INTRIGUE®
## *We'll leave you breathless!*

If you've been looking for thrilling tales of
contemporary passion and sensuous love stories
with taut, edge-of-the-seat suspense—
then you'll *love* **Harlequin Intrigue!**

Every month, you'll meet four new heroes
who are guaranteed to make your spine tingle
and your pulse pound. With them you'll enter
into the exciting world of Harlequin Intrigue—
where your life is on the line
and so is your heart!

## THAT'S INTRIGUE—DYNAMIC ROMANCE AT ITS BEST!

HARLEQUIN®

## INTRIGUE®

INT-GENR

**Harlequin® Historical**

From rugged lawmen and
valiant knights to defiant heiresses
and spirited frontierswomen,
Harlequin Historicals will
capture your imagination with
their dramatic scope, passion
and adventure.

Harlequin Historicals…
they're too good to miss!

HHGENR

# ...there's more to the story!

Superromance.
A *big* satisfying read about unforgettable
characters. Each month we offer *six* very different
stories that range from family drama to adventure
and mystery, from highly emotional stories to
romantic comedies—and much more! Stories
about people you'llbelieve in and care about.
Stories too compelling to put down....

Our authors are among today's *best* romance
writers. You'll find familiar names and talented
newcomers. Many of them are award winners—
and you'll see why!

If you want the biggest and best
in romance fiction, you'll get it
from Superromance!

*Available wherever Harlequin books are sold.*

Visit us at www.eHarlequin.com

HSGEN00

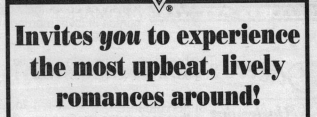

# Invites *you* to experience the most upbeat, lively romances around!

Every month, we bring you four strong, sexy men, and four women who know what they want—and go all out to get it.

We'll take you from the places you know to the places you've dreamed of. Live the love of a lifetime!

## American Romance—

Love it! Live it!

HARLEQUIN®

*Makes any time special* ™

Visit us at www.eHarlequin.com

HARGEN00